Chains of Gaia

Chains
of
Gaia

JAMES FAHY

LUME BOOKS

LUME BOOKS

For my brother,
who got me through the woods more than once

PROLOGUE
A WOLF AT THE DOOR

The Temple of the Oracle stands high on the peak of the hill of knowledge, a wild and windswept moor stretching away beneath the mount on all sides. It is an imposing building, lines of immense fluted columns rearing beneath a peaked, dark pediment, blotting out even the Netherworlde's vast expanse of sky. Great fiery torches roar in the wind, reflecting off the shining bronze doors into the night. Scarlet pennants whip and flutter continually in the high moorland gales, the cracking whips of cruel horsemen.

At the very centre of the Oracle's temple, there is a circular walled garden with a central pool, a lush overgrown space filled with the tinkling of hidden streams and the soft calls of unseen birds, the calm eye of the raging storm outside. Here, an oculus opens the roof to the starry night sky above, and in this peaceful space, deep within this temple, the Oracle sat playing chess and talking to herself. It is easy to talk to yourself when you are one woman who lives in three different bodies.

The eldest of these three bodies grumbled.

"I don't know why I bother," she muttered. Her face was lined and ancient, her hair thin and white as chalk. Her robes the darkest shade of red, like long-dried blood. She sat at a small stone table, peering at the chess board before her. "I mean; I could just see how it's going to end anyway. Any number of endings really. That's what's important isn't it?" She lifted a carved chess-piece, white as bone, and clacked it down on the board.

The woman sitting opposite shook her head slightly, a graceful movement. She was much younger, in the prime of life and startlingly beautiful. Her hair was a curtain of golden waves, threaded with gold filaments. She had large sparkling eyes which seemed slightly unfocused. Her robe, though identical in design to the elder, was a vivid bright scarlet. It practically pulsed with vibrancy.

"The problem with that way of thinking though, Youngest," she replied in a slightly dreamy voice, " …is that looking ahead so often, you miss what's right in front of you. The journey, not the destination is sometimes more important." She delicately moved a jet black chess piece diagonally across the board, her little finger held out daintily. They were well matched. This game had gone on for quite some time.

"Rubbish," the old woman grumbled. "Eyes on the prize, that's what I say. You've got to look ahead, you've got to plan your moves, that's strategy that is." She clacked another piece on the table with determination. "Strategy!"

With a smile, the younger woman took her piece, capturing it with one of her own. "Always focused on what's next. You don't pay attention to what's happening now, and you leave yourself open to attack," she said smugly. "Keeping one's mind in the present, that's the key."

The hag cackled and shifted one of her pieces, leapfrogging it over three of her adversary's and collecting them from the board with glee. "You keep telling yourself that."

"That piece can't move like that," the young woman pouted.

The elder-looking Oracle tapped her game piece lovingly. "That's Fate. She can move however she bloody well wants. I got Fate, you got Chance. Fair's fair." She nodded at the golden-haired woman's black remaining pieces. "You haven't even bothered using it yet. You've not moved Chance at all."

The doe-eyed Oracle smiled. "I'm saving it," she said secretively, " … for the present moment."

Their game was interrupted by a young girl, skipping into the room from an archway between the bushes. She was bright-eyed and rosy-cheeked, in robes of dusty pink. Her expression however was much older than suited her cherubic face.

"What is it, Eldest?" the middle woman asked, looking up from the game.

"Something has happened," the child Oracle said.

"Something always has," said the old woman, flatly, and with little interest. "And something always *is*, and something always *will*. What of it?"

The child rolled her eyes. "Well, this something has *just* happened," she said. "As in today. You must have seen it coming?"

The elderly lady shrugged. "I see everything coming. Not everything *coming* actually *gets* here though."

The child-like Oracle looked to the other woman. "And you must have felt it when it happened, didn't you?"

The beautiful woman cocked her hair to one side. "Probably, but I can't remember now."

The cherubic girl sighed with exasperation. "Didn't you feel it?" She pointed at the large circular pool in the centre of the room. All three Oracles peered at it. Its waters, usually still and glassy as a mirror, were dark and churning.

"This will be bad," the old woman sighed. "Bad for everyone. Dark, dark things are coming."

"Another shard has been found," the child said. "But the one who found it ... he isn't strong. I mean, he is, but not strong enough for a shard. He had forgotten he hid it there, forgotten what happens in the labyrinth. It will—"

"Dark things are not *coming*," said the middle Oracle suddenly, standing up from the table, a frown on her brow as she cut off the child mid-flow. The swish of her robes sent the chess pieces toppling from the board. They fell to the floor in a clatter. "Dark things are here, *now*."

All three of them heard the booming knocks deep in the temple. They echoed around the room, startling small and colourful birds from their hiding places in the foliage and sending them whipping out of the open oculus into the cold night sky beyond. Someone had come to the temple.

"I knew he was coming," the old one said grimly. "Obviously. And now ... he's here." She pursed her wrinkled mouth. "Go and admit him, Eldest, before he takes the doors off the blasted hinges. He's not one known for patience, that dark bird."

The child Oracle left without a word, and the old woman stood from the table, glancing at the spent game pieces on the floor.

"Ruining our fun," she muttered. "And to come calling at this time of night as well, honestly." She considered, clucking her tongue. "I suppose that's one way to finish the game though. Dash every piece on the floor. Chaos and ruin. Perhaps the ultimate end."

"He wants to know," her companion said dreamily. "He's searching everywhere." Her gaze focussed on the doorway. "His heart is withered from the searching."

3

"Hush," the elderly Oracle chided. "Don't you go giving away nothing for free. You let *him* tell *us* why he's here, not the other way around." She looked distracted for a moment. "Oh, and move that vase off that pillar by the wall, will you? I like that vase."

The younger woman complied without question. There was a large ornamental vase atop a plinth standing against one curving wall between the bushes. She picked it up and carried it elsewhere in the room, dropping it carefully behind some leaves by the pool before rejoining her sister.

The childlike Oracle returned, bringing their visitors.

There were five of them, each dressed in black robes over creaking dark leather armour. They were hooded and masked from nose to chin, only their dark eyes glowering out at the Oracles, alert and suspicious. Three males, two females. They moved silently, like dangerous cats. They flowed into the temple garden like ink. Black-gloved hands rested on the hilts of long thin swords, currently sheathed. It was a causal gesture, and a silent, almost polite warning.

Each of the figures wore an emblem at the throat-clasp of their cloak. A black feather in a red circle. The Oracle, all three versions of her, said nothing as these people prowled into the room, cloaks swishing, eyes taking in every detail of the inner sanctum. These were not her visitors; they were only his entourage.

Behind them entered a tall, broad figure, in dark, spiked armour. His face was hidden by a visor sculpted to resemble the grinning wicked maw of a wild wolf. His cloak was composed of countless glossy black feathers and it fluttered out behind him in whispers as he strode with purpose into the room. The air seemed to grow a little cooler. The soft swishing rustle of the many trees hushed.

"Oracle, you know I come, yet you keep me waiting at the door." His voice was a low hiss, oddly metallic in his visor. "Where is your famous hospitality? Won't you invite me in?"

"Not by the hairs of my chinny chin chin," the old woman muttered, with dark humour. She gestured with a sweeping hand at the man and his companions.

"To what do we owe the honour, Strigoi, Wolf of Eris? What warrants a personal visit to us from you and your Ravens? I doubt you are tax-collecting, and we are far from Dis here."

The wolf-headed man stalked up to the Oracle, inclining his head at

4

the pool, then at the game table, with its dropped and scattered pieces. Slowly taking in the room and its contents. He took his time answering. He was not a man to be rushed. His mana flowed out of him like a cold wind, filling the room.

"You know why I am here, one-in-three," he said quietly. "You must. There is little you don't see."

The middle Oracle nodded. "Of course *we* know, but do you?"

He turned towards her, the carved metal muzzle of his face glittering darkly in the firelight of the braziers. His eyes, if he had them, were hidden in the metal shadows of the wolf-mask.

"I have no time for games and riddles," he said. "Nor have I ever had the patience for them. I have come here, now, because another has been found. Do not deny it."

The child Oracle shrugged behind him from her position amongst his ravens. "It's not ours to deny," she said, crossing her arms. "But yes. If you're talking about a Shard of the Arcania. Most unexpected, most sudden, and of all the places …" She shook her ringleted head in wonder.

"Your mistress, Eris, sends you begging for information?" The old Oracle asked, her head tilted enquiringly. The Wolf of Eris snapped his head back around to face her. The temperature in the temple had dropped significantly further. The braziers fluttered, struggling, as though there was not enough oxygen in the room for them to burn. Shadows leapt high on the walls around them in the guttering light.

"*Your Empress* … sends *demands*," he corrected her. "You have never opposed the Lady Eris."

The younger of the adult Oracles shrugged. "We have never seen the need to. Nor have we ever condoned her. We are apart from such things. We are … a neutral party."

Several of the Ravens shifted from foot to foot uneasily. It was not common for anyone in the Netherworlde not to publicly declare undying loyalty to the Empress.

Strigoi slowly reached out and with the back of his gauntleted hand, he stroked the cheek of the beautiful woman. She neither flinched away nor moved to stop him, but stared back, undaunted, her face calm.

"You *are* … her subjects," he said slowly and clearly. "You are left in peace as long as you remain useful. Let there be no misunderstanding of that. We all of us, *belong* to the Empress."

5

"She has never tried to make us kneel and kiss her ring," the oldest Oracle mused thoughtfully. "I wonder … what do you think would happen if she did? Do you think she's considered that too? Played that scenario out? Perhaps that's why she's never tried."

"Do not needle me, crone," Strigoi whispered dangerously. "I need only one of you for information. Not all three. Remember that."

"Oh, she's terrible for remembering, that one," the child Oracle said, folding her arms. "Always looking ahead you see. I on the other hand, Wolf … I remember everything that has happened. Every dark deed from the past. Tell me, do you?"

Strigoi rounded on the child. With viper-like speed he reached out and grabbed the child by the throat, lifting her from her feet and holding her aloft as though she weighed nothing more than a feather. Her small hands scrabbled at his gauntlet as he tilted his covered head down towards her.

"Do not dare to speak to me of the past, little one," he hissed quietly, his tone low. "Deeds done are done. The past … is a barren heath. It can sustain none of us now." His Ravens had stepped backwards cautiously, giving their master room, and also bowing out of the waves of pulsing mana which flowed invisibly from him in angry waves.

Neither of the two grown women made any move to intervene. They watched the wolf-masked man shake the child Oracle a little roughly, their faces impassive and unconcerned.

"The past … *informs* the future," the girl choked. "You cannot silence it, Strigoi. You cannot silence me. Are you searching, or are you running?" She smirked at him a little.

A grunt of disgust snorted from within the wolf's mask, and with a casual toss of his arm, he cast the child aside, sending her small body flying through the air across the chamber. It crashed into the wall, just above the plinth where moments earlier, a large decorative vase had stood. On impact, the girl's body shattered like chalk with a soft whoomph. The tumbling, powdery detritus losing all colour and form as it rained to the floor, white plaster dust and rubble.

There was silence in the room for a moment.

"Well, I'm glad I moved that vase," the younger of the remaining two Oracles said in an offhand way.

The older woman looked back to Strigoi. "If you've quite finished making your point, Lord Strigoi, perhaps you can tell us what specifically you need?" She glanced at the pool, which although calming itself, was still darker than usual and somewhat agitated. "I assume that you already know *where* the Shard is, and *who* has found it, otherwise you wouldn't be here now." She looked up at him enquiringly. Behind the wolf, the youngest Oracle re-entered the room, dusting off her pink robes and looking more than a little miffed. The Ravens peered at the child curiously. Behind Strigoi's back, she made a rude gesture that caused the old woman's face to crinkle in joy. "If only the past were that easy to cast aside, darkest one," she muttered.

"What I need, one-in-three," Strigoi said firmly, in his haunting whisper. "...is information."

In the quiet temple, the flames cracked in their coals and the dark metallic face of Strigoi glinted like a demon, "What you are going to give to me ..." he whispered "... is leverage."

GREEN GIFTS AND CURSED CUSTARD

"Happy Birthday! You gossamer-winged, wish-granting, toadstool-lurking maniac!"

Henry's bellowing voice shocked Robin awake with a startled jolt. His eyes shot open, bleary and blinking, to find the unruly brown mop of Henry's head leaning over his bed inches from his face. He was grinning like a lunatic.

Robin sat up so sharply he nearly head-butted the older boy, who only just managed to deftly dodge out of the way to the side of the bed.

"Wha ... humphgh?" Robin muttered unintelligibly. The sun was streaming in through the windows of his tower room at Erlking Hall, filling his bedroom with a crisp golden light that looks suspiciously like dawn. "What ... what time is it?"

"Birthday time, crazy teenager!" Henry punched Robin on the arm. "Don't think you can go sleeping in all day now that you're officially the same age as me. You'll be moping around and feeling misunderstood any minute now."

Robin's eyes focused, and he noticed for the first time that Henry was not alone. Karya leaned casually on the dresser, arms folded and smirking, her hair still a sleep-tangled mess, and Woad was balancing impossibly on the balls of his feet on a bed knob.

Alarmed, Robin pulled the covers up tightly to his neck. "What are you all doing in my room? I'm not dressed!" he cried, in a voice slightly higher than he had intended. Henry snorted.

"Nobody is interested in your Pokémon boxer shorts, Scion, believe me," Karya said. "Henry dragged us all out of bed at this ungodly hour. Apparently it's the day we celebrate your continued existence. Strange human custom, but there you are." She shrugged, stifling a yawn.

8

"I celebrate it every day!" Woad piped up happily, rocking back and forth. The small blue faun was grinning ear-to-ear, his long tail flicking like a cat to keep his balance. "But today there should be a parade! A parade and maybe feasting in the streets!" His eyes lit up. "Oh, oh, I know, we could sacrifice a white calf?" He looked around eagerly for approval.

Henry looked thoughtful, "Or …" He pulled a brightly wrapped package out from behind his back and thrust it at Robin. "…maybe less bloodshed, and more loot!"

Robin grinned, coming around a little and taking the present. "How did you guys even know it was my birthday?"

"Your aunt told us," Henry said smugly. "She found out. You know she's no good at human customs and things, but she tries, bless her. Fourteenth of September. That's today, and you're fourteen now." He poked Robin in the side of the head accusingly. "Any minute your voice will drop like a stone and you'll stop looking like such a beautiful delicate damsel."

"Shut up, you idiot." Robin pushed his messy blonde bed-hair back from his eyes and shook the box experimentally.

"Your Aunt Irene was quite put out actually," Karya said, with a thoughtfully raised eyebrow. "When she found out, I mean. You didn't celebrate your day of birth last year, Scion. You didn't even tell anyone about it."

Robin shrugged amiably. "Well, I didn't really know much about anything," he said. "I'd only been at Erlking for two weeks at the time. I didn't know anyone really, and with Gran just dying … I didn't feel like celebrating, it's no big deal."

"It is a big deal, moron!" Henry chided. "You can't just level-up into a teenager and not make a big deal out of it. You're so weird sometimes."

"I was busy turning into a Fae at the time," Robin pointed out. He looked around at his friends. "A lot's happened since then, that's for sure."

"Yes," Woad nodded sagely. "You have stretched."

"You are a bit taller I suppose," Karya allowed. "Growing like a weed. Still as skinny as a starved redcap though. You need to eat more."

"Yes, mother." Robin rolled his eyes, propping himself up on his pillows. "So, what is it then? Is it going to explode?" He eyed the gift with suspicion.

"No," Henry promised. "But it's one of two. I've got you one for last year too, seeing as you went all thirteeny without telling us. It's downstairs. Thought you'd like to spread out the loot through the day."

"I got you something too, Pinky." Woad said. His eyes narrowed. "But ... it escaped. Don't worry though, I will catch you another one."

Robin thought it wise not to pursue this. This was often the wisest course with Woad. Instead he tore the wrapping from the oblong package, revealing a heavy leather-bound volume in bright red bindings.

"It's a book!" Henry revealed, happily stating the obvious. "We, that is, Karya mainly, said you'd like a book, because you know ..." He shrugged. "...you're bookish and that."

Karya nodded rather proudly.

Robin turned the heavy book over in his hands, reading the golden lettering emblazoned across the front.

"'Legendary Places and Loathsome Deeds,'" he read aloud. "A collection of folktales fair and foul from the deepest Netherworlde's, by Marias Goldenbough." He grinned, flicking through the pages. It was heavily illustrated throughout. "Thanks guys, this is ace. You know I love this stuff."

"We figured by now you have read Hammerhand's Netherworlde Compendium cover to cover at least eighteen times," Karya said drolly. She nodded to the book in his hands. "These are old wives' tales, but some of them are fun."

"Does it have the tale of the Bubbling Bog Hag?" Woad asked her, excitedly. "I love the tale of the Bubbling Bog Hag!"

"I believe so," Karya replied with a thoughtful frown.

"What about King Jeremy and the seven sprites?" Woad chirped. "Or The Scarlet goose? That one's creepy!" He turned his head to Robin, wide-eyed. "Oh, oh! Even better, The Cursed Custard of Cerydrwyn! Does it?"

Robin rested the book on the covers, grinning at Woad's excitement. "Tell you what, Woad," he said. "How about I let you borrow it after I've read it, eh?"

The faun made a face. "I'm not so wonderful with the squiggly reading," he said. "I never really found time to figure out all the lines. Important ... faun ... stuff ... to do, you know?"

"I'll read to you then," Robin smirked.

Woad grinned widely and flipped backwards from his precarious perch on the bed knob to land deftly on the rug. "Yes! And to Inky too!" he insisted. "Inky likes the scary stories."

"You keep that bloody pet kraken of yours away from me," Henry grumbled. "I swear, it might not be bigger than a kitten, but it's got it in for me. Every time I see it, it's hissing and banging away on the glass of its jar with those rubbery little tentacles. It's started to freak me out."

"Maybe it just wants a hug?" Robin teased. "You're so approachable, Henry. You know we all have to restrain ourselves from hugging you constantly."

"I certainly don't," Karya said, folding her arms and smirking. "I'd rather hug the kraken."

"Oi!" Henry glared.

"Enough talk." Karya stood away from the dresser. "Everyone out. I don't care how exciting it is that the Scion has lived long enough to get a shiny new number next to his name, it's still painfully early in the morning and we have to get breakfast ready. Give Robin some peace so he can get up and dressed and ..." She looked at him critically. "... Do ... something ... with that hair. Honestly."

Robin ran a hand through his blonde mop a little self-consciously. It was indeed sticking up everywhere. He sometimes suspected that Woad snuck into his bedroom at night and back-combed it for his own amusement.

"Why are *we* making breakfast?" he asked, confused. "Where's Hestia?"

"Out," Henry said, stepping away from the bed and starting to usher the others toward the door. "Our joyful and sweet-tempered housekeeper set off early with your dear old aunt. Before sun-up even. I saw them go from the window."

"Go where?" Robin's interest was piqued. It was unusual for his aunt and Hestia to go out together, especially unannounced.

"Dad mentioned something about it at dinner last night," Henry explained. "Someone's coming to the house today and your aunt wanted to meet them personally down in the village." He shrugged. "Not like Lady Irene to run errands like that, but I'm guessing it's someone important if she took her lady-in-waiting along. All very formal."

"I'm sure we'll find out in an hour or two when they're back," Karya said. "Now come on, downstairs. It certainly isn't often we get the free run of the kitchens without Hestia's eyes on us. Let's make the most of it. We'll meet you down there, Scion."

Everyone left. Robin heard their voices bickering good-naturedly as they travelled down the stone spiral staircase from his tower room to the house proper, and smiled to himself, stifling a happy yawn.

He glanced at the red book happily, sitting on his bedcovers in the golden morning sunlight. "A new year for me," he mumbled to himself,

11

sliding out of bed and crossing to the dark chest of drawers atop which lay his mana-stone. He slipped it around his neck as he did every morning, the seraphinite stone resting on his chest with comforting familiarity. "The mighty and all powerful Scion of the Arcania takes another bold step towards adulthood," he muttered, smirking. "Right after breakfast that is."

He got dressed quickly, worried at leaving Woad at large in the kitchens for too long, and dragged his fingers through his pale hair, staring at himself in the long mirror which hung on the inside door of his wardrobe. Karya was right, he really did need a haircut. It was hard to believe he'd been at Erlking more than a year. So much had changed since then.

But not, he thought firmly, *my love for Pokémon pyjamas.*

COLD BREAKFAST

"What the devil is this?"

Mr Drover, Henry's father and handyman of Erlking, entered the sunny breakfast room, shrugging off gardening gloves and peering around with raised eyebrows. He was a large, heavy-set man, with a kind face and small, sparkling eyes the same shade of hazel as his son's. These eyes were currently surveying what could only be described as a culinary battlefield.

"It's breakfast, Dad," Henry said, waving a fork at his father. "What does it look like?"

Drover bristled his moustache, shaking his head a little. "What it looks like, lad, is that the kitchen threw up in the breakfast room." He pulled up a chair and dropped into it with a chuckle, rubbing his large hands together briskly. He had been out weeding dead strangleweed in the gardens since dawn, and the autumn air had chilled his bones. "Old Hestia's liable to have all your heads on spikes when she gets back. Won't that make a nice addition to the front lawn, eh? Might scare the squirrels off at any rate."

The large wooden table, around which the four children and Mr Drover sat, was covered in food. Pancakes, bacon, eggs, sausages, stacks of ham liberated from the pantry, muffins filled with dubious concoctions of various fillings. There were at least five different pots of jam, all opened, and drinks haphazardly filling any spaces between the plates.

"We couldn't decide on what to have," Robin explained around a mouthful of pancake. "Karya wanted French toast, but Woad doesn't like eggs once they're cooked. Henry said pancakes were the best, as any food you get to throw in the air has to be a good thing, and I–"

"Alright, alright." Drover held his hands up. "I don't even want to know what the kitchen looks like. Just pass me some of that toast, will you? No, no, not the one with maple syrup, the one that's just got a whole pat of butter on it, by the looks of things."

"You should be conscious of your blood pressure, Mr Drover," Karya said conscientiously. "A man of your years and physical condition, butter can be a murder weapon."

Drover gave her a sly look, pouring himself a cup of tea. "Ain't nothing wrong with my physical condition thank you, young miss. Fit as a fiddle. A badly tuned fiddle, mind, but one that can still hold a tune or two." He slurped his tea. "And the only thing bad for my blood pressure in this house is you four rascals. Especially …" He glanced over at Woad, pointing a triangle of toast with mock-menace, "…this one here. Little blue terror."

Woad looked affronted. Or as affronted as it was possible to look with cheeks smeared with glam-glam jam. "What have I done?" he said innocently. "I am a model citizen!"

Drover laughed. "Oh dear me, if you could smell lies, I'd have to open a window right now, you little troublemaker." He balanced his elbows on the chaotic table, between the sugar pot and a stack of bacon. "Perhaps you'd like to tell me why there's a creature of the deep rolling around in the main hall in a bubble, eh? Tripped right over it. With an armful of logs I did, almost went flying. I could have done myself a mischief."

Woad looked guilty, but also a little proud. "I didn't know Inky could get up and down the stairs in that bubble. He's as resourceful as he is charming, it seems."

"That, I'm afraid, would be my doing, Mr Drover," a soft voice said behind him. A tall and willowy woman had entered the room, drifting like a ghost in a soft rainbow-hued gown. Her long pale hair floated softly around her, as though underwater, as she turned her head to calmly inspect the gastronomic destruction of the room.

"Your doing, Madame Calypso?" Drover coughed a little on his toast, startled by the nymph's appearance. Robin and Henry sat up a little straighter in their chairs, trying to look less like feral ravenous slobs. Karya shook her head almost imperceptibly to herself. *Nymphs*, she blew on her cup of tea, they had a way of fogging the male mind.

"The bubble," Robin's tutor explained, closing the door softly behind her. "The faun was carrying that creature around in a jam-jar everywhere, it didn't seem kind. Creatures of the water, such as I, we need freedom. To go as and where we please."

14

"It was my idea actually," Robin said proudly. "I was thinking how people who have hamsters and hamster-type things, they get a little clear plastic ball, don't they?" He mimed holding a little ball above his plate. "And the hamster goes inside, and it can go anywhere then, but still not get eaten by cats. If you have a cat."

Henry nodded in ardent approval. "Zorbing," he said, raising his glass in a toast. "It's called zorbing I think. Cracking idea. Genius that, Rob. Inky loves it, murderous little demon that it is."

"This is just my humble opinion, but kraken-zorbing might not go down too well with some of the ladies of the house," Drover said to Calypso. "That's all I'm saying. It's one thing for a critter to go rolling around wherever it pleases in a magic watery bubble and all. Who am I to judge?" He stroked his bristly moustache. "But when 'wherever it pleases' ends up being under-foot, well then ..." He crunched his toast decisively. "Let's just say there are less patient feet than mine to get under in this household, that's all."

Calypso nodded dreamily. "I understand your concern, human servant. Woad, you should make efforts to confine your companion to the upper levels of the house. Especially when Lady Irene's guests arrive."

Woad nodded ruefully.

"Would you like to join us for breakfast?" Karya asked. The nymph examined the packed table silently for a moment.

"I think perhaps not," she said. "It all looks absolutely horrible and badly made."

"Actually, some of this toast is salvageable," Drover said happily. "You can see where they've scraped all the really burnt bits off. Just gives it a gritty texture. Think of it as a bit of a challenge."

"As tempting as that is ... no," Robin's tutor said. "The very idea is mildly repellent." She glanced dreamily across the table. "I've only come to tell you, Robin, that in light of it being your birthday, and of house-guests arriving imminently, I have decided to cancel your training until after the weekend. You will have four days free." She gave Robin a small, distant smile. "Happy birthday."

Robin grinned at this. He had come a long way in his studies in the Tower of Water, but Calypso was an absolute slave-driver when it came to lessons. September was creeping along, and the lake was certainly not getting any warmer. Four days with no responsibilities sounded like heaven to him.

"Excellent," he said, saluting her with his orange juice. "Thank you."

"I considered getting you an actual present," she said, with a tiny frown. "But then … I didn't." She gave a small shrug.

Robin wasn't offended. He was used to his tutor's manner. She wasn't really interested in much when it came to human affairs. It was enough for him that she'd even actually considered it at all.

"These guests," Karya asked, in as light and airy a tone as the young girl could manage. "Do you know who they are?" She looked from Calypso to Mr Drover, sipping her tea innocently as she fished for information. Robin knew that Karya hated not knowing everything.

"Blowed if I know," Henry's father said. "I thought it was strange enough that Lady Irene didn't have me go pick them up myself. That's my job, that is. Driver. One of them anyway. Most peculiar."

"I have not been informed directly," Calypso said. "So I imagine it does not concern me. It probably doesn't concern you either. I should occupy yourselves in clearing up this travesty of a breakfast before certain parties return to the house, if I were you, rather than speculating. We don't want hysteria on such a pretty morning, do we?"

It was no secret at Erlking that there was little love between Robin's tutor and Hestia the housekeeper, to whom she was clearly referring. Hestia had disapproved of Calypso since the moment she arrived. The nymph didn't seem to give two hoots what anyone thought of her, which only made Hestia bristle more.

"I'll go and find Inky," Woad said. "His days of free-roaming parkour are numbered! Trust the word of this honourable faun."

"Henry and I will clean up in here," Karya said, nodding in agreement with the nymph's plan. "We'll do more birthday presents in a bit. Robin why don't you–"

Robin was already filling a plate with various foodstuffs. "Actually, I'm just going upstairs for a bit," he said. "Won't be long."

Henry frowned and rolled his eyes as Robin stood with the plate. "Yeah, yeah, we know. Off to visit Sleeping Broody are you. Good luck, Florence Nightingale … again."

Robin made his way up to the second floor, near the rear of the house where it was quiet, the laden breakfast tray clinking as he padded along the carpet of the long silent hallway. He came to a door where he paused for a moment, frowning to himself. Then with a sigh down his nose he let himself in.

The silent room beyond was a bedroom. One of the many spare and unused suites at Erlking Hall. It was sparsely furnished. Two long windows along one wall let in the bright early autumn light, which fell across the pale floorboards in bright clean bands. The room was utterly silent as Robin kicked the door closed softly behind him and crossed the floor, the boards squeaking under his feet. He set the breakfast tray down quietly.

"Today would be a good day for it," he said. "If you've been waiting to choose a dramatic moment or anything."

He looked down at the bed. It was occupied by a teenage boy, pale as snow with greyish hair, the stiff covers neatly tucked around his bare shoulders. The boy was sleeping and didn't respond. Robin watched him for a moment, looking for a flicker of an eyelid, a twitch of lips, anything.

For all intents and appearances, the pale boy may well have been dead. He certainly looked like a pallid corpse, although Robin noticed that the dark circles under his eyes had finally disappeared altogether. *If he wasn't so white*, Robin mused to himself. *He'd look the picture of health compared to when he'd arrived.*

"Just that … it's my birthday today," he said to the boy in the bed. "So … you know. Good a time as any to wake up, right?"

The sleeper made no indication he had heard a word Robin had said. He was frowning slightly in his sleep. He had been frowning slightly in his sleep for a solid month now.

Robin watched his chest beneath the crisp sheets for a moment, as he did every morning, just to check he could see their guest was indeed breathing. When he was satisfied this was indeed the case, he slumped into a chair beside the bed with a creak.

"I'm fourteen today," he said amiably. "You must be what? Sixteen? Seventeen? It's hard to tell really. You'd probably look younger if you weren't scowling all the time. But then I don't really know how Fae age. You could be a hundred years old for all I know."

He speared a rasher of bacon on a fork and wafted it tantalisingly under the sleeping boy's nose.

"Bacon today," he said hopefully. "Everyone likes bacon, right? If anything's going to guide you back to the land of the living, it's going to be delicious … crispy … mouth-watering bacon."

The silver-haired boy slept on silent and unmoving, apparently unen-amoured with bacon.

Robin persisted for a moment, listening to the soft wind outside whis-tling around the lea of the house. Then he sighed and sat back, dropping the bacon back onto the plate.

It had been a month now since he had discovered Jackalope out on the lake. Deposited by a Grimm for reasons unknown and much more alive than when last they had met. A whole month at Erlking, in this bed, in this quiet room, and he hadn't woken.

It had taken a lot of convincing of the others to allow him into the house at all. Henry had been astonished. He had assumed Jackalope, the errant Fae who had betrayed them all back in the summer, had perished in the flooded tomb beneath the lake. He had been dead set against taking the turncoat in. They should have driven him to the nearest hospital, he'd said, and washed their hands of him.

Karya had been more practical, as was her usual manner. He wasn't human for a start, and unlike Robin, he couldn't pass for one. Questions would surely have been raised at any hospital about a snow white teenager, dressed in fur scraps and with sawn off horn stubs growing out of his head.

Woad had been suspicious, certain that it wasn't Jackalope at all, but a Grimm hiding under a glamour. Aunt Irene had put that theory to bed with a few glam glam drops. It wasn't an imposter. It wasn't a trap. It was just a boy, inexpertly dressed from stab wounds and both unconscious and unresponsive.

Irene, to Robin's surprise, had asked him what he wanted to do. It was his decision, as the Scion, she had explained. Everyone had looked to him. Robin had asked immediately for a room to be prepared, and Hestia, whose healing skills were legendary, had set to work patching the boy up properly.

"It's lucky for you we had Hestia here, you know," Robin said now to the Fae in the bed, fully aware that he was only really talking to himself. He had fallen into the habit of chatting away to Jackalope in the past month, holding up both sides of the conversation sometimes. "She might not have the best bedside manner, but she's good at what she does." Absently he lifted a sausage from the plate. It was going cold but he munched on it anyway. "She healed me last year too. This was long before we met you. I'd had a run in with Strife's Skrikers. Bit of a skirmish in an airship out over the ocean in the Netherworlde – long story. She's done wonders with your stab wound. Especially considering that when Peryl stuck the knife in, she gave it a bloody good twist too." Robin had been present for the treatment, and winced now at the recollection. It had been the first time he'd seen Hestia open a wound. Considering how prissy and fussy she was about little things like house dust, she hadn't batted an eye about being elbow-deep in blood.

"Look, Sleeping Beauty," Robin said. "Everyone here thinks you're a lost cause. You've been asleep forever, you know. It's a good job there are magical ways to get nutrients and things into you otherwise you'd be in a hospital somewhere with a tube down your nose right now. Lucky us Fae are hardy folk, eh?"

Jackalope didn't argue with this.

"You're at Erlking," Robin told him for the hundredth time. "You know that, right? I know you can hear me in there, you stubborn, sulky sod." He looked around the quiet room. Dust was dancing, caught in the sunbeams from the tall windows, a silent maelstrom of peaceful, suspended gold. The room smelled of beeswax polish. It was calm and comforting. "What I mean to say is, you're safe here. Safer than anywhere else anyway." He glanced down, and lowered his voice. "It's safe to come out. No-one hates you."

He considered this for a moment. "Well …" he shrugged. "Maybe …"

Henry had told Robin more than a few times over the past few weeks that he was wasting his time. Whatever Peryl had done to Jackalope, he seemed damaged beyond repair. And he'd been pretty damaged when they'd met him already. Living in the wilds, hiding in caves and scraping out a life alone in the snow.

Robin didn't know if Henry was right or not. All he knew was that whatever bad decisions the older Fae had made, they had been made from fear, not spite. Jackalope had saved his life, when Peryl had been about to kill him out on the snow. It seemed only fair that he return the favour now. They were both Fae after all, and although they didn't seem to have anything in common, at least they could potentially bond over the fact that the same girl had tried to kill them both at some point.

"Peryl brought you here for a reason," he said to the comatose boy. "Brought you to me, specifically, I think. It's hard to explain. I know she's a Grimm, I know she's my enemy. But still … something happened with the shard when it broke in two. Something with Peryl and me, and I can't make sense of it. I could really use someone to talk about it with."

This had been a circular and one-sided conversation Robin had been having day after day. He was nothing if not persistent.

"Nothing?" he said hopefully. Still no response. "Well then …" he sighed. "I hope you're dreaming something good at least, wherever you are. Hard to tell from that scowl. I barely know you, that could be your super-happy face for all I know, right?"

Robin stood, stretching. In one last attempt, he leaned in dramatically and whispered. "If you don't wake up soon, I'm going to have Hestia come back and give you another sponge bath. Do you seriously want that? I'd rather be stabbed again if I were you."

Even this horrifying prospect didn't elicit the slightest fluttering of an eyelash from the older boy. He may well have been carved from marble.

Robin stood up straight, trying not to feel deflated. "Have it your way," he said quietly. "In your own time, Jack. I have birthday stuff to do. If you want some cake, we're all just downstairs."

FATES AND FOPS

There was indeed cake, a feast and much making of merry later that day, but before the party events, Robin was called to the entrance hall by Mr Drover.

Karya, Woad and Henry were elsewhere, no doubt still in the kitchens trying frantically to repair the chaotic damage before the return of Hestia. Drover was standing by the large doors, hands clasped behind his back. Robin couldn't help but notice that the portly man had on his smartest tweed jacket, and his hair, the tufty wisps of which were usually wild around his ears below his balding head, had been carefully combed. He seemed to be making a smart effort.

"There you are, lad," he said as Robin descended the stairs. "How's the patient? No change?"

Robin shook his head. "Still sleeping like a baby," he said. He considered this for a moment. "Well, a big, angry-looking baby, that is. Did you need me for something? I was going to find the others and help tidy before Hestia gets back."

Drover shook his head, beckoning Robin down the stairs fussily. "No, no time for that now. We'll have to hope the others have done a good job, and the faun and its pet are out of sight," he said. "Your aunt and her guests are back. I saw the car coming up the drive just now. You're the young master of the house. You need to be here to greet them. That's proper that is." He looked over Robin a little critically. Robin was relieved that he had changed out of his pyjamas. He was in dark jeans and a black sweater against the nippy September air.

"You'll pass muster I suppose," Drover allowed. "Can you not do anything about that hair though, give it a brush or something? You're as bad as my Henry. Look like you've been dragged through a hedge backwards."

Robin self-consciously ran his fingers through his hair, certain it wasn't stuck up quite as bad as Mr Drover's tone suggested. He had a horrible mental image of the man dragging a comb and hair oil through his head, plastering it down into a blonde, super neat side parting so that he looked like one of those rosy-cheeked singing children from the Sound of Music. He shivered involuntarily at the thought.

"Isn't this a bit old fashioned?" he asked, worriedly checking himself in the long mirror at the foot of the stairs. "I mean, all the staff lined up outside the house, that's the sort of thing you read about in Pride and Prejudice."

Drover grumbled into his moustache. "There ain't no expiry date on good manners, my lad," he insisted, ushering Robin towards the great double doors. "And I've as much idea as you do as to who's come calling, so best foot forward and all that. Your aunt will appreciate the effort, she will."

It was a crisp and clear morning outside. High blue skies dotted with thin wisps of woolly clouds soared over the great grey stone pile of Erlking Hall. The grassy hills before the house led down to the woods and village beyond, the leaves of the trees already beginning ever so slightly to turn. In a week, Robin thought, the woods of Erlking would be a riot of autumn colour, burnished golds and reds. Right now, the only hint that the season had turned was the chill in the bright air as he stood at the foot of the steps beside Mr Drover. They watched a car appear from the tunnel of trees which led up the hill, and crawl its stately way along the gravel to the turning circle in front of the house.

It wasn't Mr Drovers car, which was a beat up old thing. This car was black and old fashioned, but perfectly preserved, waxed and polished to within an inch of its life. It looked, to Robin's untrained eye, a little like a funeral car.

"Well blow me," Drover muttered quietly, giving him a surreptitious nudge in the ribs. "That's a vintage phantom, that is!" Henry's father had rather a mania for old cars. "A 1929 Brewster Phantom one, Henly Roadster. Good nick too. Whoever it is, they must be pretty lah-di-dah."

Robin nodded, deciding not to point out the fact that they all spent most of their time in a huge sprawling mansion.

The car came to a halt at the foot of the steps before them, and Drover made to jump down and open the back doors. Before he could though, the driver emerged, slamming the door heartily behind him.

"No no, my good fellow! I wouldn't hear of it! Too kind! Altogether too kind, but please, the pleasure is mine!"

He was a tall and bright man, all twinkling merry eyes and grinning teeth. His hair was a strange streaky mixture of orange, red and blonde, sweeping foppishly atop his head like a sculpted flame.

"It is my absolute and undying pleasure to be not only the conveyer of these fine ladies, but also the prostrate servant eager to serve in all things!" the driver said with a beaming smile and a wink. He had, Robin noticed with interest, the most dramatic waxed moustache and beard he had ever seen. The beard was carefully shaped into a point, and the long moustache was waxed into flamboyant upward curls. The man came around the front of the car at a trot, giving the bonnet a friendly double-pat, as though it were a horse, and crossed energetically to the door Drover had been aiming for.

His clothing, Robin thought, was as odd and theatrical as his face and hair. He was dressed like a dandy from another time. High riding boots, a waistcoat of cream which was positively drowning in gold swirling embroidery, and over this, an elaborate tailed frock coat of brightest crimson. This too, Robin saw, was trimmed with swirls of gold all over. The man even had great lacy cuffs at his wrists.

He gripped the door and opened it, bowing deeply and theatrically. "My most ardent apologies for the bumpy ride, ladies." He grinned into the dark interior. "Blasted country roads, you know. One does get so used to driving in town. I hope you can find it in your hearts to forgive me."

Robin's Great Aunt Irene stepped from the back of the car, taking the fop's proffered hand with natural grace.

Irene was an old woman of glacial poise and calm dignity. Her fluid exit from the car made the man seem even more animated and swaggering in comparison. She was wearing a long pale gown and a great grey fur stole, bundled around her shoulders against the air. She shrugged this up on her shoulders as he released her hand. Robin saw she was a good foot taller than the man. He was not short, Irene was a spire of a woman.

"Yes, thank you, Silas," she said crisply. "One is quite capable of getting out of a vehicle without assistance, although your eager gallantry is, of course, appreciated as always."

She gave him a respectful nod and glanced to Robin.

"You are awake, my young ward," she said in greeting. "Many happy returns of the day to you." She indicated the driver. "This is an associate of mine who will be staying with us for a while, Silas Ffoulkes. And these … are our other guests, the sisters Eumenides."

A strange and sudden chill ran down Robin's spine, like an ice cube down the collar, and he whirled. Standing behind him on the steps were three women. Or at least he guessed they were women. The word 'apparitions' seemed more suitable in his opinion. He hadn't seen them step out of the car. In fact, he couldn't see any way they could have left the car without him noticing them, but there they were all the same.

The three figures were clad head to toe in long, greying robes, every inch covered with tattered lacework like decaying funeral garb. Their heads and faces were entirely covered with similar veils. They were identical. Standing silently on the steps with their hands clasped before them in their long sleeves. They were ghastly. The ghost of Miss Havisham in triplicate.

"Mr Ffoulkes and the sisters are Panthea. Resident here in the mortal world. They have business of their own in the Netherworlde," Irene explained, speaking lightly as though oblivious to Robin's horrified wide-eyed stare. "The sisters require safe passage, and Mr Ffoulkes has been kind enough to offer to escort them. He is here also at my request for matters we shall come to later. They will be staying with us here at Erlking until Halloween. I trust you will make them all feel welcome."

"Halloween?" Robin asked anxiously, looking from the ghoulish women to the strange, bright man.

"When the stars align," said one of the sisters, in a muttered hiss like dry paper, her face invisible beneath the lace.

"And the veil between the worlds is thin," one of her companions added, though Robin could not readily say which had spoken.

"That is the best time to move between the worlds," added the third ominously. "Without drawing the unwanted attention …"

A dry autumn wind blew leaves softly across the stone steps, rustling in the silence. Robin noticed the sisters' clothing didn't stir in the breeze.

"Plus, I hear your lovely aunt puts on a jolly good spread," the man added, in a much brighter tone. "Wouldn't want to miss that, would we?" He grinned, his curling moustache bobbing as he wiggled his eyebrows playfully. He stuck out his hand to Robin. "Honour to meet you, Scion of the Arcania. Dashed good of you to have us crash at the old pile."

Robin shook the hand of the strange Mr Ffoulkes. It was very hot.

"Um … pleasure," Robin stammered.

Irene closed the car door behind her firmly, and Robin couldn't tell if it was only his own imagination, but she seemed to be giving the energetic Mr Ffoulkes a slightly disapproving look. "Shall we go inside?" she said lightly. "It's none too clement and frankly, I, for one, could do with a nice cup of tea."

Robin thought he must have imagined the glare. Why would Aunt Irene invite someone to stay if she didn't like them, after all? He glanced a little nervously at the odd silent women. But then again, who in their right mind would invite such creepy women to visit at all? Hestia appeared from the other side of the car, looking very business-like and carrying luggage, which Mr Drover dutifully bounded down the stairs to help her with.

The three ghoulish sisters leaned in to one another, muttering and whispering, then straightened up.

"There is a great darkness in this house," the middle one said, in an ominous rasp. "It seems small, but it grows in secret … There are many secrets here."

Irene blinked her sharp eyes, looking rather unconcerned. "Well yes … be that as it may, there is also tea. Shall we?"

There had been a short but heated argument, conducted in sharp whispers between Drover and Hestia in the inner hallway about who should be carrying bags, after which Mr Drover disappeared upstairs with the luggage, presumably to prepare guest rooms for these strange and incongruous visitors, and Hestia scuttled off to make tea. Irene spirited the strange ghostly sisters and Mr Ffoulkes off to the parlour, instructing Robin to make himself presentable and that dinner would be served at four. As she showed the elaborately-dressed man and his dour companions from the hall into a sitting room, she had turned and leaned down to Robin, a gentle hand on his shoulder. Her voice was very low, so that only he heard what she muttered to him.

"A necessary evil, this man," she told him. "Not a danger, only a pest, but be on your guard, my boy. And for heaven's sake, keep your faun out of sight and out of earshot until Halloween. It's best young Woad's presence here remain unknown. Magpies do covet so those things that shine."

She straightened up, giving him a wink so subtle, even Robin himself was unsure he had really seen it.

"Dinner at four," she repeated, in her normal voice.

Taking this as a cue to get out from under everyone's feet, he went in search of Henry and the others, to share the news of the new arrivals.

"What, like actual ghosts?" Henry said, frowning. Robin had found the older boy in one of the attic rooms, empty of everything but mothballs, with mismatched wooden boards on the floor and ceiling, some of which had been inexplicably painted white, and a lingering smell of pine-needles. The two boys were now sitting on the floor at opposite walls, idly throwing a tennis ball back and forth to one another across the empty space.

"No, not really," Robin explained. "I mean, I've seen actual ghosts, up on the moors. They're transparent, and well, kind of glowy." He tossed the ball overarm, it bounced once in the centre of the bare room, sending a satisfying echo around the bare plaster walls. It flew up to Henry, who caught it expertly. "They're solid, I think, these women. They just look creepy as anything. Like something that's been dragged out of a grave. All dark and ghoulish. I haven't seen any of their faces, they're all covered up like brides."

Henry looked thoughtful, throwing the ball back idly. "And they're just here for what? A social visit?"

Robin shrugged, catching it. "Passing through, apparently," he said. "You know Erlking is its own station."

The links between the human world and the Netherworlde, Robin knew, were gateways known as Janus stations. It was a network of portals, a web that tied the two worlds together at specific points, passing places. He also knew that Lady Eris controlled nearly all of these doorways. Erlking was one that she did not. "I thought you said growing up here there were always people passing through?"

Henry shrugged. "Well yeah, now and again," he allowed. "When I was little. All Panthea mind. I never saw a Fae until I met you. But I've never seen spooky-ghost-bride women before, or this other guy, whatever he is."

"He seems okay," Robin said, a little doubtfully, remembering his aunt's whispered words of caution. "Bit fancy, all gilt and teeth, and the most over-styled beard and 'tashes I've ever seen. Kind of reminds me of a game show host or something. What on earth he's got to do with those walking corpses though, I've no idea."

"Can't wait to meet them all at dinner tonight then," Henry said. "Me and dad are staying on account of it being your birthday bash and all. Shame Woad won't be able to join us though. Wonder what that's all about?"

Robin, who had told Henry that Woad had to stay discreetly out of the way while the guests were here, tossed the ball up in the air and caught it himself. "Well, you'll probably see a fair bit of them, they're all staying here until Halloween. That's a month away." Robin wasn't sure how comfortable he was with this. He secretly hoped that whatever rooms Mr Drover had prepared for the new guests, they were nowhere near his tower. He didn't fancy running into one of those women in a dark corridor in the middle of the night. And he was not at all confident he could control Woad's comings and goings for that length of time anyway.

Henry grinned. "Well, at least we've got a month then to plan our costumes for the feast. I was thinking of getting some face-paint and going as Woad. Does that still count as him staying out of sight? If I'm him, I mean? You could dress up as Karya?"

Robin glowered across the room at Henry, who grinned.

"See, mate? You've already got her expression perfect. A scowl of disapproval that could melt through walls."

"I think Calypso has enough training planned for me this month to keep me far too busy for hilarious cross-dressing, Henry," Robin said wearily.

Henry rolled his eyes. "Yeah, yeah. It must be such a massive chore for you having private lessons with incredibly gorgeous women. I feel your pain, Rob, really I do." He held out his hands expectantly, and Robin tossed the ball across the room to him. It bounced once on a white floorboard and continued on its trajectory to Henry in slow motion. "Have to say though, I thought your Tower of Water lessons would be winding down a bit, now it's autumn. I mean, you can't go swimming about in the lake much longer surely. You're going to catch your death."

"She's 'refurbished' the old pool room," Robin explained. His tutor, Madame Calypso, was only ever truly at home in or around water. It was well known that she was not overly fond of conducting Robin's lessons in the house. She much preferred to be out in nature. However, a short talk with Aunt Irene recently during a rainstorm about the perils of hyperthermia had resulted in this compromise. "I've got a few days off lessons though for my birthday, so that's all good. I reckon your dad will be busy helping out with the new guests all weekend so at least you'll be up here, right? We can have a laugh."

Henry made a slightly awkward and apologetic face. "Actually Rob," he said, a little hesitantly. "I won't be here tomorrow or Sunday. I've got some stuff to do in the village."

Robin frowned, catching the thrown ball. This was highly unusual. Although he didn't live there, Henry was at Erlking Hall almost every waking moment that wasn't taken up with school, and he slept over most weekends. This would be the third time in two weeks that Henry had been too busy to hang around.

"What stuff?" Robin asked.

The taller boy shrugged evasively. "Just some extra lessons and things, no big deal. I'm having private tuition at the weekends."

Robin's frown deepened. Henry was certainly not the most studious person he had ever met. He had spent much of the summer in summer school, when he wasn't off adventuring in the Netherworlde that is. And now he was having weekend tuition as well?

"Wow, your dad is really cracking down on the school work, isn't he," Robin said glumly. He felt a little deflated. He had been looking forward to spending his birthday weekend with Henry.

The dark-haired boy shook his head, looking a little embarrassed. "No, it's not like that, it's more of an … activity. Like a … sports thing."

Realisation dawned for Robin and he tossed the ball back to his friend. "Oh, like a football club, something like that," he said, as lightly as he could manage.

It was something of a sore point for Robin that, being the most hunted and arguably most important person in the Netherworlde, he was well guarded at Erlking. It was his sanctuary, but also, in some ways, his prison. He envied the fact that Henry, a normal boy, had a life outside these walls. Other friends, other activities.

"Yeah," Henry said, still a little evasive. "Something like that." He noticed Robin looking a little downtrodden and made a face. "Don't worry, I'll still be up in the evenings, right?" He rolled his eyes a little, leaning back against the faded and crumbling plaster. "And anyway, you've got your delicate patient to nursemaid, right?"

This riled Robin a little. Henry had made no secret of the fact that he thought Robin taking in Jackalope was a bad idea. He seemed to raise the subject at every opportunity.

"Give it a rest." Robin threw the ball back forcefully, deliberately aiming for a white board. It ricocheted speedily as though shot from a gun. "You're starting to sound like a stuck record about that. It's not like I've got him staying in your rooms and wearing your spare PJs, is it? I don't know why your nose is so out of joint about him being here."

Henry raised his eyebrows at his friend, nursing his stinging hand where he had caught the ball. "He sided with a Grimm … against us," he pointed out. Seeing Robin open his mouth to respond, Henry raised his hands in surrender. "Okay, okay. Your business, not mine. If you want to be the faerie version of crazy cat lady and take in every stray you find, it's none of my business. Just don't expect me not to say 'told you so' when everyone gets a bit stabbed."

"Nobody is getting stabbed, you drama queen." Robin rolled his eyes.

"I said a *bit* stabbed," Henry said petulantly.

"Not even a *bit* stabbed," Robin smirked, despite himself. It was always hard to take Henry seriously. "Karya has been watching Jackalope like a hawk since he got here. I think if he was showing signs of murdering us all in the night, she'd be the first to raise the alarm."

Henry made an innocent face, silently suggesting that Karya's hawk-like interest in the pale and sleeping Fae may be slightly less objective than she let on. Robin studiously ignored this, getting to his feet.

"Anyway," he said. "Seeing as you're abandoning your best friend all weekend to go play five-a-side netball or whatever, I think you at least owe it to me to help me break the news to Woad that he has to be locked in his room until the end of October. After that, it's birthday feast with all our new friends."

Henry tossed the ball over his shoulder, nodding. "Flashy gilded peacock man and the brides of zombie Dracula?" he grinned. "Wouldn't miss it, mate." The friends walked out, closing the door on the popping-corn sound of a tennis ball being pinballed between the white boards.

A SPOT OF DARKNESS

Dinner, Robin later considered, was all in all, a strange affair.

It was made stranger as, due to the special occasion of having guests at Erlking, rather than take their evening meal together in the familiar dining room as per usual, they gathered instead in the Hall of the Hunt. Robin had never eaten in here before. In fact, during all his time at Erlking so far, the very few times he had ventured into this long, vaulted hall, most of the furniture had been carefully covered with dust sheets. Henry had explained, rather alarmingly, that this was because the room tended to moult and, frankly, it looked gross. Robin had no idea what he meant, but had learnt the hard way to take such advice as writ. The fact that it had been brought out of retirement and dressed up was an indication that Hestia had clearly made every effort to get the place up to scratch to impress Irene's guests.

The Hall of the Hunt, it transpired, was a rather medieval affair. A great dark-wood dining room with flagstone floor, shimmering with numerous candles and wall-sconces. The theme of the room, as the name implied, was game. Countless rather macabre stag's heads were mounted proudly on the walls, alongside plenty of boar, fish, wild stuffed birds and plenty of other, less identifiable beasts of the forest. It was a taxidermist's dream, a gallery of stuffed wildlife, a multitude of glassy eyes gleaming down on them in the candlelight. This being Erlking, several of the wall-mounted animal heads occasionally shook their heads, dislodging dust, or rolled their eyes to peer at the diners below. An intermittent bestial snort contended with the crackling flames of the large fireplace, and the various stuffed and arranged pheasant, fowl and partridge ruffled their feathers from time to time, occasionally shedding one on the floor.

Despite its official name, Henry had dubbed it Antler-Pocalypse Hall, and with good reason. When the Fae chose a theme, Robin had discovered, they really ran with it.

A vast and imposing chandelier hung from the beamed ceiling on a long chain, swooping low over the long, dark dining table. The chandelier was composed entirely from a rather gruesome and spiky latticework of antlers, the many candles hidden amongst its angular branches sending a spider web of fractured light and shadow outwards against the walls. The table decorations themselves were likewise pointy in design and equally disturbingly organic, and the high-backed chairs in which Robin and everyone else found themselves were crested with horns like decorative Viking ships.

In this curious and rather intimidating room, Robin sat between Henry and Karya, and across the long table from Mr Drover. Robin was hoping Hestia would remember to make up a spare plate for Woad, who was currently sulking upstairs in his bedroom. He made a mental note to try and fill an extra plate himself.

Up at the head of the shadowy table, Irene herself made polite conversation with the red-haired man, who had changed for dinner into a more formal suit that, incredibly, seemed somehow to hold even more gold brocade, making him shimmer in the candle-light like a frozen firework. On her other side, the three sisters, still veiled, faceless and shadowy, sat all together, bunched up as though they wished to try and occupy only one seat.

Henry occasionally kicked Robin's shin under the table during the meal, nodding rather unsubtly or making a face when a shaking and grey hand, dressed in tattered lace gloves, emerged ponderously from the robes to stab a fork into a plateful of whatever appetisers Hestia had prepared. The three gruesome sisters, from what Robin could observe, seemed awfully fond of mushroom vol-au-vents.

He tried his best to ignore them. The women were giving him the creeps. For a birthday meal, the atmosphere was strangely uncomfortable with their presence.

"So, young Robin Fellows, you golden-haired cherub," the bright-eyed man called down the table to him, in crisp jovial tones. "Your aunt informs us that today is your birthday."

Robin nodded, grabbing a bread roll from a tray in front of him. "Yes, that's right."

"Your second here at the old Fae pile, eh? But the first you've celebrated. No party and cake last year, I understand? Kept it all jolly quiet?"

Robin felt a little uncomfortable under the man's merry stare. He didn't seem to blink very often. "I hadn't been here very long," he said, aware that all eyes around the table were suddenly on him. "I didn't want to be a bother to anyone."

The man slapped his hand on the table, as though this were the funniest thing he'd heard all day. Forks and spoons jumped and juddered with a clatter. "Not a bother!" he grinned. "A-ha-ha-ha! That's delightful. Absolutely delightful. The world's last changeling, not wanting to be a bother." He looked over to Aunt Irene playfully. "Isn't he precious? This charge of yours."

Irene's face was a study in contemplative calm. If, like Robin, she thought there was a strange atmosphere in the room, she was ignoring it with tremendously practised decorum. She sipped soup from her spoon. "Extremely precious, Silas," she agreed politely. "To many. Hence his sanctuary here."

"That's what I'm getting at!" The red-haired man pointed back to Robin, his golden cuff flashing dangerously close to a candle on the table. "Trust me, as one who knows the worth of everything, indeed whose very business is to know the worth of everything. Precious indeed! Every eye in the Netherworlde is either looking for this boy, or resting on him already, and here he didn't kick up a fuss about passing into the realm of a teenager last year because he …" his grin widened, "…didn't want to be a bother. A-ha-ha-ha! Classic. I can see why you like him."

Robin had never encountered anyone before who actually said 'a-ha-ha-ha' instead of laughing. The man named Silas had done it twice now. It was quite disconcerting.

"Can you indeed, Silas?" Irene nodded indulgently. "If Robin chose not to celebrate at the time, I feel that is entirely his business, do you not? We were all barely more than strangers last year, when he arrived." She glanced down the table at Robin, something close to approval in her sharp eyes. "We have all rather grown on each other since. There is more cause for celebration this year. Much has happened."

"A birthday should *always* be a time of joy," the man pressed, wagging his fork at Robin. "None of this false modesty. It's very unfashionable. There's never a reason to skip a party." He winked.

Robin stared at the bread in his hands, feeling everyone's eyes still on him. His face felt a little hot. "My gran had just died at the time," he said, a little louder than he had intended. "I was homeless. And I didn't know anyone. I didn't feel like celebrating much."

The man paused, fork in hand, his grin frozen momentarily on his face, but he recovered well.

"Ah…yes. Terrible business, of course. Still …" he stabbed a forkful of salad thoughtfully. "I do like a good wake. Jolly things really, once all the mumbling is out of the way and the drinks are flowing."

Robin caught Karya's expression out of the corner of his eye. The young girl was staring at the man with open disapproval. He nudged her shoulder, urging her not to say anything. He didn't know anything about these people, and the last thing he wanted was for his friends to make a scene that might put Aunt Irene in a tight spot.

"You are probably wondering, all of you," Irene said, setting down her spoon. "The nature of this visit." It was as though she had read Robin's mind. Or else she too had registered Karya's soon-to-be-vocalised indignity at the man's poor manners. She indicated the ghoulish women at her side, still bundled silently together and exuding quiet menace. "The sisters here are travelling to the Silver Sea. They have been living in the human world for quite some time now. Many Panthea do, those who wished not to be involved in the Empress' war. There are more Panthea living in the mortal realm than you might imagine. But now, they return. Erlking is the simplest way back to the Netherworlde."

"Without Eris knowing about it, you mean?" Henry piped up.

"Quite, yes," Irene nodded.

"What are you going back for?" Henry asked the women. They didn't answer, but all three of them turned their veiled heads towards the boy, regarding him silently. He shrunk back in his chair a little, as the silence stretched out uncomfortably.

"Damn fine wine this," the red-haired man mumbled into his glass, breaking the silence after a moment.

"Thank you, Silas." Irene glanced at Henry pointedly over the top of her spectacles, then she looked to Robin.

"Mr Ffoulkes, on the other hand, is here at my request," she told them. "He too is travelling to the Netherworlde, though I dare say if anyone knows of other secret ways and means to do so, it is he. I wished, before his departure from the mortal realm, to obtain his opinion on something here at Erlking. He is rather an expert at certain antiquities you see."

"I trade in the arcane and the ancient," Ffoulkes said with relish, seeming rather happy to be allowed to talk about himself. "Antique dealer, valuer of the rare, classifier of the unfamiliar. A-ha. Interesting line of work. Rather honoured to be invited here by the great Lady Irene, you know. I've been absolutely dying to have a look inside Erlking for years."

Karya nodded, as though something had just slotted into place in her head. "You're the expert, aren't you?" she said.

"The expert?" the man blinked at her politely, his grin back on his face. "How so, little girl?"

"Irene came to see you, in London, with the puzzle box we found … well, which Robin found," she replied, heroically rising above being indulgently referred to as 'little girl'. "That was you."

Robin realised what she was referring to. When they had found a sealed cylinder out on the lake in the summer, a puzzle which none of them could immediately solve, Irene had taken a trip to London to consult an expert in ancient things who might be able to help them solve it.

Robin recalled that Irene had left the actual relic at Erlking with Robin, taking only photographs with her. She had indicated that she trusted the expertise, but not the expert. If this was the same person, as Karya surmised, why on earth would Irene bring him to Erlking?

"I have something which I am hoping Mr Ffoulkes, with all his contacts, expertise and skills, may be able to help us with," Irene said. She glanced at Robin. "I will speak with you privately about this at a later time, Robin."

He could guess what she was referring to. A strongbox Robin himself had retrieved from a very hidden tomb. A box which had been considered an important treasure by none other the Queen Titania herself. Given to Robin's father and passed later into the safekeeping of another of the Fae Guard, Nightshade. The box, when they had retrieved and opened it, hadn't contained a secret weapon, a magical sword or a powerful spell written on ancient parchment as one might have expected. It had contained nothing but a list of names, and the frontispiece of an old and unidentified library book. Everyone was baffled by it.

Robin watched the glittering Mr Ffoulkes drinking his wine, looking around the room at the many trophied heads as he did. Could this glittering fop, who Robin was, rather guiltily, coming to think of as rather odious, really shed any light on the contents? Clearly Irene hoped so. The man caught Robin staring, and tipped him a friendly wink. Robin smiled awkwardly and returned to eating. The guy really was like a game-show host.

"Hey, enough about business though, right?" Mr Drover suddenly piped up, waving a spear of asparagus on the end of his fork. "This isn't just a meal, this is a gift giving, isn't it? Not every day a lad turns fourteen and I'm sure he's itching to open those." He nodded his head at the far end of the long table, across from Irene, where a small pile of brightly wrapped presents waited. Robin had been politely not staring at them ever since the strange evening meal began, but now he grinned.

"Well said, Mr Drover," Irene nodded. "Hestia, bring in the cake will you, dear? Robin, you may of course open your gifts. The one in white is from myself."

The housekeeper, who had been silently circling the table like a grumpy shark, notably avoiding passing too close to the three strange sisters, excused herself from the room. Henry, who was sitting closest to the presents, grabbed one in shimmering white and silver wrapping, large and bulky, and passed it along the table with a grin.

"That's the one," Irene nodded with a serious air of great gravitas.

Robin tore off the wrapping, intrigued as to what it could be. It turned out to be a very handsome backpack, in dark, soft brown leather, with quite a few buckles and straps.

"Awesome! It's great, thanks Aunt Irene," he said, turning it over in his hands.

"It is a Swedenborgian satchel," the old lady explained. "Given that you are of a mind to disappear from time to time, usually without permission I might add, and that I understand you often take a stack of your books along with you, I felt it might be useful. Open it and see."

Robin unbuckled the bag and peered inside. It was pitch black. He couldn't see the bottom of the bag at all. He glanced up at his aunt in confusion.

"Oh, I've heard of these," Karya piped up with interest. "Pocket dimensions, quite an advanced magic, isn't it?"

"It does have a lot of pockets," Henry nodded sagely, peering at the bag.

"No, moron," Karya smirked. "Swedenborgian space. The bag is bigger on the inside, kind of like Erlking Hall itself. You can fit tons of things in there."

"As I understand it," Irene said lightly. "It's all rather to do with fractals, though heaven knows how it works. It is enough that it does. You will be able to pack very well, should you ever need to."

"Wow," Robin said into the bag, genuinely impressed. His voice echoed back from the inside a few seconds later, as though from a great distance.

"Open this one next!" Henry said impatiently, passing a small wrapped cube over. "It's from us lot."

"You already gave me that book this morning," Robin argued.

"Yeah, well, I told you we got you two things. This is the other one. And really it's a present for all of us; you, me, Karya and … everyone … too."

Robin knew Henry had been about to say 'Woad' but had remembered in time that while they had guests, Woad did not officially exist.

Under the hastily torn wrapping, there was a stack of what looked like business cards made from weathered parchment. Confused, Robin took one out of the stack and turned it over in his hands. It was blank on both sides. He looked to Henry and Karya questioningly.

"It's instead of a phone," Henry grinned.

Robin's confusion deepened. "Notecards?"

Karya took one of them out of his hand and produced a pen from the depths of her large coat. "You know full well, Scion, that none of your modern mortal world technology works well here in Erlking, or in the Netherworlde. No phones, no TV, no computers. They all just go…to use Henry's language … 'mental'. But this …"

He watched her scribble something on the card she had taken. A couple of seconds later, the lettering disappeared, as though it had been absorbed into the parchment.

Robin peered at the card which he held. Before his eyes, Karya's words, which had faded from her own card, appeared on his, writing themselves out of thin air:

'Scion, happy birthday, hornless wonder'

"It's an enchanted roll of parchment," she explained, smiling. "Cut up into bits, one for each of us. Whatever you write on one, appears on all the others. No matter the distance between them."

"We're calling it hex-messaging," Henry said proudly. "Now I can hex you whenever, even if I'm at home down in the village and you're up here. How awesome is that?"

He grabbed a card, taking the pen from Karya and scribbled.

A few seconds later, Karya's words faded from the card Robin held and were replaced, in Henry's familiar scrawl, with:

WUU2? HP Bday m8

"You are going to have to teach me this hex-speak," Karya said to Henry, reading over Robin's shoulder. "I am unfamiliar with mortal idiocy."

"We're going to have to teach ... everyone else ... how to write," Henry replied quietly, referring to Woad of course. "We were testing this out yesterday and he just sent me an imprint of his tail."

"It's brilliant!" Robin beamed. He considered asking Aunt Irene if she wanted one of the spare cards, in case she needed to get in touch with him, but then thought better of it. If she wanted his attention, he was pretty sure she could just peer sharply at the ceiling of her study and Robin would feel it three floors above in his room anyway.

"We do not follow these human customs," one of the sisters said in a raspy, shaky voice. It was the first time any of them had spoken since they had all sat down to dinner, and in all the fun of presents, Robin had quite forgotten their ghoulish presence. All eyes now turned to them, including several of the wall-mounted stag's heads. A distant stuffed ram's head in the recesses of Antler-Pocalypse Hall gave a portentous bleat.

"But as guests," the woman continued. "We shall bestow as a gift, the one thing no-one ever truly wants."

"Socks?" Henry whispered under his breath.

"Advice," another of the interchangeable sisters said.

"Guidance," hissed the third. "Listen well, Robin Fellows. Three things you should know."

Robin noticed Irene was watching the strange women carefully, though her demeanour remained studiously calm, her fingers resting lightly on the stem of her wine glass.

"Firstly ..." the middle sister held up a lace-gloved hand. The nails were long and gnarled. Her hand trembled a little. "Air you have toiled in, and in water have you been immersed, but now you must look to earth. For soon ... soon, beneath it shall you be buried."

Robin's eyes widened.

"Aha-ha-ha. Steady on girls," Mr Ffoulkes said, with a slightly forced laugh, twiddling his extravagant moustache a little. "Let's not scare the little chap, eh? It is his birthday after all."

The women ignored him completely. The sister to the left tilted her head in Robin's direction. "Secondly," she rasped. "Know this, Robin of the House of Fellows. You have the light of the Fae within you, burning like a candle, any can see that. But we sense also a kernel of darkness deep within."

"Darkness," whispered the other two sisters behind their veils in quiet agreement.

"A peppercorn of blackness in the light. Beware that it does not grow, and snuff out the other. It is not yours. It should not be there. And it will consume you if it can."

Robin had no idea what they were talking about.

"And thirdly," the remaining sister added, her head turned towards him, though her features remained hidden and shadowy. "Choose your prizes wisely. A great choice is coming to you, Scion of the Arcania, and your decision will alter the shape of more than you can know. You are only a boy, not yet a man, but the weight of the world rests between your tender horns."

"I think … that's probably *quite* enough advice," Irene said crisply. "Always a pleasure to hear you speak of the future, sisters, you honour us with your words. However, I do rather think our attention in this present moment should be focussed less on doom and darkness, and more on cake."

"Hear hear, old gal," Mr Ffoulkes agreed heartily, raising a glass to this sentiment.

Mr Drover leaned across the table and patted the back of Robin's hand roughly. "Don't you worry about the future, lad," he said gruffly. "That's a job for us adults. That's our only job, really, eh? Your job right now is to enjoy your birthday." His eyes crinkled into a reassuring smile, but Robin saw him cast a disapproving frown at the three doom-saying spectres.

"Yeah, I'm sure Rob's chuffed to bits," Henry glowered. "You know, about being buried, consumed by inner darkness and having the fate of the world depend on him and everything."

"Henry, be quiet," Karya hissed quietly. "You're not helping." Robin had gone quite pale.

Before Robin could reply to anyone, Hestia re-entered the room with a large three-tiered birthday cake, festooned with candles, rather breaking the uncomfortable atmosphere.

"I'd rather have had socks," Henry muttered mutinously.

NYMPH AND KNIFE

Robin had been somewhat relieved to be finally released from the oddly uncomfortable dinner. Later that evening, once Henry and Mr Drover had gone home for the weekend and Karya had wandered off to find and feed Woad, Robin made himself scarce and checked again on the sleeping figure of Jackalope. This had become part of his usual evening routine. As expected, there was no change. The boy still slept, and would not be roused by any means. Hestia had clearly been in since Robin's visit this morning, as the sheets had been changed, the pillows plumped and the curtains were now drawn against the dark autumn sky. Robin left the slice of cake he had brought with him on the bedside table. It had only been a thin hope that the smell of freshly baked chocolate cake might rouse the slumbering Fae, but you didn't know until you tried, and Robin wasn't accustomed to giving up on anything.

He sat for a while, telling his sleeping and unresponsive companion in the bed all about the events of the day. Their odd new guests, how strange they were, and the worrying and rather grim things they had said. He didn't really expect any response. But it was peaceful and quiet in here, and lately he had found it a good place to gather his own thoughts.

Before he left, he lit the oil lamp on the bedside, casting the quiet room into a golden glow. He knew Jackalope didn't need it, but as far as Robin was concerned, the other boy might come around at any time, and he didn't want him waking up into unfamiliar darkness. He knew very little about Jackalope really, but he guessed he had already seen enough darkness to last a lifetime.

Not yet tired after his birthday events, Robin was halfway to Erlking's library, the sisters' odd words still ringing in his ears and with a vague plan to chat to Wally and ask if perhaps there were any beginners' books on Earth magic when his pocket vibrated, making him jump.

"Bloody Hell, Henry," he muttered to himself, reaching in and pulling out the parchment card. He had forgotten all about the hex-messaging.

Alrite? Just testin. How r u copin with the witches? – H

Robin still had Karya's pen from the dinner party. He flipped the card over, and leaning against the wall of the dark corridor in which he stood, wrote back.

They're not witches, they're something else. Haven't seen any of them since the creepy party. With Irene.

He watched the words fade and disappear. A few seconds later, Henry's handwriting appeared again.

How's Ur Boyf?

Robin rolled his eyes to himself.

Idiot. No change in Jackalope. Are you coming round tomorrow?

He watched the words fade away and stared at the empty card. Several long seconds passed with no reply. The seconds began to stretch into minutes. Somewhere in the dark corridor a clock was ticking. Robin considered that Henry was acting so oddly lately. Secretive, evasive. It was starting to irk him a little. Eventually, when Robin was just about to give up and stuff the paper back in his pocket, a reply came, and it was brisk and annoying.

Cant m8. Lessons. C U Mon.

Robin didn't reply. As far as he was concerned, Henry still had such a bee in his bonnet about them taking in the stray Fae. Well, that was his problem. If he didn't want to spend the weekend here, that was fine with Robin. He had other things to do. He didn't need Henry to have a good time.

He was just about to continue along to the library when he heard voices through the door next to which he stood. It was Madame Calypso. It had not escaped Robin's notice that his tutor had been conspicuously absent from his birthday dinner.

Robin opened the door a crack, as quietly as he could. The room beyond, one of Erlking's many parlours, was cosy and dark. Heavy drapes were closed against the evening. A crackling fire was lit in the grate, and soft sofas arranged here and there. The ceiling was a mural of clouds with painted cherubs, who were currently wheeling around the plasterwork silently, shooting tiny arrows at one another. Madame Calypso was sitting on a chaise longue, her feet tucked up under her diaphanous silk dress and a paperback book in hand. She looked as though she were studiously ignoring the man standing by the fire, who was clearly attempting to engage her in conversation. Robin saw that it was Silas Ffoulkes. The gold and red gilt of his clothing flickering in the reflected firelight.

"I have to say," he said. "If I'd known Erlking was filled with such handsome women, I should jolly well have come and visited earlier. A-ha-ha."

Calypso didn't look up. She looked utterly bored. "It isn't filled," she said flatly.

"Just a compliment, my dear lady, that's all," the man chuckled. "You really are an extreme beauty, such a thing to be locked away here from the world."

"I am not locked," the nymph replied absently, licking her finger and turning a page. "Was there something you wanted, Mr Ffoulkes? Only, as you can see, I'm trying to read. Your insistence on talking is making that quite difficult."

His smile flickered for a moment, and Robin got the distinct impression that he was used to being able to charm and twinkle whomever he chose, but he replaced it with swagger almost immediately. "Ha! I suppose it's true what they say about your kind, isn't it? Speak as you find, I see. That could hurt a chap's feelings you know, were he of lesser stock than I. Surely you must be starved of conversation at least? A little company is a good thing, isn't it?"

Robin's tutor finally put her book down in her lap, and peered up at the man, unimpressed.

"Mr Ffoulkes. I am neither locked, nor starved, nor any other phrasing you care to use which would endeavour to paint me in any kind of light wherein I am in need of rescue in one form or another, so please do stop trying. Your efforts are excruciating. I am not a damsel, in distress or otherwise, and you sir, are certainly not a knight."

The man's face darkened a little. He turned away from her to make a show of warming his hands over the fire. "A drink then?" he said after a moment. Robin was equally impressed and appalled at his doggedness. "I am not here for very long after all, and ships which pass in the night? You could at least raise a glass with me. This is a jolly draughty old house."

"I'm not thirsty," Calypso replied, picking her book up again. "And

I am a nymph, sir." She licked her thumb and flicked a page. "We don't 'pass' ships, we capsize them."

The man chuckled. "Fair enough, fair enough. Aha. Message received. I shall drink my own health then, fair one." He rubbed his hands together. "Dashed shame though, can't blame a chap for trying, eh? Rather makes one wish one was a satyr."

Robin's tutor looked up sharply. "I would watch your tongue if I were you, firebrand," she said softly. "You are a guest in this house, that much is true, but you are not my guest. I owe you no hospitality."

"I meant no offence," Ffoulkes replied, though even from his position at the door, Robin saw something like a glint of amused satisfaction in his eyes. Something almost cruel, as though he had been glad to get a rise out of the woman. "I only meant … well, it can't be easy for you." His voice was filled with theatrical sympathy. "Everybody who is anybody heard what happened to Phorbas. Terrible business that. Such a loss."

"He is not lost," she replied flatly.

"Oh yes, of course. Trapped in a sword or something, isn't he? I heard as much."

"A knife."

The man's moustache twitched with something that could have been amusement. "Sword, knife, garlic press. All details really. Either way, it's not much of a basis for a relationship is it? A soul without a body?"

"Some might argue …" the nymph replied in her dreamy sing-song voice, still intent on her book, "… that it is infinitely preferable to the other way around."

The man laughed again. He seemed to laugh a lot. Robin was beginning to notice that it was very little to do with his being amused. "Aha, so droll. But his body is gone, disposed of by the Grimms. Left in some dark wood somewhere I understand. Such a tragedy. The forces of Eris, they really don't care whom they tread on do they?"

"I really am trying to read," she said.

"Of course, you spent time with Eris' people, didn't you?" he pressed, wilfully ignoring her hints. "Before coming to your senses and getting the heck out of the war like the rest of us sensible folk."

Calypso looked up and gave the man her full attention for the first time. Robin, from his position at the door thought she actually looked a little irritated, which was a first in his experience.

"Out of the war?" she said. "Is that what you think? I chose the wrong side, Mr Ffoulkes. I do not hide from that fact. And now I am paying for my sins, such as I can. I stand against Eris. I train the Scion of the Arcania. I try to arm that boy against what I know, more than most, is out there waiting for him. If that is 'out of the war' to you, then you are an addle brained fool. As for you 'sensible folk', I can only assume that by that you mean those, like yourself, who neither stood with or against Eris, but who fled the Netherworlde to come and hide in the mortal world, hoping it would all blow over one day."

"Abstainers, my dear," he drawled.

"Cowards is the word I would choose," she replied coolly. "You do not realise. There *are* no side-lines to stand on. There is no 'safe quarter' where you can hide and wait things out. Eris means dominion. *Total* dominion. You are with her, or, like Phorbas and myself now, you are against her." She placed her book gently on the table before her. "There is no escape for those who will not fight. Those who busy themselves with gold and gilt and the distractions of the mortal realm. And that sir, is why I do not want a drink, and why I would certainly prefer the convivial company of a haunted knife or indeed garlic press, should it come to that, to the company of a swaggering dandy in love with his own voice, who cowers in the shadows and calls it common sense."

Robin had his hand over his mouth, his eyes wide. Although she had delivered this tirade in a calm and distant voice as always, she might as well have stood and slapped the man across the cheeks.

A moment passed in the small parlour, with only the quiet popping and hissing of the fire silhouetting Ffoulkes. "You are as cold as the sea that bore you, my dear," he stuttered eventually. His face, Robin noticed, had paled slightly.

"And you, sir, are a flickering candle which fancies itself a towering inferno. Good evening."

Silence passed between them, and then, after a moment composing himself, the man bowed politely, with a great deal of unnecessary flourish, and left the room, almost barrelling into Robin on his way out.

"Confound it, boy," he yelped, surprised, but recovered himself quickly, fixing his charming smile back on his face. "Sorry about that, aha-ha, didn't see you there. Such a dark and shadowy house, isn't it? Such a scamp you are, burrowing around in the corridors after bedtime." He actually reached out and ruffled Robin's hair as he passed him, as one might do to a small child or dog. Robin was too surprised to react.

"Dark and shadowy house," the man muttered to himself as he stalked off down the corridor, fussily adjusting his extravagant cuffs, his shining boots clicking on the floor smartly. "And full of cold things."

When he had gone, Calypso looked up from the sofa. "Good evening, my student," she said.

"I … I wasn't listening," Robin insisted. The enormity of this lie made his face redden instantly. "Well, I was … obviously," he admitted. "But I didn't mean to."

"Intention is irrelevant," she replied lightly with little concern. "Pay no heed to that spluttering firebrand. He fancies himself a ladies' man, and I believe I may have damaged his ego by not swooning at his handsome feet, that is all. It is nothing you need be concerned with."

"I think he totally fancies you," Robin said, unable to stop the corners of his mouth turning up in amusement. Calypso didn't look concerned with this.

"That man, Robin Fellows, has a fancy for no one but himself," she said. "He is a snake in love with the glitter of his own scales. But I am a nymph." She shrugged her elegant shoulders. "It cannot be helped. Simple elemental facts though, Robin. Water and fire do not mix well. This is exactly why I avoided dinner, though he sought me out after all it seems."

"He's a fire Panthea then, isn't he?" Robin asked with interest, coming fully into the room and closing the door behind him. "I mean, I guessed from his name, and there's that hair, and his hand was really hot when I shook it this morning, but I've never met one."

"He is indeed. And you should be careful around him," she replied lightly.

"Careful?" Robin frowned, wandering over to the fire. The autumn nights were chilly and the popping logs were difficult to resist. Irene had said something similar. "Is he … you know … a bad guy?"

Calypso gave him a weary look, her head tilted to one side. "Robin Fellows, if you haven't learned by now that the world is not that simple a place, then what hope is there for you?"

Robin shuffled in front of the fire a little awkwardly.

"There is no real evil in him," she conceded. "Not intentionally anyway. But he is an opportunist and a coward. Cowards are the most dangerous of all people, Robin. They are unpredictable." She glanced at her book absently. "I know him from old. He is also a thief. Irene will have to keep a sharp eye on him while he is here. Luckily none have eyes sharper. He calls himself a collector, but he would take anything of value if he thought it might benefit him." She glanced up at him. "Yourself included. The man is a magpie."

Robin didn't quite know what to say. He had a surreal image of being bundled into a sack and thrown in the boot of the ornate Rolls Royce, driven away at high speed and sold on for profit at some Fae-based auction.

"Where is your knife, Robin?" she asked lightly.

"Phorbas?" Robin answered as lightly as he could manage. He didn't want his tutor to know he had heard the entire exchange between her and the Fire Panthea. "Upstairs, in the drawer in my room, where he always is. Woad's up there. He's bunking up with me while Ffoulkes and the sisters are here. Aunt Irene said it would be best."

She nodded thoughtfully. "It would be wise to keep your knife there," she said absently. "Out of sight. At least until after Halloween. We don't want light-fingered collectors stealing *all* the treasures of Erlking now, do we?"

"It's of great value?" he asked.

"To some, yes," she replied.

LEAVES AT THE GLASS

Despite his concerns, the week following Robin's birthday passed without a single incident of anyone trying to steal him, or anything else for that matter. In fact, he barely saw their strange guests at all.

Mr Ffoulkes was cooped up with Irene much of the time, the two of them locked away in her study, or spotted pouring over maps in the library together and speaking in low voices. As for the strange sisters who had cheerlessly predicted Robin's imminent burial, they didn't seem to venture much from their allotted rooms at all. This was something Robin was rather thankful for. On the few occasions when he happened to chance upon them in the corridors, they paid him no heed whatsoever, gliding along like ghosts and muttering to one another in low, rasping voices.

For Robin, life at Erlking continued as normal. Water lessons with his tutor took place every other day in the newly-cleaned and refurbished pool room, occasionally with Karya observing critically from the side-lines.

It was odd, practising manoeuvres and casting cantrips without the usual noisy presence of Woad to cheer him on in his energetic way. The faun, after a day or two of being under house-arrest in Robin's bedroom, appeared to have gone a little stir-crazy. Robin returned one evening with a plate of cold-cut meats and cheese for him, only to find that Woad had filled his bed with an abundance of leaves and rather damp moss, gathered from the windowsills and roof. Woad had beamed happily, clearly proud of his efforts to make the place seem homelier. Two days later, Robin was still finding the occasional snail between the sheets.

The following day, the faun happily announced that he was keeping himself busy by helping to organise Robin's sock collection. When Robin checked his sock drawer, he found it completely empty. Looking around the room he spotted socks tucked everywhere, draped across the mirror, stretched over the bed knobs, decoratively hung from the fireplace. There was even a pair nestled high in the wooden beams of the ceiling. "I have arranged them in order of excellence, Pinky!" Woad explained knowledgeable. "Basic boring ones are easy to find, and closer to hand. The more exciting and astounding socks are higher!"

"Woad," Robin had said quietly, gazing around the room and mentally counting to ten slowly. "Why are there socks in the rafters?"

"Those are the very best! More of a challenge! Imagine your feelings of achievement once you have claimed them as your prize! How happy and honoured your feet will feel."

With a sense of resigned dread, Robin had opened the next drawer in his dresser. It was completely empty.

"Um, Woad," he asked carefully. "Where is all my underwear?"

The faun beamed from ear to ear. "Even better!" he had exclaimed. "For a treasure hunt, I have hidden that in all kinds of different rooms for you! All over the house."

Robin had slowly closed the drawer with a sigh, as from far below them in the kitchens, came Hestia's distant and startled shriek.

Henry only came up to Erlking twice in the whole week, claiming he was swamped with extra tuition. This irked Robin a little. He could do with some help finding ways to keep Woad occupied. It was a full time job. He had dismissed the idea of setting him helpful tasks like running a bath after he found a steaming hot bath happily prepared for him, complete with black water and the happily waving tentacles of Inky the baby kraken. Henry clearly had better things to do these days than faun-control, and Karya was little help. She was far more occupied sneaking around the house and desperately trying to find out what Irene's strange guests were up to. She had become a little obsessed with spying on Ffoulkes and the sisters, or 'the peacock and the ghouls' as she mutteringly referred to them. Karya hated not knowing exactly what was going on at any given time.

Jackalope remained a motionless enigma, still sleeping soundly, though Robin found the time he spent sitting in his quiet room a welcome moment of peace in the chaos of bunking with a housebound faun. In truth, Robin was trying to find ways to distract his own mind. He worried more and more about the sisters' strange warnings, and was sure that he should be learning the Tower of Earth.

It felt odd at Erlking. Autumn was painting the world gold and leaves

47

were turning to crisp paper. All was peaceful and still, and yet Robin couldn't shake the odd atmosphere hanging over the place. A sense of brooding watchfulness, as though something were brewing in the skies above. Robin couldn't shake the feeling of waiting for something. Maybe it was just the oddness of having guests, he reasoned to himself. He certainly wasn't the only one feeling a little weird. He was sure Woad was losing his marbles, especially when one evening he returned to his room to find the faun sitting on the window ledge peering out at the lawns and trees intently, his yellow eyes narrowed.

"The leaves are misbehaving," he had told Robin. "They keep moving strange. I saw a whirlwind of leaves. It crossed the grass, circled the fountain and went away again. That's no way for leaves to behave. It shouldn't be allowed."

"It's just the wind, Woad." He had crossed the room and peered out of the window over the faun's blue shoulder. There was nothing unusual out there. Just the sun setting over the forest, throwing long shadows over the lawn.

"I know wind, Pinky," the small blue boy had replied indignantly. "I know the names of all the winds, and that's no normal wind blowing leaves like that. There was a face of leaves at the window too, last night, when you were asleep, but it went away when I stuck my tongue out at it. Blew apart like …"

"Like … leaves?" Robin raised his eyebrows with a smile, making a mental note not to bring Woad any more cheese for supper.

PEPPERCORN

Robin stood knee deep in a drift of red and golden autumn leaves, a long sweeping brush in hand. He was bundled up in a large duffel coat against the blustery September wind. The leaves of the great avenue of trees which led from the Hall itself down to the gates at the perimeter of Erlking had almost completely covered the path, creating an amber tunnel filled with crisp sunlight.

Robin wasn't really sure why he was down here at the bottom of the hill near the gates, doing chores. Surely clearing the leaves was Mr Drover's job? Come to think of it, he couldn't really remember being asked to do it, or for that matter walking all the way down here. It was all very strange. But here he was nonetheless, alone with only the constant dry papery rustle of the wind in the branches before the great wrought iron gates which led out and down to the village of Barrowood. The gates were twined with straggles of dark ivy. Clumps of grey-green moss clung to the odd scarred statues atop each of the great gateposts. Although he didn't realise it at once, Robin was not as alone here as he had imagined.

That strange, prickling feeling one gets on the back of one's neck, when you know you are being watched rolled across him, making him shiver a little. Robin stopped brushing, his breath coming before him, soft clouds in the cold air, and he turned frowning, to stare at the gates.

On the other side of the curled ironwork, just beyond the boundaries of Erlking, there stood a girl. She was wearing dark jeans, a slim black t-shirt emblazoned with the jagged design of a band name he didn't recognise. She had her hands stuffed into her pockets, though the chill air didn't seem to be bothering her bare arms. Her long purple hair was blowing about her shoulders, held down by a black wool cap, her only concession to the cold. The unexpected girl was smirking at Robin through the lattice of iron and ivy.

"Hey, blondie," she called. "How's tricks?"

Robin nearly dropped his broom. He stared at the girl in disbelief. It must have been close to sunset, the days were getting shorter as autumn rolled along, and the light was slanting and rich, painting them both the colour of honey. The stone walls either side of the gate seemed almost to glow in the light.

"Penny?" he stammered. She blinked dark kohl-ed eyes at him a few times, shuffling from foot to foot in the cold. Orange leaves played around her feet, rustling in the silence.

"What are you … how are you here?" he asked.

"Wow, don't act too pleased to see me or anything will you?" she said. "Missed your birthday, didn't I? Sorry about that. Busy with stuff, you know how it is. Stuff and things. Especially things."

Robin had dropped the broom, leaving it forgotten, and walked cautiously toward the gates.

"What do you want?" he asked. "If you're here for the other half of the Water Shard …"

"Pssssh!" she blew a raspberry. "As if. Don't flatter yourself, blue eyes. I have way bigger fish to fry right now. Nah, I'm just checking in on things. You know I like to keep an eye on what's going on."

"If Irene finds out you're here …" he began.

She laced her fingers through the gates. "As if I'm here to see old lavender drawers." She smiled. "Wow, I feel like I'm visiting you in prison or something here. We should rig up telephones on either side of the gate."

"Did …" Robin wasn't sure what to say. This was all so strange. "Did you want to come in?"

Her smile faltered a little. "You know I can't, kiddo. But a sweet offer. You could come out? You know, if you wanted to?" She shrugged a little, as though it was none of her concern if he did or not.

"Why have you come here, Penny?" he asked, touching the bars from his side. They were bitterly cold in the autumn air. A large fat yellow bumblebee buzzed past his hand, weaving in and out between the gates. Robin barely noticed it.

"Oh, I haven't really," she said. "Not on purpose anyway. I just get dragged along." She nodded to her left by way of explanation, and Robin followed her gaze.

Standing further along the wide gateway, on her side of the bars, there was another 'her'. A second Penny. This one however was dressed in a crisp charcoal suit, and her skin wasn't just pale, it was as white as cold snow. Her eyes were black and cold as space. She was talking to someone on Robin's side of the gate. He hadn't noticed the other figure until now. How was that even possible?

What was even stranger, Robin realised, waving away another bee which floated around his face, was that the person this second Penny was talking to, or Miss Peryl the Grimm to be more precise, was another Robin.

Or rather, the Puck. He had Robin's face but pure white hair, bright green eyes and tall, silvery horns. Power and light practically flooded out of the boy, and his face was grim and serious.

"That's … that's me …" Robin stammered, deeply confused. "That's me over there."

"Yeah, kind of …" Penny agreed, her head tilted to one side with interest.

"And that's you," he said dumbly. His hands felt numb inside his gloves.

"Yes, Brainiac, again, kind of. That's none of our business really though, is it? I'm pretty sure they'd both be a lot happier if we were not here at all."

Robin couldn't tear his eyes away from Peryl and the Puck. Over the autumn wind and the rush of papery leaves, he couldn't hear what they were saying.

"What are they, I mean we, talking about?" he asked, looking back to the far more human-looking girl through the gate bars. Her eyes were not as black as space. They were a soft violet, and there were patches of red on her pale cheeks from the cold air. Penny shook her head. "Beats me." She sounded unconcerned. "But it's probably bad news. Maybe something to do with him." She flicked a thumb over her shoulder in a casual gesture. Behind her, half buried in a hedgerow on the opposite side of the country lane outside Erlking, Robin could make out the crumpled figure of a man, lying in the leaves and long grass. He looked to be bloodied and hurt. Robin couldn't make out much more than his general shape. There were several bees darting around near him. Wasn't it a little late in the year for so many bees?

"Is … is he dead?" he whispered.

"Nearly, but not quite," Penny told him, quite unconcerned. "Don't worry about him though, he won't be here for a while yet. But he's on his way." She didn't seem very pleased about this. Suddenly she looked at him curiously. "You've gotten taller, blondie, you're what, two inches shorter than me now? You were such a shrimp last time I saw you."

Robin stared over at the other versions of them, the Puck and Peryl, both looking powerful and otherworldly and both still deep in serious discussion. He really didn't remember coming down the avenue, or anything else about getting here.

"This isn't real, is it?" he said, with slowly dawning realisation. "None of this … is real."

"That's a tricky word, if you ask me," she said thoughtfully, after a moment's careful consideration.

He stared at the pale girl through the bars separating Erlking from the outside. Her eyes were merry and playful, just this side of wicked. The drone of unseasonal bees surrounded them. The leaves rasped against the stones in the breeze.

"What *are* you?" he asked in earnest. "Really, I mean?" It felt a moment of tremendous importance, in a way he couldn't really describe, so much so that without meaning to, the words had come out in a whisper.

She smiled at him, and her fingers brushed his gloved hand ever so slightly across the bars. "You're such a numbskull, Robin Fellows," she said. "It's like the sisters said. I'm your peppercorn, right?"

Robin woke up with a start, sitting up in bed with a gasp. His room was dark around him. The images of the dream still scattered around like startled birds in the darkness, fragmenting in a disorienting manner as he shook himself awake, still sure he could hear the low drone of bees.

It hadn't been real, any of it. Just a dream, he thought to himself. His heart was pounding. A deeply odd dream. Robin stared around the silent bedroom in the darkness, groggy and sleepy. For a moment he thought he saw a dark shape, a small moth, flitter in the grate before disappearing up the chimney, but it was gone too soon for him to tell for sure if it had been real, or a lingering fragment of dream playing tricks on his mind.

It must have been late, Robin reasoned. That still and motionless time of night, long after midnight and far from dawn. The great house was utterly silent around him. Nothing but the soft lull of the wind outside his dark window, and the distant rhythmic noise that was half snore-half purr from the small blue figure of Woad, who Robin saw was curled up and asleep in front of the fireplace in his usual spot. Woad was wearing a pair of Robin's socks.

Robin lay awake for quite some time, unable to shake the odd dream, or the curious feeling of importance it had carried, in that unexplainable way dreams do. He lay thoughtfully under the warm blankets, listening to the wind occasionally rattle the glass in the window pane and rustle down the chimney. A few errant leaves battered the glass now and then, but despite Woad's imaginings, none of them appeared to have faces. Robin thought of the injured man in his dream, and how the Puck had looked so odd to him from the outside, as alien and strange as the Grimm herself.

He couldn't remember a time, since he first arrived here, when Erlking had been filled with so many people, but even so, and despite the soft and sleepy noises of Woad nearby, he felt strangely like the only person living. Alone in the great dark mystery of Erlking.

FFOULKES SHEDS A LITTLE LIGHT

"You are not concentrating, Robin Fellows."

Madam Calypso's voice was calm and melodic as always, although it was quite muffled in Robin's ears, which were full of water. It was hard enough to concentrate on lessons at the moment, but even harder after a broken night's sleep. Woad had been snoring incessantly again. It was the last day of September and after a few weeks of sharing a bedroom, Robin was beginning to understand why some people said being an only child was better than having brothers and sisters.

He picked himself up grumpily from the tiles of the pool room, where he had just been hit full force with the watery equivalent of a fireball. His drenched clothes spattered on the floor, echoing softly into the vaulted ceiling. "I wasn't ready," he half snarled, his bad mood slightly doused by the fact that he had to stifle a yawn. Across the pool, his tutor crossed her arms, her willowy form caught in a slanted sunbeam from the tall windows.

"Nor will you be when you are duelling in real life," she said. "Do you expect your opponents in the wild to give you a ten second head start before they attack you?"

Robin pushed his wet mop of hair back from his forehead, still staggering slightly. "Well, no," he conceded. "All I meant to say was–"

Without warning he stopped mid-sentence and dropped swiftly to one knee, both arms thrust expertly before him. A hail of needle sharp ice-darts erupted from his palms, dozens of shimmering missiles whistling across the water towards the nymph. He saw her eyes widen and she twirled aside at the last moment with expert balletic grace. The icy shard-storm thudded into the wall noisily behind her, frozen porcupine quills hammering the plasterwork.

"Oh, very good," she said, a tiny smile appearing at the corners of her mouth. "That was practically wicked."

Robin grinned at her approval, getting to his feet. "Thanks," he dusted his hands together.

"Don't get too over-confident though," the nymph flicked a hand, and with a whoosh the tiles beneath his feet were suddenly a sheeny mirror of ice, causing him to slip and fall back to the ground in a graceless lump.

"Just because you've had brief communion with the Shard of Water, doesn't make you king of the oceans," his tutor smirked.

"It's too early in the morning for duelling lessons," he wheezed, thinking of his most inventive curse words. His repertoire had been greatly expanded over the summer by the discovery of a wishing well in the herb garden which echoed back your words, only littered with expletives. Henry had taken to carrying around a notepad. Before he could demonstrate his newly expanded vocabulary, however, the doors to the pool room opened with a dramatic boom, and in walked Karya, followed closely by the red-headed figure of Silas Ffoulkes. This was most unprecedented. Everyone knew that Robin's lessons, whether practical casting, Mana-management or physical manoeuvres, were private. In all the time Ffoulkes and the sinister sisters had been at Erlking, none of them had ever interrupted a lesson before. Robin secretly thought Calypso was grateful of this fact. It was her one haven from the rather annoying man, who was still insistent on attempting to charm her at every opportunity.

"What is it?" Calypso asked. "The Scion is in a lesson right now. We should not be interrupted." Robin looked questioningly at Karya, who rolled her eyes at him a little.

"Apologies," the girl said. "We've not come to observe. Though it is always entertaining to see the Scion get thrown around a bit." She smiled slightly. "Lady Irene asked me to deliver a message to Robin, and our … guest here." Her smile was a little tight. "Positively insisted on coming along."

"So *this* is where you spar?" Ffoulkes said, following the young girl into the room and looking around with greedy, sparkling eyes. "What a wondrous place! Honestly, I've been here at Erlking for weeks now, and yet every time I turn a corner, I see something new and dazzling. Truly marvellous."

"Every time I turn a corner, sir," Calypso said, hands clasped politely before her. "I seem to run into you. You certainly do get everywhere, don't you?" She didn't give him time to finish. "I'm afraid the Scion's tutelage is a private matter, not a spectator sport. I'll have to ask you to leave."

The man ignored her, looking around the newly refurbished room with bright eyes. They really had done a wonderful job of restoring the place since the discovery and removal of Inky the kraken. The mosaic tiled walls shone, the large pool was deep and green and clear. A separate area had been cleared for sparring, the tiles marked with various concentric sparring circles, where Robin was still getting damply to his feet.

"What a treasure Erlking is," the man said. "Every corner just bursting with secrets waiting to be discovered. Wonders untold."

"And as I say," Calypso replied coolly. "I do keep finding you in said corners."

Robin had noticed this too. While the sisters were reclusive, Ffoulkes was everywhere. Robin could barely enter a room without tripping over the man, peeking in cupboards, inspecting suits of armour, looking discreetly behind portraits. He was a constant bother. "He's like dust that one," Mr Drover had muttered mutinously one afternoon. "All over everything. 'Cept of course there no dust in Erlking where Hestia can reach."

"Whatever is it you think you are looking for, I wonder?" Calypso shook her head. She looked past him to Karya, clearly not interested in any answer. "What was the message you were meant to deliver?"

Karya opened her mouth to speak, but the man cut in again.

"Seems a bit silly though, really, all this dabbling around in water, don't you think? A-ha-ha," he said with a smile. They all looked at him.

"Well, you know, with what the sisters predicted." He glanced at Robin warmly. "About you shortly being … underground. Earth magic. That's the ticket now, isn't it? Best prepared and all that, surely."

"I do not teach the Tower of Earth," Calypso folded her arms. "Obviously."

"Well, no, nor I, of course." The man clicked his fingers, causing a flurry of small fiery sparks to leap and dance in the air at his fingertips like orange fire-flies. For a moment, his eyes shone with the reflection, making him look quite devilish with his waxed moustache and pointed beard. "Fire's the ticket for me, not that I'm remotely the teaching kind anyway. But perhaps your aunt, Robin, would be wise to find you a tutor more … suited … to your current needs?" He smiled at Calypso. "No offense intended, my dear lady, I assure you, I mean in addition to your good self, and, well, in addition to the butter-knife who teaches wind."

"Aunt Irene hasn't mentioned looking for any new tutor," Robin said, feeling that Ffoulkes was being wilfully rude. "I'm sure she will when she thinks it's the right time. She knows what she's doing."

The Fire Panthea looked at him sidelong, then slid his eyes lazily over to Calypso.

"Does she? Does she indeed? Your aunt is a great many wonderful things, my boy, but omniscient is not one of them. If indeed she did know exactly what she was doing, she would not have requested my assistance."

"That's actually the message," Karya cut in quickly, seeing Robin frown. He looked to her. The small girl shrugged. "She wants to see you, Scion, in her study." She flicked her golden eyes up at the flame-haired man by her side. "And this one too." She added with thinly-veiled disapproval.

"Splendid," Ffoulkes clapped his hands, rubbing them together and looking very pleased with himself. "Then the men of the house shall go together. Come along, young master. Duty calls." He smiled at Karya and Calypso. "You fine fillies stay here. Maybe tidy the place up a little, eh? Women are so much better at that sort of thing."

Robin saw Calypso's eyebrows disappear into her hairline and felt Karya bristle. He tensed, half expecting a barrage of needlepoint icy darts to rain down on the man. Karya had indeed opened her mouth to speak, but Calypso cut in.

"Come, Karya," she said in her lilting voice, as calm and treacherous as the still surface of a pond. "The air in here has grown rather stale. If the Scion is required, that takes precedent over my lessons. And if he is to take this gentleman with him, well …" She cast a sidelong look at Robin, who couldn't tell if she was annoyed or faintly amused. "…Then that is the Scion's burden to bear."

Robin was ushered out of the pool room by Ffoulkes, his face still burning with embarrassment at the insufferable man's ridiculous remarks. The fop set a brisk pace along Erlking's corridors, forcing Robin to hurry. His boots clacked crisply on the floorboards and Robin noticed for the first time that they had rather a generous heel, making the man appear taller than he really was. He wondered if he was aware how very offensive he was to everyone.

"Women are such sensitive creatures," Silas said affectionately as they walked, his voice filled with warm indulgence and an affectation of great knowledge. "As changeable as the weather, and just as unpredictable."

Robin had never thought of either Karya or Calypso as being remotely sensitive, and was about to say so, but the man continued as they turned a corner. "And yet, for all their maddening whimsy, we chase them still, do we not? A-ha-ha-ha," he chuckled, with a small and rather theatrical shake of his head. He looked to Robin. "Well, perhaps you do not. Not yet. But mark my words, my boy, the time is coming. They will rule your head and your heart if you let them. Troublesome creatures really to all mankind." He glanced down rather vainly at his own perfectly manicured nails, the heavy gilt of his lacy cuff falling over his hand. "It is rather a burden you see, when one is fair of face. A curse we must bear though, and bear it nobly." He inspected his own reflection in the shiny chest of a suit of armour they passed.

Robin thought that Silas had rather a higher opinion of himself than he deserved. The man had the most perfectly sculpted and plucked eyebrows he had ever seen. They must have taken him hours. There was enough wax in his carefully groomed moustache and beard to make a candle, and in all the time he had been with them at Erlking, Robin had never seen the man with a hair out of place, or wearing the same outfit more than once. Each costume seemed more ornate than the last. He truly was a preening peacock.

"Of course, you yourself are a blooming sprout of handsome, aren't you?" the man said, clapping Robin on the back heartily. He looked down at him, as they passed through the shadows and light of a long, many-windowed gallery.

"Not truly handsome yet, of course, still rather pretty in that disagreeable way of boys, but give it time. Let a little more of the boy fall away and more of the man appear in that face of yours, and I promise you, young master. With those eyes of yours and all the power of the Arcania you hold, why, a-ha-ha, you'll not get a moment's peace from the ladies of the world."

"I'm not really sure that sounds like as much fun as you think," Robin said, a little worriedly. "I don't get a moment's peace from my studies anyway. I'd quite like some every now and again." He was slightly put out at being called 'pretty'.

The man gave not the remotest sign he was listening. In Robin's experience, he never did.

"I expect you're hoping for a chin, yes? A strong jaw? Something with a cleft perhaps, or dimples. The fillies do rather like either in a chap. Both are deformities of course, strictly speaking, but who am I to justify the knotted and unfathomable minds of the fairer sex?'

They passed out of the corridor and crossed an inner hallway, whose circular wall was covered in a faded mural depicting some wild mountain hunt, figures on horseback circling the room forever, frozen in paint and faded to ghosts with age.

Ffoulkes stopped suddenly on his heel, clicking sharply on the black and white marble tiles so that Robin almost walked right into the back of the fop. He span and regarded Robin curiously, one eyebrow cocked and his fingers twirling thoughtfully in his carefully waxed moustache.

"Tell me, boy," he said, with a twinkle in his eye. "Living here at Erlking. Surrounded by all the magic of the long lost Fae court, basking in the ..." He glanced around vaguely at the ornate room. "... treasures, of Oberon and Titania. You must know every inch of this fantastic place, yes?"

Robin frowned. Erlking wasn't the kind of place anyone could ever know every inch of, as far as he was concerned. Indeed, it seemed to change around on a whim, feet at a time, never mind inches.

"Not really," he said. "Why?"

The man spread his hands airily. "No reason, merely curious. You have to understand of course, to a ... collector ... such as myself, Erlking is rather a wonderland. One can only imagine all the things of interest and power hidden away here." He peered at Robin again, smoothing down his embroidered lapels as he did so. "The kind of things which an inquisitive and resourceful boy such as yourself would be sure to sniff out. It must be a constant wonder to you. Such a voyage of discovery for a bright young mind."

Robin shrugged. "There are lots of odd things here," he admitted. The man was still staring at him intently, his eyes rather bright and expectant. Robin had never noticed before, but they were a dark orange, like glowing embers. "There's a bathroom upstairs near the back of the house where the taps all shriek really loud when you get into the shower." He scratched his head absently. "None of us use that anymore."

The man didn't seem impressed, he blinked at Robin, his smile still fixed beneath his moustache. Behind him, the painted figures on the circular hall chased one another silently around and around on horseback, like a mad carousel.

"Or … there's the room with all the hatboxes, I suppose," Robin continued hopefully. "That's quite fun. Henry and I found out that the different hats make you talk with different accents if you put them on. You can't really control it. Henry spent a whole day growling like a pirate a while back until Aunt Irene insisted we all stop dressing up for dinner." Robin sniggered out loud at the memory.

"Hmm," Ffoulkes allowed a tiny nod of his head. "Dressing up is fun, I'll allow. Clothes …" He indicated his own pristine appearance with a flourish. "… maketh the man, yes? A-ha-ha. I am rather looking forward to the Halloween feast here. You must have all manner of parties and events." He leaned forward a little secretively, dropping his voice low. "Tell me, have you ever enjoyed a masked ball?"

Robin shook his head. "No, not really."

"Oh they are dashed good fun, really they are," the man said with a fresh grin. "Everyone dressed up, faces hidden. Such mystery, such larks. Erlking must be bursting at the seams! There must be plenty of masks knocking around the place you could all use, yes?"

"… I guess."

"Do you know of any?" the man pressed. "Masks, that is? As I say, you know this place better than I. Inquisitive and resourceful young boy like you. Filled with the fire of youth. You would know where these things may be hidden, or stored, as it were. Come across anything of that kind during your time here, have you?"

"Masks? No, not really," Robin thought carefully. "But I could always ask Aunt Irene if–"

"No need to trouble the old girl," the man chuckled, suddenly standing up straight and waving his hands dismissively, his large cuffs flapping like sails. He was still smiling, but Robin couldn't help feeling he had slightly annoyed the foppish man somehow. "Just a thought, that's all, my boy, just a thought. Such diversions are always good fun, yes? A-ha. Might be something you could occupy yourself with on a rainy afternoon. Bit of a challenge for you. Find some masks for old Ffoulkes, eh?" He winked and beckoned Robin to continue, clopping out of the ornate hall without further ado and along the corridor to Irene's study.

"As I've said more than once since I arrived here," he continued, making

Robin wonder if he talked incessantly simply because he loved the sound of his own voice. "Such a wonderful place for a child to live. Erlking! In every shadowed nook a mystery, around every dark corner …"

They turned a corner and suddenly, to Robin's horror, were faced with a very surprised-looking faun. Woad, arms laden with what looked very much to Robin like apples recently 'liberated' from Hestia's storerooms, stopped in his tracks, looking guilty, his yellow eyes wide. One apple dropped from his armload and fell to the floor with a sonorous thunk.

"… surprising treasures!" Ffoulkes finished in a whisper, his own eyes wide as he took in the sight of the startled, frozen faun.

Several seconds of silence reigned in the corridor. Nobody moved. Robin winced internally. They had tried so hard to keep Woad out of the way while the visitors were here, on Irene's orders. Now, seeing the greedy light which came blazing into Ffoulkes' face, he understood why.

"Um," said Woad. His eyes flicking guiltily from the man to Robin and back several times.

"You … have a … faun?" the man said, still staring with great interest. "There is a faun here at Erlking!"

"Erm, yes, there is," Robin admitted. There seemed little point denying it now. Woad was standing there with an armful of apples, blue as a sailor's curse and large as life. "This is Woad. He–"

"I'm his faun." Woad finished, glaring at the man defiantly. "You're not supposed to see me. I'm very good at not being seen. I've been excellent at not being seen for weeks." He shot Robin a guilty look. "But Inky is hungry and I couldn't find any raw meat in the larder and I thought I would try him with apples."

"His faun?" the man blinked, his hands clasped as he towered over Woad in the narrow corridor.

"My faun," Robin explained. "Well, that is, my friend. Woad lives with us here and–"

"And is usually good at not being seen," Woad insisted. He was staring at the man's face. "The hair on your face is very pointy," he observed with caution. "It's as though it wants to arrive everywhere just before you do."

"Why, thank you," Ffoulkes replied, very absently, as though he hadn't heard a word Woad had said. He was inspecting Woad carefully, as one might appraise a priceless antique clock or a perfect diamond. "Such a wonderful specimen. That colouring, so light! Must be a young one. Yes!

Ahaha. And look, hardly any of the markings have come through yet, this pelt is astonishingly pure. Astonishingly!"

"Pelt?" Woad said with narrowed eyes, shuffling the apples a little in his arms.

Ffoulkes ignored him again, looking back to Robin. "Have you any idea, my boy, any idea at all, how much a pelt like this would fetch at the Netherworlde Agora? Fauns are highly prized. And one of this immaturity! So supple and soft. The mind boggles, it truly does."

"Woad isn't for sale," Robin frowned, a little aghast.

"I am using my pelt." Woad agreed eagerly with a nod. "I use it to keep all my skeleton in place, otherwise it would roll around all over the floor. I would never get anything done. It would be terribly messy."

The man grinned. "Yes, yes, of course. How rude of me," he said to Robin. "Not for sale. Of course! Why that's perfectly understandable. Who would part … with such a treasure?"

Robin was fairly sure that most people at Erlking would, and did, have other, more inventive names for Woad than 'treasure'. He had heard Hestia mutter more than a few when she thought no one was listening. Henry had written some of them down as well.

Ffoulkes loomed over, as though inspecting a prize horse. Woad leaned backwards away from him, arms still full of apples, his long blue tail swishing for balance and his eyes rather wide. "Not a single tribal marking. How unique. Not a one! Fauns, as you know, are all about scarification and decoration. This one is such a blank canvas. Tribal outcast, perhaps? How rare! How wonderful. Tell me, has it even matured into its skyfire yet?"

Robin had no idea what this meant, but he was getting more and more irritated with the man.

"*He* has not," a cool voice came from further down the corridor, before he could answer. Robin glanced past Ffoulkes and Woad, who was now backed up completely against the wall, with the glittering eyes of the Panthea roaming critically over the condition of his tail and claws.

Aunt Irene, to Robin's great relief, had emerged from her study, a few doors down the corridor. She was looking at the three of them coolly.

"Robin," she said to him. "Your faun must run along now, and do whatever things fauns do, the details of which I would rather remain a mystery to me, especially if they are to include the cultivation of skyfire." She gave Woad a sharp look. The small blue boy blinked back innocently and grinned. "Mr Ffoulkes has business with myself. You should also come along."

She disappeared back into her study, not waiting to see if they would follow. They would, of course. Irene was that kind of person.

Robin gave Woad a pointed 'we'll talk about this later' look and cocked his head meaningfully. The faun grinned and scarpered, ducking under the looming figure of Ffoulkes and dashing off with his apple bounty, bare feet slapping on the floors.

"Close the door please, Robin," Irene said politely as he and the Fire Panthea entered the cosy study. The heavy curtains were drawn against the wild weather outside, and a fire crackled merrily in the grate. Irene always had a fire lit in her study, Robin had noticed. Old people were always cold. Gran had kept the three-bar fire on in the bungalow non-stop, even in the height of summer. It had always smelled faintly of burning dust, a smell which even now he found oddly comforting.

Irene's fireplace was not a modest council bungalow affair, of course. It was a vast black marble grate, ornately carved with twining leaves and peeping faces.

"As you are aware, Robin," Irene said, indicating him to sit as she took her own chair behind her extremely orderly desk. "I asked Mr Ffoulkes to Erlking for a reason. Yes, he is travelling to the Netherworlde accompanying the sisters, whose safe passage I have agreed to for my own reasons." She pushed something across the desk toward the seated boy. It was a folded piece of paper. "But I also wished to see if he could use his expertise in the unusual and arcane to help me identify this."

Robin took the paper, aware that Ffoulkes, who was standing behind him, was leaning over his shoulder to peer down. The man smelled strongly of a peppery cologne. Rather too much of it.

The folded paper was a list of four names. Wolfsbane the Bold, Peasblossom the Architect, Matthias the Illusioner and Hemlock the Sly. Four Fae. Four members of the Sidhe-Nobilitas, including his own father. It was a list written in the elaborate hand of Lady Titania, lost Queen of the Fae. Robin had discovered it earlier in the year, safely hidden in the tomb of Nightshade.

There was another small square of card resting with the list, an old and yellowed library book frontispiece. The little card which got stamped each time someone checked out a book. The dates and names were all smeared and blurred with age and wear. This 'relic' was a mystery to all of them.

"This is about the cubiculu-argentum?" Robin asked, looking up. He didn't know what that was. He only knew what Lady Titania had written on the list of names. That its construction must be secret, and that only the four named here would be privy to its meaning and location.

"Indeed it is," Irene nodded. "As you already know, the cubiculu-argentum is an unknown factor. We don't know what it is, where it is, or what it even means. Indeed, from Titania's own words, even these four Fae, who were in some way connected to it, each only knew their own part in it. Whatever it was, or is however …" She spread her hands. "It was important enough to hide the very names of those who knew about it." She tapped the square of yellowed card. "And important enough to bury this scrap of an old book somewhere Eris would never find it."

She looked up to Ffoulkes. "The reason I have called you both here together," she said. "Is that my eyes and ears in the Netherworlde are telling me odd things. There are strange happenings and rumours. Things which may very shortly take us all away from this leisurely investigation of ours. We only have until Halloween before you leave us as it is. You have been here some time, and have so far told me nothing."

Ffoulkes grinned his most disarming grin.

"There is very little to go on, my lady," he explained. "I have been in your library, and I have made my own investigations, and I am still in the process of tracing which library this card has come from, let alone which book. These things are not simple."

"Simple or not, they are why you are here, Mr Ffoulkes," Irene said crisply. "Indeed, they are the only reason why, after many years of our association, I have finally relented and acceded to your often-repeated request to have access inside Erlking Hall. So far, for my part, I see very little return on my investment."

"Dis was not built in a day," Ffoulkes shrugged. "Tell me, what whispers are these which you have heard from the Netherworlde, which are so urgent?"

It's the bees, Robin found himself thinking, quite unexpectedly, suddenly remembering the odd dream he had had. *It's the bees and the leaves, that's the problem.*

"They are my concern, not yours," Irene replied smoothly. "My point is. I need to know, sooner rather than later, what it is you can tell me about the artefact you were brought here to inspect."

Ffoulkes seemed agitated. He twirled his moustache a little. "Aha-ha. Well, of course. And I have been able to discern a little, a very little, mind you, during my time here."

Irene raised her eyebrows expectantly.

"There is, of course, the question of a professional fee," Ffoulkes said quietly. "You have, after all, given me an extraordinarily small amount of information to go on, and my services are rather–"

"Your 'fee,' Mr Ffoulkes …" Irene cut in, rather sharply, "… as we discussed before you came here, was admission to Erlking. The leisure to walk the halls of the Fae King and Queen and, as you put it at the time, 'appreciate' the many wonders the place holds. Your fee, sir, has already been paid."

Ffoulkes face darkened. "A cosy getaway in a big old house is all well and good, my lady," he purred. "But something of this importance, I think I could name my own price for any sliver of information. Perhaps one item of my choosing? As a memento? Nothing which would be missed, of course."

"Certainly not," Irene replied flatly. "Do not imagine that I am unaware that you have been exploring this house since your arrival in September, weighing up the value of all and any goods you have seen. I do not take offence at this, please understand. It is your nature … to covet. But nothing here is mine. I am Steward only of Erlking, not owner."

A dangerous glint came into Ffoulkes' eyes. "Then one might say that you are in no position to refuse my request. If the items are not yours to keep. As you say, Irene, nothing here is … ahahah … yours."

Irene did not look away from Ffoulkes, nor did she blink. Her calm blue eyes were clear as ice.

"Indeed not," she agreed. She nodded in Robin's direction. "Everything is his."

Robin, who was already feeling uncomfortable being in the middle of this exchange, felt even more sheepish, sinking into his leather chair deeper with a creak.

Ffoulkes laughed, a merry bark. "Him? But he is just a boy."

"He is the last of the line of the House Fellows, and a Fae, direct descendant of one of the Sidhe-Nobilitas, and the Scion of the Arcania."

Irene steepled her fingers on the desk. "And even if he were not all of these things, only a fool thinks there is any such thing as 'just a boy', sir."

Ffoulkes spluttered at being indirectly accused of being a fool. The man's ego was tender at the best of times. He leaned on his side of the desk, his fingers splayed on the wood.

"I am at a loss, to be honest, as to why he is even here, in this meeting," he said to Irene. "Surely matters of such importance should be between you and I. What have they to do with a young changeling?"

"This young changeling," Irene replied, "has everything to do with this. The cubiculu-argentum, whatever it may be, is tied to his father, and others. It was the last great mystery of Titania and Oberon before they disappeared. It may explain where they went, why the war was lost. Why Eris won. And why they had to die."

She flicked her eyes to Robin. "I think any son deserves to know that."

Ffoulkes still bristled.

"So your payment, Mr Ffoulkes, shall continue to be nothing more or less than my continued hospitality here. The extent of that hospitality, and the duration of it, depends entirely upon what information, if any, you are able to give me. Right now."

Ffoulkes straightened up, clasping his hands behind his back as he sized up the old lady.

The atmosphere had grown ever more sour in the room.

"I think, Lady Irene … aha." he began, in a quiet tone. "You should realise that you have lived in the mortal world a long time. You have, in fact, become a fussy old woman. A perfectly charming one of course, but you are not what you once were, to be making threats or giving orders." A corner of his mouth turned up. "You would do well to take note of what you are reduced to. Your light, my fellow Panthea, has grown very dim and weak."

Irene stood, very slowly. Her expression could have frozen water. Tall as she was, she towered over the foppish man, staring down with cool unblinking eyes. The silence dragged on and Robin, mortified in his chair, glanced from his aunt to Ffoulkes, hardly daring to breathe. The man began to fidget, wilting under the relentless gaze. He puffed and cleared his throat. "Ahem … um … well … yes … aha …" His aunt remained impassive, a statue of regal disdain. Ffoulkes glanced away, fussing with his lacy cuffs. "Yes … well, that is … I mean …"

The door to the study swung open slowly, breaking off the man's babble.

"Would you care to leave Erlking now? Or have you information which is useful to us?" Irene asked calmly.

Ffoulkes, recovering himself, twirled his moustache and cleared his throat again. "Ahem ... of course. Yes, of course. Such larks. You always were impressive old gal, back in the day ... and still now it seems. All is forgotten."

The door to the study closed itself quietly, and Irene sat down, awfully business-like, and adjusted her spectacles.

"Excellent," Irene said pleasantly, as though nothing out of the ordinary had happened. "How very helpful of you. Do go on."

"I have no idea what this 'thing' is, of which Titania speaks in her letter, or what its purpose is," Ffoulkes admitted. "It could be anything. Something secret, naturally. A weapon, perhaps? Maybe even something that could wipe out all of the Panthea and end the war forever. A genocide machine. It's a dangerous thing to look into."

"My parents wouldn't have been involved with anything like that," Robin said hotly. The man peered down at him.

"You never knew your parents, my boy," he observed. "How could you possibly know that?"

"I just do," Robin replied, anxiety over the adults' spat turning into anger. "My dad's name is on that list. He wouldn't have anything to do with genocide, you're talking rubbish."

"Your family, Scion, are capable of more than you know," Ffoulkes replied. "Considering you didn't even know until a year ago that they existed, or that you belonged to them, I hardly think you are best placed to judge their moral character. Indeed, certain branches of the Fellows tree–"

"Enough," Irene said. "Robin. Let Ffoulkes continue please. And Ffoulkes ..." She looked at the man darkly. "Let us keep to the subject in hand, if you don't mind."

Robin seethed quietly, and Ffoulkes smoothed his lapels.

"My point ..." he said. "Before I was passionately interrupted by this admirably forthright young man ... is that although we don't know what it is, or what part each of these individuals have to play in it, we can safely assume that it is in some way tied to this card." He tapped the faded square of card on the table top. "And more specifically to the book it came from.

A human world book, it seems, which the King and Queen of the Fae, for whatever reason, seemed to think was important."

"So far this is all rather obvious conjecture," Irene noted. "Have you been able to identify the book?"

"No," the man replied flatly. "With this level of evidence to go on, I would think no-one could." He held up a finger. "However, dating the paper, looking at the type and construction etc., I have been able to surmise that this particular stock dates to the 1900's."

"The book is from the turn of the last century?" Robin asked.

"Well, it was printed then at least, or rather, the book itself may have been older, but that was the date at which it was filed in a library."

"Which library?" Irene pressed.

"The British Library," Ffoulkes revealed, sounding rather pleased with himself. "You can just make it out in the corner of the smudge, that little inked semi-circle there. It's almost completely faded of course, but you can still see a third of the design, if you tilt the card to the light. It's a library stamp, an old one. They don't use it anymore, but I would stake my reputation on it being the stamp used by the British Library in London around the turn of the twentieth century."

"Well …" Irene removed her spectacles and cleaned them on a hand-kerchief. "That is something at least, although it does not narrow it down much. I understand the British Library carries rather a fair number of books. Anything else?"

"It was last checked out in nineteen twenty-six," Ffoulkes elaborated. "This final smudge at the bottom. Your eyes are not as keen as mine. None are. But I can just about discern it. In those days, there were no computerised records. One signed a name on the book-plate here."

Robin peered down at the card with great interest. He could still make out nothing but old and faded squiggles.

"Does it say who it was?" he asked. "Who last checked out the book, whatever it is, back in the twenties?"

Ffoulkes shook his head. "I've studied a great deal of handwriting in my time, young man. I cannot make out this signature. It is too damaged. I can however, from the shape and composition, tell you three things. It was more likely a man than a woman, a fully adult and well-educated man by the penmanship still visible. He also most likely had a military background of some kind. One can always read these things. And lastly, although the name itself is too poor to read, it is a fairly short one, and appears to begin with a 'G'."

Robin was actually a little impressed if Ffoulkes had truly been able to read all that just from studying this smudged bit of card. Of course, there was always the possibility that he was making the whole thing up just so Irene didn't kick him out of Erlking.

"This is quite a great deal more information than I might have hoped for," Irene said graciously.

"It is?" Robin sounded doubtful. "But we aren't any closer to knowing what book it's from."

"True," Irene allowed. "But we do now know that it is a book of some age, which was entered into the British Museum at the turn of the twentieth century, and that the last person to check the book out, before it found its way somehow to us, was an adult male of potentially military background in nineteen twenty-six, and that his name may have been 'G'." She shrugged. "It is more than we did know."

Robin was frustrated. "But that just raises even more questions."

"Yes," Irene allowed. "One finds that is often the case, when the most interesting questions are asked." She stood, and very formally offered her hand to Ffoulkes, who shook it genially like a perfect gentleman.

Robin thought he may never really understand Panthea. A moment ago, the two of them had been at each other's throats, and now here they were being completely convivial. Perhaps all adults were like that, he thought. Maybe that's what adulting was, in the end.

"Thank you for the light you have shed, Mr Ffoulkes. It is most appreciated. I hope you enjoy the rest of your short stay with us."

"Thank you, madam," Ffoulkes responded. "For the light you have restrained. I may have spoken out of turn."

"May have?" Irene raised her eyebrows. To Robin she said, "After our guests have left us, I shall travel to London. Make some further enquiries. You will be required here, Robin."

Robin nodded. He hadn't really expected to get a trip to London out of the proceedings anyway.

"I expect I shall return before Christmas," Irene added reassuringly. "As I said. There are … other concerns in the Netherworlde at present which may be escalating. I will expect things here at Erlking to remain calm."

No sooner had she spoken, than the door of the study burst open with a bang, making them all turn and stare.

This time, however, it was not a subtle flow of mana which had opened it. It was a faun. Woad stood in the doorframe, looking out of breath and pale, his eyes as wide as saucers.

"The faun!" Ffoulkes exclaimed in surprise. "The faun has returned!"

"Woad?" Robin stood, staring at the little blue boy, whose face was a mask of drama.

"Pinky! Quick! Come quick!" Woad said breathlessly. "It's the old ladies! The ghostly creepers!"

Irene had also risen from her chair. "What on earth is the meaning of this?" she asked frowning.

"The sisters?" Robin asked.

Woad nodded frantically. "Upstairs!" he panted. "We found them! Karya and me! You have to come! They have discovered Jackalope in his bed, and they are eating his soul!"

RUDE AWAKENINGS

Robin hadn't waited to see what Aunt Irene said. By the time he reached the sickroom at the other end of the house, following the scampering Woad, he was heavily out of breath.

Karya and Henry were already there, both standing in the doorway looking pale and concerned. Robin hadn't even realised Henry had arrived at the house.

"What's going on?" Robin panted. Henry held his hands up innocently. "Couldn't find you when I got here, mate. Thought you might be up here with silver-top, but when I got here, those women were inside and they wouldn't let me in. I found Karya." He flicked a thumb in the girl's direction.

Robin pushed past the two of them and stared into the room. It had started to rain outside, and the drops were hitting the long windows of the sickroom noisily, their shadows making the light ripple across the floorboard. The Eumenides sisters were gathered around the bed, grey and looming shadows, blocking Robin's view of Jackalope.

"I've tried talking to them," Karya said, sounding both exasperated and annoyed. "But they won't tell me what's going on." Louder she said, rather pointedly into the room. "Although I'm fairly certain they shouldn't be in here!"

One of the sisters waved a gnarled and wispy hand over her shoulder dismissively. "We do not speak to people who are not real," she muttered from beneath her veil.

Robin closed in on the three haunting figures. "You leave him alone," he said angrily.

"This one …" they rasped in a low voice, "… has been left alone too long. Alone is all he knows. Is all he has become."

The irritation which had risen when Ffoulkes had insulted his parents down in Irene's study was back, rising in Robin's chest like an angry and agitated bird, beating dark wings against the inside of his ribcage.

"I mean it!" he snapped, edging closer to the bed, undaunted by their grisly presence. "If you hurt him–"

"Or suck out his soul!" Woad added helpfully from the safety of the doorway.

Robin was aware he was gritting his teeth. He didn't like these visitors, any of them, if he was honest. This was his house, and they were poking about in his business. He couldn't remember feeling this angry. His mana stone beneath his t-shirt felt as though it were a hot and jittering stone, and the idea came into his mind, surprising himself, that he should just form a Waterwhip and lash the three ghoulish women out of the way, or form a Galestrike and blow them against the wall. That would teach them a lesson. Not to treat him like some insignificant buzzing insect. They hadn't even looked around at him. He was the Scion, by the gods.

Without realising fully what he was doing, his hands were already starting to move, to form the basic cantrip. He heard Karya call his name, a worried hitch in her voice, and ignored her.

"We are not trying to hurt the creature," one of the sisters whispered, finally turning around to look at Robin. She noticed his hands, and her head beneath its veil tilted slightly to one side in a thoughtful and questioning manner. "We are trying to help it."

"What are you doing, child?" another sister said, glancing up at Robin. "We feel your power flow. Are you so quick to strike? To rush in and ask no questions?"

Robin paused, the cantrip still half-formed in his hands, blinking. He felt furious still, but also confused. He stared down at his palms as though they belonged to someone else. The flickering mana dancing between his fingertips was his own, but it looked darker somehow, a flickering pulse of angry energy.

"Steady on, Rob," Henry said carefully from the doorway.

Karya took another step into the room. "What do you mean, you're trying to help him?" she asked.

The women glanced at her, then back to Robin, who had lowered his hands, shakily.

"Answer her," he demanded.

"We do not speak to that one," one of the sisters hissed, though Robin could not tell which had spoken. "She is no-one and nothing. Speak into a void and you will only hear your own echo."

Robin glared at them. "Then you will answer me," he snapped. "I am the Scion." His voice sounded odd, even to himself, as though it were coming unbidden from somewhere deep inside.

"I am the Puck."

All three women turned at this, giving Robin their full attention, although it was impossible to see their faces.

"Ah, there it is," said one. "That peppercorn of darkness in the light."

"We are healing him," another said. "In so much as he can be healed by the likes of us … or anyone."

Robin shot a look across the room at Woad, who looked a little sheepish. To the women he asked. "How did you know he was even here?"

"He called out to us," one of them replied simply. "He has been calling out for some time now, though he does not know it, of course. We heard him." She tapped the side of her head with a bony finger. It clacked audibly. "We can bear it no more."

The woman nearest to Robin raised her hands in supplication. "Dim your fires, young Scion," she said softly. "There is no ill intent here."

Reluctantly, Robin unclenched his hands, forcing himself to relax. He felt his mana, which had gathered around him like the low brooding rumble before a thunderclap, slowly dissipating. It raced out and away from him like static electricity, charging the air in agitation. He swallowed, feeling as though he had a golf ball lodged in his throat. That he was literally forcing the Puck down. In the see-saw within, as the Puck descended, Robin rose back to the surface.

"Okay," he said, a little shakily. He was aware that his friends were still watching from the doorway, all three with worried expressions. Had he really looked that bad? Everyone lost their temper from time to time, right? It wasn't a crime.

"Okay," he repeated, when he was sure that his voice was his own again. He glanced down at the still and sleeping Fae in the bed. "Help him how? Wake him?"

"Simple as spit," they replied.

"Hope it's not true love's kiss," Henry mumbled. "He'll be waitin' a long time for that."

73

"Henry, you're not helping." Karya jabbed him in the ribs with her elbow.

One of the women reached out her hand, hovering it over Jackalope's chest, just above the neatly tucked bedsheets. The fingers shook slightly.

"It's time to come back, little Fae," she said. Before Robin could reach out or speak, she clenched her hand into a fist and brought it down hard, cracking it against the boy with surprising strength. His whole body shook and juddered, and then, to Robin's wide-eyed astonishment, Jackalope coughed.

The women drew back as one, gliding away from the bed as the white-haired boy coughed and spluttered again. His eyes flickered, face deepening into a frown and he rolled first onto his side and then straight off the bed, falling to the floor in a tangle of sheets.

Henry, Woad and Karya rushed into the room as Robin pushed past the women, dropping to one knee by Jackalope's side.

"He's actually moving?" Henry sounded astonished.

"He's choking," Karya said. The coughing fit continued. Jackalope had struggled to his hands and knees, hands splayed out on the floorboards as he retched, his pale spine arching.

Not knowing what else to do, Robin slapped him hard on the back. He seemed to be choking.

Something flew out of the boy's mouth and rolled across the floor. It looked as though he had just coughed up a small ball of dark, rumpled paper. Karya and Henry had both dropped to the floor with Robin, as their patient took several deep and shuddering breaths.

Woad scampered over to the small dark object and with a look on his face that was both revolted and fascinated, nudged it with his foot.

They watched, transfixed, as the object shivered, and unfurled itself. What they had taken for paper was wings, dark and glossy. A large black moth sat on the floorboards, experimentally beating its dusty wings slowly, as though it had just emerged from a chrysalis.

"Grimm magic," Robin heard one of the women hiss. "This was buried deep." They had retreated further, gathering around the doorway. "We have done as he asked. He is purged."

The moth suddenly fluttered to life, lifting off from the floorboards into the air. With wings fully unfurled it was large, as wide as Robin's hand span. They watched it flit fitfully into the air and circle the room a few times, before it made a bee-line for the open fireplace.

"Stop it!" yelled Karya, and she, Robin and Woad all skittered across the floor, grasping for the insect in vain, Jackalope momentarily forgotten. It ducked and whirled between their outstretched hands, disappearing up the large chimney in a whoosh.

"Damn it!" Karya snapped.

"I will catch it!" Woad growled, and without a second thought, he leapt into the ashy grate and scampered up the chimney after it, dislodging soot and cold embers. He vanished in pursuit, a ferret up a drainpipe, forcing Karya and Robin to shield their eyes from the grimy debris that erupted from the hearth.

"That was one of Peryl's moths," Karya said, coughing a little as the dust cloud settled.

Robin turned away from the fireplace, meaning to ask the sisters how they had known what to do, but they were gone. They had slipped out of the room as silent as ghosts, leaving the door to the corridor open.

"Rob?"

Henry's voice, sounding oddly muffled, snapped Robin's attention away from the door and back to the bedside. He froze.

Jackalope was awake. He stood facing Robin and Karya, who still knelt in the soot by the grate. His eyes were wide and wild, silver irises flashing from the boy to the girl and back in confusion and panic. He looked unsteady on his feet and sheened with a cold sweat. Of more immediate concern was the fact that he held Henry before him like a human shield, one arm pinning Henry's arms flat to his body, the other tightly around his neck in a headlock.

Henry's face was an odd shade of red which made the Fae's pallid complexion look even more ghostly as he glared over the boy's shoulder at Robin and Karya.

"Jackalope," Robin said slowly, moving to rise from his knees.

"Don't!" Jackalope shouted, his voice, unused for so long, cracking hoarsely. "Don't you move! I'll snap his neck."

Robin froze in mid crouch, his heart pounding. Slowly, he raised his hands, showing the other boy he was unarmed.

"Just … wait a second," he began.

"Where am I?" Jackalope demanded. His voice still raspy and a little shaky with disorientation. "What is this place? Who are you people?"

"Just let Henry go," Robin said. "Let's talk. You're confused, I can see that. Let's–"

"Shut up!" Jackalope was trying to watch both Robin and Karya at the same time. Henry struggled in his grip, but the older boy, though he looked unsteady on his feet, was clearly far stronger. "Stop talking. Where are my things?"

"How are we supposed to answer that without talking?" Karya asked calmly, standing up slowly. Jackalope flinched at her movement, stepping backwards, dragging Henry with him, until his heels met the edge of the bed.

"I said don't move," he growled, twisting Henry's neck in a jerk.

"Yeah," Henry gurgled furiously. "Don't move, eh?" he suggested.

"My clothes and weapons," Jackalope said. "What have you done with them? These garments are strange to me. This place is strange."

"Those are Henry's pyjama bottoms," Robin explained, arms still held up peacefully. "Your wolf-rags weren't very practical. You're at Erlking. Please calm down, it's okay, just–"

"Why the hell is he wearing my stuff?" Henry managed to gurgle angrily.

"I know you," the white-haired boy said, coughing. "I know all of you."

"We're friends," Karya said. "You're amongst friends. You've not been well."

"Friends?" Henry choked. "Might be … a strong term." He tried to wrench himself away again, lifting his foot to stamp on Jackalope's bare toes, but the Fae, weakened and unsteady as he might be, had quick reflexes and dodged the move.

"I don't have friends," he growled at them. "And that's not what you are. You brought trouble to my door. I was safe and secret until you came, out of the snow."

"Technically, it was you who brought us to your door," Karya pointed out.

Robin stood beside her, slowly. "You need to let Henry go. Right now," he said. He knew the other boy was just scared and confused. He should be trying to reason with him, talk him down, but he was suddenly awfully impatient with that idea.

"You brought Peacekeepers onto the mountain," Jackalope said accusingly. "You forced me from my home. And now you bring me here."

"To Erlking, yes," Karya said, again with a reasonable tone. "Best place to heal, safest place to be … arguably. You were injured by our enemy. Badly injured. You should have died."

Robin was staring at Henry, his best friend's face was a mixture of pure panic and outrage. It made anger bubble up in his stomach.

"I won't ask again," he said through his teeth. "Drop Henry, or I will make you."

Jackalope glared imperiously at him, silver eyes flashing. "Make me?" he spat. "You couldn't tie your own shoelaces on the Gravis Glaciem. How do you think you can make me do anything?" He sneered at Robin. "Stupid child."

The rage erupted in Robin, flashing up through his veins like boiled mercury. Enough was enough. He threw out a hand, intending, with cold, detached precision, to cast a hard Galestrike at the other Fae, a javelin of invisible air to knock him off balance and onto his back.

What erupted from his palm, however, was not an invisible jet of air. A fat black whip of churning darkness, like inky smoke, shot across the room, the lashing tentacle of some deep-water beast. It was partly air, shot through with glittering shards of ice, making its sinuous form glitter like the night sky as it flew across the room, a striking cobra of pure mana.

The air in the room crackled and hissed as Jackalope stumbled backwards, Henry twisting out of his grip just in time to duck and throw himself to the floor before the blast caught the side of his face.

The black, whip-like coil roared like a thunderhead as it caught around Jackalope's throat, lifting him from his feet. It flung him hard across the room, slamming him bodily into the far wall, making the rainy window rattle and plaster dust rain down in chunks from the old ceiling. Robin held the boy there a second, then, too shocked at what he had done to sustain the cantrip, he dropped his hand, flinching back as though he had touched a hot stove.

The mixture of smoke, churning air and water dissipated, and Jackalope was dropped to the floor like a rag doll, hitting the boards with a loud thud.

"Bloody hell, Rob," Henry gasped, rubbing his throat as he got to his feet shakily.

Jackalope was also standing, one hand propped on the wall and the other massaging his own neck, which looked red and chaffed. His bare shoulders were covered in plaster.

"Scion," Karya whispered. "What did you do?"

Robin didn't know. His heart was hammering, and he felt weak and watery. He hadn't meant to hurt the other boy, just to knock him over. At least, those were the thoughts in his head now. A moment ago, to his shame and horror, he genuinely hadn't cared if Jackalope got hurt. He hadn't even cared if Henry had gotten caught in the crossfire. He stared down at his hands, which were shaking. They looked like alien things to him. Treacherous.

"Robin, your eyes are green," Henry said in wonder.

"What is the meaning of this?" A voice from the doorway made them all look up. Even Jackalope didn't make a move, but stared at the figure of Aunt Irene, who, having followed Robin and Woad, had just arrived at the room, Mr Ffoulkes in tow.

Her sharp eyes took in the scene. The tumbled bedsheets, the soot-covered floor by the fire, the cracked plaster on the walls and the hunted-looking feral Fae half crouched in the corner.

No one spoke.

"I see," she said after a moment. She looked to Jackalope. "I am glad you are awake. You are at Erlking Hall. In the mortal world, more or less." She glanced at the other three. "These here have been your nursemaids. Watching over you and keeping you from harm. You are a guest here, for as long as it suits all parties. Stand down."

Jackalope glared at her, still looking like a wild animal, although being thrown against the wall appeared to have taken a lot of fight out of him.

"You. You are not Fae," he spluttered. "If this is Erlking–"

"I am the guardian of Erlking," Irene cut him off sternly, her voice, though still calm, could have sliced steel. "And all in it. I will not have ..." She glanced around at the dust still falling from the ceiling, "... boisterousness of this kind." Her eyes settled on Robin. "Even from ... especially from, you."

Robin didn't know what he could possibly say to make the situation better, so he said nothing. He wanted the ground to swallow him up.

"Don't blame, Robin," Henry said gruffly. "Blame Snow White here. He's the one who went all mental and tried to strangle me."

He stared hotly over at Jackalope, who glared back, uncowed.

"And I want my bloody pyjamas back!" Henry added, a little childishly.

"Only maybe not right this second," Karya added quickly.

"I do not care who started what," Irene said, bringing their attention back to her. She fixed Jackalope with a firm look. "I am Panthea, yes. I am Irene of the Hours. I will have order here. No harm shall come to any at Erlking while I watch over it." She noticed he was still rubbing his neck. "No serious harm, that is. You are no prisoner here. You are a guest.

If you wish it, your things will be returned to you immediately and you are free to leave." She raised a finger to silence the Fae, who had opened his mouth to speak. "However," she added. "Before you decide what you want and how you want it, you will do me the courtesy of speaking with me. Alone."

"You can't keep me here," Jackalope said quietly. His eyes flicked over to Robin. There was high colour in his white cheeks. "You shouldn't have brought me here."

"They didn't," Irene said simply. "You were brought here by the enemy of the Fae. By the enemy of all of us."

He looked back to her, confused.

"And I do not know why," Irene said, cutting off his question. "But I believe it may be in your best interests, as well as ours, to find out. Don't you?"

She waved a hand invitingly at the corridor. Jackalope stood uneasily, and warily hobbled across the room towards her. "We will talk," he said grimly. "I promise nothing but that."

"I ask nothing but that," she said, nodding slightly. She beckoned to Karya. "Karya, please be so good as to take Henry down to Hestia if you will. That bruising around his throat looks sore. Perhaps a poultice? Or at the very least some tea with honey."

Karya nodded, and she and Henry followed Irene and Jackalope out of the door.

"Robin," Irene said, turning at the door. She looked at him very thoughtfully and carefully for a moment. She must have been able to see the discomfort on his face. "Please clear up this mess before you join us." She indicated the room. "And do not look so downcast. If there is one thing I can tell you, it is this. There is no mess made, that cannot be put right, if one is willing."

Robin nodded. He wanted to apologise to Jackalope and to Henry, but they were already gone, ushered out of the room by the adults. He heard Henry and Karya's voices as they passed along the corridor.

"I don't get it. I really don't get it. Why does he even want him here? He's a menace. Unstable. After that lovely cuddle from a sweaty psychopath, I trust the paranoid maniac even less."

"You really don't see anything do you?" Karya replied wearily to Henry, as their voices faded away. "He's Robin. Robin without the luck that he had. Robin was lucky. Luckier than most Fae. He could easily have been Jackalope instead."

Robin stared around at the now empty room, feeling a little empty. Was that true? Did he feel responsible for Jackalope because his life, the death of his brother, all the years in the camps of Dis … It could easily have been his own fate?

Robin was an orphan. He had never known his parents, and his only loved one, Gran, had died, leaving him to figure his way as best he could. He had never thought of himself as lucky before. But now, in comparison, he felt embarrassed that he had ever had a moment to feel sorry for himself. Compared to some in the Netherworlde …

"Well done, Scion," he muttered to himself as he began to gather bedsheets from the floor. "Way to earn someone's trust, eh? Throw them against the wall. Nice move. He's bound to want to join the family now."

He shook his head, trying not to think about what had happened with his temper and his mana as he cleaned and tidied.

When he had finally got the room in some semblance of order, there was a 'whoomph' behind him, making him turn in surprise.

Sitting in the fireplace, in a brand new and quite expansive cloud of soot, was Woad. He was grey and black with grime from the chimney, his yellow eyes staring out of the darkness of his own face as the cloud settled on the floorboards.

"Moth got away," he shrugged.

Robin and the others didn't find out what was discussed behind the closed doors of Aunt Irene's study. She and Jackalope were in there for a long time, during which Robin and the others sat together in the hallway, drumming their fingers. They couldn't even hear muffled voices. The rain was coming down in sheets now, darkening the late afternoon sky into an unnaturally early twilight. Karya had lit some candles to chase away the gloom, their flickering light bouncing off the panels, and Woad sat curled up on the deep windowsill, arms wrapped around his knees and frowning moodily into the weather. He was still sore about his failure to capture the moth.

Henry and Karya had other things on their mind. Robin's outburst.

"But … that was the Tower of Darkness," Karya said. "I'd bet Henry's life on it."

Henry gave her a sidelong glance. "Why my life?"

"Well, I'm not certain enough to bet my own," she explained. "But the point is, Scion, you haven't learned *any* Darkness magic. How did you even do it?"

Robin had no idea, as he explained for the hundredth time. He hadn't meant to do it at all. He'd just been so annoyed. And it hadn't been pure darkness, there had been air and water mixed in there too.

"But you totally pucked out," Henry pointed out. "I mean like, full puckage almost. I saw your eyes, Rob. They were bright green, and your hair was almost white." He shrugged a little. "No horns or anything, granted, but still. I've only ever seen you like that when you touched one of the Shards of the Arcania. How did you hulk out without one?"

"I don't know!" Robin insisted, frustrated. "Look, I'm not kidding, I really have no clue. It … it felt like I wasn't in control. Like the Puck was just … taking over." It was hard to explain. "It was like I was being pushed aside and out of the way inside myself."

Karya and Henry both gave him odd looks. Henry looked impressed, but Karya was frowning.

"You do realise, Scion," she said. "This 'Puck'. He's not a *real person*. It's just a name you made up, right? When you channel mana like that, you're still *you*."

Robin looked at the flickering candles. "I'm not so sure," he said. "It doesn't feel that way. Think about it. I can randomly read ancient languages I've never learned. I've solved puzzles I had no business knowing the answers to. I knew how to summon you with Eris' flute. There's all kind of weird things that have happened since I came here that I just don't have any answers for."

"Puck-based phenomena," Henry nodded. He looked thoughtful for a moment, then grinned. "But it was still wicked how you flung him across the room like that, even if I did nearly lose half my face in the process."

"It was not wicked," Karya argued piously. She paused, considering. "Well, maybe it was, but not in the way that you mean," she allowed. "It was dangerous."

"Do you think I don't know that?" Robin ran his hand through his hair, still agitated. "What if I'd properly hurt him? Or Henry? Or any of you?"

"We're made of strong stuff, Pinky," Woad said from the windowsill. "Don't worry about that. Worry about what the old lady is going to do when she gets you alone. Fighting in Erlking!" He sounded a little gleeful at all the excitement and scandal.

81

"It'll be a poker chasing for sure," Henry nodded, looking sympathetic.

But as things turned out, Robin was not chased with a poker, or any other blunt instrument. Nor was he really reprimanded in any other way.

When Aunt Irene came to find them, she announced that after consideration, Jackalope had decided he would leave Erlking, as soon as his full strength had returned. This may take a week or two, and in the meanwhile, there was to be no fighting, no arguing, and certainly no magic. Mr Drover, she advised them, had headed into the village to pick the boy up some suitable mortal-world clothing, as he was too tall to wear anything of Robin's, or even Henry's. Hestia was preparing a temporary room for the boy, to which he had already retired, and did not, for the present, wish for visitors.

The only mention Irene made at all of Robin's outburst was to speak with his tutor and arrange extra mana-management lessons in the blue parlour, to assist Robin with his control. Robin groaned at this. There was truly nothing more boring that mana-management. But he had the good sense to know he had gotten off lightly, so his groan was very quiet indeed.

Unwelcome guests in the house, a brooding and solitary Fae locked away upstairs, and extra lessons. October was going to be hard work.

FIVE'S A CROWD

September blew and blustered its way wildly into October, and the grounds of Erlking Hall eventually turned to gold. Papery leaves dressing the woods in the old hall like gilded crepe.

For the first few days of the month, no-one saw hide nor hair of Jackalope. He kept almost exclusively to his room and they were all on strict instructions from Aunt Irene to leave him well alone while he adjusted to his new surroundings. He was not used to company, or indeed civilisation, she explained. Henry's father agreed with this rule. "You can't bring a wild fox into your house and expect it to be a labrador," he said sagely one morning at breakfast, pointing a triangle of toast at Robin and the others, a wise, bread-bearing sage. "It'll tear up the furniture and pee on the floor, and it'll be your fault, not its."

Everyone agreed that nobody wanted torn furnishings or damp floors, so to speak.

Robin's increased mana-management lessons with Calypso were excruciating. The nymph had draped the already stifling Blue Parlour with swathes of relaxing and soft silk, taking away every hard edge and corner, so that entire room seemed more like a diffused cloud than a study room. The air reeked thickly of calming incense and Robin tried his hardest to meditate, or whatever on earth he was expected to do during these sessions. If Calypso herself was concerned with his outburst of uncontrolled mana, she didn't show it, though that came as no real surprise to the boy. For most of these sessions she sat curled up on a chair behind the sofa on which Robin dutifully lay, usually quietly reading a book to herself while the hour of the lesson ticked away. Robin suspected she enjoyed the peace and quiet, as it was one of the few places in Erlking where she was safe from the unwanted attentions of the ever-insistent Ffoulkes. From time to time, she chuckled to herself at the whale music playing softly in the blue parlour. Robin suspected the whales had said something amusing.

Of Karya and Woad, Robin saw little during the day. Now that he had been sighted, Woad was on even stricter instructions to stay discreetly out of the way, despite Mr Ffoulkes asking after his whereabouts at every possible opportunity. Karya spent much time in Erlking's library with Wally, the enchanted stag-headed suit of armour who had seemed to have fallen into the unofficial role of librarian. She was busying herself looking up anything she could about the nineteen twenties and the British Library, eager to shed more light on the mystery of the bookplate after Robin had told her the slender facts Ffoulkes had uncovered for them.

As for Henry, as October rolled on, he came up to Erlking only intermittently. Robin found this irritating and quite childish. He was clearly avoiding running into Jackalope, his conspicuous absence an obvious snub to their reticent guest. But Henry was supposed to be his best friend and Robin couldn't help but feel a little abandoned. The dark-haired boy was forever 'busy' or 'taking extra lessons down in the village'. He seemed to have gotten a bee in his bonnet about something or other, although he was cagey enough about what he was filling his time with. Robin wasn't going to ask if Henry wasn't going to tell him. It was fine during the week, when Robin was busy with practical wind and water casting in the Atrium, or duelling in the ballroom or the pool. But ever since Robin had arrived at Erlking, Henry had always been there at weekends. Now he seemed engaged elsewhere, or when he did turn up, late more often than not, he seemed tired and distracted.

Robin couldn't help but worry that their friendship had somehow weakened. Although he didn't admit it, even to himself, the worry lurked in the back of his mind that maybe Henry had made some better, more normal friends, away from Erlking. Was that what he was spending his time doing? Playing computer games and football and other normal human things with someone else? Avoiding telling Robin to spare his feelings. The idea of that made Robin feel worse, like he was some housebound invalid who needed to be pitied and carefully handled. He wondered if Henry's visits, when they did come at all, were nothing more than a duty for him.

With the others occupied and a lot of time to himself between lessons, Robin took to walking the grounds alone, kicking through great drifts of crunching brown leaves with his head tucked into a scarf, the cold nipping at the tops of his ears. It was bitterly cold out, but he felt cooped up in the house, despite its size. He had read his books from cover to cover, and there were only so many times he could polish Phorbas. He needed the fresh air to clear his head.

He wondered and worried about many things. If he might dream of Peryl again, or what the moth meant. Why he kept focussing on the sisters' dark prophecy that he would be buried, or when next he might feel himself slipping and losing control of the Puck.

This last issue niggled him so much, that he even swallowed his pride and admitted this fear to his tutor one afternoon.

"Sometimes I worry that the Puck is stronger than I am," he said. "His voice is getting louder."

Calypso had considered this for a second, standing with her arms folded by the poolside.

"If *he* is getting louder, *you* will not be heard by treading softly, Robin Fellows. You must shout!"

And with that she blasted him mercilessly off his feet with a well-aimed Waterwhip.

Robin saw nothing of the strange sisters, even at mealtimes now. He only remembered they were in the house at all when he occasionally turned a corner to see the greyish hem of a long skirt disappearing around another bend or through a decorative archway with a papery whisper, encouraging him with a shiver to alter his route. And as for the exhausting Mr Ffoulkes, he, it seemed, had finally found someone willing to listen to his bluster and pomp. Having discovered a captive audience in the housekeeper, Hestia, he now spent much of his time in the kitchens, regaling the woman with various long-winded and highly unlikely stories and anecdotes. Robin could hear his voice bouncing down the hallways, often accompanied by Hestia's uncharacteristic titter, making his skin crawl. Those two were made for each other, he shuddered.

It was a particularly windy Sunday, leaves blown against every window in rattling waves, when from sheer curiosity, Robin found himself outside the room that had been allocated to Jackalope. He paused at the door, hand raised to knock, and considered if this was a good idea or not. The only person who had seen him since his talk with Irene had been Hestia, bringing his meals up on a silver dome-covered tray like he was some shut-in invalid. As far as Robin knew, the older boy hadn't ventured from his room at all. He hadn't shown the slightest inclination to join the rest of them or to explore the house.

Well tough, Robin thought decisively. He was bored and irritable. You can't just skulk around forever.

He knocked on the wood. When, after several long seconds there was no response, he pushed open the door.

"Hello? It's just me," he called out. "I'm coming in, okay?"

He had half expected to find the boy asleep. There had been no response to his knocking, and he had grown so accustomed to seeing the Fae motionless like some carved statue in the past few months. But Jackalope was up, standing at the window and peering out at the blustery autumn. He looked very odd to Robin, dressed in human world clothes of dark jeans and a pale grey hoodie, his hands thrust into his pockets. He might have passed for human at a glance, had his hair not been such an odd light shade of grey and sprouting sawn-off horn stubs. He didn't look around as Robin entered. He gave no indication that he had even noticed his visitor.

"Is it okay if I come in?" Robin asked again, closing the door behind him.

"Could I stop you even if I wanted to?" the older boy replied flatly. "This is your house. Go where you wish."

"You're looking … better," Robin said, ignoring this less than friendly greeting. And it was true. The tall Fae looked much less wild and frantic. He was staring out at the gardens pensively.

"After you strangled me with dark magic, you mean?" Jackalope said. "Yes, I suppose I do."

"Sorry about that," Robin said, matching the other boy's flatness of tone. "You kind of brought it on yourself though, grabbing Henry that way. We were only trying to help."

The Fae at the window sighed and finally looked at Robin, his expression curious. "Yes. I suppose you're right," he admitted. He considered a moment. "I should apologise to the human boy. I forget they are so frail."

Robin was surprised by the frank admission.

"I don't think calling Henry 'frail' is going to make him warm to you, you know," Robin pointed out.

"Why did you do it?" Jackalope asked. He leaned back against the windowsill, folding his arms.

"You provoked me, I just said."

"No, not that." The Fae shook his silver head, clearly not interested in discussing their earlier scuffle. "Why did you ... take me in? Your aunt told me what happened. How you found me on the lake. You could have left me there. Why bring me into your home? I betrayed you. All of you."

"Well ... at least you admit that," Robin shrugged. "I don't know," he admitted. "It was just the right thing to do, I suppose. People generally do the right thing, right? You could have left me in the snow, let Peryl bash my head in with a rock, but you didn't."

"So now we're even?" Jackalope asked.

"I suppose," Robin frowned. "Jack, look. You don't *owe* me anything. I'm not expecting anything from you. None of us are. Like Aunt Irene said, you're not a prisoner here. You can leave if you want to."

"And yet you harbour no hatred toward me?" Jackalope was frowning, his expression intense, as though trying to figure out if Robin were an idiot. "I sided against you. With a Grimm of all people." His stare was challenging, defiant, athough beneath his tone, Robin thought he sounded a little revolted with himself.

"People make bad choices when they're scared," he reasoned.

"I wasn't scared," Jackalope said firmly, his silver eyes flashing.

"Okay, okay ... desperate then, out of options, whatever." Robin held his hands up. "No, I don't blame you. I left you for dead down in the tomb remember, when it was flooding. I wasn't completely myself at the time. It's hard to explain. There's kind of another 'me' in me, and he's pretty hardcore. But I shouldn't have left you down there, regardless." He shrugged. "We all have things we wish we'd done differently."

Jackalope looked away out of the window again, frowning. "Leaving me there makes sense. It was your best chance of getting out. I would have done the same in your position, in a heartbeat."

Robin smirked. "Looking after number one, eh?"

"You can only rely on yourself in this life," the other boy countered decisively. "If you think differently, here in this place, you're wrong."

"Stick around and find out," Robin said. "I know you have it in your head that Erlking is the worst possible place for you to be, but trust me, it's not."

Jackalope sneered, looking out at the russet treetops of the forest beyond the lawns. "It's a noble offer, but this isn't the place for me ... I don't belong here."

"None of us do, really." Robin said, raising his eyebrows. "That's kind of the point of Erlking. We're all outcasts here."

Jackalope made a noise down his nose. "But you're different." he said. "You're all 'good' people."

Seeming to shake himself out of his thoughts, he ran his hands over his head, making him look for a moment just like a normal teenager.

"Well, are you going to stay up here until Halloween, brooding out of the window like you're in some Bronte novel," Robin asked, leaning on the doorframe with his arms crossed. "Because if you are, that's fine. I mean, I've got to hand it to you, you've got the brooding at windows look down pat. I can even dig a bonnet out for you if you want."

Jackalope glanced over at Robin's dry teasing.

"Or are you going to come and help me annoy our housekeeper? She keeps flirting with one of our guests and clearly doesn't have enough to do." He smirked. "It's quite ghastly, really. She's a pain, but a good cook."

Jackalope considered this for a moment, still looking out over the distant trees and the grey, scudding clouds above. Eventually, he turned away from the windows, hands thrust into the front pockets of his jeans.

"Well," he admitted with a kind of reluctant and haughty stubbornness. "I am a bit hungry."

The short glowering woman was busy with a mountain of dishes, up to her elbows in soapy water and looking harassed as ever. Hestia eyed both boys suspiciously as they entered the kitchen, and upon Robin's request for a quick sandwich, made many loud and put-upon noises, listing the lamentations of pandering to the whims of what she referred to as 'the bottomless pits of teenage boys' stomachs'. Hestia had never yet made Robin so much as a crust without complaining about it. It was almost her own special seasoning.

She watched them, sitting at the kitchen table, wolfing down their food, her black beady eyes filled with scowling interest, speaking only to demand they both take their elbows off the table top.

Jackalope devoured his food with record speed, wiping his mouth with the back of his sleeve. He looked up at the housekeeper with his own frowning, serious stare. "This is the best food I have ever had."

Hestia peered at him oddly, as though he had spoken a foreign language.

"It's just ham and cheese," she replied, quite defensively. Jackalope pushed his plate toward her.

"Make me another," he demanded.

"'Please' …" Robin muttered under his breath to the other boy around the corner of his own sandwich. He was waiting for Hestia to explode in anger.

Hestia stared at the empty plate, and then at the pale boy with his direct and unblinking stare. She seemed to be noticing how thin he was.

She snatched the plate with a put-upon tut, and made Jackalope a further three sandwiches without complaint. Robin was aghast. Had he himself dared to speak to her in that tone, he would certainly have got a clip around the ear.

She didn't make Robin any more of course, just Jackalope, her new BFF apparently.

Jackalope, after some cajoling, joined Robin and Woad that evening in Robin's room. The wind was howling fiercely in the night, and battered even the windows of the high tower with the odd smattering of dry leaves. The fire roared and the silver-haired boy sat silently before it, staring into the flames and apparently content to be still and silent, while elsewhere in the room, Robin read to his faun from the book he had received for his birthday.

"Can you read The Subtle Gnome?" Woad asked, sitting cross-legged on the bed. "Inky likes that one."

Inky the kraken, encased in his large enchanted bubble, was rolling from the head of the bed, where Woad sat, down to the footboard, where Robin perched, and back again. Woad had explained that when the creature got restless like this, he needed entertainment or feeding.

"Kind of like me."

Robin flicked through the book. "There's always The Cursed Custard of Ceridwen. We only got half way through it last time."

The faun shuddered. "And half way we will stay, Pinky. I'm still having nightmares about ducks."

"What about this one?" Robin suggested, turning the page. "The Banshee and the Bard?" He looked up at Woad. "What's a banshee anyway?" he asked. "Are they Panthea?"

The faun shook his head. "There's more in the Netherworlde than Fae and Panthea you know, Pinky," he said. "You're still such a clueless lump. Redcaps, lantern-claws, sloe, bog-hags. These are all their own critters, and banshees are just the same."

"They are restless spirits," Jackalope said from the fireplace.

Robin looked over. "Do you want to come and listen?" he offered. "There's plenty of room. We've been reading a story every night."

"I'm a little old for slumber parties and fairy tales," Jackalope replied. "Anyway. I can hear you from here. Banshees. They're vengeful things, I think. Ghosts. I remember stories about them from when I was a child. Before the war."

Robin frowned, dislodging Inky from under the pillow where he'd gotten stuck. "We've met a ghost. He was really nice. Helped us out of a tight spot, didn't he?" Robin nodded to Woad, gently rolling Inky to him.

"Yeah, but he was just a dead version of himself. Banshees are what happens when ghosts forget who they were," the faun replied, nuzzling the bubble. "Aren't they, my ickle wickle Inky boo?" The bubble wobbled manically in ecstatic kraken frenzy.

"If they exist at all," Jackalope said. Robin raised an eyebrow questioningly. "No one's ever seen one."

Woad sniggered. "There's even more in the Netherworlde that's just legends, Pinky."

Robin rolled his eyes. "Well, fake fictitious banshee ghosts sound like a safe bet, then. Are we sitting comfortably?"

"Don't blame me when you're having nightmares about ghosts stealing your face and making you live your worst fears," Jackalope said with a shrug.

Woad shuddered. "It can't be worse than … the custard."

Robin looked down at the illustration in the book. It looked like a grim reaper, looming over a helpless victim. Only a rough sketch, with long, cruel-looking claws poised to strike. Nothing visible under the hood but two pin-pricks of light in a black void.

"Maybe," Robin decided at length. "We should read the Subtle Gnome tonight."

When the weather was dry and fine, Calypso took their lessons outside, into the grounds. She had set up several scarecrow targets for Robin at the end of the long lawn beneath the trees, and he took them all down, day after day, with Galestrikes, Waterwhips, and Needlepoints. Jackalope, whose health was fast recovering, also used this space for training. The boy had no mana-stone and thus no magic, but Robin and the others soon discovered he was rather agile, and his aim and accuracy with a thrown knife was impressive.

Woad enjoyed outside lessons. He would tire of watching the two Fae after a time, and scurry off into the autumn woods or down to the lake, claiming he was teaching Inky to be a proper companion and hunt squirrels. The wobbling watery ball of tentacles bouncing alongside him like an energetic puppy as they disappeared into the trees.

Sometimes, Karya came out to watch Robin and Jackalope train, offering rather sharply critical observations of Robin's skills, and quiet rather awkward compliments on Jackalope's manoeuvres as he scissor-kicked a scarecrow to pieces or deftly dropped a target with a hurtling blade.

Henry sometimes came around, though he largely rolled his eyes at the two Fae and their combat skills, sitting moodily on a log with Karya.

"I think they're both quite good actually," Karya replied to his grumbles.

"Yeah yeah, bloody superheroes, both of them," Henry half-joked picking at the bark of the log with his fingernail. "Don't see why Jackalope has to do all his twirly tai-chi knife juggling with his shirt off though. It's bloody freezing. He's just ridiculous."

"He lived on the Gravis," Karya argued defensively, pulling her own large coat around her against the cold. "This is just probably warm to him, that's all."

"Yeah sure," Henry muttered, giving her a sly, sidelong look. "I'm sure your sudden active interest in outdoor sparring and combat training is completely professional."

The tips of Karya's ears reddened and she stood up quickly. "I'm going inside," she said haughtily, nose in the air. "It must be nearly suppertime anyway."

Henry got to his feet too, stretching. "I'm not staying for dinner," he said, a bit apologetically. "Got some stuff to do."

He shouted Robin to tell him to come inside and eat.

"You too, Jackie Chan," he yelled to Jackalope. "Put your abs away and get indoors, before Hestia bakes you a shirt made of cake or something."

As Robin and Jackalope tidied away their tools and straightened the scarecrows, Robin noticed the older Fae staring off into the trees, his expression wary.

"What's up?"

Jackalope shook his head. "Something moving in the trees," he murmured distractedly. "Watching us."

Robin shrugged. "Probably just Woad on his way back from the hunt," he reasoned. "He's decided Inky clearly isn't enough of a cold blooded killer. He's quite proud about being the first person to train a land-kraken to terrorise squirrels."

Jackalope shook his head, looking curious. "It looked like leaves."

Robin raised one eyebrow. "Well ... it is a wood, Jack," he said. "Leaves are pretty normal. Generally speaking, they move about in autumn too, generally downwards."

"These leaves were moving sideways," the silver-eyed boy said blankly. "Like a whirlwind shaped like a man, stepping between the trees. But ... they've gone now."

Robin couldn't see anything out of the ordinary. He wondered if Jackalope was pushing himself too hard, determined to get back to full strength in time for Halloween, so he could pass through to the Netherworlde and leave with the other guests. He seemed determined to leave as soon as possible.

"I think the only solution to this terrible, leaf-based mystery," Robin said, feeling his mana stone cold and heavy on his chest after the day's exertions. "Is a good dose of Hestia's roly-poly pudding."

This information managed to tear the other boy's eyes away from the trees. "I have never heard of such a pudding," he frowned, seriously. "This is interesting to me."

A THIEF AT ALL-HALLOWS

The morning of Halloween, Aunt Irene announced rather abruptly that she would be travelling. She had business in the South where she hoped to shed more light on the mystery of the library book. She would be taking rooms in London, she explained, and spending a great deal of time at the British Library, where she intended to unearth as much information on the cataloguing system of the nineteen-twenties as possible. As riveting an adventure as this sounded, she explained to Robin over breakfast, he would not be accompanying her. His duty was to remain at Erlking and, as the nominal highest ranking Erlkinger, to see to the eventual departure of their guests after the traditional Halloween feast that evening.

She left, along with Henry's father, on what had turned out to be a crisp and bright morning, taking Mr Ffoulkes' vintage car, much to Mr Drover's secret delight and the Fire Panthea's earnest insistence. He would no longer be requiring it, he assured her, his business in the Netherworlde would take up much of his time, and the car had only recently been acquired anyway. Robin couldn't help but wonder at that often used term, 'acquired', and silently hoped that Aunt Irene and Mr Drover were not pulled over by the police during their trip to the capital.

The running of the house in Irene's absence was left as always to Hestia, and Madame Calypso was to remain in charge and ensure guardianship of the children.

This was not a task the nymph was particularly happy with, pointing out to Irene as they filled the large car with luggage, and not bothering to lower her voice, that her only responsibility in the house should be the Scion. The others, the nymph insisted, were perfectly able to govern themselves, with the exception of the faun, who, she allowed, was determinedly ungovernable.

It occurred to Robin as they stood on the steps, watching the car being loaded, that he hadn't actually seen Woad at all since the night before. He had muttered something about being off on a 'top-secret mission', which was a phrase he used commonly when hunting squirrels, and hadn't been seen since. He hadn't been in Robin's room when Robin fell asleep, and he hadn't been there this morning either. There had been nothing but a few crusts of jellied bread on the table in the breakfast room this morning. Scant but convincing evidence that the messy creature had been around at some point.

"Just make sure that nobody throws anyone against a wall again," Irene patted Calypso's hand a little absently, unruffled by the nymph's protests. "And no impalements please."

With a farewell to Robin, Karya and Jackalope, she and Mr Drover left, the autumn sun flashing from the rear window of the old rolls as it disappeared away under the brown crisp avenue of trees.

Robin glanced up at the sky after the car had gone and the sound of its engine had faded under the long avenue of trees which led down the hill. There was a definite chill in the air, and the clouds were pale and almost glowing, a sure sign of snow in the offing.

"Well," Calypso eyed them all hazily. "Erlking has stood for time immemorial. I trust you three not to tear it down while I go down to the lake for a swim."

"A swim?" Karya wrinkled her nose. "It's freezing. You'll be breaking through ice to get to it. I've never known a colder autumn."

"I have swum in the northern oceans of the Netherworlde," Calypso replied. "Where the ice is thicker above you than a castle wall, and as green as glass. The mortal world is a mild enough place." She glanced back to the house thoughtfully. "And anywhere is preferable to the presence of a spluttering firecracker, today of all days. I will be glad when it is over, and our guests have gone."

Robin, Jackalope and Karya retreated back inside out of the cold, leaving the nymph to dodge responsibility and Mr Ffoulkes, in her own way, and wondering how to fill their time until tonight. Henry would be up after school later. He had promised to make it to the Halloween feast. Hestia had indicated that she was preparing a great and impressive spread in honour of those planning their leave for the Netherworlde at midnight.

So, it was with some surprise, these plans already laid and agreed, that

Robin found Ffoulkes standing at the top of the grand staircase, wrapped in a great, fur lined overcoat of golden suede and brocade, with several bags and cases at his feet.

"Off is she? The old gal? A-hahah," he called down to them. "Fair play to her. Busy one, your aunt. But so good of her to let us stay. I only hope I offered some small guidance while we were here in these most luxuriant halls. And, of course, that we were not too much of a bother."

"What are you doing?" Karya said, frowning up at him with her small hand on the bottom of the bannister.

Ffoulkes beamed his toothy grin and clapped his hands, rubbing them together. "Well! The thing is, I thought we'd get off too. The sisters and I. No time like the present, eh? Wouldn't want to be a bother with the lady of the house gone and all. And my business in the Netherworlde is rather pressing."

"We understood you would stay for the feasting tonight," Jackalope pointed out, crossing his arms. "The mortals have a great tradition of it. There is to be much food to honour the dead and spirits. I aim to experience this thing they call 'jelly'. That is the plan."

Foulkes shook his head dismissively, picking up his heavy cases. He had a small backpack nestled between his shoulder blades also, lost in the furry folds of his decorative coat. "That does sound smashing!" he said. "And yet, the Netherworlde calls. As the sisters would say, 'when the stars align', yes? Ahaha. I have business in the Agora town and if I'm to get there on time, we really should leave now. Such a shame, so sorry to be dashing. Shall we?" He turned and disappeared from the top of the staircase, not waiting to hear a response from any of them. He was headed, Robin guessed, for the red door at the end of the corridor upstairs which served as Erlking's own Janus station.

"Come along, young master of the house," the Fire Panthea's jolly voice floated back. "The sisters are waiting already. They travel awfully light. Just a few wispy rags. You know, I don't know how they manage it."

Hestia had appeared from a side room, as was her wont when trouble was in the offing. Robin explained what was happening, and the short housekeeper looked both surprised and affronted.

"Leaving? Now? All of them leaving?" she stammered. "But ... but ... Hestia has prepared the feast! The gammon is salted! The potatoes are boiling. Seven ... *seven* meringues have been prepared! And for all of this I do nothing? None of it to feed our guests? All of it only for ..." she stared at Robin, Karya and Jackalope in disbelief. "…for you? It is not for *you* that I work my fingers to the bone all through the night!"

Bustling and bristling, she followed Robin and the others hastily up the stairs and along the twisting corridors of Erlking, grumbling all the time, until all of them reached the long passage at the end of which lay nothing but an unassuming red door. It was plainly decorated, yet a doorway to another world nonetheless. Before it stood Foulkes, practically hopping from one foot to the other in his strange eagerness to leave, and beside him, still and silent as the grave, the shadowy silhouettes of the three sisters who had raised Jackalope from his slumber.

"Aha! Here at last. The man of the hour," Ffoulkes said, cheerily. "Capital! Capital! I believe this doorway opens for you, Master Robin, yes? Scion and all?"

"I do not understand this hurry," Hestia said, sounding a little devastated and affronted. She was looking from the man to the sisters in confusion. "The feast? The feast tonight! A proper send off was prepared. There are … there are *rules* to hospitality."

"More like guidelines, my dear woman," Ffoulkes insisted dismissively, with a beaming smile. "And we must bend them a little, I'm afraid. Terribly sorry, of course. The Netherworlde calls, and a good business deal never waits, as they say."

"Maybe we should fetch Calypso?" Karya said quietly to Robin.

"No time for that, cherub," Ffoulkes said loudly. "The sisters and I are away, and that's all there is to it. Although, of course, please do give my most ardent apologies to that wonderful vision of a lady, that I could not offer her words of parting in person." His face became grave. "In truth, it is likely she knows already of our leaving, and the thought of our separation may be something too great for her to bravely bear." He nodded gravely at his own words. "No, no. let her mourn our leaving in private. Women's hearts are such fragile things."

Robin suspected the most fragile thing in this corridor was probably Ffoulkes' jaw, should Karya get within swinging reach.

"The veil is thin from dawn on allhallows to midnight," one of the sisters whispered quietly. "Any time is good to leave. The alignment of the stars is fair."

"You see?" Hestia said quickly and hopefully. "There is plenty of time to stay. Won't you be our guests this evening? So much work …"

"Alas," Ffoulkes said, his voice perhaps a little firmer than intended. For a second, his eyes flashed orange. "Now is our time." He looked to Robin, his mask of carefree geniality firmly back in place, though it had slipped for a second, and they had all seen it. "Scion of the Arcania? If you would be so kind as to do the honours?"

Robin hesitated. There was something not right about all this. The sudden leaving. It all felt wrong. Not that he'd be sorry to see the back of the man.

Ffoulkes noticed the boy's hesitation. He tilted his head to one side enquiringly, his waxed moustache twitching with a smile.

"Not a problem is there?" he asked. "We are after all guests at Erlking, not … ahahaha … prisoners?"

There was nothing really Robin could do. He couldn't argue with this fact, and he could hardly stop them from leaving early, even if he'd wanted to. No matter how much it might upset Hestia and all the work she had put into the Halloween feast. It was incredibly rude of Ffoulkes, but it wasn't actually a crime.

He reached past the sisters and placed his hand on the silver doorknob with its intricately carved letter J. There was a flash under his palm, like a ripple of static electricity, and he felt his mana stone pulse as Erlking reacted to him. There was a click, loud in the quiet corridor, and the doorway slowly opened.

Beyond the portal, it was daytime in the Netherworlde too, although from the warm breeze that rolled over him, it was significantly less chilly. Golden light flowed in what looked to be a short corridor of black stone, through a galley of high arrow-slit windows on one wall. A few paces in, and a wide stone spiral staircase, worn smooth and dipped like melted butter under the eons of many feet, wound down and away from them. The inner walls were scattered with overgrown ivy here and there.

This door, to Robin's knowledge, had never yet opened onto the same part of Netherworlde Erlking twice. It seemed to connect to a different portion of the immense, crumbling palace each time.

The smells of the Netherworlde, rolling through the door and over Robin, were the same though. Deep spices, honey and cloves, wild fresh grass, and something undefinable that never failed to make his heart ache a little.

The women passed silently through the doorway and out of the mortal world. The last of the three peering down at Robin through her veil.

"You have been fine hosts to us, little Scion," she whispered raspily. "We have tried to repay your hospitality as we could." She glanced back at Jackalope, standing in the corridor between Hestia and Karya. "In doing so, perhaps we have set events most calamitous in motion. But fate is blind, and the games she plays must play out. We are all merely pieces on her board. Remember that." A bony hand reached out and laid on his shoulder. Robin managed to suppress a shudder, not wanting to seem rude.

"But remember also, that with the right strategy and chance, a pawn may one day topple a queen."

The gnarled hand slid listlessly from his sweater with a rasp, and the woman moved on. "Or even … an empress," she hissed.

Robin watched the three spectral women glide away down the stone corridor of Netherworlde Erlking, passing in and out of bands of golden sunlight until they reached the spiral staircase and disappeared silently from view. Compared to the tedious Ffoulkes, for all their creepiness, they didn't seem too bad on the whole. They had helped Jack after all. If only they hadn't predicted Robin being buried alive, he might have actually warmed to them. But things like that can stick in the mind.

"As the ladies go, so must I," Ffoulkes said, clapping Robin on the shoulder heartily. "Be a good boy, eh?" He glanced down at Robin's sweater and jeans ensemble critically. "And do work on developing a sense of style to match your bearing, eh? Clothes maketh the man, am I correct? Aha."

Something rolled between Robin's feet and bumped against the brushed patent leather of Ffoulkes' shoe. They both peered down curiously.

It was a globe, like a cloudy glass crystal ball, smoky and churning beneath its surface.

"Oho," Ffoulkes exclaimed. "What's this then?" He tapped the orb with the tip of his shoe, and it rocked back a little, then rolled itself back at his foot a little urgently.

"Oh, that's Inky," Robin said, surprised. "It's a kraken, well, a baby one anyway. Woad's pet. We made him a travelling bubble so he can get about."

He was aware of Hestia's outraged stare behind him. They had managed, up to this point, to hide Inky's existence from the housekeeper.

Ffoulkes shifted his backpack slightly and drew back a little, frowning good-naturedly at the ball. "Well well!" he said. "Will wonders never cease?

This place, honestly. It really is filled with the strangest things. Little chap seems to have taken rather a shine to me."

"Inky doesn't really take a shine to anyone," Karya observed, glancing back along the corridor to see if Woad had finally appeared. Usually the two were never very far from one another.

"I'm afraid you cannot come on this journey with me, little one," Ffoulkes said, good naturedly. He pushed the orb back again a little more forcefully, as though shooing a bothersome cat. "Run along now, eh? That's a good … squid."

Robin bent and picked up the ball of water containing the kraken, cradling it in his arms and peering at Ffoulkes curiously. The ball was practically vibrating, as though Inky were thrashing around inside. He could even hear the faint screeching hisses. The creature was very agitated.

"Not that I wouldn't enjoy such an exotic familiar on my travels," Ffoulkes insisted with a laugh. "But I have a terrible reaction to seafood."

He took a step backward, so that one foot crossed the threshold of the doorway and into the Netherworlde. At that moment, something odd happened. Every light along the corridor on the mortal world side of the portal flickered in its sconce. There was a low, creaking groan from the walls and floor, as though the house were settling in a storm.

"What was that?" Jackalope growled warily, his silver eyes darting around. "Dark sorcery."

"The wind, surely," Ffoulkes said, as the lights flickered again and the timbers groaned, low and quiet. "Winter is nearly here, it's a draughty old house, aha."

But when Robin glanced at Hestia, he was surprised to see her face was white and set rigid. At first, he assumed that she was still furious about the discovery of the kraken, but then he noticed she wasn't paying any attention to the watery ball in his hands at all.

She was staring at the Fire Panthea with wide eyes.

"Hestia?" Robin asked. "What's the matter?"

The housekeeper didn't reply. Slowly, she raised an arm and pointed an accusing finger at the man. The lights in the corridor flickered again.

"You!" she said, and her voice shook tremulously. "You are stealing? From Erlking? You think to take from the bastion of the Fae what is not, and should not, be yours?"

Ffoulkes spluttered. "What? What are you … Of course not." He sounded positively scandalised "What absolute ... what nonsense! What on earth has gotten into you, dear lady?"

Inky wriggled in Robin's arms. It was a struggle to keep hold of him, like a greased bowling ball with a mind of its own.

"These walls do not lie to *me*!" Hesita said shrilly, as Erlking groaned around her. "Not to old Hestia. These walls know everything, and so do I. The second your foot passed the boundary. You are ... you are a *thief*, sir!"

Ffoulkes wrapped his fur coat tighter around his throat, looking rather affronted and sticking out his chin defiantly.

"How...how *dare* you!" he snapped. "The very arrogance! Unimaginable accusation. I–"

"The hospitality of Erlking has laws!" Hestia snapped. Any vestige of the woman who had, only moments ago, been crestfallen that she would have too many baked potatoes and not enough guests, had fallen away utterly. Robin had never seen her look so righteously furious. Her little eyes flashed. "You have broken those laws! Return what you have taken ... or I shall take it back myself!"

Ffoulkes broke into a grin, sneering at the small woman with clear and undisguised disdain. His air of shocked innocence fell away in the face of her threat.

"You? What a tremendous insult," he said. "A glorified washerwoman? A maker of sandwiches and a scrubber of floors?" The man looked angry, as though tired of playing the charming guest. "You threaten action on me? I am of the House Ffoulkes, of the Black Glass Halls! I can trace my linage back to–"

"If you've stolen something, give it back," Robin said firmly, cutting him off. Ffoulkes had been coveting every item, painting, vase and object in the house ever since he'd arrived. Hestia's accusation didn't seem remotely outlandish to him. It would certainly explain his sudden urgency to leave as soon as Aunt Irene was out of the house.

"Glorified washerwoman?" Hestia trilled, her voice painfully shrill. "Washerwoman, he calls old Hestia! Hestia is more to Erlking than you imagine, sir. I am housekeeper. I am the *keeper of the house*! And of all things in it! You will *not* take in secret what is *Erlking's* to have. I will take it back from you."

Hestia snapped her angry little fingers, and a whoosh of air flitted past Robin's face. Ffoulkes voluminous fur coat billowed open, expensive buttons popping off and clattering away to the floorboards in a merry tinkle.

Beneath the coat, tucked into the man's waistcoat, a bulky object was stuffed. They all stared. Hestia held out her hand, eyes still wild with indignation and the pale artefact flew out from its hiding place, sailed through the air and landed in her hand. Ffoulkes made a desperate attempt to snatch it mid-air but Hestia's cantrip had been too fast.

It was odd, Robin later thought. He had always known Hestia was a Panthea, but it had never occurred to him before that she might have any actual skill with any of the Arcania. That however, had been a perfectly executed and controlled Featherbreath.

"Give that back!" Ffoulkes snapped indignantly.

"Well!" Hestia peered down at the object, flabbergasted and outraged. "And here it is. Shame on you, sir. Shame!"

It was, as far as Robin could make out, a mask. One of those rigid ones which covered only the eyes and top of the nose. He had seen them used for festivals in Venice, or at masquerade balls. This one was carved from a wood so ashen and white it looked like polished bone, powdery around the dark eye-holes. Its surface was carved in the shape of spiralling leaves, and above, where it would rest against one's eyebrows, there were thin carved tendrils, interlacing and swooping upwards like the branches of a tree.

"Why are you stealing a mask?" Robin asked, shocked.

"I … I'm not," Ffoulkes said stutteringly, in the face of all evidence otherwise. "Your aunt gave me this, as payment. She must have forgotten to tell you before she left. That's all this is." He made a very unsuccessful attempt to cajole his features back into a charming smile. "Just a misunderstanding."

Karya, standing next to Hestia, was staring at the innocent looking mask with wide eyes. "Is that … what I think it is?" she gasped. The housekeeper nodded, looking utterly scandalised.

Robin felt out of the loop. He had no idea what it was, other than an old mask. But looking at it tipped a memory. He stared back at Ffoulkes. "My aunt didn't give this to you," he accused. "She specifically said your payment was just being at Erlking, as agreed. I remember her saying it. And you've been looking for this mask since you first got here, haven't you? Admit it? You even tried wheedling it out of me, asking me all about masks and masked balls and all that nonsense, fishing for information. You were trying to find out if I knew where it was."

Ffoulkes glowered at them all indignantly. "I deserve payment!" he snapped, pulling his coat tight around him once more. "No one else in the mortal world could have given that silly old woman as much information about that scrap of paper as I did! No-one! I demand that mask!"

He gritted his teeth. "Do you, any of you ... idiots ... have *any idea* how much this is worth to the right people in the Netherworlde? How much money I could make from this? It's the find of a lifetime!"

"The treasures of Erlking are not yours to pawn!" Hestia snapped. "You have betrayed every sense of hospitality here, and you will leave! Now, sir!"

Ffoulkes lip curled and he suddenly looked quite ugly, his face peevish and naked of affectation.

"Years! Years I've been trying to get to Erlking," he snapped. "Just for a chance! For a peek in all its corners! At all its treasures. And knowing ... knowing ... that *this mask* was here, somewhere! Of course, I agreed to help your aunt! That feeble minded old coot! I jumped at the chance to come here and help her with her ridiculous library card! For the prize of course!" he sneered at Robin and the others.

"Honestly! Why else? Why else would I bother to come here? Out of the goodness of my heart?" His orange eyes blazed. "Leave London, willingly? To come up to the back end of beyond, where the only culture is in the tasteless cheese in the larder? To walk these draughty halls, to put up with squawking children underfoot? Draughty beds? Not a decent bottle of brandy in the whole sorry pile?" He pointed rudely at Hestia. "And having to put up with the terrible cooking of this sour faced, miserable old crone here?" he said savagely.

Hestia looked shocked by this outburst. To Robin's surprise, Jackalope leapt to her defence. "Nobody," he growled, glowering dangerously at Ffoulkes. "Nobody cooks more magnificently, than this sour faced, miserable old crone! I should cut out your tongue, you insolent dog!"

From somewhere about his person, there was a flash, and to everyone's shock, a knife was in Jackalope's hands. He must have lifted it from the kitchen at some point.

"I should cut out your tongue," the silver-haired Fae repeated, through gritted teeth. He looked quite feral. "Even if I must use this ill-crafted mortal dagger to do it with!" He glanced as Hestia. "Say the word and his tongue is on a plate!"

Hestia, holding the mask to her bosom, actually looked for a second as though she were considering this.

"Jackalope put down the knife!" Karya snapped. "You're not helping. You can't solve everything with stabbing! Honestly!" She snatched the knife swiftly out of his hands, like taking a toy from a naughty child. "This is a cheese-knife anyway, you moron, what are you going to do, pare him to death?"

"What is that?" Robin demanded, nodding at the mask in the housekeeper's hands.

"It is the Mask of Gaia, boy," Ffoulkes spat. "Priceless! Lost for centuries. Forged by one the elementals themselves! Owned for time eternal by the dryads of the Elderhart! Rumoured to have been gifted to the Fae during the war and hidden here at Erlking." He was eyeing the mask with a hungry, maniacal gleam. "It's worth is ... incalculable! And it has been here, unused and hidden in a mothballed box for time out of mind! No good to anyone!"

"It ... is ... not ... yours!" Hestia said firmly. "Leave Erlking now. You bring shame to your own name. Shame and disgrace, you peddlar of stolen goods."

Ffoulkes straightened up, pushing Robin roughly back into the corridor with the others. He took a step back into the house, his face very dark and serious.

"You catch me off balance with a simple cantrip, but you think you can best me?" he said quietly.

The air around him in the corridor grew darker, as he clenched his hands. Flames flickered into life across his fist with an audible 'whoomph', their shining tongues flickering over his fingers. His narrowed eyes seemed to glow, brimstones in the darkness of the doorway.

"*They* probably cannot. But *I* can," said a voice behind Hestia. From beyond the gathering at the doorway, a thick jet of water, stronger than a riot cannon, blasted past Hestia, causing Jackalope and Karya to duck as it roared overhead. Robin threw himself against the wall, as the deluge filled the corridor and hit Ffoulkes full force, knocking him off his feet and onto his backside against the wall, the impact making the lampshades shake.

Spluttering and drenched to the bone, his flames extinguished in sooty damp clouds, the man coughed and glared furiously down the corridor.

Calypso stood between the children and Hestia, her hand still outstretched. She didn't look very impressed.

"Would you like to take me on? Mr Ffoulkes?" she said calmly and quietly. "It would be the first time I've found your company entertaining since you arrived." She blinked at him, looking archly bored. "I can wait for you to dry out if you like, though heavens knows, that may well take years."

"You ... you *witch*!" Ffoulkes spluttered. He scrambled to his feet, bracing himself against the wall. His fur coat was saturated, clumped together, making him look like a drowned otter. "I'll boil every molecule of your hateful, watery–"

The man didn't get to finish his threat. At that second, Inky, still struggling in Robin's hands, exploded from his watery bubble with an enormous splash, drenching the boy as the cantrip collapsed.

The kraken, no bigger than a house cat, leapt out of Robin's arms as though on springs, and soared through the air towards the horrified face of Mr Ffoulkes, its tentacles flailing wildly.

There followed a rather frantic struggle between man and beast, as the kraken, firmly attached, writhed and beat at the man mercilessly, delivering slap upon slap with its many leathery tentacles to his head and body, while intermittently sending out great cloudy jets of black ink, spraying the Panthea from head to foot.

"Get it off me!" Ffoulkes screamed in a most high-pitched and undignified way. "Get it off! Get it off! It's possessed! It's insane!"

"It's ... trying to get the backpack," Karya said, her face a mask of shock.

Indeed, the furious crustacean was struggling to grab at the straps and to prise the sodden pack from the man's back. It was only with dawning realisation that Robin saw what was going on.

"Hey!" he yelled. "That's *my* backpack!"

It was indeed the Swedenborgian satchel which Aunt Irene had given him for his birthday in September. Robin lunged forward and grabbed at it. Inky already had several suckered tentacles wrapped around the strap and had managed to wriggle it from Ffoulkes' soaked, ink-black shoulder. Robin tore it away, slipping on the wet floorboards, and fell backwards onto the soaked and inked floor, clutching the backpack to his chest.

Inky the kraken immediately left off its violent attack, detaching itself from the now bruised and bewildered Ffoulkes, giving one last jet of ichor-like ink directly to his face. Blinding him completely, it slid across the wet floorboards to Robin's feet, tentacles slapping across the boards urgently.

"You were taking my pack with you?" Robin was aghast and confused.

Inky had wrapped several of its limbs around his ankle, starting to climb up his leg.

Ffoulkes struggled, spluttering and dazed to his knees. He looked a terrible sight. His clothes were ruined, his face a mass of blotted ink and bright red circles where Inky's suckers had slapped at him. His usually perfect moustache and beard were sodden and as a wild as a hedge. Perhaps the most alarming thing was that his hair was gone, revealing a smooth bald dome, spotted with ink and covered in a pattern of kraken-whip marks.

"He's bald?" Hestia gasped, clutching the mask she held to her chest, as thought this was the most shocking development so far.

Ffoulkes staggered, searched around on the floorboards before him with shaking hands, grabbing at what looked like a squashed and very drowned rat. With the last shreds of his dignity, he thrust the sodden toupee back onto his head.

"Why were you taking my bag?" Robin cried indignantly, flipping open the straps. Inky gave a high, keening hiss, and as the satchel flopped open, all became clear. A thin blue arm flopped out of the dark mouth of the bag. Robin, too shocked to speak, grabbed it and pulled, and in a great ungainly heap, the figure of Woad, fast asleep and snoring, came tumbling impossibly from the Swedenborgian space, sliding out of the small backpack like a baby cow being born, straight into Robin's arms.

Everyone stared at Woad, snoring and oblivious, one foot still inside the satchel. Inky leapt from Robin's leg to land on the faun's stomach, curling itself into a tight ball and snuggling against the boy's tummy. It made an odd happy noise, almost like a gurgling purr.

Everyone present looked up slowly at Ffoulkes, who still knelt in the doorway, drenched and ruined. He grinned at their dark looks sheepishly.

"You ... stole ... Woad?" Karya said, very quietly.

Her expression, matching everyone else's present, was murderous.

Ffoulkes wrung his hands. "Be reasonable ..." he stammered, ink dripping off his chin. "A-haha. The pelt you see ... it would fetch such a good price ..."

"Erlking revokes its hospitality to you," Calypso said. By her side, Hestia nodded. It was the only time Robin had ever seen the two women agree on anything before.

"Now wait!" Ffoulkes struggled to his feet, wavering uncertainly. "I am not leaving here with nothing!"

Karya, Robin saw, had a look of pure fury on her face. Through gritted teeth she hissed at the man. "Oh yes, you are."

She dropped to one knee, slapping her palm against the floorboards, her amber bracelet flashing like fire. The floorboards bucked underneath them, making them all stagger, and then they rolled towards Ffoulkes in a great undulating wave, gathering speed and force as the shockwave flew down the corridor. Boards flipping up one after another with great booms. It caught underneath him, catapulting him off his feet and sending him flying backwards into the air, through the doorway and empty-handed into the Netherworlde. He landed on the flagstones with a winded 'oomph'.

As the floorboards settled, the red door of Erlking shook a little, and then of its own accord, slammed firmly shut.

There was a sigh in the air for several seconds. The floorboards settled. The walls ceased their creaking. The flickering lights became steady once more.

The Janus Station had closed. Ffoulkes had been thoroughly expelled from Erlking.

"Is your blue creature alive?" Jackalope knelt by Robin, peering curiously at the snoring faun. "It sounds in terrible pain."

"That's just his snoring," Robin said, struggling to extract himself from beneath the drowsing boy. "Woad always sounds like that." There were smudges of jelly on the blue boy's cheeks, and Robin remembered finding the half-eaten crusts that morning. "I think he was just drugged. Drowsing herbs, I'm guessing."

Calypso stared around at the corridor. It was drenched. The doorjamb was smeared with firey soot and ink stains covered everything. The floorboards looked buckled as from a recent earthquake, and several of the light fittings were askew. There was a cheese knife lying with its point sticking in the floor, still vibrating.

She sighed. "Your aunt has been away for less than an hour, Robin Fellows," she said. "This is why I do not care to be left in charge of things."

"We must get the faun downstairs," Hestia fussed. "I can bring him round. Though Hestia is tempted to leave him this way and have a little peace in the house for once!"

Robin glanced at the mask the housekeeper still held. "What is that thing?" he wanted to know.

"There is clearly much to discuss," Calypso told him. "But one thing at a time, please. Someone detach the kraken from the faun ..." Inky growled softly. "...If you can. Downstairs, and then we talk." Her limpid, hazy eyes took them all in one by one. "We have a larger problem anyway."

"Larger problem?" Karya looked up at the nymph from Woad's side, where she was stroking the sleeping boy's hair out of his eyes with uncharacteristic affection.

Calypso nodded. "I was on my way to the lake," she explained. "You think I returned to the house for no reason? I sensed a presence at the perimeter." She looked to Robin.

"I came to tell you all that there are redcaps at the gates."

UNDER GEAS

The nymph would not be drawn any further until everyone was downstairs, decidedly calmer, and Woad had been attended to. Her only response to Robin's questioning as he and the others followed her gliding form down the grand staircase that the 'creatures at the gate could wait'.

Jackalope carried the limp form of Woad in his arms, with Karya at his side, still looking an odd mixture of furious and concerned. Hestia followed the whole troupe, still clutching the odd wooden mask she had reclaimed from the thief Ffoulkes, and complaining loudly about the wet and inky footprints they were all leaving on the floor.

Woad was carried to the main entrance hall at the foot of the stairs, where he was set gently onto a decorative chaise longue. Robin's tutor looked over him thoughtfully for a moment.

"Is he okay?" Karya asked.

The nymph nodded. "He is drunk on drowsers, that is all. Mixed with glam jam and butterwing seeds, by the smell of it." She glanced up at the housekeeper. Robin saw Hestia was still shaking slightly, though whether from her earlier and uncharacteristic use of magic or at being called an old crone by the vile Ffoulkes, Robin couldn't tell.

"Keeper, you have the skills to revive the faun. Bring him to his senses?" Calypso asked her. Hestia nodded. The nymph held out a delicate, pale hand, and the housekeeper handed over the wooden mask, sniffing a little and straightening her apron fussily.

"I didn't like to do that," she said, tremulously. "Hestia doesn't like having to do the Towers. Terribly messy things. But what am I to do? When thieves attack the house? While the mistress' back is turned? I have my duties."

"You did great, Hestia," Robin said reassuringly, wanting nothing more than for her to stop flapping and attend to Woad.

She shot him a withering stare. "And who is asking you opinions?" she fussed. "Trouble follows you. Always, I am left with messes to mop wherever you tread, Robin Fellows. You are not master of this house for five minutes once your aunt is out of it, and calamity! And am I thanked for it? No! Such a nice man he seemed." She wrung her hands together. "So charming! So dashing." Her lips pursed. "And Erlking has the finest brandy!"

"A vile snake," Jackalope said with feeling. "A true fox in furs. You should have let me take care of him."

"Robin's aunt made it quite clear there were to be no impalings," Caylpso said, her voice calm and reasonable in contrast to the other two. "I will at least keep that basic promise, if nothing else. Although if you are going to threaten worms like Ffoulkes, perhaps we should look into arming you with something rather more fitting than a butterknife."

Jackalope's eyes narrowed, his face deadly serious. "It was a knife ..." he said with grim feeling, "... for cheese."

The nymph's soft green eyes flicked to Robin. "Perhaps, for the time being, Phorbas would be advantageous in teaching the elder Fae a little control?" she suggested. She saw Robin's immediate unspoken resistance to the idea of giving up his blade. "Phorbas is a trusty weapon," she assured him. "He will steer a hand wisely, not rashly, Robin Fellows. A loan only. I feel it would be a wise preventative to anyone getting, as young master Henry would put it, 'even a little bit stabbed'."

Hestia bent over Woad, fetching smelling salts from a pocket in her apron, and began to fuss about bringing him to his senses. While she was busy, Calypso drew Robin and the others to one side. She held out the mask for all to see. It was a rather pretty, if curious design.

"All this trouble over a little trinket," she said, her voice faraway and daydreamy. "From the moment that man set foot in this house, I knew he was after something." She sighed lightly. "Lady Irene had no choice however. It is ... unfortunately ... true what he said. He is indeed an expert in rare things. Perhaps no one else could have pointed her to the London library." She turned the mask over in her hands, shaking her head in soft wonder. Still, to try and bolt with it as soon as she leaves. The man is a cretin as well as a coward."

Karya couldn't help but smirk a little. "Agreed," she said. "But he did look in rather a wonderful state when we sent him packing. I rather enjoyed that, you know. Clothes maketh the man, do they?"

"Henry is going to be *livid* that he missed this," Robin said, wondering if it was lunchtime yet, in which case Henry would probably be having his school dinner and therefore free to receive an urgent hex-message.

"What is the artefact?" Jackalope wanted to know, peering intently at the mask. "He said it was of great value."

"Oh, it is," Calypso said. "Great value and great power, looked at from certain angles. A dangerous thing in the wrong hands, which is no doubt why it has been hidden away here at Erlking for so long. The last person to have knowingly handled this was the Fae explorer, Hammerhand himself." She glanced at Robin, seemed to consider something for a moment, and then decisively passed it to him.

"As with all things at Erlking, this is your property," she said simply. "It is called the Mask of Gaia. An almost legendary thing. It was crafted by old beings of the Netherworlde. Older than the Panthea and the Fae. Long ago, carved from wood taken directly from the Elderhart. For a long time, it was a treasure of the dryads."

"What's a dryad?" Robin asked, turning the mask over in his hands. "And what's an Elderhart for that matter?"

"Dryads are a type of earth Panthea, Scion," Karya explained. "They are to Earth what nymphs are to Water. They are at one with the trees, forests, nature at its deepest roots. They are very, very reclusive. The Elderhart is a tree, or rather a great circle of trees. Enormous. Some people don't even think they exist, that it was only ever a myth. They were said to be the mother trees of all the Netherworlde, the first. The greatest forest in our world shares its name."

"Well, the elder trees clearly exist if these dryads carved this mask from them, don't they?" Jackalope mused.

"But why is it legendary?" Robin asked his tutor.

"Because it is imbued with true-sight," the nymph explained. "Varnished in the clearest sap of the Elderhart and blessed by the very elemental of the earth itself, when the elemental still walked the world, long long ago. It has great power to the wearer."

Robin held the mask up, inspecting it. It was quite light. "True-sight? What you mean like x-ray vision or something?"

Calypso shook her head. "The mask shows the wearer the past, memories, the truth of a thing, or the truth of a person," she said in low tones.

"A terrible thing. Never put it on. Not unless it is absolutely needed. The power in it resonates with your own mana, and as I am sure you have been told before, as Scion of the Arcania, you have the greatest store of mana of any of us."

Robin frowned to himself. *The truth of a thing*? He held the mask up and peered through the eyeholes, holding it carefully away from his face so as not to 'put it on' by accident. He swung it around, catching Karya in his sights.

"Don't you damn well dare!" she said, batting it down, almost out of his hands. "The truth of a thing is a private affair. How would you feel if I could look straight into your head and saw all your deepest secrets and things, eh? It's rude to pry."

"And dangerous," the nymph agreed. "Many claim to seek truth, my student. But truth is rarely what people wish to find, in the end. Truth can be ugly. "

"I can see why the dishonourable thief wanted this," Jackalope said with guarded wonder. "Imagine what some might pay for such a thing. What even Eris would give for such a tool."

"Don't get any ideas, treasure hunter," Karya gave him a sidelong look. "This is Robin's by right, no-one else's."

"But surely it really belongs to these dryad people?" Robin asked Calypso. "It's their magic mask, right? Why should it be at Erlking? Shouldn't it be returned to them?"

The nymph made a face, indicating that whether it stay or return was none of her business or concern. "It was entrusted to Erlking long ago, clearly. War was upon the world. Perhaps it was safer here." She looked thoughtful. "I wonder where Ffoulkes finally found it?"

"Um ... He didn't ... I did," said a voice behind them. They turned as one to see Woad sitting up, looking a little drowsy, but awake and fine.

"You little blue terror!" Karya said, though there was relief underneath her indignant tone. "You went and got yourself kidnapped?"

"Why were you helping that weasel, Woad?" Robin wanted to know, though he too was mainly relieved to see the faun was okay. Woad absently stroked Inky, who still curled contentedly in his lap. He looked a little sheepish.

"Well...he bet me I couldn't find it," he said. "Firey-moustache-man met me in the corridor. Late last night. I was just sneaking down to the kitchens for a snack…" His eyes flicked guiltily to Hestia, who looked silently outraged. "Anyway," he said hurriedly. "That bit's not important. Firewhiskers, he was up and prowling about. Weird, I thought. He said he was looking for a mask, but then … then he said that it was a very special thing, and not just anyone could find it. Only the very best and cleverest kind of person. When I asked him about it, he was really annoying. Kept telling me not to bother myself. That it was beyond my grasp. Mine! Me, a faun!" He sounded affronted, his yellow eyes wide. "I'm the best at finding things! I could find the flicker in a candle, I could. I could find the hair on a fish, the song in a stone! He just laughed at me and bet me I couldn't. Said if he lost the bet, he'd make me a sandwich himself."

Robin rolled his eyes. "He played you," he sighed. "And drugged a sandwich, knowing you'd find it. Then he'd have the mask and a faun as a bonus. Cheeky sod even stole my satchel to stash you in."

Woad nodded. "Swedenborgian space is a very strange place to be," he said seriously. "I think it's given me indigestion."

"But *where* did you find it?" Karya asked. "Ffoulkes has been searching for weeks, clearly, and none of us have ever seen this thing before now."

"Oh, it was easy." Woad pointed behind them at the main doors to the house. "Hidden in plain sight, of course. No-one ever looks at things properly around here. No one 'cept me."

Jackalope opened the front doors of Erlking, letting in a chilly breeze, and he and Robin stepped outside onto the stone.

"Look up, numbskulls," Woad pointed. Robin followed the faun's direction.

Above the great doors to Erlking, in the stone arch into which the entrance was set, there was a carved face, a swirling circle of leaves, a man with a beard of foliage. It had been the very first thing he had seen when he had first arrived here. He still remembered Mr Drover explaining that it was a sculpture of the oak king. Now, Robin saw, a portion of the circular carving was missing, like a piece of a jigsaw puzzle. He currently held its eyes in his hands.

"Right over the doors," he said wonderingly. He looked at the others. "So, what do we do now?"

"About the mask?" Calypso asked. "Put it away, if I were you. Keep it safe. All things come at the appointed time, Robin Fellows. If it has come to you now, perhaps Erlking meant for it to be found at this time."

She glanced past the boys, through the door at the wide sweeping avenue of trees. "Besides. We have other, more pressing matters, which require our attention."

"Yes," said Karya. "You said someone is at the gates. Redcaps?"

Jackalope bristled. "Redcaps are vile creatures."

Robin was beginning to think that Jackalope considered most things 'vile creatures', but in this particular case, he agreed. He had met redcaps before. Withered, mean little creatures who lived deep underground in the Netherworlde, burrowing beneath graves to make their homes. They were bright red, like lobsters, with long hooked noses and chins, and black eyes, meanness and sharp teeth in downturned mouths. Henry had described them as evil garden gnomes.

The last time he had had dealing with the redcaps, they had helped him out, in their way, but they had also betrayed him to Mr Strife.

"Redcaps are a blight," Hestia piped up, tucking away her smelling salts. "They come to steal the cabbages from the gardens. Mr Drover, he puts up horseshoes on wire. Nasty tinkling things, to keep them out. No redcap has set foot in the grounds of Erlking for a good long while."

"And they are not within the grounds now," Calypso told them. "As I said, they are at the gates. I believe they are waiting to be admitted. They seemed official, as though they were here on business."

Robin wished fervently that his aunt had not left. She would know the right thing to do. But with her and Drover gone, technically, he was master of Erlking. Everyone was looking at him, waiting to see what he said. He twirled the mask in his hands a few times, then passed it to Karya.

"Pop this in my satchel for now," he said. "We'll worry about it later. Right now, I think I ought to go and walk down to the gates and see what these things want with us." He reached into his back pocket and drew out Phorbas, looking for a moment at the slim, ornate dagger, and hoping he was making the right decision. He passed the knife to Jackalope, who took it silently, but with a questioning look.

"You come too," he said. "Keep that out of sight. Hopefully, we won't need it, but Erlking is the home of the Fae. We should present a united front. This cuts more than cheese."

Jackalope curled his lip, making it perfectly clear that of the many things Erlking was, he clearly didn't consider it a 'home', but he nodded anyway and tucked the knife into his jeans.

"Surely we should all go?" Karya said. "Calypso too?"

Robin shook his head. "No. I remember redcaps. I think they'd see that as a sign of weakness, all of us together. Better just me for now. I have to show them I'm the master of Erlking after all."

Karya gave him an appraising look. "You're becoming more a Scion every day," she mused. "Last time we met redcaps, you were so green behind the ears, all you could do was mumble like a clueless moron." He couldn't tell if this was a compliment.

"Whereas now, you can meet them with chin held high," Woad piped up encouragingly from the sofa. "Like a well-informed moron instead."

Robin walked down the long avenue of tree to the gates below on legs which still felt a little shaky. The deception of Ffoulkes, the discovery of the mask, and the fact that they had almost lost Woad … all of this was still running through his head. And now redcaps? It had been a busy Halloween morning. His body, filled with adrenalin which had nowhere to go, was making him jittery. Jackalope stalked by his side in silence, Phorbas glinting in the sun in his belt buckle. Robin guessed that the older Fae thought it prudent, if redcaps were afoot, that the knife be on display, just to show that the two were not unarmed. Robin wasn't expecting aggression, however. As they passed through the corridor of dead and crunchy leaves, the autumn colours drab and rusty above them, thin flakes of snow began to fall, floating through the air as light as pollen, and Robin had the strangest sense of deja-vu.

When had he last been at the gates of Erlking? Had there been pollen? His memory came flooding back. Not pollen … but bees, and Peryl.

"Someone's injured," he muttered aloud, remembering the man sprawled in the hedge in his dream. "An old man." He felt Jackalope's questioning stare.

"How would you know that?" the silver-eyed boy wanted to know.

Robin shook his head, in an attempt to shrug off the dream. In his mind, he heard Peryl's voice. "He's not here yet … but he will be, soon."

"I just do," he replied. He wished Aunt Irene had waited another day before leaving. She was the calm, still sense of order at the heart of Erlking. With her absence, Erlking felt to the boy like a ship unanchored, free to be tossed by the waves.

The gates, just as in his dream, were large, black iron affairs, wreathed with trailing ivy, each stone gatepost in the high outer wall topped with a curious gargoyle. There were no bees.

114

But there were two redcaps. Short, leathery-skinned creatures with long, wicked faces and skin as red as blood. They were wrapped in tattered black furs against the October cold. Their tiny eyes regarded Robin and Jackalope brightly, narrowed with either suspicion and malice, as they approached.

They were holding something up between them, a lumpen shape.

"He arrives at last," one of the redcaps rasped, its voice insectile and filled with dry clicks. "The Scion of the Arcania," his voice sounded full of scorn.

"And another," the other redcap muttered, peering darkly at Jackalope, whose hand had drifted to the hilt of his dagger, hovering over Phorbas. "Another knight of Erlking, perhaps?"

"I am Robin Fellows," Robin said, stepping up to the gates with as much authority as he could muster. He was painfully aware that his jeans were still damp and ink-stained around the shins. "Why have you come to Erlking?" He looked over both creatures. He didn't think he'd seen them before. Robin had spent some time deep in a redcap burrow the previous year, but the creatures seemed largely interchangeable in appearance to him.

"You are collecting Fae, it seems," said the one who had spoken first, nodding to Jackalope. Its mouth split in a horrible smile, revealing small, yellow teeth. They dropped the lumpen shape they were hoisting between them on the ground with little ceremony. It banged against the outside of the cold gates.

"We have brought you another."

Robin looked down, eyes wide. It was a man … no a Fae. Unconscious and wounded, dried blood crusting the emaciated frame of his dark skin and curling horns. Thin flakes of snow drifted into his eyelashes and settled in the grooves of his curling ram's horns.

Robin realised that he knew him. He'd met this Fae before, once, in the Netherworlde, near the Temple of the Oracle.

"Hawthorn?" he breathed.

The redcaps leaned forward, poking their extremely long noses through the iron bars.

"Let us in, Scion of the Arcania," one of them demanded. "We bring this offering. The Netherworlde requires saving, and you … You owe us a debt."

* * *

It was several hours into the afternoon before Calypso finally emerged from the parlour into which the redcaps, with their uncanny strength, had carried the unconscious form of Hawthorn the Fae. As soon as the boys had returned to the house with their new visitors and the unconscious man, she had summoned Hestia and all of them had been behind locked doors ever since, leaving Robin, Jackalope, Karya and Woad to pace and speculate as the afternoon drew on and the thin October sunlight faded from the sky.

"I don't understand it," Karya said, for the hundredth time, pacing the dark floorboards of the hallway outside of the parlour doors. She had walked back and forth impatiently for what seemed like eons now. "Hawthorn? The very same Fae we met out on the moors, the one who showed us how to pass through the caverns beneath the Singing Fens …"

"And almost got us all killed by forgetting to mention the harpies," Woad added from his perch on the bottom step of Erlking's grand staircase. Inky, safely back in his enchanted bubble, rolled lazily back and forth between the faun's bare feet. "Don't forget the harpies."

"What on earth is he doing here? And with redcaps of all people?" Karya mused.

"I guess we'll find out, won't we," Robin replied a little distractedly. He was scribbling on his parchment, sending what felt like the hundredth hex-message to Henry, who hadn't replied so far.

Get up here will you? All hell has broken loose!

And hex me back as soon as you get this!

He suspected Henry had gone to school without his enchanted card. It would be just like him to leave it in his other trousers. Robin checked the clock in the hall. It was nearly five pm. School was out, surely Henry should be home by now? Down at his cottage in the village. Why hadn't he got these messages? Or was he wilfully ignoring them?

"Henry's going to be livid that the Halloween feast is cancelled," Robin muttered. Jackalope, who had been perching silently on an armchair by the door, idly spinning Phorbas on its tip and fraying the cloth of the seat covering, looked up, his brow knitted.

"Cancelled?" he said. "No-one said it was cancelled, did they?"

"Look, I know you're in love with old Hestia's cooking," Robin said with a sigh. "And this was meant to be your going-away party too, but I think we have bigger things to worry about right now, don't you?" He watched his scribbled lines sink into the parchment and disappear.

116

"This Fae," Jackalope asked. "The old man they have brought. He is a free Fae? Like myself?"

"An outlaw, yes," Karya said, stopping her pacing. "Living in the wild, like most of your kind who aren't in camps somewhere. Evading the Peacekeepers and trying to stay out of trouble."

"Seems that trouble found him," Jackalope observed. "By the state of him. Although, at least he still has his horns. He must be wily to have survived the Netherworlde for so long."

"Grumpy old lady H will make him better," Woad insisted with a nod. "It's what she does. Bakes pies and sets bones. Darns clothes and sews wounds. She holds Erlking together, and everyone in it. She does a lot of it while shouting at us. You will see."

Jackalope snorted. "This place falls to pieces without Irene to keep order. You all treat it like a sanctuary. It is not a safe place."

Karya fixed her golden eyes on him, dangerously narrowed. "We're at war, Jackalope. There is no 'safe place'. You just have to decide where to stand and plant your feet."

"Well, I plan on planting mine far away from here, and all this madness, and all of you," the Fae glowered back at her.

Robin opened his mouth to interject, but at that moment, the parlour doors opened. Hestia emerged, her arms full of bloodied and dirty towels, which she spirited away toward the kitchens. Calypso floated through the doorway looking unruffled as usual.

"Is he okay?" Robin asked, getting to his feet immediately. The nymph nodded.

"His injuries were superficial," she said. "The Fae was mainly exhausted, though he has suffered in his escape, or so he tells me." She shrugged with one shoulder. The sufferings of others not being one of her greatest interests. "He is awake."

"Escape from where?" Karya asked. Calypso ignored her, her soft eyes never leaving Robin.

"He, and the redcaps, wish an audience with you, Scion," she said. "You must hear what they have to say." She looked to the others, all peering at her with expectant faces. "Alone, if you please. The redcaps are private creatures, especially in their … dealings. They wish only to speak directly with the Scion of the Arcania." Her opinion of redcaps and their dealings was evident in both her tone and expression.

Karya nodded in understanding, and looked at Robin critically. "At least smooth down that bush of hair before you go in there," she instructed him.

Robin, not quite knowing what to expect, closed the parlour doors behind him. The room within was quiet. Hawthorn the Fae was sitting up on a long sofa, his wounds cleaned. He looked tired. Threadbare and hungry, but he had looked that way when Robin had last seen him too. It was possibly merely the way he looked. It was still an odd experience to Robin, seeing another Fae, especially one with horns. Hawthorn's curled and nestled in his ragged mop of hair, their lustre catching the late afternoon sunlight as he turned his head with interest to watch the boy enter.

Seated close by, each in low armchairs, were the redcaps, who had removed their black fur coats. This hadn't improved their appearance much. Hestia had lit some lamps against the falling light outside, and the room was a series of cosy pools of light in shadow, deepening by the moment as the early British evening fell over the hall.

"Ah, the prophesied one," Hawthorn said, his voice languid, if a little raspy. He regarded Robin through heavy-lidded eyes, his head tilted slightly like a cat. "Robin Fellows. You have grown taller as I have grown thinner since last we met."

Robin looked from the Fae to the redcaps, who were eyeballing him in thin-lipped silence. Their eyes were like chips of shining coal. He was unsure what was expected of him.

"It's good to see you again," he said. "You're very welcome at Erlking, Hawthorn. You can rest here, and heal, if you need to."

Hawthorn gave a short dry laugh. Robin didn't understand what was funny. "You are your father's son," the man said. His voice was a little mocking, but Robin saw genuine warmth in his eyes. "What a fine lord of the manor you have become." He coughed a little, beckoning Robin into the room. "He always had that earnest face too. Come, sit," he said, beckoning Robin into the room. "Your offer is most graciously delivered, and extremely tempting, I admit. I have no time to rest on my laurels however, and nor do you. I heal quickly. Quicker than you might imagine." He glanced at the two redcaps. "Though I owe much to Terp and Tine here, of course." He nodded at them graciously enough, though Robin sensed the man's caution at associating with redcaps. "Had they not found me on the edge of the forest when they did…had they not brought me here, well …" He gave a thoughtful tilt of his head. "This would be a shorter tale to tell. Necessity makes for some odd bedfellows indeed."

Robin pulled up a footstool and sat before the sofa, still wondering what on earth redcaps were doing helping a Fae in the first place. They were not, as far as he knew, known for their charity. He looked to them for explanation, though he still had no idea which of them was named Tine and which Terp. They could have been clones of one another. Twin goblins with pinched and rosy faces.

"Calypso, my tutor, said you'd escaped?" he asked. "Escaped from where? What happened to you?"

Hawthorn sat up fully, swinging his thin but strong legs off the sofa and pushing himself up on his elbows with a grunt.

"Long story very short," Hawthorn said slowly. "You know from when last we met abroad in the world, you and I, that I live free, despite Eris' wishes. Well, even I have bad luck sometimes." He sighed. "I was captured. Months ago, while out on a routine forage for supplies." His lip curled in a distasteful way. "Foolish of me. I had grown overconfident in myself, having eluded them so long. But they are still combing every inch of the Netherworlde for the last of us, Eris' death-hounds I mean. The Peacekeepers."

Robin knew of this already. Most of the remaining Fae who had not been killed in the war when Eris rose to power were now enslaved. Many of them living in horrific slave camps, imprisoned as Jackalope had once been, before his escape. The few remaining free Fae who had managed to escape this purge were now outlaws, living wild and hiding in the wilderness, often alone and desperate. Eris' forces of Peacekeepers hunted them relentlessly.

"Peacekeepers took you by surprise?" he asked. Hawthorn looked insulted.

"Not just Peacekeepers, young one," he said. "I am a Master of Earth. I may be old, tired and half starved, but I still have all the wits and wiles about me that I did when I served the King and Queen as Sidhe-Nobilitas." He looked around the room. "This was my home for a long time, Erlking. Seems strange to be back here, after so long." He looked back at the boy, shaking his head. "A knight of the Fae is not so easily taken by mere scarecrow-dolls."

"Of course, sorry."

He sighed down his nose. "No, it was the Ravens themselves. Of all the luck in the Netherworlde, perhaps I have the least." Hawthorn gave a humourless laugh. "It was Strigoi and his unit who finally captured me. That black dog and his own hunting party. Didn't expect to run into him in that part of the world. Took me by surprise. Even I am not match for that one."

Robin's interest deepened at the mention of the name. "Strigoi?"

The weather-beaten Fae studied Robin's face a moment in silence. It was an odd sensation. Like being appraised by a large and dangerous cat. Hawthorn was as quiet and unguarded with his mannerisms as Ffoulkes had been false and brash. He seemed to wear his emotions quite openly on his face.

"I see from your expression that you know of whom I speak?" he enquired. Robin nodded.

"I met Strigoi in the summer," he explained. "He and the Grimms captured me too. But I got away."

Hawthorn seemed impressed. "Then that is something else we have in common, my boy. Strigoi is the most dangerous of all Eris' razor blades. He is not a man to be trifled with. Perhaps you really are the one the prophecies spoke of after all, if you can escape him, little sapling that you are."

"I didn't do it alone," Robin said quickly. "I had help. My friends."

Hawthorn nodded. "Well," he allowed. "I didn't." He shrugged. "I was taken to the Hive."

"What's the Hive?" Robin wanted to know.

"It is a prison," the Fae explained darkly. "The largest and most secure outside of the city of Dis itself. It is situated deep within the southern-most reaches of the great Elderhart forest, far west of us here at Erlking. In a poisoned part of that wood. A great windowless, doorless pyramid, squatting on a bald hill. Filled with despair. Impossible to breach."

"It is where the Empress Eris puts people to be forgotten," one of the redcaps, Terp or Tine, rasped with a wicked smile. "A dark hole of shut-in security, filled with the lost and abandoned. A grave for the living, and guarded by the swarm. The swarm and its new queen." It cackled at Hawthorn. "You must have annoyed the Empress very much, faerie-man, to end up there."

"I was Sidhe-Nobilitas once," Hawthorn said. "Like this boy's father. The ultimate enemy of Eris and everything she stands for. She hates us. Of all the Fae still evading her particular brand of 'justice', we few still living from that line vex her most. And Strigoi?" His hooded eyes narrowed in undisguised hatred. "He hates us all the more. Vile thing that he is … low beast."

"But how did you escape?" Robin asked. The Fae shook his head.

"There's one way in and out," he said. "Cunning and timing, that's how." He waved Robin's question away.

"What is important is not my capture or my escape, this explains only why I was deep in the forest at all. What matters here is what has happened in the Netherworlde since I escaped, since I ran, fleeing deep into the Elderhart, and … what I found there."

"Or what found him," the redcap corrected. Its companion nodded in agreement. "That is why we bring him to you." Its eyes were drops of ink, shimmering in the lamplight.

"A darkness roams the forest, Scion of the Arcania," Hawthorn said grimly. "A great and terrible beast. It has laid waste to much, it has even attacked the deep dryads themselves. But of late, not content with merely destroying the great forest and any who dare to travel through it, this creature has left the confines of the Elderhart. It is becoming bolder, and now it plagues the villages and towns which skirt it too. It has ventured out onto the great grasslands more than once, each time bringing destruction untold."

"A beast?" Robin asked, looking between all three of them, his eyebrows raised in question. "What kind of a beast?"

Hawthorn reached for a cup of water which, left by Hestia, stood on a table by the sofa, and took a long sip. "When I stumbled upon it, I did not clearly see. Something huge. A snake perhaps, or something like one. Claws and teeth and shuddering motion. It rarely leaves survivors, so eyewitness descriptions are unclear."

"Many believe it is a drake," one of the redcaps rasped.

"No drake has been sighted south of the Gravis Glaciem for four hundred years," the other argued. "Some say it is the forest come to life. A living tree-snake. Leaves and bark and rock. Biting and clawing."

Hawthorn ignored the bickering twosome. "Regardless of what 'many believe' or 'some say', one thing all agree on is that this creature is dangerous. Something has happened in the forest, boy," he said. "Something terrible. A Shard has been found, a Shard of the Arcania, and a monster has awoken. Villages burn. Livestock is slaughtered. It terrorises those who live within and without the forest also. Wherever it goes, the vegetation dies, tree and field and glade withered in its wake. The very life sucked from them as a vampire sucks blood." He looked thoughtful. "And the dryads? The great guardians of that forest? They do nothing about it. No word from their noble king. They are silent on the matter."

Robin's eyes were wide. A Shard of the Arcania had been found?

"It is a problem even for the redcaps, drake or not," Terp or Tine said, nodding gravely, his long red nose bobbing. "My people, we live under the earth, yes, safe in the deep, moist dark, where it is good and it is quiet. But we have one town above, up on the surface, only one."

"Spitrot," the other continued. "It lies on the eastern border of the great forest. Far from the Hive, far from the deep dryads even. It is the place we use when we need to trade with surface dwellers. For the exchange of the riches of the earth, for meat, for treasures."

He leaned forward, his long, dark red talons worrying the arms of the chair with a creak. "A week ago, Spitrot was attacked by this scourge of the forest. Many redcaps were killed. Many." It made a grizzly face. "The town … is in ruins."

"These two here," Hawthorn explained. "When their town was attacked by this creature, they were part of a hunting party. Redcaps who entered the great forest in vengeance, chasing the monster. Hoping to capture and kill it." His face was serious. "They found it alright. They are the only two of that party left alive."

The redcaps growled low. "There were sixteen of us," one said. "The beast took us, one by one. In the shadows of those great trees. It is large, it is violent, and it is destroying all. We fled to save our skins." He pointed a finger. "And that is when we stumbled on this one, a Fae, bloodied and delirious, wandering the woods, another victim of the beast."

Robin processed what he was being told.

"So if a Shard of the Arcania has been found in this huge forest, and somehow a scary forest-monster-killing-machine has turned up at the same time, it's a pretty safe bet that the two are connected, right? You think maybe this thing causing chaos in the Netherworlde is somehow using the Shard? Using its power for its rampage?"

"The dryads of the Elderhart," Hawthorn said. "They have a settlement deep in the forest. They are a secretive people, but old. They ruled all the forest once, though since Eris rose to power, they have struggled to maintain even their own small borders against her forces. Especially since the Hive was constructed and the southern portion of those woods fell to Eris. You would think they would take action against this beast of the forest themselves, but they have not. It is believed that, fuelled by the power of the Shard, the creature is growing. Becoming more powerful, larger, more dangerous still."

"They cannot take action," the redcaps told Robin. "These dryads. They have a king. And the king is missing."

"The dryad king … is missing?" Robin tried to keep up.

"Taken by the beast, it is feared. It is they, the dryads, who are to blame for this calamity. Who else could unleash such a force? This monster ravaging the land is surely a wild wood spirit run out of control. They are leaderless without their king, helpless to stop it." The redcap made a distasteful face. It pointed at Hawthorn. "As were we. So, when we find this Fae in the woods, our own kin slaughtered, and our home above ground, our town of Spitrot, burning still, he says one thing to us."

"Erlking must help," the other redcap said.

Hawthorn looked deep into his glass, then up at Robin. "I was indeed delirious," he said. "By this point, I had been on the run from the Hive and the swarm, and hunted by this great forest scourge in the deepest part of the woods. I admit I was close to death, with no water or food, and little mana remaining." He shrugged. "In my addled mind, I must have believed Erlking to be what it once was, a grand fortress, filled with the finest Fae, with the Sidhe-Nobilitas, with the King and Queen themselves." He looked a little distant, glancing around at the parlour. "But those days are long gone."

"But a Fae still remains at Erlking," the redcaps said wickedly. "Not just any Fae, but a Fae who owes a debt to the redcaps. And a debt to the redcaps cannot be undone. All know this."

Robin felt a lump of dread settle in his stomach. When he had first met the redcaps, not knowing their ways and traditions, he had promised them anything in exchange for information. Karya had been horrified at the time. A promise to a redcap could not be broken. The redcap leader, a bloated, purple old creature named Deepdweller, had been clearly pleased to have the Scion of the Arcania in his debt. He had not yet collected on it, until now it seemed.

"We have consulted with Deepdweller," one of the redcaps said. "He remembers you well, Robin Fellows," it grinned. "Oh yes, very well. He had heard of your achievements since last he saw you. And he remembers your debt to him. Deepdweller does not forget."

"What does he want?" Robin asked.

"Vengeance!" the other redcap hissed. "Our town is destroyed. Our people dead. Without a link to the surface world, we cannot trade." It spread its long fingers wide. "He wants you to find this forest demon. This blight killing travellers, stealing useless dryad kings, and terrorising the grasslands. Do what the dryads, in their leaderless bind, cannot. Do what the redcaps could not. Find it, stop it and kill it. Before it destroys every settlement in and around the Elderhart lands."

Robin stared at them, aghast. He had no idea how he was supposed to do that. Did these creatures think he was some kind of storybook hero? Riding off on a white horse to slay dragons and save maidens? He swallowed hard, looking back to Hawthorn for guidance, but the Fae was watching him thoughtfully.

"What will you do, son of Wolfsbane?" he wondered aloud. "Will you refuse the redcaps' call? Or will you honour your word? A Shard of the Arcania has been found in the Netherworlde. It has released something terrible and destructive. Many are dead or lost. This Shard, like all the others, was awakened by you . Your actions send ripples through the Netherworlde, whether you intend it or not."

"Ripples of fire, destruction and blood," one of the redcaps muttered. "This forest beast must be killed. The Shard must be recovered from it. Taken from it! Claim the Shard, take the monster's power away. End this haunting of the forest and avenge us."

"You should know, Scion, that I strongly believe Strigoi hunts it too," Hawthorn said quietly. "I know how to read tracks. He and his ravens are in or close to the forest. If he is there, you can guarantee that Grimms will not be far behind. A Shard hangs in the balance."

He set down his cup on the table and sat back, wincing a little, though he looked more healed than he had even since Robin had entered the room. "Not only that, but the deep dryads are defenceless against the forces of the Hive to the south, lost as they are without a king to lead them. What is your decision?"

Robin considered, in the quiet gloom of the room. Not many other fourteen year old boys were given such decisions to make. Being asked to go and hunt what sounded like a monstrous nightmare in another world. Other fourteen year olds had pop quizzes and acne worries. They worried about liking the right kind of music or if there was decent wi-fi nearby. Robin looked down at his hands, feeling his mana stone resting softly on his chest, and knowing that Karya and the others were out in the hall, wondering what was going on.

But I'm not other fourteen year olds, he thought to himself. *I'm Robin Fellows, the Scion of the Arcania, whether I like it or not. What would the Puck have to say if I decided to say no? Aunt Irene isn't here to answer for me. I'm the main representative of Erlking. And I owe a debt.*

"I'll go," he said quietly. "I will repay my debt." He looked up at them. "Though, I don't know how, or what I can actually do? The Shards are awake because of me. Whatever happens because of them, well, that's my responsibility, isn't it?"

Hawthorn smiled grimly. "Wolfsbane through and through," he nodded. "Well said, young lord."

The old Fae looked at the two recaps very sharply. "I mean no disrespect to you, or your kind," he said. "I'm grateful you brought me here, you could have just left me in the forest where you found me. But understand this. If the Scion accepts this burden. If he ends the scourge of the forest, then his debt to your people ... all of it ... is at an end. Agreed?"

The two redcaps looked slyly at one another. "Agreed," they nodded. "We have no doubt he will put every effort and resource into this endeavour. He will find there is as much at stake for him as there is for us."

Robin was barely listening to them, he was fumbling with his mana stone, trying to quell the rising tide of worry that he had just basically agreed to go monster hunting in the Netherworlde. Alone against some boogeyman beast that so far had killed everyone and everything it touched. Was he completely mad?

Hawthorn peered so hard at the boy, clearly seeing the worry he was trying to conceal on his pale face. After a moment, he nodded to himself slowly, his old eyes crinkling.

"Listen to me, Robin Fellows," he said, kindness at the edge of his gruff tones. "The Elderhart is vast. The largest forest in all of the Netherworlde. It lies across the plains of grass, and the river Nyx. It is a ride of many days on fast horses from here before you even reach its borders. There are many dangers before you even arrive at the treeline. And once you pass its leafy edge, you will then be in the realm of dryads and the Swarm, both worrying concerns. The Elderhart may be breathtaking and wild, but it had no paths, and much darkness and danger there, even without this scourge."

"If you're trying to make me feel better about this, it's really not working," Robin said.

The Fae shook his horns. "No, Son of Wolfsbane. What I am saying is this. I will accompany you, if you will have me. I know the land well, better than most. I can at least get you there."

Relief and surprise flooded through Robin. "But, aren't you injured?"

"I will be well enough to travel again by the time the moon rises tonight," Hawthorn replied, shrugging off Robin's concerns. "I am used to the wilds. I told you, I heal fast, and your nursemaid here at Erlking is incredibly skilled. The short angry one. Although her bedside manner is rather grating."

"You must leave tonight, Scion," the redcaps demanded harshly. "There is no turning back on the agreement now. And there is no time to waste. We shall report back to Deepdweller and confirm the terms of the debt are agreed."

"Tonight?" Robin's mind raced. "But … I mean … I don't have a plan yet. I've got no idea what to do when we get to this forest. I don't even know anything about the place, or about dryads, or how to kill a Shard-possessed beast. I need time. To study, to find the books I need in Erlking's library and—"

"You have none," the redcaps both said at once, utterly dismissive. "The time to act is now. Blood seeps into the soil even as we speak. You need books? Bring them. You need plans, make them on the way. But tonight is Halloween, and the veil between the mortal realm and the Netherworlde is at its thinnest. Best time to cross without alerting the Empress to your use of a Janus."

"This charmless pair are right," Hawthorn nodded. "If Strigoi is already in the area. You don't want to give him a heads up that you're on your way, believe me. I don't wish to cross paths with that one. Leave under moonlight, travel carefully. Soft and silent into the forest. That is how we must tread." He sighed, leaning back slightly with a creak onto the sofa. "We must leave tonight, though I admit, I dearly wish for some decent sustenance before we do."

126

Robin stood, his mind already racing, making a mental list of things he might need, and how he was going to go about telling the others he was going.

"Well," he said. "Seeing as you're here now, and this goes for you redcaps too…we do have a spare Halloween feast prepared which no one is eating. It would be a shame to let it go to waste. Please, be my guests."

The redcaps' beady eyes lit up hungrily. "There is … meringue?"

THREE FAE AND A FAUN

As night fell and Erlking played host to the most unusual Halloween guests, Hestia plying them with all manner of food, visibly relieved that her preparations would not go to waste after all, Robin explained the situation to Karya and the others.

"A marauding monster in the Netherworlde?" the girl repeated, her brown set in a frown. "Something that has come out of the forest? And they think it has been awoken by the finding of a Shard of the Arcania?"

"How is any of that your concern?" Jackalope wondered, tucking heartily into a plate of Halloween sausage rolls. Robin gave him a weary look.

"Because people have been killed by this thing," he explained. "Whatever it is and wherever it has come from. Redcaps and Panthea alike. It's destroying villages and it's made this forest a dangerous place. It's even killing the woods in parts. It's my concern because, if I hadn't woken up the Shards in the first place, then chances are it never would have appeared at all."

"The Elderhart forest is a pretty dangerous place at the best of times, Scion," Karya said. "You're way in out of your depth. It's the largest forest in the Netherworlde. Bigger than some of your countries here in the mortal realm. There's more in there than rumoured dryad settlements, that's to be sure." She drummed her fingers on the tabletop in an antsy manner. "Very few people have passed all the way through the forest and come out to tell the tale. I think Hammerhand himself is the only person who knew how to navigate it. Who knows what else lives in there? It's a vast, vast kingdom."

"One with no king," Woad pointed out. He had taken a plateful of pigs in blankets from the table and waggled one at Robin before popping it into his mouth. "Well, not since he probably got eaten by this beastie. Although the Hive has a queen now apparently. Horrible-sounding place."

"Look, it doesn't matter how dangerous a place it is," Robin argued. "Or what might be lurking in there. The point is, one of those lurking things got out and is being powered by a Shard. I have to try and stop it." He glanced up at the far end of the table towards the redcaps, who were noisily devouring the feast and chattering in low voices to one another. "It's not like I really have any choice at all in the matter, is it? I owe the redcaps a debt."

Karya nodded. "I knew no good would come of that," she sighed. "I knew it. It was only a matter of time before they collected on it. Redcaps always do. Vile little things. But to be honest, I was hoping they would eventually ask for some treasure from Erlking, not for you to go off into the Netherworlde on a dragon-slaying quest that sounds like a suicide mission."

"Nobody said it was a dragon," Robin said quickly and worriedly.

"So don't go," Jackalope said. "Why do you all make things so complicated? Let someone else hunt and kill this monster."

Karya glanced at the boy, her stare hard. "It's not that simple," she said. "Do you know absolutely nothing about honour? Responsibility?"

He narrowed his eyes back at her. "I know about survival," he said. "And I'm not stupid enough to stick my neck out for people I don't even know."

"See, this is why you're not the Scion," Woad muttered conversationally around a mouthful of bacon-wrapped sausage.

"I can't 'let someone else deal with it', Jack," Robin said, exasperated. "What if Strigoi or the Grimms find this thing before I do?"

"Maybe it would kill them," Jackalope shrugged.

"*Or* maybe they would gain a Shard." Robin shook his head. "Too risky. I can't have that on my shoulders as well as these people being hurt in the Netherworlde." He put his hands flat on the table. "I'm going, that's all there is to it."

"What does your tutor have to say about you wandering off in the Netherworlde into the maw of certain danger?" Karya asked.

"Calypso?" Robin shrugged. He had explained things to her before they all retired to the hall for the feast. "You know her. She sighed a little, then told me to take a coat. It's cool weather there this time of year apparently."

"That does sound like her," Woad grinned.

"She's upstairs now," Robin continued. "Packing some books, supplies and maps, she said. Wanted me to stay down here and keep an eye on our

129

guests, specifically the redcaps." He lowered his voice, glancing up the table at them. "Apparently, they shouldn't ever be left alone at Erlking. Their thievery would make Ffoulkes look like an honourable knight. I don't think Hawthorn is too happy about being rescued and dragged here by them. He's been polite to them, but he hasn't been gushing about owing them his life or anything."

"That's because he knows they'd collect if he did. Some people are smart enough not to get themselves into debt with redcaps." She pursed her lips at him and he made a face in return. "Calypso has a point though. I wouldn't leave them alone here either. They would steal the shine off a silver candlestick, that's for sure," Karya said.

She folded her arms and thought for a moment. "At least you won't be alone out there," she said.

"Hawthorn knows the way to the forest," Robin agreed. He barely knew the Fae, he was practically a stranger, but he had helped them once before … kind of. He seemed trustworthy … sort of. Robin tried not to worry about it too much. The man had known his father, that must count for something, surely. "He said he would guide me there."

"Not him, dolt. Us," Karya rolled her eyes.

"You think you could leave us behind?" Woad giggled. "This faun will never miss an opportunity to go to the Netherworlde. The shadows are softer there, the grass is greener." He looked critically at the remaining scraps on his plate. "And the food is definitely more faun-centric."

"And the wildlife, the people and even the terrain are all much more likely to kill you all," Jackalope interjected with scorn. "But I was due to take my leave tonight anyway. To cross over into the Netherworlde. Before that fiery thief mucked things up. I will come to the grasslands with you if you are crossing over. I want to put some distance between myself and this place."

They all glanced at him.

"But that's as far as I go," he said firmly. "We part ways then. I'll find my own way in the world, and I can guarantee you it won't be in any stupid direction that takes me within fifty miles of a deadly forest full of monsters. I didn't sign up for any of your ridiculous adventures."

Robin grinned at them all.

"You do know none of you are contractually obliged to follow me into danger, right?"

"Yes we are," Karya said simply, her face as serious as ever. "That's what friends do. We're all coming and that's that."

It wasn't as simple as they had hoped.

The sun had set and the moon risen long ago. To everyone's relief, Terp and Tine, the wickedly gruesome redcap twins took their leave of Erlking, both bowing deeply to Robin as they left and promising, with hints of an underlying threat, that news of his repayment would be conveyed immediately to Deepdweller, who would be watching closely to ensure the terms of the favour were satisfied. Very closely. And woe betide if it wasn't.

He was glad when they were off the property.

Hawthorn spent some time talking alone with Calypso, whilst the children pored over a large yellowed map which Karya had fetched from the library with the help of Wally. She had laid the huge map out on the dining room table, using leftover cups and plates from the hurried Halloween feast to pin the corners flat.

Robin was unfamiliar with the Netherworlde's geography. He had no idea how far it was to this forest. Karya showed him where the ruins of Erlking stood on the map, with the large Barrowood Forest at the north-eastern base of its hill. The first time he had travelled beyond the human world, she explained, they had passed through this wood, and then on further east, over the high moorlands, seeking the Temple of the Oracle. From there, northeast to the Singing Fens and the mountains beyond. The second time Robin had encountered the Netherworlde, they had been much farther afield still, in the far far north, up by the high snowy tundra of the Gravis Glaciem.

This trip, she indicated seriously, using a spoon as a pointer, to which still clung a small modicum of jelly, would take them in a different direction. From Erlking's ruins in the Netherworlde, they would need to head southeast. It was grasslands there. The odd farm and village, but largely a wild and open wilderness, with only a few small woodland areas. Not much cover to evade any Peacekeeper patrols. Wild hills and grass, like a prairie. After a few day's march through this high sea of tough grass, they should reach the low, undulating hills, the most famous of which was Briar Hill, a legendary place in Netherworlde lore, though merely an abandoned ruin these days. They would avoid the hill altogether, she explained. Abandoned places tended to attract revenants and other unpleasant things.

Robin nodded, following the line across the map she was tracing with the spoon.

Beyond the hills, she told them, was the Redcaps' solitary surface town, Spitrot, or whatever was left of it anyway. It stood close to the borders of the Elderhart Forest itself. She tapped the map firmly, and Robin's eyes roamed over the ink and parchment, taking in the forest.

It looked huge. It rolled across so much of the map, a huge swathe of tiny inked doodled trees and a blob of jam.

"It seems such a long way," Robin said, slipping his pack onto his back. He was incredibly grateful for the Swedenborgian satchel. Hestia had filled it with enough food for a month at least, and Calypso had provided Robin with an armload of books and maps, including his trusty edition of Hammerhand's Netherworlde Compendium, along with the book of Netherworlde legends he had received for his birthday. All of it fit easily into the pack and seemed to weigh nothing. The pack also held the Mask of Gaia, so recently discovered. It might be safer at Erlking, but they were heading into dryad territory and it was a dryad treasure, after all. It might come in useful.

"It is a long way," Karya agreed. "But not to worry, I can tear us back and forth between here and the Netherworlde, and cut our journey time to nothing. Just like we did when we needed to get to that human city, remember?"

"That won't be an option," Hawthorn said, the long-limbed Fae walking up behind them and peering down at the map. His feet were utterly silent on the floorboards. Robin glanced up at him, noticing how much healthier he looked already. His old face was lined, his eyes still hooded, but they glimmered. The Fae, it seemed, really did heal quickly.

"Why not?" Karya bristled. "You haven't seen me in action."

"It's not a matter of skill," the Fae replied calmly. "We have to leave now, because Allhallows is the point at which the two worlds touch naturally. Using a Janus station is smooth and quiet, and unlikely to be noticed by Eris at this time. But you cannot then tear back and forth between the worlds, flipping us across them like a skipping stone on the surface of a lake."

"I assure you, I can," Karya insisted haughtily.

"Not without causing ripples," the Fae shook his dark head. "Big ones. And ripples are the last thing you want when there are sharks in the water."

"You mean Strigoi," Robin said, rolling up the map. He took Hawthorn's point. "He'll sense we're in the neighbourhood."

"He probably will anyway," Hawthorn said. "He sniffs out his quarry. They don't call him the Wolf of Eris for nothing. But let us not actively invite calamity. Softly and without tearing, that is how we shall go. Best not to telegraph our position any more than we have to."

The Fae patted both Robin and Karya on the shoulder. "We leave now," he said. "I want to put some distance between Netherworlde Erlking and ourselves before the sun rises over there."

"But Henry isn't here!" Robin argued, as the others shouldered their backpacks.

Henry still had not replied to his hex-messages. Robin couldn't understand why. His father was down in London with Irene. The cottage he lived in would be empty and dark. It was incredibly unlikely that the boy would choose to go back there after school rather than up to Erlking, especially when there had been a party planned, and yet he hadn't arrived.

"We can't leave without him. He'd be livid."

"We must," Hawthorn said simply, bowing politely to Calypso and Hestia and thanking them for their aid and hospitality. The entire company began to make their way up the stairs, to the red door of Erlking through which the sisters and Ffoulkes had not long since passed.

"Henry is my best friend," Robin argued. "He'll want to come. He wouldn't miss a trip to the Netherworlde for anything."

Jackalope raised his eyebrows. "Perhaps it is for the best that the human is not here," he said. "The Netherworlde is no place for such soft creatures. It is not safe."

"Nowhere's safe according to you," Karya grumbled. "At least Henry wants to be with us."

"Apparently not," Jackalope retorted. Robin glared at him.

"Your human friend will have to follow after us, if he is so insistent," Hawthorn said, as they reached the door. "Your tutor and the keeper of the house can let him know what has happened, as and when he arrives."

Robin placed his hand on the door, feeling the familiar heady rush of mana as the will of Erlking flowed through and around him. The handle vibrated and the door swung open with a whoosh.

"But he won't be able to," Robin realised. "This door only opens for me. He can't use Janus stations. I don't even know where the next nearest one to Erlking is in the mortal world. I'm pretty sure he doesn't either. He's going to be stuck here, on his own."

The view beyond the red door, the portion of Netherworlde Erlking they could see, was impressive. This time the portal had opened onto the top of a wide sweeping staircase which fell down away from them, shadowy polished obsidian flanked by great black pillars, dotted here and there with crumbled masonry and stones. At the foot of the steps, some distance below, Robin could see an archway through which silvery moonlight streamed, and the pale movement of grass under a breeze. It seemed to lead out to a courtyard.

"Robin is right," Karya said. Her face was set as she seemed to be considering something. "Henry won't be able to join us. Not on his own."

She looked around at them all. "I will stay."

"What?" Robin frowned.

"I'll wait here for Henry, we'll follow you." She glanced at Hawthorn before he could argue, "And yes, we will have to use my skill at tearing to get through to the Netherworlde, but you should have a decent head start on us by then. It certainly shouldn't telegraph the location of either you or the Scion to any unwanted eyes."

"I'm going with Pinky!" Woad said swiftly, stepping to Robin's side. "He won't last a minute in the Netherworlde without a decent faun."

Karya nodded in agreement. "You'll have Hawthorn, and Jack, for a short time at least. We will find you in the Netherworlde, Scion. Don't worry about that. We'll catch straight up to you."

Robin knew there was no time to argue with this.

"I don't want you to wait for Henry," he told her. "I want you to go and find him, can you do that?"

She frowned at him in confusion.

"I can't explain it," Robin shook his head. "He's been acting odd, I know, but this, not turning up for the Halloween feast? Not answering hex-messages?" he shook his head. "It's just not like him. I'm worried. I can't help thinking something's happened to him."

"Something like what? He probably just had a snooze when he got home and hasn't woken up yet. You know how tired he's seemed lately."

Robin couldn't explain it. "It's just a feeling. A bad feeling. Go to his house. Make sure he's okay?"

She nodded. "I will, and we will find you. Now can you stop worrying about everyone else in the world for once, and go and throw yourself into the jaws of certain danger please. It's getting close to midnight."

Hawthorn and Woad had already stepped through the shimmering doorway, standing at the top of the long staircase in the Netherworlde, the night wind toying with their hair. Jackalope looked to Calypso and Hestia.

"I have not deserved your hospitality," he said a little stiffly, and bowed slightly to them.

The nymph put her head slightly to one side. "We will meet again, I'm sure of that, mana-less Fae," she said. "Though whether hospitality will play any part in it, who can say?"

Hestia came forward, a little awkwardly, and pushed a package into Jackalope's hands. It was brown greasepaper, tied up with string.

"What is this?" he frowned at her.

"It is just extra supplies," the housekeeper waved the question away. "Do not be getting ideas of a high station. There is food enough in everyone's packs, but you … you are not coming back. Meat. A jar of good salt. Every meal, even one in the wild, can be a feast with the flavour of good salt. A few odds and ends. Enough to keep you going until you find somewhere … to belong." She sniffed and folded her arms crossly.

Robin gawped at Hestia's random act of kindness. Jackalope however simply nodded.

"You are a good person," he said to her quietly. His voice sounding a little thick. "Your kindness is misplaced." He stowed the package in his backpack. "But I will not forget it either."

He turned away quickly without a backward glance at Erlking.

"Be careful, Scion," Calypso said, as Robin crossed the threshold. "You aunt will not be pleased to hear that you have gone to another world to hunt a killer monster with a strange Fae. I would advise you to attempt to return before she does. Preferably with all, or at least most, of your limbs attached."

Robin nodded, unable to suppress a smile at the thought of Calypso trying to explain his absence to his aunt.

"See you soon," Karya said, as the door closed. "And for goodness sake, try not to get killed."

"Not even a little bit stabbed," he promised with a smile.

CENTAUR OF ATTENTION

The great dark steps led Robin and the others down and eventually out into a crumbled, gravel-strewn courtyard. Hawthorn led the way across the moonlit space, explaining that he wanted to be out of sight of Erlking as soon as possible. It was the most dangerous place for any Fae to be. Eris' eyes were always on it, day and night. They must move swiftly and quietly.

Robin stared up at the high black stone walls as they passed between them, abandoned, crumbling and ghostly. Their shiny surfaces glinted in the moonlight like glass and he caught glimpses of his own reflection ghosting along beside him, the uneven walls refracting his image so that it seemed a crowd of Robins jogged along with him, flittering and broken.

Once they were clear of the fortress proper, Hawthorn led the two Fae boys and the faun swiftly down the great grassy hill of Erlking through the shadows, to the river which circled its base. The hill, here on the Netherworlde side of things, was much larger and steeper than the hill on which the manor house stood back in the mortal world. The grass was wild and tall, higher than Robin's waist, and it whispered about them as they passed, a pale sea, constantly in motion with the night-time breeze.

Despite the circumstances, it felt incredibly good to Robin to be back in the Netherworlde at last. His heart was beating fast. It was hard to explain, but it felt more real than anywhere else. It was as though everything in this world was in slightly sharper focus to him. The dark grassy hills, the shadows of the Barrowood trees, stark and black in the night against an autumn sky. The heavens above them seemed strewn with jewels. The moon hung low above the travellers, a great yellow harvest crescent in a blanket of velvet. There wasn't a single cloud, making it feel as though the sky above them stretched out in all directions forever, an endless vault above, glimmering down on the silent haunting wilderness below.

Jackalope was sullen and silent as ever, stalking through the grass behind Hawthorn, his body language clear. He was on high alert, expecting an ambush or attack at any moment. Years of hiding had given the silver-haired Fae a distrust of open spaces with little cover. Too exposed. The blade of Phorbas the knife glinted in his hand. Robin was still unconvinced that it was a good idea for Jackalope to carry it, but he had decided to trust his tutor's instincts.

Woad, on the other hand was having a whale of a time. He ran back and forth through the long grasses like a happy puppy, criss-crossing the paths of the others and sending up great clouds of pollen and stray leaves into the clear night air. His running making the grass hiss dryly. Occasionally, he turned a somersault like a demented acrobat.

"Can you control your faun?" Jackalope hissed to Robin in a whisper. "He is hardly subtle."

"I can't help it!" Woad grinned with glee. "I'm back home. Smell that?" He breathed deeply and theatrically, puffing out his thin blue chest. "Honey and apples and spices and tin! The air of the Netherworlde! You never need to eat again. You could live off it alone and grow tall as an oak!"

"Hush, Woad," Robin insisted, unable to stop a grin. The Netherworlde did have a smell. To Robin it smelled like a home he'd never known. Like mystery and magic.

"All I smell is soil and river water," Jackalope grunted. "And jelly. But I think I got a little of that on my shirt. Are we headed for those trees?"

Hawthorn, leading them down to the riverbank, nodded. They were headed away from the Barrowood, he told them. The opposite direction. There was a shallow ford here at the base of the Erl King's Hill. They could cross the encircling river there, and beyond that, if they kept on until daybreak, was the grasslands.

The river was indeed shallow, and clear as crystal. It was also, as Robin discovered, absolutely freezing, coming up to his knees at the deepest point and soaking into his jeans, making them flap about uncomfortably as they climbed a small slope on the far bank and passed between the shadows of thin and gnarled trees.

"At least it's a warmer night here than back in the mortal world," he noted. The breeze was indeed gentle, despite the clear air. The trees through which they passed were abundantly crowned with thick, dry leaves, shining where they caught the light.

"The Netherworlde seasons are always out of balance with the human's," Woad nodded sagely. "Sometimes they're ahead, sometimes behind. No icy nips here. No snow in our sky."

When they reached the crest of the wooded hills, Hawthorn stopped and looked back. From here, they could see the Erl King's Hill, some distance behind them now and crowned with the vast black ruin of the Fae fortress. It was nothing but a broken shadow against the starry sky. Still and haunted.

"It's still beautiful," Robin said, noting the thoughtful look in Hawthorn's eyes.

"It was magnificent once," the elder Fae replied. "A shining jewel." He looked lost in memory for a moment. "I was nobility here. In another life." He sighed. "In another Netherworlde. Before the uprising, before Eris' war destroyed everything."

Robin considered the willowy man. Hawthorn looked like a creature haunted. Dressed as he was in scraps of leather and cloth. Tangled hair, weathered skin. Living like a wild thing. Always hungry and never resting. It was hard to imagine him as a bold knight of the Fae, dressed in the same kind of finery he had seen his own father wearing in his book of Fae Families.

"The war took something from all of us," Jackalope said, unsympathetically. "Some more than others. At least you still have your horns. And your mana-stone. We should keep moving. There could be spies. Grimgulls."

Hawthorn nodded, and they moved on. Soon, Erlking was out of sight and far behind them, hidden by tree-dotted hills, shadow and time.

As they walked through the night, silent and stealthy as bats, Robin wondered if Karya had found Henry. Whether they were already in the Netherworlde, following them. He wondered if hex-messaging might work across different worlds, but they were moving at too brisk a pace to stop and write. He also wondered about this mysterious beast. This forest scourge. A creature somehow fuelled by a Shard of the Arcania. Destroying the forest and anyone near to it. He had no plan, no idea how to actually find it, and even less of an idea how to begin to stop it if they could.

He watched Hawthorn's slim back as they marched onward through the night, the feline Fae slinking from shadow to shadow noiselessly before them all. He would lead them to it. He had almost died escaping this 'Hive', the prison of Eris, and yet he was willing to head straight back into danger, for the sake of what? Helping the people of the Netherworlde? The common good? Or was it simply that he didn't want the Shard falling into the hands of the Grimms? Robin realised that, although this man had helped him once before in the past, in truth he knew very little about him at all.

And yet here he was, following this near-stranger into the deep wilds of another world. He tried not to think about how unwise this might be. He was fairly certain Aunt Irene would not have been impressed with his decision.

They eventually stopped, much to the relief of Robin's aching legs, just as one end of the sky was beginning to blur with light grey, signalling the death of the night and the promise of dawn to come. The narrow hollow was dotted with crumbling rocks, some taller than Robin, sticking up out of the grass like sharp mossy teeth. Woad scrambled over and between these huge menhirs, perching atop the tallest one like a gargoyle and peering all around.

As he had designated himself the sentry, the other three set to gathering sticks and moss, and Jackalope lit a small fire with envious and practised ease. Robin was relieved to sit down on the soft grass. It had been a long night.

"It's a fair distance yet, young one," Hawthorn said, noting Robin's tired face. "Many miles to go. But don't look so downcast. We shan't need to walk the full distance. The Tower of Earth is our ally."

"I don't know any Earth magic," Robin confessed a little awkwardly, rubbing his hands together at the fire. Hawthorn looked shocked.

"But, you are the Scion, are you not?"

"I haven't got a tutor," Robin explained. "Only Air and Water so far. No-one to train me in Earth. There's only Karya who knows anything about it, and she says she can't teach me. I asked her, not longer after Ffoulkes and the sisters arrived. She doesn't know how she does it herself. She just can."

Hawthorn looked enquiringly to Jackalope, who was leaning back against a rock, just outside the circle of firelight.

"Don't look to me," the grey-headed boy said. "I don't even have a mana stone. I'm about as magical as a human. Though not as defenceless as one, obviously."

"Well," Hawthorn considered for a moment, peering into the small crackling fire. "I'm no teacher, but my mana is Earth." He looked up at Robin through the flames. "No formal lessons, of course, but there is nothing like learning on the job, Robin Fellows."

Robin blinked in surprise. "You can teach me Earth?"

He felt stupid for not realising earlier. Of course, Hawthorn's Tower of expertise was Earth. When last they had met, he had sent Robin and Karya on their way on an enchanted rolling stone deep beneath the caverns of the dark Netherworlde. Robin felt a glimmer of hope.

"I can give you a few basic moves. Here's a cantrip for you," Hawthorn said. He drew out from his back, beneath his ragged cloth shirt, a long bow, inlaid all along with red gems. Robin had seen him with this before too.

"My mana stones," the Fae explained. He quickly notched an arrow, and aimed it at the tall mossy menhir atop which Woad currently perched.

"This cantrip is called Golem" he explained, and as the stones in the bow flashed, he let the arrow loose. It whipped through the air and exploded against the stone with a crack, disappearing utterly.

Woad let out a short cry of shock as beneath him, the huge stone heaved itself out of the ground with a ponderous rumble and rocked alarmingly, a loud grating making the ground beneath all their feet shake.

The rock rolled onto its side, the faun leaping off and to safety with some very inventive curse words which he had clearly learned from Henry. Robin watched as the menhir continued rolling ponderously, end over end, like a tall egg. It circled the three Fae at the campfire, making a full circuit up and down the grass, then it rolled away and up the hill with impressive speed, coming abruptly to rest on its narrowest tip at the very crest of the hill.

The rumbling stopped.

"A simple trick to animate and move stone," Hawthorn explained. "This was of course a very basic demonstration, but still, it's a handy cantrip to learn. It can help you build a wall very quickly, block a passageway, or like now…" His mana stones flashed again, and this time, three of the huge rocks moved at once, groaning and grinding as they lumbered, possessed, along the hollow floor. Two of them came to rest on either side of Hawthorn like great bookends, and the third, longer and thinner that its squatter companions, thudded against them, and then began to climb their sides, rolling up between them until it rested heavily on top, suspended by the two points.

The dust and noise settled, and the Fae was sitting in a stone arch, like a mini portion of Stonehenge.

"...a rudimentary shelter," he finished, smiling. "Of course, in times gone by, when the Arcania was still whole and magic flowed through the land with ease, the Master Earth users could build whole monuments. Temple and towns, using mana alone. It was quite a sight to behold... provided of course you were at a safe distance so as not to be crushed."

He gestured at Robin, as Woad clambered with interest onto the newly formed rock shelter, sniffing at it suspiciously.

"Now you try."

"But...I haven't got a clue how," Robin said. "I don't know where to start."

"Pinky isn't really a fast learner," Woad said, quite unhelpfully. He had laid down on the roof of the shelter and was peering up into the ever-lightening pre-dawn skies above. "It took him forever to learn Air, and even longer to learn Water."

"Earth is simple," Hawthorn assure Robin. "Though by that, I do not mean it is easy, merely uncomplicated."

"What do you mean?"

"Air, " the Fae said. "As I'm sure you learned, is all about thought, yes? Very intellectual, Air magic. All calculations and control, subtlety and precision. A lot of reading, a lot of theories, more of an intangible art form than anything else."

Robin nodded in agreement.

"And Water?" Hawthorn continued. "Nothing to do with conscious thought, all to do with instinct, emotion. The natural flow of things. More like...well, like meditation. Learning to release your feelings and emotions into the mana and trust it to shape your element."

"Yes, that's what Calypso has been teaching me," the boy agreed.

The old Fae made a face. "Wishy washy nonsense, both of them," he whispered, laughing softly.

Robin was shocked. Hawthorn held his hands up apologetically.

"I jest...I jest! But there is some truth in what I say."

Jackalope frowned down at the knife in his hands, which he had been twirling idly, catching the firelight.

"I do not think the Scion's first tutor agrees with you, old timer," he said. The knife was vibrating a little in the boy's pale hands. "He seems a bit...put out."

141

"I mean no offence to Phorbas," Hawthorn said politely. "My apologies, knife." The blade stopped vibrating like a tuning fork. He looked back to Robin. "What I mean to say is that, compared to the complexities of Water and Air, Earth is less cajoling persuasion and more…well…more force, if I'm totally honest."

"Force?" Robin said worriedly.

"Pure will," Hawthorn nodded. "Authority! Intent! Your will must be as strong as a mountain, as deeply planted as the roots of the greatest tree. As solid as the earth itself. Earth magic responds only to strength. Strength of intent. Determination and command. When you perform Earth magic, you are not 'asking' your mana to do something for you, you are telling it. In no uncertain terms."

This explains why Karya is so good at it, Robin thought absently to himself.

"The rocks don't want to move, you see," Hawthorn explained. "They are rocks. They generally don't. They have a strongly held belief in 'not moving about the place.' But you have to make sure your will, your directed mana, your determination, your absolute and unshakable conviction that they *should* move, and that they are damn well *going* to, is stronger than their resistance not to."

"I don't really understand," Robin admitted, with raised eyebrows.

"You gotta show them who's boss!" Woad piped up, giving Robin a thumbs up from his high perch.

Jackalope smirked and leaned back against the rock behind him, clasping his hands behind his head. "Unlikely," he said. "The Scion here probably cares about the rock's feelings too much."

Hawthorn indicated a small boulder sitting in the long grass, not too far off.

"Try it," he insisted. "Focus your mana, form your command before you cast, and be very, very certain that it will be obeyed. So certain that the very idea that it won't be obeyed is unthinkable to you. Cast a golem cantrip. *Make* it move."

Feeling very self-conscious with all eyes on him, Robin nodded, and fished out his seraphinite mana stone from beneath his t-shirt. He clasped it in one hand, holding out his other arm towards the rock, and focussed, trying to clear his mind.

He mustered all of his willpower, blocking out everything else, reminding himself that he was the Scion. That he had communion with two of the Shards of the Arcania. If anyone could command the earth, it should be him.

He silently shouted at the rock to move, feeling a thrum of mana pulse invisibly out from his palm like the shockwave of a banged drum. He cast the golem cantrip with as much force as he could muster.

Opening his eyes, he saw the rock shudder a little, like a shivering dog. It didn't move an inch however.

Jackalope laughed and clapped his hands.

"Priceless!" he cried, shaking his head at Robin's expense, as Robin's cheeks flushed crimson with embarrassment. "And this is the saviour of the known world? Beware the great Scion of Erlking!"

"Hush up, meanie," Woad called down sharply. But Jackalope seemed intent.

"Redeemer of the Netherworlde! Wobbler of small rocks. They shall call you the stone-trembler."

Unbidden, Robin's embarrassment flared into anger, rising suddenly up from deep within him quite unexpectedly. His teeth clenched, and his head was filled with such a fury at the cynical Fae. Why couldn't he ever say anything nice? After all they had done for him, and all he could do was mock and sneer and scowl. Someone ought to wipe the smile off his face.

A thought, only half-formed, was in Robin's head. To cast golem at the stone against which Jackalope leaned. How funny it would be to make it move, to roll away from him so that the boy fell flat on his back. That would teach him a lesson. Who'd be embarrassed then? It would serve him right, the sly, selfish-

Robin's hand was moving before he even really noticed it, Jackalope's laughter still in his ears through the haze of anger. He threw out his arm, intending only to cast Golem again, with all his might.

Instead, to his horror, and the shock of Hawthorn, a deep blast of thick darkness roared from his palm, a jet of powerful shadow, filled with grit and rolling stones, grinding noisily. It arced over the fire, scattering the flames in sparks and flashes, and descended on Jackalope like a bolt of black lightning. The Fae, acting on instinct, ducked the blast at the last second, his silver eyes wide and shocked. The blast hit the rock behind him, which exploded into countless tiny fragments with a deafening boom and a huge cloud of dust.

Woad shrieked in alarm, as the shuddering explosion rolled out in a shockwave, bending the long grass outwards all around them. He leapt from the shelter where he was perched, just as it too exploded to fine grit, along with every other rock, large and small, in the hollow of their camp. They set off all around them, bursting like fireworks, as the dark angry jet of mana dissipated with a hiss.

Horrified, Robin fell backwards, staring at his own shaking hands in disbelief. The anger had gone, as swiftly as it had come, leaving him feeling empty and hollowed out. His skin, he saw, was white, almost glowing.

"Filius Canis! What are you trying to do?!" Jackalope yelled, scrambling furiously to his feet. Phorbas was in his hand. He was covered in dust and grit. "You madman! Are you trying to kill me?"

Robin opened and closed his mouth a few times. "I…I didn't mean…" he started. The words came out strangely. They didn't sound like his usual voice. There was a whisper beneath them, two voices talking at once. The other, Robin knew, was the Puck.

"Can't you even take a joke?" Jackalope shouted, still shaking with shock.

"Jackalope, be still," Hawthorn said. He had gotten to his feet also, his hair full of grit and rock dust. Small stones still rained down around them all, falling like volcanic pumice and pinging off his horns. He was staring at Robin in surprise and open wonder. "Look at his face, he didn't intend…"

"I don't care *what* he intended," Jackalope pointed the knife at Robin. "You! You need to learn to control your temper. You're not safe to be around!"

Robin could tell by the way Hawthorn and Woad were staring at him that he didn't look himself. He knew what they were seeing. White hair, cold skin and bright green eyes. Robin could still feel the mana rushing though his body like adrenalin. It was intoxicating, like a powerful wind. He swallowed hard, squeezing his eyes shut and pressing the palms of his hands against them. Willing himself to calm, to push the Puck back down deep inside. To make his eyes blue again. Go away…go away… just…let me be me again.

Around his head he could feel the breeze of the Netherworlde night toying around horns that were not there.

"Just…I didn't mean to…give me a moment.." he managed out loud.

"It seems the Scion has no shortage of mana," Hawthorn said at length, his voice careful and thoughtful as he surveyed the devastation around them. "Although maybe a little more mana-control would be desirable."

"That was Darkness again, Pinky." Woad had appeared in front of Robin, crouched on the floor before him. He took Robin's hands in his own small blue ones, and pulled them gently away from his eyes. "Mixed with Earth."

The faun was searching Robin's eyes, looking a little worried. The dust was settling all around them in clouds. Woad smiled tightly.

"See? All better now. Blue eyes are back. Just a slip. Like unexpected bubbles in the bath. Can't be helped sometimes," he sniggered.

"Just a *slip*?" Jackalope sheathed his knife, brushing scree and gravel from his shoulders. He still looked shaken and furious. "You have no control. You're like a bomb waiting to explode!"

"I've been taking extra mana-management classes," Robin said, looking to Hawthorn. He felt a desperate need to explain, how he was filled with this strange other self. "It's…there's something in me. A darkness. The sisters saw it. They were right."

"Sisters?" Hawthorn enquired.

"Spooky Morai" Woad explained, letting Robin's hands go as both of them stood. "All dusty lace and doom-speak. You know how some of these soothsayers are. Though they did make silver top here cough up a big bug, so I guess they weren't all bad."

Hawthorn looked deeply confused, but Jackalope cut in before either Robin or Woad could explain further.

"I don't know what your problem is," he said, grabbing his pack off the floor and hoisting it onto his shoulders. "But I'm not staying around to find out. I saved you in the snow, you saved me at Erlking. We're even, like you said. I came to the Netherworlde with you but this is as far as it goes. That was always the plan anyway. I'm leaving."

"You're really leaving?" Robin said. "To go where? We're in the middle of nowhere, on our own."

"I'm used to that," the older boy replied sharply.

"You're a big bag of wind, hornstumps," Woad said testily to the tall boy. "If you stopped sulking and feeling sorry for yourself for just one minute, you would see that you need us."

"Need you?" Jackalope scoffed, his eyebrows disappearing into his hair. "Me, need you? I need to get thrown across a room and slammed into a wall? I need to get almost blown to pieces by this maniac? I don't think so."

"Everyone needs people," Woad said insistently. "Even annoying, selfish ones. We all occasionally nearly blow each other up…so what." He shrugged as if this happened every day. "That's what friends do."

"I don't need *friends* like you," the Fae replied. "Really. And *you* don't need friends like me."

"You think you're not good enough for us," Robin said with sudden conviction. Jackalope froze, his pack half on his shoulders.

"It's true. You're all spiky edges and snide insults, but it's all one big act," Robin continued. "You think you don't deserve to be happy, or safe, and you're too afraid to even admit it to yourself."

Jackalope glared so furiously at Robin that it seemed inevitable that he was about to lunge and take a swing, but he just sighed down his nose, his lips pressed together in a thin line.

"You are an idiot, Robin Fellows. And even worse, you think you're one of the good guys."

"I am," Robin said. "Or at least I try."

"Well…" Jackalope turned away. "I'm not. No matter how much you and the other knights of the gossamer-winged table want me to be… Farewell, Scion."

He made to walk away, but the old man raised a hand.

"I'm afraid that's not an option right now," Hawthorn said. He was looking off toward the top of the hollow, where the pale skies were beginning to bleed with lemon yellow and salmon pink as the sun prepared to rise. The three boys looked at him curiously. He was standing very still, his eyes roaming the edge of the hollow they camped in, leaning on his bow and sniffing the air.

"I'm afraid our little magical mishap just now may have drawn some unwanted attention. We all need to leave…right now."

Following his lead, they scrambled stealthily up the grassy hillside, out of the dell, now strewn with shattered rocks, Woad kicking dirt over their tiny campfire as they left.

"What do you mean?" Robin asked. He felt rather dizzy and jelly-legged after his puckish outburst.

"What kind of attention?" Jackalope asked.

"There!" Hawthorn, cresting the hill, dropped suddenly into a crouch, dragging the boys down with him on either side. The grass up here was longer, and damp with morning dew.

The land before them was thinner of trees. There were long undulating hills, studded with the occasional rocky outcrop. They rolled away under the pre-dawn sky. Silhouetted against one of these outcrops, some way off was, what at first glance Robin took to be, a large pale horse. But as it turned, he saw that its pallid muscular torso blended into that of a man's, white as milk and long armed. It carried a wicked looking spear, and atop its head, a long freakish looking helmet, pyramidical in design, so that it resembled the long muzzle of a horse.

"A centaur!" Woad hissed in alarm.

"Has it seen us?" Robin asked, his heart pounding. He had encountered these creatures before, in the war camps of the Grimms far in the snowy north. They were violent, brutish and vicious. Part horse, part stag, part human in appearance, but not a shred of humanity within. The blood-thirsty war horses of Eris.

"Undoubtedly," Hawthorn whispered. "At the very least it will have heard your little mana-tantrum just now, and cannot have failed to have seen the smoke and dust. It is a scout."

"Mana-trum," Woad giggled quietly to himself. Robin shushed him.

"A scout for others. But how many?" Jackalope cursed.

"They travel by herd," Hawthorn said. As he spoke, the distant centaur suddenly reared up on its great hind legs, rolling its forelegs in the air against the sky. It threw back its nightmarish head and shook its spear in the air, uttering a bellowing call, part scream and part roar.

"And it has found our scent!" Hawthorn hissed. He dragged the boys to their feet and turned, setting off through the long grass as the creature leapt down from the rocks and galloped away, disappearing behind two hills.

"Hurry! All of you! We have to get to clear ground, out onto the grass-lands proper, away from the trees. It has gone to fetch the herd."

They ran along behind him, panic rising in Robin as his satchel bounced on his back.

"Away from the trees? Shouldn't we be hiding in the trees? We'll be completely exposed otherwise!" Robin gasped, struggling to keep up. Hawthorn was fast.

"They'll sniff us out," he called back, dismissing the idea immediately. "Then we'll be trapped, skewered on spears."

"As opposed to being run down and trampled," Jackalope said. "Is this a preferable fate? We're never going to be able to outrun them. Not in the open! I don't know if you noticed, old man, but they have more legs that we do."

A thunderous noise came from the distance, far off, but growing. Robin, despite a small voice in his head telling him it was a very bad idea, risked a glance behind them.

The sun had breached the horizon, turning the sky to blood and fire as it rose, and pouring over the distant hills came a herd of centaur. Twenty ... no closer to thirty of them, Robin guessed as he scanned the hillside. They flew down the grassy slope like water.

"They haven't seen us yet!" Woad said encouragingly. "They have our scent, but the gap is too great. Centaurs are not the best with eyesight, nothing like a faun, but they have noses like bloodhounds. The grass is long."

"But they're going to close the gap!" Robin argued. "They're headed this way. Where are we running to?"

"I feel the 'from' is more important than the 'to', at the present time," Hawthorn replied. "And we only need enough distance that I can stop for a moment."

"Stop?" yelled Jackalope, crashing through the grass at Robin's side, their shadows elongated before them in the light of the rising sun as they ran. "Are you completely insane?"

"Debatable," the Fae responded. "But if we can find a clear enough space, I've a way we can outrun them, at least for a while. We can make for the nearest safe place."

"Safe place?" Robin gasped, out of breath.

"Briar Hill," Hawthorn explained. "Stop talking and run."

"Briar Hill ..." Woad pointed out, crashing through the long grass. "... is not a safe place! It is a haunted and cursed place!"

"Woad," Robin gasped, watching the small blue creature dart ahead like a swift rabbit as the thunder of the centaur herd grew louder behind them. "Right now, it sounds better than here!"

EQUIS TERRAE

"Stop!" Hawthorn panted. "This will do." They had erupted from a small copse of trees into open ground, the last of the sparse shelter behind them.

High, undulating moorland, blanketed with tall yellow grass stretched out before them, golden in the rising sun. The hills seemed to stretch on forever, rising to distant smoky shadows on the far horizon which looked like cliffs and quarries.

Jackalope and Robin almost barrelled straight into the back of the suddenly stationary man. Woad scampered past, propelled by momentum, a small blue streak of energy.

"Here? What? There's nothing here!" Jackalope panted.

Robin glanced behind. He couldn't see much through the trees, but the sound of the centaurs' hooves was a distant thunder. He could feel it vibrate through the soles of his shoes.

"They're coming," he gasped, nursing a stitch. "They're fast."

Woad had stopped, scanning the horizon. His sudden eruption into the open grasslands had started a multitude of tiny birds and they rose before him in their thousands, a black, scattered cloud, cawing and complaining. Robin watched them fill the sky, wheeling in great swooping arcs, arabesques of living smoke dancing in the sky against the crimson heavens. He had seen something like this on television once with Gran. One of the nature programmes she liked to watch. Starlings they were called, he remembered. They massed and danced like this back in the human world too. People would travel for miles to see them do it.

It would have been more relaxing had the imminent probability of being trampled or speared by monsters not been more pressing on his mind. The sight of the birds however, and their majestic, cacophonous dance against the wild, open skies, made Robin's heart hurt unexpectedly.

In that moment, he simply wanted his Gran back. He would have given anything to be in the lounge of the small bungalow, his dinner on a tea tray on his knees as he sat beside her on the lumpy old sofa watching starlings on TV, filtered through the calming voice of David Attenborough.

Hawthorn was peering at him oddly, as though he sensed his strange emotions.

"Scion," he said. Robin couldn't draw his eyes away from the birds, scattering now, their vast cloud sweeping out and away across the horizon. "Robin," Hawthorn said, softer.

The boy dragged his eyes from the sky and looked at the Fae. "Are they going to catch us?" he asked. What he really wanted to say was 'are we going to die', but he felt superstitiously as though saying this out loud would make it too real.

"Not today," Hawthorn said firmly. "No son of Wolfsbane is falling to centaurs while in my care. Your father would never forgive it."

He stuck his longbow into the ground, forcefully, driving the sharp tip into the soil. "All of you, come close to me. Stand here, at this spot."

They gathered close to Hawthorn uncertainly. He set off, dragging the bow behind him, scoring a deep groove in the soil, leaving them to watch in confusion as his thin limbs carried him around in a graceful arc.

"Stay within this circle," he said, pointing to the rough depression he had just made. "Don't break it."

"What are you doing?" Jackalope asked.

"A cantrip, Earth magic. But very powerful, so I need more mana than I have. I'm going to use yours too."

"Ours?" Woad said. "Like … a mana-cocktail?"

"Exactly." Hawthorn moved to the middle of the circle, dropping into a crouch and planting both hands firmly on the ground. He wriggled his fingers into the long grass, worming them into the soil.

"I don't have a mana-stone," Jackalope argued. "I don't do magic, remember?" He waggled Phorbas. "Just stabbing."

"Doesn't matter. You still have plenty of mana, whether you can use it or not. That will do."

"How does this work?" Robin asked, reaching for his own mana stone. He knew that mana could be shared. Karya had used mana from Phorbas the knife to save their lives once, drawing power from his mana stone to 'flip' them across leagues when her own store was depleted.

"How about I explain the ins and outs of it to you later, Robin." Hawthorn said. "When we're not in quite such a pickle? Right now, we need steeds. This cantrip is called Boulder-dash, and it hasn't been attempted since before the shattering. This might … sting a little."

Robin opened his mouth to reply, but Hawthorn released a pulse of mana deep into the earth and it boomed through the circle like a shockwave, blowing the grass outwards in all directions and filling the air with an electric charge. More clouds of starlings erupted from the grass around them, hurtling off into the distance, their countless wings filling the sky with noise.

The wave of mana engulfed the three boys, rooting them to the spot, and Robin gasped as though punched in the stomach. It felt as though all the air had been ripped from his lungs, and a great, crushing weight had descended on his back. Buckling, he fell to his knees in the dirt, struggling to breathe as he clutched for his mana stone. From his blurred peripheral vision, he saw Jackalope and Woad the same. Jackalope was on his hands and knees in the grass, pale and shaken, his gritted teeth grinding in pain. On his other side, Woad had dropped into a tight ball on his haunches and had his head buried under his arms protectively. He could see the faun's milky mana stone flashing rapidly and erratically, like a lighthouse sending frantic morse code.

The pain was unbearable. Robin's own mana stone roared in his fist, the silver and green stone rolling with motion within, a contained storm, as the power of the cantrip flowed through his body, electricity in his veins, his lungs crushed, heart feeling as though it might burst out of his chest. Robin, unable to speak, squeezed his watering eyes shut. *Bloody … magic*, he thought to himself. *Why is it always so … painful?*!

He could feel his mana being torn from his body, draining out and down and into the soil beneath them, leaving nothing behind but a chilling, empty feeling inside. It was like bleeding to death.

And then, just when he felt he couldn't stand it a moment longer, it stopped. A golden-green flash flickered in the circle, bright against his eyelids.

Gasping and drawing in air like a man who had almost drowned, Robin's eyes shot open. Hawthorn was getting shakily to his feet. He looked unsteady and weak, but his long deep eyes were blazing. His arms were covered with dirt and soil to the elbows. It fell from his shaking hands in clumps, wisps of smoke and steam rising from his grubby fingertips. Beneath their feet, the ground began to shake and buckle.

"Get back," Hawthorn wheezed, staggering away, bow in hand.

Robin wasn't sure he could stand at all. He was dizzy and tingling from head to toe, but the discomfort was gone. Flashes and blurry spots clouded his eyes, but he felt Woad's hand on his arm, hoisting him to his feet.

"Pinky, watch your step," the faun said in a wobbly voice.

Shapes were erupting from the ground beneath their feet. Two of them. Large things, making the earth and soil buck and heave like water. There was a rumbling roar, and Robin and the others watched in astonishment as two great forms clawed their way out of the earth to freedom, as though digging themselves out of their own graves.

They were beasts. Lions, Robin thought, but much bigger than any lion he had ever seen in the mortal world. Each was as large as a police horse, great muscled flanks shaking off avalanches of soil as they climbed out of the ground, still flickering along their edges with green mana.

"They're … they're made of earth?" Jackalope wheezed hoarsely.

It was true, Robin saw. These were not living creatures of flesh and blood. Each of the two vast lions was sculpted from the ground, rocks rolling just beneath the rich black skin of soil and dirt like large bunched muscles. Branches and roots crisscrossed their hides like sinew, tying their forms together, poking from the surface here and there, questing tendrils of tubers, shoots and vines, flexing and shaking as the beasts stood before them. Their vast heads, dark and delineated with grit, pebbles and dirt, were rock and stone, each long tooth in their maws a mica-flecked dagger of slate, and their vast and shaggy lions-manes were composed entirely of the coarse yellowed grass of the hills.

"Well, that worked better than I imagined," Hawthorn said, as one of the huge beasts stretched, shaking off excess dirt with a flurry of motion. The other creature roared, its loud voice deep and rolling, a landslide. "Quickly now! Climb on."

"Climb on?" Robin yelped. The monstrous lions turned their great heads toward the sound of his voice, regarding him with hard black eyes of darkest solid coal.

Hawthorn swung himself up onto the back of one of the steeds. It didn't seem to mind, or indeed to notice.

"Hurry," he said, beckoning to them. "They won't hurt you. They're not alive. Boulderdash is a travelling cantrip. It's just animated earth. Well, rocks and twigs and bits of old root too, you get the idea. Your father was excellent at this once, Robin. Before the shattering, of course. He always summoned a land-dragon. I could never quite match it." He held out his hand. After only a moment of hesitation, Jackalope crossed the grass and grasped it, swinging up beside the older Fae. There was plenty of room for two atop the wide back of the curious creature.

Robin considered that out of the options of large and vicious-looking earth-lions or a herd of murderous centaur, they would be better off taking their chances with the former. On legs that still felt more than a little drained and watery, he ran over to the other creature and, grasping the long tangled grass of its mane, he hauled himself up onto its wide, knotted back. Woad landed behind him immediately, holding onto his shoulders.

"These are fast," Hawthorn assured them. "Very fast. But they won't last forever, even with mana from all four of us. We make for Briar Hill!"

"Faster than centaurs?" Jackalope asked, as Hawthorn dug his heels into the rocks and wood that formed the steed's flanks. "It's a long way to Briar Hill from here."

"Well, let's hope so, eh?" Hawthorn replied, as the great cat leapt out of the circle, and began to run with thunderous booming paws swiftly across the hill and out onto the wide hilly prairie. "Just like riding a horse!" he called back reassuringly to Robin and Woad.

Robin, wide-eyed, gripped the thick yellow brown mane in fistfuls. "I've never ridden a horse!" he called, slightly hysterical. "There's not much call for it in the inner-city!" He had no idea how to make the Boulderdash cat move. It was wider than a horse's back, his legs dangling over its great sides as he felt it growl and creak beneath him, like a forest in a storm. But if his father could do it, then so could he.

"Yahhh!" Woad bellowed at the top of his lungs, holding on to Robin for dear life and kicking his bare heels into the cat's huge earthy flanks. The creature reared up with a deafening roar, and with a lurch that almost threw the two boys from their seats, it set off after its companion, thundering across the ground.

The cantrip beasts were fast. Agile and fleet, their great paws slamming on the ground, heads low and wooden, tree-root tails flickering behind them like great whips as they tore across the uneven ground at tremendous speed. The grass was a blur beneath them, the wind streaming tears from Robin's eyes so that he had to hold his head low and close to the mane to keep out of it. The great creature smelled of deep soil, tree sap and freshly cut leaves. It was an oddly warm and comforting smell, he had time to think, as he clung on for dear life.

"This …" he muttered giddily into the grassy mane, "… is nothing like riding a horse!"

Hawthorn and Jackalope had already made good ground on them and were some way ahead, speeding tirelessly across the grasslands, sending up clouds of startled and complaining birds now and again, through which Robin and Woad's sentient ride leapt with undaunted determination.

The creatures were running full pelt, their footing sure as they leapt up and down the undulating hills, from grassy tussock to rocky outcrop, splashing through the occasional hidden mire in the long grass.

The earth rolled under them at thundering, rhythmic speed, landscape flashing by, and the morning sky, blue now, arched above them cool and high with shredded cloud, an autumn cap of fresh, wild air.

Over the roar of the constant wind, and the pounding of the cantrip's great paws, Robin could occasionally hear Woad whoop and holler with sheer glee, though his voice was whipped away and over the hills almost immediately.

Robin couldn't help but grin at the euphoric speed. He tightened his fists in the grassy clumps of the creature's mane, clinging to its back with his legs as they bounded onwards.

"Come on, leafy Aslan," he muttered breathlessly. "Don't let us down."

Robin had no clear idea how far it was to this Briar Hill, nor why Hawthorn seemed to think they would be safe from the pursuing centaurs there. He vaguely remembered Karya mentioning that it was a good few days' hike at least. But that had been on foot across the grasslands, not pelting across the countryside at full magical-herb-cat speed.

"They're behind us," Woad said after some time. The sun had fully risen by now, and the wide grasslands were bathed in a crisp light, making the tussocks shimmer like spun gold. "They're not giving up."

Robin risked a glance over his shoulder. On the horizon behind him, far across the rolling plains, he could make out the herd of centaur, a pale army of racing death. They were raising a cloud of dust in the air behind them, and there was the occasional flash where the sun hit their spears.

"I think they're gaining on us, slowly," Woad shouted to Robin. "First,

I couldn't see them. Then I could see them, but not hear them. Now I can hear their hooves."

"How can you hear anything over the noise of this thing?" Robin shouted back over the roaring wind. The creature they rode groaned and rumbled like a thunderhead with every movement, its magical parts grinding grittily together with every swift motion. Its rapidly falling feet were a constant thudding tattoo on the ground beneath them, and above all this, the wind roared like a freight train. Robin felt it burning his cheeks red, and they surely hadn't been riding even two hours yet.

"Fauns have the best of all ears," Woad replied. "You should hear your stomach gurgle at night. I can hear it from two floors away. And that's just a stomach, not a pile of horsey death."

Robin watched their tenacious pursuers for a moment longer, then looked forward to Hawthorn and Jackalope still ahead of them, tearing through the grass.

"Do you think we can make this thing go faster?" he shouted to Woad. "I want to get alongside. I've never driven a … whatever this thing is again…before."

Woad considered this for a second. "A Boulderdash. We could try saying 'ya' again, only louder?" he suggested.

"Woad, I don't think–"

"Yaaah!" Woad bellowed in Robin's ear.

The Boulderdash cantrip growled and, to Robin's surprise, the lion lowered its head further, dropping its shoulders so low that Robin almost toppled forward over the creature's head. Considering the fact that they were moving along in a blur, this would not have ended well for him. He clung on grimly. Their beast sped up somehow, and, leaping between rocks and over clumps of heather with feline agility, it gradually drew alongside its companion.

Hawthorn glanced over at them. His face was very calm, as though he did this sort of thing every day. His hair whipping about his horns.

"Not bad are they?" he bellowed to them, reaching down and patting the flank of his steed, setting loose a clump of soil and dust. "Better than walking, that's for sure. Though they are a bit unforgiving on the old backside, eh?"

"The centaurs are still following us, Hawthorn," Robin yelled back, as the two great cats galloped alongside each other. "Woad says they're closing in. How much further until we get there?"

Jackalope, sitting behind Hawthorn, looked backwards, his ashy grey hair flicking into his eyes in the slipstream.

"Centaurs don't tire," he yelled. "They're bred in the pits of Dis. Engineered for war. They will follow us until their legs give out and they collapse dead."

"That's very helpful, Jack," Robin bellowed back, giving the pale Fae a thumbs up. "Cheerful contribution as always." He looked to Hawthorn. "Will these things last?"

"Not forever," Hawthorn replied reluctantly.

"We must have been riding for hours already," Robin yelled.

"Definitely," Woad agreed. "My butt is completely numb. I think my tail might actually fall off."

"How fast are we going? Eighty, ninety miles an hour?" Robin asked Hawthorn, ignoring the faun's complaints. "So we've covered nearly two hundred miles of grassland, give or take. How far is this hill of yours from Erlking?"

"I don't know miles," Hawthorn shrugged. "We measure distance in the Netherworlde in days. Erlking is four day's march from the hill. That's with resting and sleeping, of course. These earthy beauties don't need to do either."

This wasn't very helpful information to Robin. "What do we do if the cantrip runs out before we get there?" he said.

The old man looked at him sidelong. "We get run down by centaurs and killed," he replied bluntly.

"And what happens if they do catch up to us?" Jackalope said. "If these things are slowing down?"

"Then we hold them off!" Hawthorn replied, beginning to sound a little testy. "Honestly, the pair of you. Are you constantly worrying about what *might* happen and what *could* be? Can you not concentrate on what *is*? The future is a promise and the past a memory. They're not real places, so don't give them all your attention. All there is for us is now, always. A great continuous rolling moment. That's quite enough to deal with."

Their rides had crested the top of a tall smooth hill, and more of the grasslands were laid out before them. Hawthorn pointed ahead. "There, look. Between those two small hills on the far horizon. Once we cross those, when we pass between them, Briar should be visible."

Robin dismayed at the distance. The grasslands were huge and empty, wild ground undulating away. Here and there were occasional low bushes or stubby trees. There was a small purplish blur in the distance which might possibly have been a tiny wood, but that was the only place of any substance to focus on. He could barely make out the smokey shapes of the hills Hawthorn spoke of. He had been on high moors before, back in the human world. Nothing made you feel smaller or more insignificant. It was like being in a desert, but of grass and gorse. At least back there, in the mortal realm, even on the moors there was the occasional road, even a motorway, to hint at civilisation. Here, there was nothing like that. Just wilderness, untamed, immense and majestic. Sweeping golden-brown nature rolling away beautiful and heartless on all sides.

"Hold them off how?" he wondered.

"By resting, and recharging your mana," Hawthorn advised. "We have little else to do but hold on tightly, after all."

He was right of course. What else could they do? They rode on in silence, Robin occasionally glancing behind. The centaurs still followed, a wave of pursuing death, but there was still enough distance between them that he couldn't make out their faces, or their odd and disquieting masks.

If Karya were here, he thought to himself, *she'd have a plan, a strategy.* She always did. Hawthorn seemed such a wild spirit. He had been living in the wilds of the Netherworlde for so long, used to the constant danger, dodging and avoiding capture. It was understandable that he would live only from one minute to the next.

Well, Karya isn't here, Robin remonstrated himself angrily. *It's just you, the dour frosty Fae, and a faun, so you'd better think of something yourself. If they do catch up, within say … deadly spear-throwing distance, for instance. What will you do? How will you defend yourself? Harsh language? Distracting mime?*

He wondered desperately where Karya and Henry were. Whether they were even in the Netherworlde yet. And if they were, if Karya had the sense to be tracking him using her method of tearing back and forth between the worlds to cover ground. The last thing he wanted was for her and Henry to run into another centaur patrol.

Time passed. The land rolled beneath them and the sky overhead, and slowly, the centaurs gained. It was barely noticeable at first. The tireless, rhythmic thudding of the Boulderdashes' huge paws, the rocking sway of their bodies, was almost hypnotic, as the grasslands thundered by. Clouds drifted in from the east, sending long spiralling fingers stretching across the cool skies. After a time, a light, silvery rain began to fall, thin and fine. It glistened on the hills and rocks, making them glitter and shine when the sun broke through. Robin watched the great shadows of the clouds roll over the vast expanses of countryside, like ghosts of drifting continents.

But each time the land dipped or rose, and they lost sight momentarily of the herd giving chase, they would be visibly closer once they reappeared. The noise of the centaurs was a dull and constant thrumming of hooves, tireless war drums, and they were only getting louder. The occasional angry bestial bellow could be heard now and again. The magical steeds Robin and the others were fleeing on were definitely tiring. Almost imperceptibly, they were decelerating. Slowly but surely, the gap between them and their pursuers was closing.

"Look!" Woad exclaimed. The rain had long since stopped, and the autumn sun was shimmering down onto the wet ground through a gauze of cloud so thin and smooth, it seemed like muslin stretched above them, suspending the orb of the sun like a softly cradled egg yolk.

"What is it?" Robin asked, looking back.

"They're going away … I think," Woad said uncertainly.

He seemed to be right. They had finally reached the low hills which Hawthorn had pointed out to them earlier and, as the two great lions dipped between them, the high coarse grass whipping and whispering against their sides, the centaurs broke off.

They were in fact veering to the left, banking like a great flock of birds, slowly disappearing behind the hills.

Robin shouted this information to Hawthorn, who looked back also, his face grim and serious.

"Are they giving up?" Robin asked, hardly daring to believe it.

"Centaurs don't 'give up'," Jackalope said, his eyes skimming the high hills now rising up on either side of them.

"It's unlikely," Hawthorn agreed. They had lost sight of the centaurs altogether now. Nothing stretched away behind them but miles and miles of empty hills. "This could be extremely bad."

The lions emerged from between the two hills, and Robin saw that the land on this side of them was far more broken than the great savannah they had just navigated. Here, great jagged cliffs and outcroppings rose out of the scrubland. On the far horizon, the world was dominated by a steep rise, the hills sloping up and up into true highland, and all along the edge of it was a solid golden line, fuzzy and hazy in the light.

"That is the Elderhart forest," Hawthorn announced, pointing forward at the very distant wall of autumnal vegetation. "Miles to go yet before we reach its borders. But look! At last!"

It was clear what had caught Hawthorn's attention. A short way off, maybe four broken dips and rises of crumbled, grassy hillock, the land rose in a great solitary hill. One side of the hill seemed missing, as though a giant had taken a great bite out of the earth. Atop this uneven spur, there appeared to be a town. Robin could see the shapes of rooftops and towers, black and indistinct from here, silhouetted like a crown set atop the unbalanced rise. It looked like old Viking settlements he had seen in books, fortified, walled and remote.

"Briar Hill," Woad grinned. "We're almost there!" He patted the side of the lion with affection. "Good kitty! I'd give you some catnip, but I think you've already got a bit growing in your mane here." Clumps of dry soil and twigs came away in his hand, blown away by the passing wind, and Robin looked in concern. He had been noticing deterioration in both of their strange steeds for a while now. Clumps of the grass which formed the creature's mane had started coming away in his hands. The tightly packed stones under the skin of soil before him seemed looser and less smooth.

"I think ... these things are falling apart," he shouted to the others.

Hawthorn nodded. "Not far to go! Once we reach the hill, we will be fine! We can ..."

He trailed off, making Robin look up in question, and his heart froze.

In front of them, flowing out from between two rocky hills, spreading from the left to block their path, were the centaurs. They appeared like a nightmarish wall, dead ahead of them.

"That's not good," Woad observed quietly, his fingers digging into Robin's shoulders.

"Where did they come from?" Jackalope cried. "They must have doubled around. Known a faster way between the hills."

The cantrip lions made no attempt to stop, they barrelled forwards relentlessly, delivering their cargo directly to the centaurs ahead.

"What do we do?" Robin asked urgently.

"We go through!" Hawthorn answered, his mouth set in a thin line. He had lowered his head, close to the lion, his spiralling horns aimed forward.

"Through?" Robin stared at the centaurs, now rushing up to meet them. There were more than thirty. Their ranks tight. Their pallid horse bodies were sheened in sweat and covered with dark splattered dirt and mud from the long chase. He could hear their roars as they shook their spears in fury and triumph. Hot gushes of breath escaping their long nightmarish triangular masks in clouds.

"The lions will not last," Hawthorn said firmly. "The Boulderdash is falling apart, you must have noticed. No time to change course. Nowhere else to go. Heads down and everything you can to clear a path. No matter what happens, get … to … the … hill!"

Robin nodded, swallowing the hard lump that seemed to have risen and lodged in his throat. It felt like charging into battle. But the numbers were decidedly uneven. He wondered briefly what he'd be doing right now, if Gran had not died. If he'd never come to Erlking. Sometimes a normal life seemed so preferable, and decidedly less deadly.

But he wasn't a normal boy, a small voice, quiet but insistent, said inside his head. It was the voice of the Puck. He knew it was really just himself, but it never sounded like he did. You are the Scion, it said. You are the son of the sidhe. Your father rode land dragons made from earth and root and rock, and you will not disgrace the line of Fellows by faltering in the face of monsters.

Robin set his jaw. "Woad, hold on," he shouted determinedly back to the faun. "I'm going to clear as many as I can. I need you to do what you do best."

He felt the faun's confusion. "You need me to whistle?"

Robin sighed. "I need you to cause chaos!"

The lions rushed across and pelted down the grassy slope as the centaurs reared up to meet them. The air hung thick with bestial smells. Robin felt his mana stone slapping against his chest like a fist with every swift stride of the steed.

Wait, said the Puck in his head, *not yet, just wait, closer…*

They were almost upon one another. Robin saw the centaurs raise their spears, levelling them at their prey, animal grunts and whinnies of delight erupting from them, bouncing against the rocky roars of the indignant lions. They were close enough that he could see the designs of the tattoos cut into their human-like torsos, the detailed scarification, tribal and geometric. He could see the red and bloodstained wildness of their eyes.

Now! the Puck shouted in Robin's head. Holding on tightly to the loose and fraying mane with his left hand, Robin leaned out to the right as far as he dared, dangling off the side of the lion, his hand outstretched to brush the long grass which sped underneath them. His fingers whipped through the grass, immediately soaked with the rains that had fallen. With all his might, he concentrated and cast needlepoint into the grass, heaving himself back upright with a grunt and throwing his arm out in a wide arc.

His mana pulsed, flashing through his body and into the spell, and a thousand icy darts flew up out of the grass all around them like arrows, shooting with whistling velocity towards the herd.

Ice rained everywhere as the tiny javelins struck their marks left and right, piercing countless flanks, jabbing into torsos and arms, spearing and stabbing the centaurs in a horizontal rain. Many of the beasts cried out in guttural pain and shock, stung by a thousand magical wasps, barbs glittering all over their bodies. They reared up on their hind legs, bellowing, turning instinctively to shield themselves from the attack, barrelling into one another.

Robin and Woad's lion leapt into the air, crashing through the first ranks, knocking several of the disoriented creatures flying with its massive paws. They landed in the midst of their enemies, scattering them. Their steed roaring and pushing through the jumbled crowd of bumping flank and stamping hooves.

"Now, Woad!" Robin yelled forcefully. He felt more than heard the faun's mana stone flash behind him, and from all around them, in the packed chaos of the herd, there were flashes of foxfire, wisplight and bangs of small flame, clattering amongst the creatures like devilish fireworks.

More confusion and surprise bellowed from the centaurs, their animal minds confused and startled by the sudden lightshow. Through the press of bodies, Robin saw Hawthorn's lion some way off, also shouldering its way through the blinded stung creatures. He focussed his mana and sent flying several Galestrikes, aiming low at the enemies' legs. Toppled and off balance, many of the centaurs fell or reared up amongst their fellows in panic, dragging others down with them.

Several of those creatures closest to Robin made a swipe for him, long pale hands, barbed with steel, reaching out hungrily to pull him from the lion, but their steed swiped at them with its great rocky claws, batting them away, leaping at them and knocking them to the ground. Bodies rolled underfoot as it plunged onwards relentlessly.

Robin cast Featherbreath, a multiple point cantrip, sending it out randomly in every direction around them, not bothering to aim, not caring where the spell might find its marks. Where the cantrip hit, it lifted spears from the ground, wrenched them from centaur hands, and sent them all spinning away up into the air in a great multitude. He cut off the cantrip as they passed, and the weapons, no longer held aloft by his force, fell back to earth, deadly javelins, scattering the enemy even more as they strived to dodge the deadly rain of their own steel. Woad sent another flurry of foxfire into the fray. It was as though someone has lit a pack of joke shop bangers and cast it into a thick crowd. Harmless explosions, loud bangs and bright flashes, faun trickery at its best. But the centaurs were animals at heart, startled and panicked by the fire and the noise.

A shout of triumph somewhere in the chaos drew Robin's attention. He saw a flickering line of red lights, realising they were the inlaid mana stones that Hawthorn carried along his bow. The elder Fae was doing the same as they were, blasting his way through with confusion and cantrips. Robin saw Earth magic all around them, unfamiliar to him but effective, clearly Hawthorn's doing. Sink holes opening up, tripping the centaurs and sending them sprawling, parts of the hillside spontaneously erupting into landslide, or turning inexplicably to thick mud.

We're almost through, he thought. Much of the chaos was now behind him. A final line of centaurs, five in all, were holding fast, determined, their spears raised and their hooves dug firmly into the ground.

"Get out of the way!" Robin shouted furiously at them. He could feel his stores of mana dwindling, but he was determined. These things just kept on coming, it was infuriating. He was aware that his heart was pounding and he was gritting his teeth, anger surging up inside him. "I said get out of my way!" he yelled, and with all of his force and the last of his mana, he cast Breezeblock at them. The wall of immovable air hit the centaurs like an invisible battering ram, scattering them like skittles, actually lifting their huge bodies from the floor, sending them crashing away to either side, as the two lions burst through this last defensive line together, finally free of the melee, with open ground ahead of them.

Robin felt his head swim and dark spots blur in front of his vision. He had used too much mana. Only Woad's steadying grip, hauling him upright on the lion's back, stopped him from falling altogether from his perch.

"Inspired!" Hawthorn bellowed, suddenly at his side. Robin looked up blearily. The Fae was looking at him in wonder, eyes flashing as he rode alongside. "Like a knife through butter! Ha!"

"We're almost there!" Woad said with an outburst of relief and joy. It was true. They were at the foot of Briar Hill itself.

"They're following, regrouping!" Jackalope yelled, looking back from behind Hawthorn. Robin had time to note that Jack's blade, Phorbas, was wet and dark with ichor. Evidently, he had helped Hawthorn to hack through the crowds too.

"It doesn't matter now!" Woad said jubilantly, his voice a little shaky as the lions, slowed by the skirmish and the crowd, were loping along at a relatively slow speed, bouncing them up and down. "It doesn't matter because—"

The faun never got to finish his sentence. At that moment, with a great rumbling series of creaks and groans, the Boulderdash cantrip finally failed, and the rapidly deteriorating lions of earth, twig and stone, fell to pieces beneath them.

They came apart like broken toys, still running forward, flanks crumbling, roots snapping and rocks falling apart in a landslide of scree, sending Robin and the others tumbling to the ground, rolling over and over on the rough earth in a cloud of mud and dirt.

Coughing and spluttering, Robin got waveringly to his feet, wiping soil from his face. The impact had winded him and he felt bruised everywhere. His backpack had been thrown from his shoulders and he saw it lying in a pile of rock and dirt a few paces off. Stumbling towards it, he called out to the others.

"Is everyone okay?"

"Fan-tastic," Woad coughed sarcastically, digging himself out of a pile of roots and grime. "How about you, Jack? Didn't hurt your pretty face on the ground, did you?"

"Shut up, you jabbering blue idiot," Jackalope complained gruffly, appearing out of a cloud of dust as Robin hauled his pack back onto his shoulders. He was stumbling a little and covered in dirt, but seemed otherwise unhurt. Hawthorn was beside him.

"What now?" Jack said, spitting out soil onto the floor. "Our rides just crumbled. Last stand? Fight for it?" He was clutching Phorbas tightly, his knuckles white. His face was set in a firm and challenging scowl as he stared back at the approaching centaurs, but despite his brave front, the hand gripping the knife was shaking a little.

"We are on the hill," Hawthorn said with authority. "Up to the wall, all of you. Make for the gates. The centaurs will not pass that boundary. Last stands are for fools. Fly and fight another day."

He ushered the three of them on before him, sending them scrambling on foot up the steep slope of Briar Hill.

Robin didn't look back. With Woad on his left and Jackalope on his right they half-ran, half-stumbled up through the steep grass. The footing was maddeningly uneven, the ground growing in closely knit tussocks and clumps which seemed designed to trip and hinder them.

So close, he thought furiously, dragging himself breathlessly upwards. It was like being in one of those nightmares where you're being chased and can't remember how to run. Behind him, he heard the flick and swish of a loosed arrow, and knew that Hawthorn was following them, sending bolt after bolt from his bow at the centaurs climbing the hill behind, trying his best to give the boys time to reach the abandoned town above.

When they were almost at the top, and Robin could make out the broken wooden doors that once marked the entrance to the long-dead town, he shoved Woad and Jackalope on ahead.

"Go! Get inside! Both of you!"

Woad glared back at him wide-eyed. "You too, Pinky! Come on!"

"In a second," he replied, breathless. "I'm not leaving Hawthorn behind. The centaurs are on top of him. Just go will you! I can't help him and worry about you at the same time."

Woad looked as though he was about to argue again, but Jackalope grabbed him roughly by the arm, nodding to Robin and dragging the faun up forcefully to the gates of the town, much to Robin's relief. He turned, looking back down the hill. In the sunlit glow of late afternoon, Hawthorn was picking his way up towards him, walking backwards and loosing arrow after arrow at the centaurs. They met their mark, jabbing into flank and leg, but more often his arrows were being batted out of the sky, glancing off spears.

Several of the creatures were close enough to throw, and Hawthorn twice barely dodged a launched spear, landing inches from him, thudding into the dark soil hillside. He wasn't going to make it. There were still too many of the enemy, and they were too close. They would reach him before he could reach the top and safety.

Robin couldn't let that happen. This man had been a friend of his father. He had risked everything bringing them here, had abandoned the safety of Erlking without a moment's hesitation to lead Robin and the others into the Netherworlde. All to stop Eris gaining a rogue Shard, without a moment's thought for his own safety. Robin wasn't going to let him die protecting a bunch of children on some remote hillside miles from help, miles from anywhere.

He felt his mana stone. It was cold and dead. Utterly spent from the skirmish in the valley below.

Not good enough, he shouted at himself internally. *There's more. Reach deeper. Are you the Scion or aren't you?*

"Hawthorn!" he yelled. "Get up here, now!"

The Fae glanced up, waving at Robin to get inside, to safety, but Robin ignored him. He glanced back at the town, at the high wall of roughly hewn stones now at his back. Each stone was as large as a man. What was it Hawthorn had said about the Tower of Earth? Will. Determination. The utter unshakable conviction that the magic *would* work. That the mana *would* flow. That the earth would *obey*.

He thrust his arms in the direction of the wall, making his hands into tight fists in mid-air, and tugged.

You will *move for me.*

With a roar, a great section of the wall burst apart, exploding outwards in a shower of brick and mortar dust. Robin felt a flicker deep inside, a spark, and it ignited. Mana pouring through his body from deep within like liquid fuel set alight.

With a grunt, he turned on his heel and threw his hands out in the direction of the centaurs. A high, keening buzz was in his head, and wetness on his upper lip told him his nose was bleeding. He let his fury at the creatures flow through him, embracing the anger and darkness rising in him, feeling it giving him strength, and the huge rocks which had been torn from the wall behind him rolled past him, down the hillside in a deadly avalanche. Several soared over his head, landing amongst the centaurs like bombs, exploding into the earth. More thundered, end over end, guided by his will, crashing into the creatures and sending them tumbling back down the hillside. Hawthorn stood stock still in the middle of the deadly landslide, watching the huge boulders fly past him, the landslide parting around him like a rock in a stream, leaving him utterly unharmed as it smashed and crashed into the screaming, bellowing enemy. Hawthorn was staring up at Robin, open mouthed, his eyes filled with disbelief at the force and scale of the Golem cantrip.

Cacophony and destruction rained around Robin, watching his enemies fall before him, toppled by the deadly missiles, crushed or driven back under the unrelenting fury of his mana. It felt good. It felt righteous and powerful. The might of the Puck, merciless and unbowed.

He saw Hawthorn making his way swiftly up the hillside towards him, not a single pebble touching the man in the ongoing storm of rock churning the hillside.

"Robin," he heard the old man call in something like wonder, breathless. "You have horns."

As Hawthorn reached him, Robin felt the great well of anger and power within him ebb. His eyes refused to focus. He tried to smile triumphantly at Hawthorn, the Golem cantrip still laying waste to the enemy below them, scattering the remaining centaurs, driving them back down the hill, but he couldn't manage it. He was exhausted suddenly. More tired than he had ever been. He felt blackness rushing up to engulf him, and blearily saw Hawthorn close the last few steps between them just as his legs gave way beneath him.

Strong, rough hands caught him under the arms as he fell, and Robin distantly felt himself being lifted, carried like a child through the open gates of Briar Hill.

"You rest," he heard Hawthorn say quietly, exhausted himself and struggling for breath. "You did well, boy. You rest now, son."

Robin gratefully sank into blackness and silence.

BRIAR HILL

"Is he dead?"

Jackalope's voice sounded both distant and detached, rising out of watery darkness.

"Of course he's not dead, numbskull!" Woad's voice drifted in. "He's not the dying type. Don't be stupid!" And then, quieter. "He's not dead, is he?"

Hawthorn's calming voice joined them. "No. Don't worry. He's just … drained, that's all. There. I think I got most of the blood off."

Robin felt as though he were struggling to swim upwards through black water as thick as treacle. He became vaguely aware of himself. He was sitting, propped or leaning against something. His arms and legs felt heavy, as though someone had cut the strings of a puppet. With no small effort, he forced his heavy eyelids to open. The faces of his companions swam into view against a background of deep red sky glowing behind them.

"There. See? He's awake," Hawthorn said, though he sounded a little relieved underneath his confidence. Robin felt a damp cloth pressed against his forehead. It was incredibly soothing.

"What … where are we? Are we safe?" His mouth was dry and felt full of cotton wool.

"Safe is a fairly relative term," Jackalope said.

"Yes, Robin. Safe for now," Hawthorn assured him. "How do you feel? Could you take a little water?" He turned his head to Woad. "Fetch more water from my skin," he instructed. "In my pack."

The faun scampered away.

Robin gingerly lifted a hand to his head. It felt bruised. The bright and crimson sky was stinging his eyes. "Did I–"

"Faint?" Jackalope interjected bluntly. "Yes. You dropped like a stone."

Robin scowled. "I was going to say 'pass out'," he muttered. This somehow sounded better to him.

"We are at Briar Hill," Hawthorn told him, as Woad returned with a water skin. He passed it to Robin, who took it gratefully.

"Sips, not gulps, please," Hawthorn instructed in his crackly old voice. "You've been out of action for several hours. The sun is setting."

The water was wonderful. Robin felt utterly parched, and it seemed to wash the cobwebs out of his head. He sat up a little stiffly, running a hand through his messy blond hair, and secretly relieved to find there were no horns there.

"Sunset?" he said, coughing a little. "The centaurs?"

"They have gone," Hawthorn explained. "They would not enter Briar Hill, even in daylight. They are a superstitious bunch, but they have been circling the hill all day. Now that night is falling, they have finally left. They won't even stay close in the dark."

This was tremendously good news to Robin.

"So, we're rid of them?" he said with relief, looking around at the others.

"I doubt that," Hawthorn replied grimly. "It's likely they know they have us trapped up here. They will have gone to fetch reinforcements. We rather decimated their ranks, after all." He was looking at Robin curiously. "When you have come around properly, there are things we must speak of. They are not merely chasing us for sport. There is more to it than that."

He patted Robin lightly on the knee. "But first, we eat. Jackalope has built a fire. Come and enjoy the delights of Briar Hill before we lose the light altogether."

Robin soon discovered that they were in a town square, long since abandoned. The ground below was packed earth, and all around them rose the empty wooden shells of buildings. Hollow glassless window-frames stared down at them like haunted eyes. Many of the low buildings, crammed together, were roofless or partly tumbled down. Grass grew long within their walls, and ivy trailed over their crumbling timbers, as though the earth were reaching up and slowly trying to pull the ghost of the town down under her green skirts.

It was utterly silent and still in the empty square. Not even a bird sang. Clumps of tough-looking grassland flowers grew here and there through paving slabs and blocked narrow alleyways, long since disused. Their questing tendrils pushing determined through cracks in the stones.

The still, silent place was incredibly eerie, especially in the setting sun. The sky overhead was blood bright, crimson and dramatic. Shining through empty frames and broken walls in thick beams dancing with ghostly dust. The buildings cast elongated evening shadows across the square, questing fingers of darkness creeping over the long abandoned cobbles.

Jackalope had indeed started a fire, near the front of an old building that may once have been a town hall. He and Woad were busy rooting through Robin's near-bottomless satchel for food and drinks.

He joined them, feeling more steady with each step he took toward the fire.

"Why won't the centaurs come here? Into the town?" he asked, looking around them. It was quite creepy, like something from an old black and white zombie movie, but he was still surprised. Centaurs didn't seem the nervous type to him. More the hard-headed, bloodthirsty murderous type.

"Don't know your history, Pinky?" Woad teased. "Shame on you. You've always got your nose in your books, haven't you read about the hill?"

Robin shook his head, which he immediately realised was a bad decision as it made his vision swim. He dropped down next to Woad, as Jackalope began to spear dried fish Hestia had packed for them onto sticks for roasting over the fire.

"It's a dark place," the faun said. "The world is full of them. Some places are just … bad. Like the brown spots on a good apple. They dip down heavier than other places, and all the shadows just roll into them and pool up."

"Briar Hill has been many things to many people, Robin," Hawthorn said, sitting cross-legged on the floor opposite the three boys. He passed Robin the large leather copy of Hammerhand's Netherworlde Compendium which had tumbled from his satchel during Woad and Jackalope's rummaging. "Few of them good," he added.

Taking the book, Robin sat by the flickering flames in the sunset of the abandoned town and leafed through the waxy pages until he came to the relevant entry.

Frowning at the spidery script on the yellow vellum, he read aloud as the others listened.

"West of the ruins of the once great Fae palace of Erlking, amongst the great and rolling grassy hills, now home to herds of wild beasts, there rises Briar Hill, a strategic military outpost of some fame during the ancient Fae wars between those people and the invading Whitefolk. Once home to a monastery housing the mysterious and now long defunct Brothers of Shadow, the ruins of Briar Hill have since seen many incarnations. A military fort; a refugee camp for Fae fleeing from the south at the outbreak of the war; and later, and perhaps most grimly, as an internment camp run by the Peacekeepers for the 'processing' of captured Fae prior to transportation either south to Dis or further west to the Hive. Long since abandoned and left to ruin, the structures atop Briar Hill are now tumbled stones, reclaimed by nature and said to be haunted by banshee. None but the foolish or those desperate for shelter now venture near the hill after dark, for fear of encountering these vengeful spirits."

He looked up from the book. "Cheerful stuff," he quipped. "So which are we? The foolish or the desperate?"

Hawthorn chuckled. "Hammerhand knew his lore, especially about the wild beast. These grasslands are full of centaur, although these ones seem very organised. I wonder who is leading them, and what they are doing out here in the lonely places."

"We read about banshee," Robin looked to Woad. "Do you remember? Back at Erlking. You said they were old wives tales."

Woad shrugged unapologetically. "I didn't say old wives were liars, did I?"

"So this town has been a prison, a death-camp, and some kind of secret society," Robin said. "Where did all the people go? Why was it abandoned?"

"They went to the camps of Dis," Jackalope said. "This was mainly a Fae place originally. There are countless towns like this in the Netherworlde now. Empty." He scuffed his boot in the dry dirt. "Dead places. The Fae who had lived here for hundreds of years all rounded up and marched off like animals by the Panthea. Men, women and children alike." He flicked his silver eyes at Woad.

"No offence to you," he added gruffly. "I know you're Panthea, but a lot of your kind, even those who didn't actively believe in Eris' cause, they didn't do anything to stop it, the persecution of our people. So called 'fae sympathetic' Panthea, watching in silence as their Fae friends and neighbours were taken in the night." He snorted in distaste, poking the fire.

"I'm the first to side with the Fae, believe me, but many Panthea were simply terrified to speak out against Eris," Hawthorn counselled, even-handedly. "Many of them still are. They have families of their own to worry about too, and it isn't just Fae like ourselves who disappear in the middle of the night." He peered into the small fire, looking sad and tired. "Fear closes lips that should roar and stays hands that should tear."

Jackalope looked up angrily. "How can you sit there and defend them?" he asked. "Those who did *nothing*? The poor, frightened Panthea?" His lip curled. "They're as guilty as Eris' supporters. Am I supposed to feel sorry for them because yes, fair enough, they might not have stopped it, but hey, they felt just terrible about it on the inside? That makes it all okay?" He snorted down his nose.

"I used to hate *all* Panthea," Hawthorn said. "For many years after the war. Some of the Fae resistance still do." He sighed a little in the setting light of the sun. "But stories have more than two sides, boy. Some of them have more sides than a glittering diamond. Things are not simple or clear in this world or in any. You are too young to know that yet perhaps."

Jackalope looked around at the ruined town. His face was thoughtful, distant. The empty shell of the town had clearly stirred up memories of his own

"The night they came to our village," he said quietly after a moment, not looking at any of them. "A town like this one … They were taking Fae families from their houses, dragging us into the street in the dead of night." He took a bite of his grilled fish, speared on the kebab and chewed it thoughtfully. No one said anything.

"They took me and my brother," he continued. "I was very young at the time of course, but I remember it so vividly." His hard silver eyes flicked up to Hawthorn across the flames. "We lived next door to a Panthea family at the time. They had children our age. We used to play together all the time. Two boys." He swallowed his fish, looking down at the roasting stick. "They were my friends. Their mother fed us at their table." He smiled humourlessly, his eyes scanning the broken walls. "She made the best scones. I can still remember the taste. Full of cream. Lovely woman. We didn't know they were different from us. We were just children. Children are blind to these things." The smile dropped and he looked back to them, his silver eyes like mercury in the flickering firelight.

"That night, when they dragged us out through the street like dogs, the Peacekeepers rounding up every Fae in the village, just as they were doing everywhere, in every town … it was a spectacle. All the village was up in the middle of the night. For the horror show. They were out in the streets, the people of my small town. The Panthea, at doors and windows. Some only brave enough to twitch behind curtains. The Peacekeepers drove us

Fae down the main street, hands bound behind our backs like animals, shoving us into barred wagons. We passed my neighbour's house."

His sharp eyes flicked from Hawthorn to Robin. They were hard and harsh.

"The children, my friends …" he smiled grimly. "Both of them … they stood encircled in their mother's arms. All three of them huddled in the doorway, watching our dark procession. They looked horrified. The youngest boy was crying, I remember that. Even the mother's face was like ash." His eyes cast downwards, looking at the soil between his own feet.

"My brother was quiet, full of dignity. He always was. I … was very young. I caused a fuss."

Jackalope wiped his nose with the back of his hand.

"Kicking and screaming, a puny child trying to fight the Peacekeepers every step of the way. All tears and snot and terror. Embarrassing. I saw our neighbours as we passed. The mother? She looked right at me, holding her children tight. Right at me. And you know what she said to them? As she turned them inwards, burying their faces in her skirts?"

The fire popped and hissed under the crimson sky.

"She said 'don't look'," Jackalope said, thickly into the silence. "Don't look at them, babies." He threw another stick on the fire, sniffing. It caught and kindled, popping and hissing.

"This woman who had fed me, this woman who had nursed my bruised knees a hundred times, fed me at supper like one of her own, chatted to my brother at the market every day. There were tears standing in her eyes, and she said to her children 'don't look.' She said 'turn away.' Do you know what her tears were worth to me?"

A long and uncomfortable silence spread further out from the fire.

"Nothing," he finished bitterly. He looked at Hawthorn, his eyes like hot stones, challenging the older Fae. "There's another side for you to add to your glittering diamond stories, old man."

He got up, dusting off his knees. "I'm not hungry," he said thickly. "I'm going to go and have a look around."

"Be wary," Hawthorn called after him as he stalked away. "And stay within the walls."

"This town has been a death-camp," Jackalope called back. "The worst thing that could happen here already has happened." His boots scuffed at the dry dirt, kicking loose and long forgotten cobbles ahead of him into the deepening evening gloom. "And now here we are, the last three Fae, hiding like rabbits in our own ruins." He laughed humourlessly at the irony of this, as he disappeared into the shadows beyond the circle of firelight.

They ate in subdued silence for a while after he had left. The light drained from the sky, cloaking the town in quiet shadows around them as night fell.

"We are not the last three," Hawthorn said quietly to Robin, some time after Jackalope had gone off to wander the empty streets alone. He had been watching the boy's face as they ate. Clearly, he could sense how troubled he was. Hawthorn reached for one of the seared fish sitting above the flames. "There is a resistance against Eris, a gathering of Fae. Scattered we may be … yes. But it *is* there. I am part of it, and we plot and plan. Fear not, Robin."

"I'm not afraid," Robin said, glancing around at the shell of the town. "Erlking is a resistance too. Of Panthea. And not silent or scared ones either." He looked directly at Hawthorn. "Eris *will* learn that fear cannot control people forever. Fae or Panthea. I'll never let it control me."

"How did you do that?" Woad asked, crunching into his dinner noisily. "Back on the hill, with the rocks? You had no mana left, but then boom!" The faun mimed a big explosion with jazz-hands. "You dragged half the walls of the town down on those angry horse-men. Talk about mastering an element."

Hawthorn was looking intently at Robin as well, clearly just as curious.

"I … I don't really know," he replied, honestly. "It's like I just … found more?" He shrugged. "I don't know how to describe it. I was so angry. We were so close, and you weren't going to make it. It wasn't fair. My mana seems to be doing this. When I get … emotional. Mad, I guess."

"There was darkness in that casting," Hawthorn said, though there was no judgement in his voice, merely an observation. "Looking up the hill at you, I saw. You were not yourself. Just … fury and power."

"That's the Puck, not me," Robin said quietly.

"Well, whatever it was, and however you did it, you saved my life without a doubt," Hawthorn said. "You have my thanks for that. These powers of yours could be a tremendous weapon against Eris, for the resistance." He shrugged. "That is, if you could learn to control it better. It's never a good sign when cantrips cause nosebleeds and unconsciousness."

Robin wasn't sure how much he liked being referred to as a 'weapon', and the gleam in Hawthorn's long eyes was a little bright for his liking. He shuffled uncomfortably and took a bite out of his fish as the last rays of light left the sky above, washing a band of deep twilight purple over them.

"Before, when I woke up," he said, eager to change the subject. "You said you thought the centaurs were chasing us for something more than just the fun of it?"

The older Fae nodded his ragged head. "Centaurs can and do hunt for fun, and they are territorial. They tend to stick to their own hunting grounds. The amount of distance we covered in this chase, it is larger than any centaur's usual patch. Many times larger."

"So, they were determined," Robin reasoned.

"More than that," Hawthorn insisted. "They were hell-bent on catching us, and I want to know why."

"It's obvious, isn't it?" Woad said. He sat across from them, cross-legged in the crackling spluttering light of the campfire, waving his fishbone at them. "I mean, look at you two. Two Fae. Big one been thorn in Eris' toe for years, finally caught, escaped, probably showing everyone up in the process, I bet there were some red faces at the Hive. Then you have the cheek to come waltzing back into the Netherworlde right away, larking about like you own the place."

He nodded to Robin. "And little one, well, you're the Scion. You're like the grand prize in the competition right? The shiny trophy Eris wants to put on her great big mantelpiece of evil. If I was a centaur, I'd be chasing you both too."

Robin thought this was a fairly reasonable explanation, but Hawthorn's furrowed brow made it clear he didn't agree.

"But they wouldn't *know* who we were," he argued. "Not from the distance they started chasing us. Centaurs don't have fantastic eyesight, they're not the brightest bulbs in the great Dis fairground. When we were sighted, all they knew was that magic had been done, and that there were four vagabonds, easy prey."

"So what's your explanation then, longbow?" Woad asked.

"Centaurs may not be big thinkers, but they are creatures of magic," the old man reasoned. "They were, as Jackalope said, bred in the pits of Dis amongst the Shidelings. Magic flows in them and more importantly, it *calls to them*. For them to pursue us so far and so determinedly, they must have sensed some strong magic … old magic even. It's like blood in the water to sharks. They wouldn't have been able to resist."

174

The faun shrugged. "Well, I am a particularly exceptional faun," he said humbly. "But even I admit that my cantrips are not that amazing. Even Pinky here isn't going to win any awards when he's not flashy shiny psycho-puck."

"I agree," Hawthorn looked to Robin pointedly. "Is there anything you can think of, Robin? Something you want to share?"

Robin was bewildered for a moment, but then Hawthorn's words, 'old magic', made him remember something. He almost dropped his fish.

"What is it?" the Fae pressed, his head cocked to one side with interest.

"Well …" Robin hesitated, but then reached for his satchel and began to rummage through it. "I had forgotten all about it, to be honest. But I brought this along too. Do you think it might have been this they could smell?"

He pulled from his satchel the wooden mask. The treasure which Ffoulkes had spent months searching for at Erlking and had tried to steal.

"Woad found it," Robin explained, holding it up in the firelight. "Calypso said it was old and very powerful. Some kind of–"

"Legendary mask of the dryads," Hawthorn finished, wide-eyed. He leaned forward to inspect it. Robin half-expected him to take it from him for a closer look, but the old Fae made no move to touch the artefact.

"This is the Mask of Gaia, Robin Fellows," Hawthorn said after a few moments. He looked up at Robin, his eyes full of wonder. "This is a tremendously valuable object."

"We know," Woad said lightly. "Creepy guy tried to nick it off us, to sell at the black markets. Tried to nick me too. I'm also valuable. *Tremendously*."

Robin looked down at the pale wooden eye-mask. "I don't really know much about it," he admitted, still wondering if this mask had been drawing the centaurs with its waves of old magic. "I was just told that it's been lost for a long time, and it's very … well … magical."

Hawthorn sat back on his haunches. "It is unique," he said. "And it most certainly explains our dogged pursuers. This mask was gifted to the very first king of the dryads by an elemental themselves. An *Elemental*, Robin Fellows!"

Robin looked a little awkward. Sometimes, being raised in the human world made him feel like the eternal new kid at school.

"What's an elemental?" he asked, smiling sheepishly.

Hawthorn blinked at him emptily for a moment. "Apologies," he said. "I forget that you know so little of our world, of your own world." He smiled a little. "The elementals, Robin, were perhaps the most powerful entities in all the Netherworlde once. It is said they were here not only before the Panthea, but before the Fae as well. Old things. Very old. They were eternal, they were endless, and it is said that it was they who first forged the very Arcania itself. They who gifted it in the early days of the world to the Fae, and set it to the service of Oberon and Titania."

"There were only ever seven elementals, Pinky," Woad explained. "I remember my bedtime stories. One for each element. They put their very essence into the Arcania when they forged it. They were like gods … or ghosts."

"So, where are they now?" Robin asked, the mask in his hands, possibly made by some kind of ancient god, older even than the Fae, suddenly felt heavier.

Hawthorn spread his hands to the sky. "Gone!" he said. "All of them. Long, long gone, shortly after the Fae took ownership of the Arcania. They were never seen in the Netherworlde again. They likely never will be. Legends of Fae tell us that once they bequeathed the Arcania to us, our tool to rule and shape the world, they had no further need to be here, no further purpose, so they left."

"Shame really," added Woad, "What with the Arcania shattering thousands and thousands of years later and starting a big old messy war. Would have been handy to still have them around really, wouldn't it? They could make a new one." He looked thoughtful. "Or maybe stick the broken one back together with … mystic … god … glue?"

"The salient point …" Hawthorn ignored Woad, "is that each elemental is rumoured to have gifted not only the Arcania itself to the Netherworlde, but also an artefact, a tool to rule, if you will. The legendary Sword of Vulcan…the Shield of Ether…these things are myths." He nodded to the mask.

"As is that. The Mask of Gaia."

"This thing was to help people rule the world?" Robin asked. Firelight danced over the wood.

"Legends tell that it holds the truest of sight. That it can show you the truth of a thing, of a person, a place. What better or more valuable thing is there?" His eyes glittered. "Imagine what the resistance could do with this? Knowing without a doubt who was friend or foe? It could aid us greatly against Eris."

"No wonder Eris' centaurs could smell it then," Robin said. The hungry look had come into Hawthorn's eyes again, making Robin feel a little uneasy. It was a little too reminiscent of Ffoulkes. He must have drawn back a little, holding the mask to his chest without realising he was doing so, as the older Fae looked up and caught his expression.

His own face was hard a moment, but then it softened, and a smirk crept into his lips.

"You need not fear my motives, Robin Fellows," he assured him. "I want only justice for our people. For the Fae to reclaim the Netherworlde and take back our homeland. I understand however." He indicated his own ragged appearance. "After all, what do you really know about me? I am just a wild and untamed vagabond, who shows up bleeding on your doorstep with redcaps, and offers to take you deep into the dangerous wilderness, hunting a dangerous magical monster?" He laughed a little. "Your thoughts are written on your face. Now you are wondering if this was wise? If, now that I have you far from home and out in the Netherworlde, I might try to take from you what I want?" He nodded in understanding. "You are right to suspect," he said. "It is a wise thing, caution. Do not trust all you meet. But I swear on my former honour as a Sidhe-Nobilitas, I mean no harm to you or yours, Robin of Erlking."

"Why did you come with us?" Woad asked. "We're headed straight back to where you've been imprisoned. You didn't even think twice about coming."

"Because I know the way and you did not," Hawthorn said simply. "And because if this monster, this scourge of the woods that we seek, if it really is in possession of a Shard of the Arcania, then Eris *must not have it*. That's more important than my safety."

Robin felt a little guilty for his suspicions. The man had saved them all from the centaurs after all.

"A Fae," Hawthorn said firmly. "A *true Fae*, that is, will *never* betray another Fae to Eris." His face darkened, becoming set in hard lines. "Nothing could be worse. There are far fewer of us in the world, Robin Fellows, than once there were." He waved a hand. "Perhaps living amongst the Panthea at Erlking has made you suspicious. You should live amongst your own kind, then you would see."

Robin nodded. "The Panthea at Erlking are all good people," he said insistently.

"As am I," Hawthorn nodded. "Rough and unpolished, yes, but basically good." He nodded at the mask. "And I will prove it to you. Don the mask. Look at me, Robin, son of Wolfsbane. See me as I am and as I was, and you will see there is no malice in me. Not for you, or for your friends."

Robin peered back down at the wooden mask, so elegantly simple, laid in his hands. Its oval, carved eye-holes, the swirl of the wood-grain, and the delicate branches swooping up to cup the forehead of the wearer. Forged by strange creatures of the Netherworlde older than even the Fae. It seemed warm in his hands. Without thinking, he nodded, lifted his hands to his face, and placed the mask across his eyes.

Hawthorn smiled grimly at him.

"Respice, adspice, prospice," he said softly.

The wood seemed to shiver and writhe, moulding to the size and shape of Robin's face perfectly to frame his eyes. He felt the questing tendrils of the carved branches come alive, snaking across his forehead and burrowing into his thick blonde hair. Curiously, he looked across at Hawthorn, sitting like an old ragged peddlar under the bruised night sky. Ghost buildings at his back and a spluttering fire at his feet.

And then there was a flash across the boy's vision, green and gold, and he was blinded.

MEMORY AND MURDER

Robin blinked rapidly, disoriented. There was a great rushing noise in his ears. Hawthorn still sat across from him, but as Robin stared, a curious thing happened. The scene began to change. The gaunt and malnourished figure of Hawthorn filled out, his hollow cheekbones and thin arms swelling with health, and the dust and dirt of the road melting away from his dark skin until it shone, the shade of honey and oak. His tangled mat of hair resolved into a crown of lustrous brown curls around shining, polished horns, and his ragged, colourless clothes, half-destroyed and weathered by his time in the wilds, blurred and were replaced with elaborate armour. It was black and red, trimmed with silver in spiralling leafy patterns. The backdrop of the campfire, of Woad, and of the nighttime empty shadows of the ruined town of Briar Hill all melted away like a watercolour wash, swirling and reforming to a different place altogether.

Robin stared wide-eyed. The hill was gone. He was in a room, bright and lavishly appointed, in broad daylight. The floor beneath him was not packed earth, but marble, and the walls around him were circular, decorated with detailed frescoes showing ancient forest hunts. High above, a ceiling of white plaster arched, from which hung an ornate decorative cauldron of gold, filled with flickering candles which made the shadows in the plasterwork above them dance.

I'm in a tower? Robin thought, blinking and shaking his head.

A memory, the voice of the Puck whispered in the back of his mind.

One tall window in the encircling wall, thin and empty of glass, showed a high blue sky beyond. The stone floor was littered with thick and expensive rugs, and the air smelled faintly of soft herbs. Frankincense and candlewax.

Robin opened his mouth to speak, and found, to his alarm, that he could not. He was utterly voiceless. Nor could he move a muscle, other than turning his field of vision a fraction to the left or right of Hawthorn. He tried to look down at his feet, feeling oddly unbalanced as he realised that he could not tell if he was sitting or standing, only to find that he had no feet, or hands. In fact, his body was entirely absent.

I'm just observing, he thought. *Like a ghost. Where are we?* The room, in all its grand palatial splendour, was furnished with old pieces, but without the ability to look far from Hawthorn, he could make them out only in the blurred edges of his peripheral vision. The grand Fae, looking so strange in his noble grandeur, was sitting on a chair in this room, beside what looked to be a large bassinet.

Somehow, Robin could feel the man's emotions. Hawthorn was troubled, deeply worried and anxious, though he sat stoically, waiting for something.

We're in Erlking, Robin realised suddenly, staring at the Fae, who looked right through him, his own face lost in thought. *This is Erlking before its destruction. I can feel it in Hawthorn's mind.*

The noise of a door opening behind him startled Robin, and he heard heavy boots enter the room, though, frozen as he was, he was unable to turn to see who had entered. Hawthorn leapt to his feet, bowing ever so slightly. Robin felt a mixture of relief and concern flow from the Fae.

"You've returned," he said.

A voice behind Robin replied. It was deep and assured, but there was an undercurrent of worry in it as well. "Yes. The child? He sleeps?"

A shiver ran through Robin's consciousness. Hawthorn had taken a step or two toward the large and ornate crib, allowing it to come further into Robin's fixed view.

"He is well, Lord Truefellow," Hawthorn said, nodding. "I have not left his side, as you instructed. None have come. He sleeps like all babies, without a care or a worry."

Robin knew at that moment, the man standing behind him was his father. He strained with every fibre of will to turn his non-existent head, to see him. But this vision, or whatever it might be, kept him firmly fixed on Hawthorn.

"Is it true then?" Hawthorn asked, reaching into the crib gently. He rose, and in his arms was a tightly swaddled infant in blankets as pale blue as a spring sky. The regal-looking Fae held the child gently. "They have gone? Really gone?"

Robin's father must have taken a step closer, as he suddenly appeared on the edge of Robin's vision, standing beside him, mere inches away. He was tall, with long blonde hair. He was wearing what looked like armour, similar to Hawthorn's, but covered at the shoulder with a purple cloak. Robin strained to look to his left, to see his father's face, every part of his heart ached for it. But he could only make out the maddening line of his profile. He saw his father nod in response to Hawthorn's question.

"It is true, Lord Hawthorn," he said grimly. "The King and Queen have … gone. As is the Cubiculum. The palace is in uproar."

"Eris?" Hawthorn asked.

"No-one knows," Truefellow replied with a shake of his head. "There are conflicting reports. Rumours only. It is as my wife said. Order had fallen. Chaos reigns."

"I felt the shockwave even here," Hawthorn said, holding out the baby gently. Robin saw his father reach forward and carefully take the baby, holding it gently as though it were a precious treasure. He watched his infant self, carefully passed into his father's arms.

"There is something more," Hawthorn guessed. "Something you are not telling me. Where are the servants?"

"The servants have fled," his father replied, folding the infant Robin onto his shoulder with practised ease. The child mewled a little, nestling into his neck. Robin saw his father's hand, decked with jewelled rings, cradling his back, almost the size of the new-born baby.

"All of the Panthea have fled. They have left our service. They are going to her, I suspect. And yes, there is more I have not told you."

"The magic is gone," Hawthorn guessed, a wave of despair rolling out from him. He strode to the tall window, leaning on the sill and looking out at the Netherworlde beyond. Infuriatingly, this dragged Robin's vision along with him, tugging his father back out of sight. "I tried a simple cantrip, when I felt the shockwave, when Oberon and Titania … Nothing. I can do nothing. Not a single spell."

"It is the Arcania," Robin's father said. His own voice sounded hollow, a little shell-shocked. He jogged the baby gently, almost absently in his arms. "It is shattered, my friend."

Hawthorn spun at the window, staring right through the ghostly Robin. His face was pale. "Shattered?"

"Gone," his father confirmed. "And with it, our last defence against Eris. We are helpless. Exposed."

"How could they do this?" Hawthorn asked, reeling from this news. "The King? The Queen? How could they leave us?"

"Hawthorn," Robin's father spoke firmly and calmly, forcing his friend to focus on the matter in hand. "Eris *will* come. It is not safe for us here, for any of the Sidhe-Nobilitas. Not any longer. We must leave. If we are to survive, we must gather and go. Now."

Hawthorn looked aghast. "Flee Erlking?"

The infant Robin began to cry softly, and Robin heard his father shushing him. Making soft, comforting noises.

"Retreat and regroup," his father assured him.

Another, new, voice spoke at the unseen door. A second person had entered the tower room.

"Truefellow, Hawthorn, we are gathered in the chamber of the Arcania. You must come now, both of you." This new voice was deep and calm, and strangely hollow. All of them sounded in shock, clearly reeling from the events.

"Have you heard?" Hawthorn asked this newcomer. "Have you heard this? The King and Queen? The Arcania?"

"I have," came the calm, sad reply. "There is no time. We must mourn later. Eris' forces are already on their way. Lord Truefellow, your wife awaits you."

"Where is she?" Robin's father asked.

"The Lady Dannae is with the Oracle, and the keeper of Order. She consults with them, with the stone. What you say is true. We must all flee. Into the wild. There are places we can go. But the child…" The voice trailed off.

Robin saw Hawthorn look up with interest. He felt, rather than saw, his father turn behind him to face this newcomer, presumably another member of the Sidhe-Nobilitas, Robin reasoned.

"What of my son?" Wolfsbane asked.

"He will not survive in the wilds, Truefellow. It is too dangerous. You know this. He must be made safe. He is too young … I have spoken to Dannae–"

"You have decided this for me, have you?" Robin's father answered, a little sharply. "You and my wife?"

"Brother," the calm voice at the door said slowly. There was so much sadness in it. Robin didn't understand. "My lord, I have followed your shadow into every battle. You have *always* heeded my counsel. You *know* there is no other way."

"He is right, Truefellow," Hawthorn said, agreeing with the newcomer. "Eris will kill the child. She will kill anyone she finds. The baby is worth too much." He nodded towards the door.

"He is right. He is always right. We must go. To the Arcania chamber now. The Oracle will guide us."

"Give him to me," the voice said, and Hawthorn moved forward into the centre of the room to watch, allowing Robin's vision to slide tantalisingly to the side of the room. He still could not see fully but, from the furthest corner of his vision, he could make out his father opposite another Fae, dressed in identical armour but with a darker cloak. This man had darker, curled hair, but his face, like the face of Robin's own father, was nothing but a maddening blur.

Robin saw the shape of his father bring the small bundle up to his own face. He may have rested his forehead against the blanket, or perhaps he laid a kiss on the head of the small child, it was too difficult to make out. But even swimming in the periphery of sight, the gesture was filled with an unbearable sadness. He saw the dark-haired Fae with outstretched hands, and his infant self being passed over gently.

"The mortal world," the man said reassuringly, as though the words held magic of their own. "He will have a chance there. He will be safe. The Oracle has opened a way for me. I will take him to the woman. Your people need you here, for the evacuation."

"Ride fast," Robin's father said, and his voice was so quiet it was almost a whisper. "Protect him. He *will* live. Protect my son. Find a way to get him to safety."

Robin saw the other man nod and bow as he cradled the baby. "With my life and my death," he vowed solemnly. "*Aut viam inveniam aut faciam.*"

He turned and left, taking infant Robin with him, and Hawthorn began to walk over to Robin's father, arm outstretched to place a comforting hand on his shoulder. Sadness flowed from the Fae and Robin felt it roll over him as though it were his own.

And a piercing scream ran through his head.

GUILTY FACES

A disorienting flash of green and Robin felt his own fingers fumbling at his face. He tore off the mask, blinking rapidly. Erlking, his father…all was gone. He was back on Briar Hill in the dead of night. Cold autumn wind blowing around the dark eaves.

Hawthorn had stood, his sudden movement breaking off the strange window to the past. He looked worried.

Robin stared down at the mask in his hands. An inert, innocent piece of carved wood, but one that had just transported him across time and memory. He could still hear the echo of his father's voice.

"What was that?" Woad said. He was also on his feet, Robin saw, his back to their small circle of firelight, staring off into the dark haunted shadows of the ruined buildings.

"What was what?" Robin replied groggily. He felt slurred, as though he had just woken from a dream too suddenly. He could still faintly smell the incense of Erlking, feel the sunlight on him.

"The scream," Hawthorn said grimly. "Jackalope!"

Robin realised with a start that it had been the scream which had snapped him out of the power of the mask. He had imagined it had been somehow part of the memory, something from long ago, that cataclysmic moment when the world of the Fae was falling down around their ears. But no, it was here and now, and as he stumbled to his feet as well, the mask slipping groggily from his fingers, it came again. A shriek of pure terror, broken in voice. Somewhere in the darkness of the ghost town.

"That *is* Jack," he said, eyes wide. He'd never heard such a howl of pure terror. "Where is he?"

"Trouble," Woad said, setting off swiftly into the shadows without waiting for the others. "That's where he is! Come! Hurry!"

Hawthorn and Robin ran after him, their feet scuffing up dirt and dust in the darkness. Robin's heart was pounding. What was going on? Were the centaurs back? Had they somehow breached the walls of Briar Hill sometime in the night?

The dark streets and alleyways were a maze of moonlight and shadow. Woad scampered ahead, vaulting over low, broken walls and tumbled fences knotted with blackened ivy. They stumbled from light into darkness, picking hastily through empty shells of homes, dodging around rotted and warped furniture in the gloom, each calling out to the missing Fae. After the second scream, they had heard nothing more, and the longer their search continued, the more worry and fear built inside Robin.

"Where the hell is he?" he gasped, as the three emerged from the broken walls of a dwelling, finding themselves in a cobbled side-street, the ground half-swallowed by the relentless return of nature. "Why won't he answer us?"

"Maybe he can't," Woad said grimly. He was sniffing the air in the gloomy street. "This is bad. This is a bad smell, Pinky. He came this way, but something is all over the top of everything else. Another smell on top of his. Blood and darkness and sharp sorrow."

Hawthorn held out his hands, stopping the three of them together in the night-time street. "We will cover more ground if we split up," he said. "It's not a big place. He won't have left the walls."

"Split up?" Woad said. "Split up in the incredibly dark and spooky abandoned town in the middle of the night where we hear screams and I have *literally* just said the air smells of *blood and sorrow*?"

Hawthorn blinked at him.

"Works for me," Woad shrugged. "I'm bound to find him first. I'm a champion finder of things. I found that mask, I found–"

"Not the time, Woad!" Robin said urgently. He pointed along the length of the street. "I'll go this way, Hawthorn, the other. Woad, you're the nimblest. Climb high, wherever it's safe to do so. See if you can get a better view of the layout of this place."

Hawthorn nodded and set off at a run without further question.

"If any of us find him, shout the others," Robin called.

"Or scream in a terrified way, depending on the situation!" Woad's voice floated back as he disappeared swiftly into the shadows of a tumbled hovel of old grey bricks, scrambling up the sheer wall of the house like a monkey.

Robin ran the length of the old street, concentrating on not tripping on the uneven, broken cobbles and dodging the thick determined tussocks of moorland grass which protruded obscenely here and there, slowly eroding the town of Briar Hill.

This was such a bad idea, he thought to himself. *Split up? Have I learned nothing from pretty much every scary movie I've ever seen?* But what choice did they have? Something bad had happened. They had to find the Fae.

The path he took led him through twists and turns between the timbered ghosts of old buildings. The only sound was the slap of his trainers on the slippery dark cobbles and his own laboured breath. Minutes passed. He couldn't hear the others. His mana stone bounced against his collarbone beneath his t-shirt. Where the hell was Jackalope? Robin gritted his teeth. The older Fae was beginning to feel like more trouble than he was worth. When he wasn't being snide or dismissive, he was a walking sullen silence. When he wasn't irritating someone or other, he was disappearing in a huff, making them all panic.

But that scream had been so full of horror. Robin couldn't imagine what would make a person make such a noise.

A spluttered whimper from a darkened doorway made Robin scoot to a halt so suddenly that he almost lost his footing. It had been a sob, the most pitiable sob.

Robin ran in through the doorway. The room within was shadowy and large. The ruined building must have been a warehouse once, a winter store for grain or supplies perhaps. It was filled with inky shadows, criss-crossed struts and beams, but much of the high ceiling above had crumbled and toppled in long ago so that the moonlight fell down in grey and ghostly shafts through a latticework of black timbers.

In the centre of this room, in a patch of bare earth, the figure of Jackalope lay. The boy was on his side, knees curled up and arms over his head defensively, as though he were taking a beating. Robin didn't see why.

"Jack!" he gasped, a mixture of relief and worry fighting inside him as he ran into the room.

The grey-haired boy looked up from behind his defensive arms. His eyes were wide with fear and wet. His face a mask of shock.

"No! Don't come here. Run!" he yelled, his voice breaking.

Robin skittered to a halt, eyes darting everywhere in the darkness, trying to find the attacker. There was nothing. No danger he could see. There was only Jackalope, fetal on the floor in the middle of an open crumbling barn.

Robin edged towards the fallen boy, turning a slow circle as he did so. The hairs on the back of his neck were bristling. Jackalope whimpered quietly, drawing in on himself as if in pain. "Hold on, Jack," Robin said. "I'm here. I'm here now."

He reached out for the prostrate boy. In the shadows, he couldn't see any wounds, but the silver Fae whimpered again as though he were being cut open. He shuddered violently under Robin's hands, breath coming in tiny painful gasps. "Jack, we have to go!" Robin said desperately, wondering if he had had some kind of a fit. He tried to drag the boy up, but Jackalope was a dead weight on the floor. "Jack, please, there's nothing her–"

A movement cut him off. For a fleeting second, from the corner of his eye, Robin had seen something floating above them. Just a glance. It had been a white swish, stark against the gloom. He stared up at the open and broken roof in confusion, watching the shadows deepen as cloud banks drifted by. Jackalope had stopped gasping now but still refused to move from the floor. In fact, he huddled down tighter than before, head locked firmly under his arms.

I need Hawthorn, Robin thought. He would know whether Jackalope had tripped over a magical booby trap or inhaled guano or whatever was wrong with the boy. "I'll go get help," he said to the stricken boy, giving his shoulder a reassuring squeeze. He rose, spinning on his heel, as the clouds finally gave way and silvery light suddenly flooded into the room, illuminating Jackalope with a spotlight of moonbeams.

Horror crawled up Robin's throat, constricting his chest, as an apparition appeared. Illuminated by the moonlight, it floated directly above Jackalope. It was a shifting ethereal haze, purest white, a nebulous cloud with only the vaguest sketchy form of a person. The only seemingly solid part of it was its hands, long wicked claws which Robin now saw by the light were currently burrowing into Jackalope's hair.

Robin staggered back a step, drawing the thing's attention away from its quarry.

Twin pinpricks of eerie white light were all that told Robin that the creature had eyes at all, as it turned its head slowly and ponderously to regard this newcomer. It was utterly silent.

The horrible sight floated in the darkness above the Fae, white and sickly, a grim reaper in negative.

"Banshee," Jackalope managed.

Robin, frozen to the spot in shock, opened his mouth to reply, but the hovering spectre had sensed his presence, and its glowing head whipped in his direction. Fear hit Robin like a cold wave, almost knocking him over. Pure, childlike fear over which he had no control.

I am the boogeyman, the silent creature seemed to whisper in his mind, wordless and primal. *I am the thing under the bed, the darkness in the wardrobe. I am the tree-branch scraping your window pane at night. The face in the forest shadows.*

Malevolence rolled from the airborne creature like dry ice, covering both Jackalope and Robin in a fog of terror and the banshee, distracted by this new morsel, left the cowering Fae in the dirt and swooped instead towards Robin, disappearing completely in the shadows.

Its speed was alarming after its languid hover. It darted through the air in a flurry of whispered movement, a silver fish in a dark sea, and barrelled straight into Robin, knocking him on his back on the floor.

The banshee, ghostly as it appeared, had substance. Enough to drive the boy down onto the ground, and to grip his shoulders with its long, horribly inhuman fingers. Robin felt them grapple him through his clothes, so cold they burned in agony. The greedy clutch was so tight he felt certain at any moment to hear the snap of his own collarbone.

A wordless cry escaped him, half panic, half horror, as his hands came up blindly to defend himself, but his grasping fingers found only fog and smoke.

All else was forgotten in the darkness of the old barn. There was nothing in the world but Robin and the nightmare which pinned him like a butterfly, seeping terror from his every pore. The banshee lowered its long neck down, closer and closer to Robin's face, and for a moment, he saw the creature's features swirl beneath the white fog, like muddled paint, lumpen and unformed. And then, as the long talons reached up and closed tight around Robin's throat, the head of the monster jerked, and the smoke dissipated, revealing a face within.

Robin's heart almost stopped.

It was Gran.

His own grandmother, dead and gone, stared back at him. The same sharp eyes, every wrinkle and crease of her face the same as ever, more real and detailed than even he could remember. But Gran had always smiled, her lips turned up lopsidedly, and her eyes, for as long as Robin could remember, had been much younger than the rest of her face, filled with a twinkle of mischief, set in wrinkles like crepe paper.

The Gran above him now, blotting out the world and choking him hard enough to make blurry dark spots appear at the edge of his vision, was different.

Her face was set in hard lines, stern and repulsed at the very sight of the boy struggling. Her lips were drawn back in anger, and her eyes…her eyes were like cold marbles, filled with fury, and a pure and fierce hatred.

"Dead!" she spat, her voice, so familiar to Robin, was tinged with a bitter malice he had never heard from her in life. "Dead! Because of you! You brat!" She shook him roughly.

Robin tried to respond, but all he could do was gasp for air, choking weakly. This couldn't be real.

"All my life, wasted! To keep you safe? And for what? I'm worm food! A life of loneliness for me! Coddling a clueless, ungrateful, selfish brat! Never safe, never resting!" Her eyes burned with pure hatred.

"Not that you cared! Spoilt infant! I never wanted to take you in! Never! They made me! Threatened me! And then what?" Her lips drew back, her dentures grinding together so fiercely, she seemed like a wild dog. "What reward for me, at the end of my life? Protecting a worthless rat from an unkind world? Killed! Cast aside like some old furniture in the way, just to get to you, the special one, the chosen saviour! The only important thing in the world? Hah!"

Robin tried with shaking hands to prise the long claws from around his neck, but they held his throat like an icy vice.

"Not that you stuck around long to shed tears!" Gran spat, teeth grinding. "Oh no! Off like a rocket to a new life, couldn't wait could you? Held you back, did I? Smelly old bat! Good riddance to her. Much better off without!" Her voice had risen, screaming hatefully at him. Her cold eyes blazing. "You horrible, selfish creature! You ungrateful brat! I am dead! Because of you! It is your fault!"

Tears were swimming in Robin's eyes as he gasped for air. He shook his head as much as he could, squeezing his eyes closed against this horror.

"You're … wrong!" he wheezed. "I didn't kill Gran!"

Beneath the great weight of fear and guilt which pressed down upon him from above, there was something else rising within him.

189

The peppercorn of darkness, the strange, solid core of anger which had been flaring on and off since summer. It rose through the ghostly pressure of the banshee like a determined bubble in deep dark waters. For once, Robin didn't fight it. He needed it, this alien anger deep within him. It was not cowed by this spectre. It was not afraid, but defiant. Robin welcomed it, feeling the rage flow through his system, a wash of bracing ice, wiping his panicked mind clean. It gave strength to his hands and suddenly he found himself prizing apart the grip of the banshee.

"I *didn't* kill her!" he gasped, jaw clenched as he strained. "She would never say these things! It wasn't my fault!"

The face above him wavered a little, as though in a heat haze, as the banshee struggled momentarily to regain its grip on him. The features blurred, and Gran disappeared, replaced with another face, dark and bearded, glaring down at him furiously. It was Phorbas.

Robin was so surprised that he flinched, losing his grip on the banshee. The creature with the satyr's face slammed his head down against the hard earth, making him dizzy and nauseous. From above him came his old tutor's familiar voice, filled with cold menace.

"Oh no?" he said, snarling down at his old student. "Maybe that helps you sleep at night, Master Robin. Poor innocent child, yes? But what of me? What of old dear Phorbas, eh?"

The orange eyes of the satyr were wide with rage and indignity. "Fool I was, to accept your aunt's calling! To agree to put my neck on the line, to shepherd a snot-nosed orphan! A brainless, hornless Fae without the sense to tie his own shoes? And look where it got me! Murdered before I ever reach Erlking! My body and soul torn apart!" His brow beetled furiously. "This is the fate of those who help the great Scion. All who stand with you, you will doom! All who aid you, they will die! You, Master Robin, walk ignorantly on a path of broken bones ... and call it clover!"

Fighting off the overwhelming fear, Robin pushed back up against the creature. "Get away from me!" he screamed, horrified to hear his own voice in his ears, sounding more like the desperate whimpering pleas of a child than the defiant yell he had aimed for. "Please! Stop! I didn't mean for Phorbas to die! I didn't know ... I–"

The banshee grinned down at him, cruel and cold. "Didn't mean ... Wasn't your fault? Do you know *how many* have died for you, Master Robin? Do you know how many more *will*? Can you count that high?

190

Can you bear to? You are the calamity of the Netherworlde, not its saviour! You will lead everyone to death! To ruin! Is it not easier to die now? Give in! Sacrifice yourself for them! Spare them the pain by doing the one decent thing you can! Die, and spare the world your selfish trail of des–"

The banshee did not finish its tirade. Something had barrelled into it, knocking it aside, and the two shapes rolled off and away from Robin in a confused tangle of flailing limbs and glowing white wisps, leaving Robin lying on the ground, shocked and shaken, his hands at his own throat.

With a start, his heart thudding enormously in his chest, he realised he had been choking himself, clawing at his own neck, and he coughed shakily, rolling weakly and blearily onto his side.

It was Jackalope. The boy had forced himself up off the floor and had leapt on the back of the banshee while it had Robin in its grip. Like a feral animal, he had wrestled it away. The two figures now rolled in a glowing flurry of limbs and anger, in and out of the dark shadows and filtered moonbeams, the banshee disappearing surreally. Robin saw the flash of Phorbas the knife in Jackalope's pale hands, slashing furiously at the banshee's form. The knife was having no effect however. It was like cutting fog.

Robin heard scuffling from the doorway of the old building and turned quickly, still coughing, certain in his horror that a second banshee had arrived.

To his relief, he saw Hawthorn and Woad, evidently drawn by the noise of the struggle. They stood rooted in surprise, witnessing the scene within. Robin gasping and struggling to his knees in the dark, and Jackalope, the unlikely saviour, wrestling the apparition further in the shadows.

Robin forced himself to stand, shaking off the images of Gran and Phorbas from his mind. His heart felt bruised, the feelings of guilt and pain still fresh. Unbidden tears were rolling down his cheeks, their harsh and horrible words still ringing accusingly in his ears. But he had to focus. He had to help Jackalope.

Across the room, the banshee had gained the upper hand, and was rising slowly into the air, shining like a sickly moon, lifting the boy with it, huge claws around his neck. Jackalope's legs dangled and kicked uselessly in mid-air.

Robin heard Jackalope utter a strangled cry of pain, deep and hopeless, as the formless mist fell from the creature, and Robin stared up at its wavering face.

It was a Fae. Male and dark-haired. A young man, curling black horns rolling back from above his ears. He glared down at Jackalope from within the flowing white smoke. His pale, silver eyes filled with judgement and hatred.

"Murderer!" he spat. Jackalope stared back into the banshee's face, at the older boy with this shimmering silver eyes. His own face was ash. Pure shock, crumbling and undone.

"Slaughterer!" the apparition said, hissing the word through his teeth. "How can you bear to live with what you did to me? Snake! Betrayer! Killer!"

Robin peered between the two in confusion. The face of the banshee was so like Jackalope's. The eyes identical, the skin pale, they could have been...

"Brothers," Robin whispered into the darkness.

"You filthy coward!" the banshee roared. "You murdered me! You low, vile creature!"

A moment of silence hung in the air as the banshee loomed over its captive, judgement made solid in the gloom.

And then something barrelled past Robin, a smudge of blue, blurred and rapid.

Woad had run up behind them, vaulting past Robin and launching himself into the air. The small faun somersaulted through the latticework of moonbeams, crashing into Jackalope and the banshee like a bowling ball into skittle pins, breaking the silence of the ghastly moment and knocking the Fae to the floor.

Winded, Jackalope rolled away, clattering against a tumbledown pile of rotten old furniture and sending up a great cloud of dust.

The banshee howled at the loss of its prey. The noise, deep and utterly inhuman, shook the rafters, making the floating dust vibrate madly in the moonbeams. Robin fell to the floor clutching his head. It was like being physically struck.

Woad too was huddled on the floor, arms wrapped about his head as though he was trying to stop it from splitting. The banshee turned on him slowly, the mournful cry mercifully fading, and casually backhanded him with a clawed hand. Robin tried to stand as Woad crumpled backwards, but his legs were numb, his vision swaying back and forth wildly, and he managed only to propel himself face first into the dirt, ears still ringing.

The apparition floated above Woad, it's movements nightmarishly slow, and pinned him to the floor, gnarled hands tight around his throat, as it had done the others. The faun glared up at it, a smudge of blood at the corner of his mouth, as it lowered its head towards him hungrily. Woad froze, staring wide-eyed and frowning up at the creature.

There was no face. The banshee has stopped. It hovered, suddenly motionless, above the faun lying at its feet. There were no features that Robin could see at all, nothing but a blank mask of unbroken skin, into which Woad trained his fiery, unblinking eyes.

Nothing moved in the room. The only motion Robin could see was the rapid rising and falling of Woad's chest as he panted for breath beneath the floating horror.

It was as though someone had pulled the plug on the creature. The banshee hung perfectly still and silent in mid-air. Not attacking or retreating. Showing nothing to its intended victim. No face, no apparition. Even the smokey cloud of its body had stopped in mid-air, frozen in its ceaseless billowing.

For several seconds, nobody moved.

"Banshee stares at me, I'll stare right back," Woad declared defiantly, his bright yellow eyes glaring up fearlessly at the looming spectre. "I'm not the blinking kind of faun."

With his free hand he gestured to the others. "Now would be a good time!" he added, a little urgently.

Hawthorn rushed forward past Robin, and he saw that the old Fae had his travel pack slung across his shoulder, and was reaching into it as he ran towards Woad and the paralysed, deactivated banshee.

He withdrew a jar, large and filled with something white. Robin realised it was the salt which Hestia had gifted to Jackalope as they had left Erlking.

Hawthorn lifted it aloft and hurled the jar overarm at the creature. It sailed through the air like a spinning grenade, exploding on impact as it crashed into the banshee, covering both it and Woad in a large white cloud of salt.

The banshee reared and screamed, shaking dust from the rafters, and making Robin cover his ears again against the deafening sound. It released Woad, flailing around as though it had just been drenched in acid. Its folds whipped and snapped, steaming and smoking. And then, before their eyes, it dissolved, burning away and breaking apart like paper to a flame, grey ash blown to the wind in crumbling and dissipating fragments, until nothing remained but flickering embers and a long, fading scream of sorrow.

The salt settled like snow on the dirt around Woad.

Robin hurried over and helped the faun up, grabbing him by both arms and pulling the boy to his feet.

"How did you … what did you do?" he spluttered, his heart still racing.

Woad shook like a dog, dislodging salt in a flurry of flakes. "I'm not scared of myself," he muttered by way of explanation.

Hawthorn appeared at Robin's side, looking down to Woad. "Banshee. The creature can only show you your guilt, your own fears." He managed a grim, lopsided smile in the dark. "This one has neither. As innocent as a babe."

"But not," Woad pointed out, brushing salt and dirt from his arms, "as helpless."

"They show the darkness within," Robin said quietly, remembering what he had read about banshee back in Erlking. "They confront you … with your darkest deeds."

He turned slowly, followed by the others, to see Jackalope, standing in the shadows. The boy was wavering and unsteady, his breath coming in ragged heaves. He still clutched Phorbas, and there was blood and dirt on the side of his face. He stared at them all across the darkness. His silver eyes wide and hard behind the messy tangle of his hair.

"Well," he said eventually, when the silence in the room had grown long. His voice was flat and hollow. He still looked incredibly shaken. "There you have it. Now, you know."

"That was your brother," Robin said, his voice was quiet, but it carried in the darkness. Jackalope didn't reply immediately. The knife shook slightly in his hand. Nobody spoke.

The room was very still and quiet around them, hushed in the absence of the monster, but a terrible dread and dawning realisation hung over them all. The air was thick with it.

"Why did the banshee show you your own brother?" Woad asked.

Jackalope's eyes flicked to the faun, and then back to Robin. His lips were tight and pale.

"He called you betrayer," Hawthorn said in a low voice. "Deceiver? What is it that passed between you, boy?"

Jackalope took a stumbling step back from them, deeper into the shadows. He was still gripping Phorbas tightly, his knuckles white as bone as he tried to keep it under control. He shook his head, almost imperceptibly.

Hawthorn frowned. "Jackalope," he said, quietly. "I will have answers. I must."

Robin knew only too well what Hawthorn had said earlier. His views on betrayal. The lowest act a Fae could visit on another. Robin felt as though his stomach was sinking.

"Will you?" Jackalope replied hoarsely. "Must you?" His mouth cracked in a grim and shaking smile. There was no humour in it, and finding no footing on his face, it fell immediately. He had tried for haughty, but clearly so shaken by the banshee's attack, he could not hide his true horror.

"Answers can be dark. Not what you want to hear, that's the problem." He looked from Hawthorn to Robin, his silver eyes piercing and defiantly dry. "Like your nymph said, Scion. Truth can be ugly, right?" He was staring hard at Robin, as though daring him, challenging him to look away. There was such anger in his face, and such fear. "I kept telling you. I told you all a million times. I'm not one of you. Not one of the good guys. We can't all be perfect heroes like you, Scion of the Arcania."

"He called you murderer, Jack," Robin said. His own voice shaking a little. "Why did he do that? What happened? Just tell us. It's oka—"

"What did you do to him?" Woad asked, interjecting.

Jackalope looked small and lost and very alone, standing in the moonlit shadows of the ruined warehouse. He glared at each of them in turn.

"What did I do?" he whispered. "What did I do?" He sheathed the knife with shaking fingers, then looked back up at them, his eyes red. Robin had never seen such despair.

"I killed him," he said flatly. His words were swallowed in the dark.

"I killed my brother," the boy said again, raising his voice, as though forcing himself to say it out loud. "There. There's the ugly truth you've all been so desperate to hear. Murdered my own brother. Now you know." He panted a little, swallowing. "I killed him, in order to save my own worthless life. Is that what you want to hear?"

Robin opened his mouth to reply, but no words came. He felt as though the blood had just run out of his body and into the ground. This couldn't be true.

"See?" Jackalope said, lifting his chin at them. His mouth curled into a sneer "Didn't I tell you I didn't belong? That there was no place for me at your wonderful Erlking? Now you understand why. My brother is dead … because of me. At my hand."

He stared down at his own hands, and for a second, his face looked utterly empty. Devoid of anything, just a mask.

That boy has blood on his hands. The voices of the sisters rang in Robin's memory. He didn't want to believe it.

"It's not true," he said simply. "You're lying. Why are you saying this? You can't have–"

"What would you know?" Jackalope snapped. "You know nothing, Robin Fellows. You grew up loved, safe! I grew up in hell! I would have done anything to get out of the camps of Dis … *anything.*" His shoulders slumped. "And I did. I killed my own kind. The only person who I ever meant anything to."

"A Fae … murdering a Fae?" Hawthorn said, his voice dark and a little shaken.

"I betrayed my brother," Jackalope said, shuffling backwards. "To save my own skin. To protect my own hide. *That's* who I am … that's *what* I am … and now you know."

Robin felt sick. Woad was staring at the dirt at his own feet. At Robin's other shoulder, Hawthorn tightened his grip on his bow.

"I'm not like you people," Jackalope said grimly. "I can't take back what I did. Not ever. I'll never be one of you. I told you I didn't deserve your kindness, didn't I? I never asked for it." His eyes met Robin's across the room. They were shining. "I never asked for any of it … I don't belong here."

He turned and walked, stumbling out of the warehouse and into the ghostly ruins of the town beyond, headed in the direction Robin knew was the gates of Briar Hill.

"Wait, where–" Robin began, but Hawthorn lay a firm hand on his shoulder.

"Let him go," the old Fae said quietly. "Let him crawl back to the shadows. Alone in the wild as he has been before. As he wishes to be again. There is no place in our company for a kinslayer and a coward." His face was lined with anger only barely held in check. "There is no greater crime, to betray your own. To kill to survive. He knows the cost. It is his to bear, forever."

Jackalope had already disappeared from sight, leaving them, swallowed by the dark night.

Robin felt numb. He didn't want to believe any of it. Nearly everyone had warned him against the silver-eyed Fae at some point or another. Everyone had secrets, right? Dark moments in their past, but this? He could barely process it.

Behind him in the silence there came the soft scrape of broken glass and he turned to see Woad, squatting sadly on his haunches, rifling through the salt-strewn earth. He was collecting the shattered shards of glass, the jar which Hawthorn had thrown. He frowned at the faun questioningly.

"It was Hestia's gift to him," Woad said quietly, slowly dropping the glinting broken pieces into Robin's knapsack. "It was pretty. Seems a shame to leave it behind, even if it's broken."

"I can't believe Jackalope," Robin said hoarsely, looking up to Hawthorn, desperate for some explanation. He couldn't finish the sentence, couldn't bring himself to say that the boy had killed his own brother.

The older Fae's face was grim and stern. His long eyes narrowed. He looked old and tired. Very tired indeed.

"War makes people do things they could never imagine," he replied quietly. "Darkness is always waiting, within us all, just below the surface. We fight to keep it there. To stay in the light." He shrugged, sighing heavily. "Some of us lose that fight."

He walked out of the warehouse, beckoning for the two boys to follow him.

"There is no greater crime than betrayal," he said with feeling. "I know this first hand. Come. Let's return to the campfire. The night is not over yet and there may be more banshees on the hill. We should set a watch between us, try and get some sleep. We will leave at daybreak."

"Jack's left now," Robin said, as he and Woad followed. "Will he be okay, out there in the night?"

Hawthorn looked terribly sad. The night around them was oppressive and deep.

"I imagine not."

OLD ACQUAINTANCES

Dawn, when it finally came, brought Robin no answers. It brought trouble.

He had slept only fitfully after the events of the evening. His mind torn back and forth between Jackalope's horrible revelation and the memories of the vision he had seen under the mask. Memories of his father and Hawthorn, the shattering of the Arcania. Hawthorn had insisted he use the mask, assuage any reservations he might feel about his trustworthiness. Robin had been left in little doubt. He had seen how gently the Hawthorn of the past had cradled his infant self. He had seen how his own father had clearly trusted him more than any other to keep watch over his son, and he had felt the man's emotions. But Robin felt so unsure about everything else. How could he judge anyone, really, when people could be hiding secrets like Jackalope's? Hawthorn had said that war makes people do terrible things. Robin had no brothers of course, but could he imagine killing Henry or Woad, just to save his own life? He thought not. He certainly hoped not. He would die first himself to protect them if it came to that.

Had Jackalope's aversion to people, his self-enforced retreat from the world, living a hermit's exile alone up on the Gravis Glaciem all those years, been more than just fear of being recaptured? Had it been punishment meted out by his own guilt? Shame?

Robin had no answers to any of this.

The sun had breached the walls of Briar Hill at dawn, thin fingers poking through a cold and clammy mist, forcing away what had seemed an endless night, and Robin finally stirred from his place by the long-dead campfire, only to find Hawthorn absent, and Woad shaking him none too gently by the shoulder.

"Wha … what is it?" he asked blearily, sitting up. His back ached from sleeping on the cold floor, as though knots of moorland gorse had dug into his spine and cobbles had left an imprint on his ribs.

"We have company, Pinky," Woad said grimly. "Bad news at the gates. Come!"

He set off with no further explanation, and Robin clambered to his feet, peering after his friend in confusion through the thin mist which filled the town square, making it seem even more ghostly and unreal that it had in the night.

He was about to call out to Woad's retreating figure, when there was an alarming vibration in his back pocket.

Robin jumped, startled fully awake and convinced that he had just been bitten on the rear by a grass-snake or some other strange creature, but then, with dawning realisation, he reached into the pocket of his jeans and withdrew a small square of yellowed parchment.

His birthday present. He had forgotten all about it. The card vibrated again in his hand, fluttering in agitation as if caught in a high wind. It was a hex-message.

Robin flipped it over and watched as Karya's unmistakable spiky hand-writing slowly appeared before his eyes.

Scion. Where are you?

It took him a moment to quickly locate a pencil in one of the many small pockets of his satchel, looking up distractedly through the mist where Woad had disappeared between the sketchy buildings. He shivered a little in the damp morning cold. Leaning against his pack for support he scrawled a reply on the reverse.

Have you found Henry? Is everything okay? We've had a lot of
trouble. Centaurs.
I think we're in trouble again now.

The words disappeared as he wrote them, sinking into the paper. He waited a moment in the pale golden fog of the dawn, impatient for a reply. When none came immediately, he shouldered his pack and set off after Woad towards the gates at a jog, the card gripped in his fist.

The reply came as he weaved his way through the streets and buildings, Briar Hill oddly muffled and silenced around him. He would be very glad to see the back of the place. Frustratingly, Karya's response was not answering his questions, but demanding answers of her own.

Where are you, right now? Exactly?

Robin, paused in the street, flipped the card and leaning against a wall, scrawled on the reverse.

Briar Hill, at the main gates to the town. Are you nearby?

The reply did not come until Robin, having weaved his way through the odd ghost town, reached the gates, and was approaching the figures of Hawthorn and Woad, who he saw were standing between the gateposts, looking out and down the hill into the mists at something.

Don't move a muscle. Sending help.

Robin shook his head, unsure what to make of this. It would have to wait. He stuffed the card back into his jeans as he came up alongside Hawthorn and Woad.

"What's wrong?" he asked. "What is it?"

"They are back, Robin," Hawthorn replied, still staring down the hill. "And they are not alone."

Robin peered down at the landscape. The autumnal grasslands, with their rising swathes of heather, their dips and hollows and rolling vistas, were lost in a low ground mist, hilltops emerging below them here and there in islands in the fog. It looked like an old Japanese silk painting. The sky above was hidden by the thin mist, cocooning the three travellers and the town they stood before in a vapour through which the sun's rising light streamed like scattered gold-dust.

Robin saw at once what Hawthorn referred to.

Centaurs. They had returned. In far greater numbers. They circled and strode about in the mist below them, shadowy shapes half glimpsed. Through the morning fog it was impossible to tell how many were down there, but it was a lot. Maybe a hundred, maybe more. The ground was a low muffled rumble of thunder with their ceaseless hooves.

"We're surrounded," Woad said. "I've been all along the outer wall.

Like a desert island and sharks. Only sharks with spears. That's not a good thing."

"What did you mean they're not alone?" Robin asked, his eyes roaming over the half-hidden army below them. Their silhouettes faded in and out of view in the rolling mists. Shadow puppets on a muslin screen, backlit by the lamp of the sun.

Before Hawthorn could answer, a chill, deeper than any morning mist could account for, rolled up the hill toward the town gates where Robin and the others stood. It hit them in a silent wave, making all three shudder. The centaurs closest to the front had parted, their vast, armoured heads bent low in deference, forming an empty corridor in the ranks leading up to the base of the hill. A figure on horseback was emerged from between them.

"The mask," Hawthorn whispered. "Keep it safe. He must not take it from us. At any cost."

"He?" Robin asked, and then a lurch in his stomach cut off any further questioning. The figure on horseback came forward, resolving out of the mists into clarity like a conjuring trick, the darkest of shadows.

The man on the horse was clad in black, spiky armour, oiled and insect-like. A long feathered cloak, darker than a crow's-wing fluttered from his shoulders, drifting behind him in the mist. The hard iron-masked face of a grinning wolf looked up at them all inscrutably. Strigoi.

The man brought his horse to a standstill, the steed stamping restlessly in the mist. The centaurs were silent at his back, and for several seconds, he did nothing but stare up at them, the blank eye-slits of his iron mask unreadable, frozen in eternal scowl.

When he finally spoke, his voice was a low whisper, but despite the distance and the fog, it carried clearly to their ears.

"Well," he said softly, a cold rasp. "What treasures there are to be found, in the wild places of the world."

With a rustle of his cloak, he swung down expertly from the horse, landing heavily, his great armoured boots thudding solidly into the soft loamy earth.

"I scour this land, seeking a Shard," he said, his tone thoughtful and cold. "A Shard awakened and living in a beast. But instead, one of my hunting parties ..." With a lazy wave of his metal-gauntleted hand he indicated the horde of centaur at his back. "They tell me instead that they have run errant quarry to ground. Flushed from the underbrush. Outlaws." His masked face peered up at the companions standing by the town gates above, curiously. Its grinning maw making every word he spoke seem mocking. "Not a Shard, but still … a prize nonetheless."

"There is nothing here for you, black worm," Hawthorn called down the hill defiantly. "Your mules will not set their tender hooves on haunted soil, and we have the higher ground."

Strigoi's wolf-face tilted thoughtfully to one side. "An old man, a tender Fae-thing, and a blue runt. What odd companions you make. I was told there were four. Another Fae." His eyes roamed the hillside slowly, as if searching for another member of their party. "Imagine," he whispered up to them. "Three Fae abroad in the world like wild animals, loosed from their cages. Not knowing their place is not in the wild, but in irons."

"Your horse-brained beasts cannot count, clearly," Hawthorn said. His voice was filled with hatred. Deep resentment. Robin knew that it had been Strigoi and his ravens who had captured and imprisoned him previously. No wonder he hated the servant of Eris.

"Be that as it may," Strigoi said. "I caged you once before, fallen lord. Not long ago. Sent you to the Hive to dwell on your crimes." Strigoi stepped forward, away from his horse toward the steep slope of the hill. "You are a slippery one. You pathetic rebels always are. Slippery as eels. I think this time you will not escape the Hive. Fool me once, shame on you … etcetera." He pointed a long finger up the hill at Robin.

"And you!" he said, a note of sudden triumph in his cold hiss. "Troublemaking Fae-spawn. You are the worst of them all. Snuffling through the Netherworlde like a blind piglet. A creature unchained. There is a price on your weak and feeble head that even I cannot ignore."

He glanced back at his army, still lost in the mists. "What sport my centaurs might make of you, if only our Empress did not wish for you unspoiled. It seems a shame to deprive them of it. It would be fun to watch them fillet you."

Robin refused to be cowed by the menacing servant of Eris. They may be surrounded, and he would be stupid not to be scared, but he would certainly not give Strigoi the satisfaction of seeing it.

"As I remember," Robin called down, his voice sounding defiant. "Last time we met, you were sprawled in the mud and snow. More like a pig than I ever was."

He heard Woad gasp quietly next to him. The herds of centaur shuffled uneasily, and the temperature of the chill seemed to drop even further.

"And you fled," Strigoi noted darkly, outwardly unruffled. "A running, whimpering coward." He laughed harshly, low and quiet. "Delusional child … playing at heroes. Saviour of nothing."

The wolf mask leered at him, black iron and frozen malice. "We will see who is the beast on their knees in the mud, Robin Fellows. You will come before the Empress of the Netherworlde on your belly, like a worm, and before I am done with you, you will beg like a dog to be allowed to kiss the hem of her robe."

"Why don't you come up here and say that?" Woad yelled angrily, half-stepping in front of Robin protectively. "Maybe you're as scared of ghosts as your evil donkeys, eh? Or is it that you're worried we might have a can-opener, you … big metal moron?"

Strigoi ignored Woad's anger completely.

"I do not parley with animals," he said simply, directing the statement to Hawthorn. "I wonder though, how shallow are the beasts? This noble and united front they present. Foolish yes, but how easily they might sacrifice one another, to be spared my judgement."

He pointed up at Hawthorn. "Old one. You have tasted the nectar of the Hive already. You know its bitterness, its despair. You know the world that awaits you back there. Tell me…if I were to spare you. To set you free to roam the barrens like the aimless, sad beast you are, would you give up your spoils, I wonder? Would you surrender your charge to me?"

Robin glanced at Hawthorn, but the older Fae did not look back. He was staring down the hill intently at Strigoi, his face hard. He may be dressed in rags, his face lined and cheeks hollow, but Hawthorn's bearing was still as regal as it had appeared to Robin in his vision of the past.

"*Te futue et caballium tuum.* You will not take this boy from me," he said firmly. "You will not lay one black claw on either of them. I will not trade my life for theirs. Your offer is insulting. Not all of us are so easily bought and sold, dark one." His bow was clutched tightly in his right hand. With his left, he raised his arm, fingers splayed toward the lurking menace below.

"I would die to protect either one of these children from you … and your Empress."

"How predictably noble," Strigoi replied, sounding rather bored. "Cling to the shreds of your ideals, fallen race, if you must. But know this. You will die only when I allow it." His voice was low and full of spite. "The Hive is a place you may come to know well, a longer stay is in order, I feel. And these spawn you value? Resist if you will, you know you cannot best me. I will pry them from your broken fingers."

"Try," Hawthorn said. "The higher ground is ours." His hand flicked suddenly and the line of red gems along his bow flashed as he cast his mana. Between them, the Fae atop the hill and the servant of Eris at its foot, the earth cracked and shook, tearing open in a great fissure. From out of this maw, rocks and boulders flew, spewing out of the earth. Stones the size of cannonballs, deadly missiles aimed at Strigoi and his army.

As quickly as Hawthorn had cast, Robin saw their enemy raise his hand in response. A similar flash in the pommel of Strigoi's sword and the air shimmered around him, an invisible dome of pure mana wavering like a shield. Several of the boulders and rocks smashed and crashed into this barrier of will, exploding into harmless dust against thin air. Others flew over the dark man's head, landing with crashes amongst the centaurs in the mist, who were not so protected. The great beasts reared up in alarm in the deadly hailstorm, crashing into one another to avoid the heavy rain of rocks. Strigoi ignored their commotion behind him. He hadn't flinched at all.

"Yes, you do have the high ground," he hissed over the cacophony of stone. He hadn't taken his steady gaze from the three on the hilltop for even a moment. "Allow me to remedy that."

Strigoi clenched the fist of his outstretched hand, the metal gauntlet shrieking as his fingers ground together, and he pulled his arm back sharply.

Hawthorn, at Robin's side, was lifted clean off his feet, plucked upwards like a helpless puppet. He flew through the air and down the hill in an ungainly tumble, landing with a crash in the mud at Strigoi's feet, dragged by concentrated, invisible mana.

"Hawthorn!" Woad cried in alarm. Robin could hear the old man wheeze, winded as he struggled to clamber to his feet. Strigoi, looking down at him, splayed his fingers wide and lowered his hand a little in the air, as though about to deliver a blessing on the old Fae's head. Hawthorn collapsed back to the ground with a grunt, crushed by some terrible unseen weight, his face ground into the earth under the sheer force of Strigoi's mana.

"Stop it!" Robin yelled. "Leave him alone!"

The wolf head looked back up the hill to the two boys, as the man effortlessly kept the Fae pinned to the ground like a butterfly.

Every carved corner of the grinning wolf-mask seemed to be grinning hungrily at Robin, filled with mockery and cruelty.

"It is simple to teach a beast to crawl," Strigoi whispered. "Beasts want to, deep down. They only need be reminded of their position. As do you, so called Scion. Will you walk down the hill; I wonder? Submit to me as the submissive slave you know you ought to be? Or must I drag you by the neck also? Strip you of your defiance and your ill-placed dignity? Shall the choice be yours?"

Woad grabbed his wrist. "Pinky, he will kill us."

"Oh no, faun," Strigoi called up. His hearing clearly as keen as his skills with the Arcania.

"Your precious, delicate master is to be delivered to the Empress. Alive and … relatively … unspoiled. You, on the other hand, you I may very well kill."

Robin stared down the hill, at Hawthorn, captured and held. They were in the middle of nowhere, he thought. There was nowhere to run, even if they wanted to. Strigoi was only toying with them for his own sport. He could drag them down the hill at any moment he wished. But he wanted Robin to choose. He wanted to break him. It was what he did.

But if I do go willingly, what then? he thought. Woad would be killed. Hawthorn sent back to the Hive prison. Strigoi would find the mask. What would happen if that fell into Eris' hands?

As though the dark man was reading his mind, the Wolf of Eris held out his other hand, his black-feathered cloak billowing behind him. He beckoned Robin.

"You know you have no choices here," he said. "You will come with me, if I must kill everyone here, and break every bone in your body to make it so."

The armoured fingers glinted in the sun streaming through the fog.

"You are alone in the world, Robin Fellows," Strigoi said. "Alone in the wilderness. And no one can help you. Submit."

Robin glared at the man with boiling hatred, his fists balled at his side. He opened his mouth to prepare to tell Woad to run. He didn't know how hopeless that would be. But Robin could fight. He would fight Strigoi and the centaurs alone. He knew his mana was no match. He knew he couldn't win. Hawthorn's easy dispatchment had proved that. But maybe he could buy Woad enough time, even if only seconds, if he could cause enough confusion with cantrips and chaos, to at least give the faun a fighting chance to get away.

But before he could say a word, his hands half-raised to begin casting, there was a great rumble beneath his feet and the entire ruined town of Briar Hill shook, making timbers creak and groan. Small landslides cascaded down sloping roofs. Ancient chimneys behind them toppled and fell, crashing into empty buildings.

The centaurs below whinnied and reared. Strigoi's own horse cantered about in panic, and Woad grabbed Robin by the wrist, just as the earth opened up beneath him in a sudden large sinkhole, dropping them both down and into its dark mouth.

Shocked, Robin had time to glance down, at the ground opening up beneath him. A great pit had opened suddenly, right at the top of the hill where they stood. Portions of the rocky wall either side of the gates collapsing noisily as the earth disappeared from under it. Down there in the soil of the deep sink-hole was a tangle of green and vibrant vines, monstrously large, writhing over one another like a great nest of snakes. Robin and Woad, their footing stolen from beneath, tumbled into them, feeling the strong whips of vegetation and root wrap around them, dragging them down further. He heard Hawthorn and Strigoi both yell over the roar of the landslide. Above them, the earth which had gaped wide to welcome them, suddenly closed up again, shutting out all light and noise, plunging them into suffocating darkness as the two boys were swallowed whole by the ground.

LOVELY, DARK AND DEEP

Robin awoke to a low rumbling continuous thunder, being juddered to the bone from side to side. A very sharp pain in his head made him wince as he reached out with both hands to find himself sitting on a curved and lumpy surface. It felt as though he was in a pile of ropes. It was pitch black.

"Woad?" he called in panic.

"I'm here," came the reply, very close to his ear. "Wherever *here* is."

Robin reached out, feeling lumpy surfaces close on all sides. What on earth had happened? They had fallen into the ground. Swallowed.

"Can you make some light?" Robin asked, talking loudly to be heard above the close, continuous thunder. It sounded like they were inside a storm cloud.

A tiny flash of Woad's opal mana stone blinded him, and then a soft glowing wisp of light appeared in the faun's hand, illuminating their surroundings with a bluish, flickering glow.

"Where are we? What happened?" Robin stared around. He didn't try to stand up. There wasn't room. "Hawthorn?"

They were in a small space, perfectly spherical, as though packed inside a giant ball. The curved walls all around them were comprised entirely of thick, tightly knotted vines. They shook and rumbled, and there was a sense all around them of great motion. Occasionally, Robin's stomach lurched. He looked at Woad, wide-eyed. The faun looked more than a little disoriented.

"Did you …" Robin asked woozily. "Did you pass out too? My head is blurry."

Woad looked terribly affronted. "Fauns do not 'pass out'!" he exclaimed. He looked around their curious alien environs. "I may have taken an impromptu and very short power-nap, but that was just to regain my strength."

Robin decided there were more important things at hand than arguing with this.

"What is that noise?"

"We appear to have been eaten by the ground, Pinky," Woad supplied helpfully, looking suspicious. "And we're moving under it, at very high speed. My guess is that churning rumble we can hear is soil passing over this…thing. We're burrowing."

"We're moving?" Robin asked, steadying himself against the sway of their organic prison. "How can you tell?"

"I can feel it in my stomach, can't you?" asked Woad, giving him a look as though he were an idiot. "Honestly, you really are a brainless pteranodon sometimes. Whatever this thing is, it's going fast. Through the ground like prunes through grandma, a rolling rootball."

"Are we sinking?" Robin felt more than a little claustrophobic at being buried alive. He pictured them rolling deeper and deeper into the earth, the weight of rock and soil above them increasing with every second.

"No, not really, we're moving sideways. You really have no sense of direction, do you?"

There didn't seem to be anything to do but sit, listening to the rapid roar of ground soil washing over the strange orb which enclosed them. Robin watched Woad's face in the soft flickering light of the faun's cantrip, wondering worriedly how much air there was in their odd cage.

"Well, the spooky old ladies at Erlking were right after all, weren't they?" Woad said after a short while. "They said you'd be under the earth soon."

"Bully for them. I didn't think they meant like this," Robin admitted. He still had his pack with him, he noted with some relief, but in the same moment he realised that he had lost Phorbas. Jackalope had taken the knife with him when he had left in the night.

He felt bleakly lost without his blade.

Calypso is going to kill me when we get back, he thought bleakly, then amended this. *If we get back. We have quite possibly been eaten by a burrowing plant.*

"We left Hawthorn," he said. "We just … left him … with that creature and his army."

"It wasn't really our choice. Don't worry too much. That old guy is tough as boots," Woad replied, sounding remarkably unconcerned.

208

"He's survived Strigoi dog-face before. And escaped right from under his nose. He'll be fine … probably."

Robin didn't feel quite so sure. Strigoi clearly didn't like having been made a fool of by Hawthorn's previous escape from custody. He had a horrible feeling the vengeful servant of Eris might decide to make an example of him this time around. What would happen to him then? He voiced these concerns to Woad, who shrugged after a moment.

"Then I suppose he'll have his shaggy Fae head on a spike along the walls of Dis, as a warning to others," he predicted. "Either way, it's not something we can do much about from inside here anyway, so I don't see how worrying will help. Hawthorn clearly wanted us away from that mad crow-feathered psychopath, and away we are. We should probably be more worried about ourselves at the moment." He considered this for a moment, frowning seriously in the glimmer of his own magic light. "Although I don't really see what we can do about our own situation either."

Robin rolled his eyes at his unhelpful companion. "Well then, maybe we should just not worry about anything at all then, eh?" he said, sarcastically.

Woad beamed at him. "That's the spirit, Pinky!" He tapped the side of his head. "Now you're finally starting to think like a faun."

"God help me."

Eventually, after much rocking and high speed shuddering through the black tomb of the earth, just when Robin was beginning to worry about how much longer Woad's light cantrip could last and how much more disturbing this surreal experience would be in the dark, there was an uncomfortable lurch in his stomach, telling him that the ball of woody vines had slowed and seemed to have changed direction. It was a little like being on a rollercoaster car which was shut in with no windows. He could feel the movement, even if he couldn't see it.

"We're going up," Woad said hopefully. "Back to the surface?"

Moments later, there was a muffled crash outside the spherical walls, and their odd transportation lurched to a halt altogether. With a slow creaking of vines, the roots around them unfurled from above, like the opening petals of a great flower. Daylight streamed in, much to Robin's relief, momentarily blinded them both, and sweet, fragrant fresh air, which both boys took in great lungfuls.

As the sphere around them collapsed outward into a star-pattern of pale roots and thick fibrous vines, Robin and Woad stood up unsteadily, blinking in the brightness.

Robin had never tasted fresh air so gratefully.

They were in a large swathe of long green grass, dotted here and there with swaying clumps of poppies, countless red blood drops on a wide green skirt. The sky above them was free of mist, a high cobalt autumn bowl of blue. And to their left, at the edge of the flower-filled grass was a forest, composed of the tallest line of trees Robin had ever seen in his life. The trees soared into the sky, taller than the tallest redwood, and their foliage was a rusty golden riot of autumn leaves, reds, yellows and amber, all flashing and shimmering in the bright sunlight. The line of trees edging the long grass stretched away unevenly, further than Robin could see in both directions.

"Welcome to the Elderhart forest, you two," a familiar voice said. Robin turned away from the trees. Standing off to one side, not far from where their ball of vines had surfaced, spilling freshly turned black soil onto the green carpet like a giant molehill, there were two figures. One of them was a stranger. A very strange-looking stranger. A man, or at least male. He was easily seven feet tall, with long arms and legs. His skin was dark and whorled like the patterned bark of a tree, tinted a mossy green. His hair, a wild cascade of unlikely greens and golds, matted like wild grass to his head, and was trussed up here and there with strands of ivy and gold. This mane rested atop extraordinarily long and pointed ears. His face was handsome, in a long, fox-like way, glowing like polished green oak, although it was hard to make out much of his features, as most of his face and much of the skin of his body, Robin saw, was covered in paint of some kind. Tribal whorls and patterns in swirls of berry red and charcoal black chased across the huge man's face and body, lined with chalk and flecks of gold like crumbled autumn leaves.

The stranger was dressed, after a fashion, in the same way that trees themselves were sometimes dressed in moss and vines. 'Decorated' was probably a better term. Across his shoulders and down his back there fell a long glossy cloak of what seemed to be iridescent silk. The cloak made him look quite regal, in a primal way.

He looked exactly how one might imagine a forest might look, if it decided to come alive and go for a stroll.

The eyes of this improbably tall man were trained sharply on the two boys. They were a deep emerald green, without pupil. They were faceted, like a dragonfly's. As Robin took in the sight of this odd person, he realised that he hadn't seen the man blink yet.

The figure at his side however, was significantly smaller, dwarfed by the pagan god nearby. Dressed in a long coat of patched furs and animal hides. It was also wonderfully familiar.

Robin didn't think he'd ever been more grateful to see anyone in his life.

"Karya!" he cried, tripping over the roots as he stumbled out of the collapsed root ball, over the disturbed soil and into the long grass. "It was you? You saved us?"

The girl nodded, glancing at Woad, and looking concerned. Her brow furrowed. "Why are there only two of you?" she asked. "You told me you were on Briar Hill. Where are Hawthorn and Jackalope?"

Robin shook his head, unsure where to start. "A … a lot has happened," he began haltingly. "Karya, where's Henry? I thought he'd be with you? And where on earth are we? And who …" He looked up at the intimidating, silent figure of the huge man beside his friend.

"A lot has happened at my end too," Karya said grimly. "Evidently, we both have much to tell each other, Scion. Not much of it good. But this is not the time. It's not safe here, out in the open. Not with the beast abroad. We need to get into the forest, off the grasslands."

"How did you drag us under the earth, boss?" Woad said, excited. "That was powerful mana right there! We must be more than half a day's hard ride from Briar Hill here."

"Oh, that wasn't me," Karya told him. She indicated her companion. "This is Praesidiosilvestris. Or Splinterstem, if you're wanting to save time … which we are. Best not to trip over the high tongue, Scion, you'll only hurt yourself. He was good enough to fetch you, once I determined where in the Netherworlde you were. He's a dryad. The steward of Rowandeepling in fact. I will explain more once we are out of the open."

The dryad nodded sombrely to Robin and Woad.

"It's an honour to meet you," he said. His voice was very deep. "Your friend is wise however. It is not safe to linger out of the trees. The scourge will scent us. We will meet the fate of others." He looked around at the open meadowlands, soft green grass and wildflowers, his alien green eyes gleaming. "Plus, I dislike this open space. It is not natural to be so far from the wood. It makes me feel adrift."

211

The dryad, Splinterstem, beckoned them to follow and set off through the long grass without another word, scattering crimson poppies before him.

"But–" he began. Karya gave him a sharp look.

"Save your 'buts'," she insisted. "It's safer in the forest, there's more cover. We'll talk on the way." She seemed to consider her words. "Well, not 'safer' as such. In fact, it's pretty lethally dangerous within a hundred miles of this forest scourge in any direction at the moment, but it's at least easier to hide if we come across trouble. Come on."

"Come on where?" Robin asked, as they made their way from the open sun and began to pass into the cool dark green shadows of the monumental trees.

"To Rowandeepling, of course," Karya replied. "To the secret and safe sanctuary of the dryads. That one we talked about, where no outsider is ever allowed in." She smirked a little. "Well, unless you're as persuasive as I am, that is."

Woad sniggered behind him as they moved into the trees. He gave the faun a questioning look, wondering what he could be finding funny in this situation.

"'Save your buts', she said," Woad explained, sniggering again. "But she's the one who just saved them for us."

The forest soon closed around them, and as they walked single file behind the tall and strange figure of the dryad, Robin had time to marvel at it. He had never seen anything so immense and wild.

It occurred to him that, although he had explored the tangled woods of Erlking Hall, and although he had played in other woodlands as a child (Gran being awfully fond of the Macc forest, or rather certain restaurants on its borders), he had never before walked through a forest in the mortal world that had no path. It seemed natural to him for woods to be filled with dirt pathways, usually well-trodden and often signposted here and there with blazes and different coloured arrows pointing out circular pleasure walks for daytripper and dog-walkers.

Even in the Netherworlde, when he had trudged through the Barrowood with Woad and Karya, they had been following a beaten, meandering trackway of sorts. But here, in the vast and untamed primal spread of the Elderhart, there was no path.

Their route took them through bushy undergrowth and alongside tufty, overgrown roots. A great golden carpet of deep autumn leaves covered the floor as far as the eye could see between the endless trees, piling up here and there against the great dark boles like crispy sand dunes.

The forest itself was nothing like the picturesque woods of Erlking, or even the dark and twisted tangle of the Barrowood. It was enormous in every sense. The trunks of the trees were improbably massive, like buildings carved out of wood. They shot up all around them into dizzying heights, tall piercing columns turning the forest into a hushed city, their interlocking web of branches far overhead providing a russet and orange sky, constantly in distant, whispering movement.

Sunlight filtered down in thick, glowing beams, tinged golden by the leaves which drifted softly through it, a perpetual soft and papery snow. A constant lulling haze of autumnal butterflies.

The dryad set a swift pace through this unspoilt, autumn paradise, and they struggled to keep up. Their marching took them around, over and, on occasion, under great tree roots, occasionally rearing up out of the earth to form natural archways, bridges or tunnels. These were thick with lush moss and tiny flowers, or else hung with secretive curtains of vines and ivy. It was a dream of a forest, every child's delight.

As they moved doggedly forward, further from open ground and deeper and deeper into the mysterious sylvan wonderland, Robin filled Karya in on events since they had parted.

Karya actually stopped dead in her tracks when Robin related the news of Jackalope's to her, so that he almost stumbled into her back, knee deep in papery rust coloured leaves.

Splinterstem, their dryad guide, who had uttered not a word since they entered the forest, stopped and looked back at them questioningly.

"I can't believe it," she said quietly.

Robin nodded understandingly. "I know. It's a lot to take it. I mean, we all knew he was a little, well, harsh, but even I would never have suspected—"

"No, no," she cut him off impatiently. "I don't mean it's hard to swallow. I mean I can't believe it. At all. You're wrong."

Robin blinked at her, searching her soft golden eyes. Countless papery leaves fell silently all around them. She was frowning at him.

"I'm pretty sure I heard what I did," he said carefully, not wanting to upset her. "I mean, I was there. He told us himself. He was pretty insistent."

"Then he's wrong too," Karya insisted stubbornly, the tips of her ears a little pinker than usual. "He has to be!"

Robin didn't think it was really the kind of thing you accidentally misremembered, killing your own brother. He told her as much.

"Jackalope is a lot of things," she retorted firmly. "Sullen, proud, more than a little rude and yes, quite annoying. But I don't believe for a second he's a murderer."

"You are aware you just pretty much described yourself, aren't you?" Robin raised his eyebrows. "Minus the murdering thing."

"I would have felt it in him." She shook her brown tangle of hair irritably. "There's a darkness there, I'll grant you that much. A weight. Guilt clearly, but … murder?" She shook her head again, ignoring Robin's attempt at a playful barb.

Woad, who was bringing up the rear of their marching party, popped his head around Robin's shoulder.

"Are you sure that you just maybe don't *want* it to be true, boss?" he suggested, in a quiet voice that, for him, was almost meek. He shrugged. "You know, on account of him having those shiny silver eyes and cheek-bones and looking heroic with his shirt off and stuff?"

Karya's cheeks flushed and her mouth set in a thin line. She glared witheringly at Woad.

The faun held his hands up defensively, shamelessly using Robin as a human shield.

"I'm just saying!" he squeaked. "People see what they want to, right? Many a bad judgment made in light of a bishy dish? Remember that time Pinky kissed a Grimm?"

"Oh be quiet, Woad," Robin groaned.

Karya folded her arms. "So, he's gone then? Just like that? Out in the wilds, alone again?"

Robin nodded. "To be fair, that was always his plan anyway. To leave," he said sadly.

Karya turned away, signalling the dryad to continue deeper into the winding wilds of the forest.

"I know," she said quietly, sounding ruffled as they set off again. "But I suppose I just didn't think he actually *would*."

The morning wore on as they picked their way deeper through the woods, up and down the undulating land beneath the trees. The going was uneven, the floor of the forest rising and falling in great hills and valleys, an undulating sea, and not once so far had there been the slightest break in the trees, not once even the smallest open space or clearing. The sky was hidden from them by the canopy high, high overhead, so they traced the passage of time from the slanting of the sunbeams, the hidden orb in the sky moving the ghostly bars of light which penetrated everywhere as surely as the shadows of a sundial.

Robin continued with his tale, avoiding for now any further talk of Jackalope, a sore subject for all involved. He explained to Karya about the centaurs' return, and that they had brought with them the unwelcome and worrying presence of Strigoi himself.

"That at least makes some kind of sense," Karya confirmed, as they slogged up a wide long hill, leaning on tree boles and grabbing at low branches for support as they forged onwards through the woods. "The Shard of the Arcania is in the area, lodged in this great dangerous monster. Eris would surely send no one less than Strigoi to recover it. He's clearly been using the centaur herds to scour the hills. They're good at scouring…both in the search and torture sense. Unlucky for you lot to run into them."

"Good thing you and leafy Mr Mossface grabbed us when you did," Woad said. He was the only one of them who didn't seem out of breath. "And none too soon either. We were in a bad situation. They would have had us spear-ka-bobbed in another moment or two."

"We didn't all get grabbed," Robin interrupted the crude faun. "Hawthorn got captured. We left him with Strigoi."

"It's not like you had a choice," Karya said pragmatically. "You're no match for Eris' wolf. None of us are."

"Doesn't mean I don't feel terrible about it," Robin argued. "We just abandoned him."

"Good. He would want you to," Karya insisted. "If what you've told me is correct. He would gladly trade his freedom again to ensure that both you and that mask you carry are far out of Strigoi's reach. He told Strigoi he'd defend you both to the death. With the both of you gone, he didn't have to. It probably saved his life."

"They seemed to have some kind of personal beef if you ask me," Woad observed. "The old man and Evil-in-a-Can."

"Beef?" Karya asked, scrambling over roots. "What does bovine produce have to do with Strigoi?"

"More of a personal dislike than a merely political one," Robin elaborated, rolling his eyes at the girl. "I noticed that too."

"I doubt very much that Strigoi has ever left a pleasant impression on anyone he's ever met, to be fair," Karya reasoned, as they finally crested the current hilltop. "Even the Grimms are afraid of him. Hawthorn has his pride remember. He's lived free in the wilds since the war. Wily and clever. Strigoi was the one who finally caught him and slammed him in the Hive not too long back. That's not going to endear him to the Fae at all." She brushed errant leaves from her hair where they had fallen and become tangled.

"And for his part, I expect Strigoi will have lost face letting him escape in the first place. No one's ever escaped from the Hive before. It's a windowless, doorless pyramid of death." She looked thoughtful. "I still don't quite understand how he managed it. Given everything, it's unsurprising there's more than a little bad blood between them."

"We have to help him though," Robin insisted. "If they're taking him back to this prison. I'm not just going to abandon Hawthorn and give him up for dead."

"Hmm." Karya was noncommittal. "Honourable of you, Scion, but one thing at a time. Our business with the dryads takes precedence. You have a beast to hunt and kill, a deal with the redcaps to repay."

Robin balked at Karya's dismissive tone. They scrambled down the other side of the hill, kicking up rich golden leaves as deep as their knees. "Look, I know I owe the redcaps, and I know that killing this monster will get me off the hook, but priorities change. Someone we actually *know* is in danger here."

Karya stopped and turned again, looking troubled.

"That's just the problem," she said, shrugging in her huge coat. "More than one person we know is in trouble here."

Robin studied her face. The high canopy above undulated in the breeze, rolling dappled light over the company.

"What is it?" he asked, getting a bad feeling in his stomach. "Karya, what aren't you telling me?"

Karya sighed, and signalled to the dryad to stop.

"We'll make camp here for a while," she told him. "We all need a rest, I think."

Splinterstem nodded courteously.

"I'll go get some firewood for a fire!" Woad suggested happily.

The dryad straightened up to his full intimidating height, narrowing his green, insectile eyes at the faun. They glittered in the forest light. "No fires," he said sternly in his deep voice.

Karya dropped to the floor, sitting on a tangled root. "It's Henry," she said.

"Henry? What about Henry?" Robin demanded.

"I'm afraid ... he's been taken by the redcaps," Karya explained. "Sit down, Scion, for the sake of the fates. Your hair's all stuck to your forehead with sweat. You need to rest. Sit and I'll explain."

Robin sat beside her on the log. He dropped his pack heavily to the ground. "What do you mean taken by redcaps? Taken where? Why on earth are you only telling me this now? This is Henry we're talking about!"

"Yes, yes, I know," she snapped. "I wanted to hear your side of things too. To see whether you'd seen or heard anything through your trip. You didn't wonder why he wasn't with me?"

"Forgive me for being distracted!" Robin said. "I've had one friend admit to murder and run off into the night, and another captured by the Darth Vader of the Netherworlde. There's a lot going on! Taken by the redcaps?" he repeated, pointedly. "What for?"

The dryad had wandered some way off, standing still as a tree in a distant patch of golden light and looking upwards quietly at the canopy far ahead, as though tactfully giving the children their privacy. Woad sat cross-legged on the mossy floor opposite his friends, looking worriedly from one to the other.

"For insurance, it seems," Karya sighed. She had produced a small leather thong from somewhere within her hide coat and was using it to tie her wild mass of hair up in a pony-tail, dragging it off her neck. It was hot and still here in the great forest, despite the season, and the long morning's march through the uneven woodlands had taken its toll even on her. Robin noticed for the first time as she tied up her hair that her mana-stone bracelet looked almost black instead of its usual fiery amber. She had clearly recently used a lot of mana. He was suddenly concerned.

"Hey, are you alright?" he said, making an effort not to snap at her. "You look kind of drained."

"I've been busy," she replied matter-of-factly. "Look, I'll tell you both what I know, which isn't much." She sighed and rubbed her eyes briefly with the heels of her hands.

"Halloween night," she recapped. "You left with Hawthorn, off to the Netherworlde, but Henry hadn't turned up at Erlking, right? We all agreed this was odd."

They nodded.

"I'm sure on some level we were all just thinking he'd been avoiding the place because of Jackalope," she said. "You know what a sulking childish ninny he's been since the Fae woke up. He's always making excuses not to come, or not to hang around as much, you must have noticed. He's been pretty absent since the school year started."

Robin had noticed this of course, but hearing others confirm it still stung a little.

"So obviously, I offered to stay behind. The plan was, I go to the village, grab Henry and tell him what had happened, slap some sense into the idiot, and then the two of us would catch up to you lot in the Netherworlde, using my tearing skills to travel." She frowned darkly, her gold eyes glimmering.

"Well, that wasn't to be. When I got down to the village, the cottage was dark. Mr Drover is away down in London with your aunt of course, but Henry, if he wasn't at Erlking, should have been there, home from school by then. The door was open.. It was still snowing back in the mortal world and it was all over Mr Drover's hall carpet." She glanced up. "Which is horrible by the way."

"Is that relevant?" Robin pressed.

Karya shook her head apologetically. "I searched the cottage, no Henry, but the place stunk of redcaps. In the kitchen, there were signs of a struggle. A chair overturned on the flagstones, a smashed cup on the floor. But no sign of Henry, or of the redcaps. I tried to hex Henry but his parchment was there on the bloody floor. They were long gone."

"But I don't understand!" Robin argued. "Why would the vile little buggers take him? I'd already agreed to do as they said. When they came to Erlking to collect on their debt. I said I would honour it! I promised to come to the Netherworlde and stop this monster, didn't I?" He was furious. "Didn't they trust me? Isn't my bloody word good enough?"

Woad shook his head in bewilderment. "Poor Henryboy," he muttered quietly to himself. "He is so popular with the bad things."

"Popular?" Robin said, aghast. "He's captured more times than the Doctor's bloody assistant!"

The faun looked up confused. "What doctor?"

"Never mind," Robin waved the question away irritably. He looked desperately to Karya. He was furious with the redcaps, but with himself too for thinking they would be reasonable or honourable. They had made deals with the redcaps in the past and been betrayed before, and now that he thought of it, when the two redcaps had left Erlking, they had seemed decidedly smug, and had assured him they had their 'insurance'.

Horrible, deceitful little things! They must have already waylaid Henry at that point. Maybe had him tied up in a bush or goodness knows where like a trussed pig, before they even dragged Hawthorn to the door, acting like good Samaritans.

"Where would they take him?" he asked Karya. "How do we get him back?"

"They would take him underground," Karya explained, picking thoughtfully at moss growing on the bark of their log. "The network of barrows and tunnels which the redcaps own, they run further than anyone knows, all under the Netherworlde. They would have to get to a Janus station first, to cross over from the mortal world, the same one they used to get to Erlking. And then once in the Netherworlde, they would need to get to a barrow entrance."

She smiled grimly. "I knew I had limited time. Once they got Henry underground, we would never find him again. Never. Not unless Deepdweller wanted us to. And if for any reason we failed to kill this thing marauding the forest, they'd keep him forever."

"So you gave chase, boss?" Woad asked grimly.

Karya nodded. "Your aunt was away so I couldn't use the Erlking station. Hestia couldn't contact her either … bloody farce! I mean, what is the point of leaving a number if you're not there to answer it? Anyway, I left Hestia's trying and gave her Henry's hex-message parchment in case she got through. I knew that the nearest Janus station to Erlking, the one they must have used to get to the human world with Hawthorn in the first place, was across the moors, near to the village known as Howarth. It's above the village, in a fairly remote spot by a waterfall. I tracked the redcaps there. The smell of Henry was mixed with them. When I flipped over to the Netherworlde, I followed their tracks on this side. Smells are stronger

219

here. The air is clearer. They were easy to follow and, as I suspected, they were headed for Spitrot. It must be the nearest way into their warrens."

"But Henry isn't with you," Robin pointed out. "And that's a lot of ground to cover on foot with a prisoner in tow. It took us forever just to get to Briar Hill, which is only half the distance, and we were riding extremely fast cats fuelled by the mana of four people."

Karya shook her bracelet at him testily, rattling it in his face. "Why do you think I'm so drained, hornless wonder?" she rebutted. "I've been snapping back and forth, tearing across two worlds non-stop like a bloody ping pong ball, trying to cover as much ground as possible to find them. To head them off. I completely exhausted my mana. But … I did eventually find the redcaps. Terp and Tine, or Swar and Feega, whatever the hell they called themselves."

Woad's eyes lit up. "That's good news! And Henryboy?"

Karya shook her head. "It's *not* good news," she said. She looked at Robin. "I didn't find them alive."

Robin felt his blood run cold.

"Centaurs," Karya said. "I'm almost sure of it. The tracks were muddled and confusing, the earth all churned up, but I can read a fight written in the earth like you can read one of your books, Scion. It's clear as day to me what happened. The redcaps, with their bartering chip, ran into some trouble of their own. One of Strigoi's centaur patrols, same as you did. Only unlike you, they didn't have powerful Earth mana to help them escape." She looked stern. "Centaurs kill for sport. The redcaps are dead. Very … extremely dead. I found their heads on spears driven into the ground." She shivered a little. "Still had those silly winter hats on top. But good riddance to them, treacherous little demons. The good news … kind of, is that there was no third spike." She looked at both boys. "No Henry."

"He got away?" Robin asked. It seemed unlikely, though he was massively relieved to hear that his best friend had not been decapitated by evil horse men.

"Henryboy has a good head on his shoulders, after all," Woad nodded sagely, giggling a little with nerves. Both Robin and Karya gave him a sharp look.

"I couldn't track Henry," Karya admitted, sounding extremely irritable to admit her own limitations. "There were too many prints, too much churned earth, and it had rained heavily. I couldn't pick out Henry's smell or even guess in which direction he had fled." She looked genuinely worried. "They wouldn't have taken him prisoner. He's just a mortal. They're not highly prized here. If he hadn't run off, I would have found his head.

Robin took a moment to digest this grim news. "So what you're saying …" he said slowly, "is that Henry, *our* Henry, who let's remember, once got lost in the herb garden at Erlking for a solid hour," he sighed. "Is lost and alone somewhere in the wilds of the grasslands?"

Karya shook her head. "Not the grasslands, I don't think," she said thoughtfully. "As I told you, I'd been travelling all over, following these tracks. The Elderhart forest is large, it sweeps alongside the edge of much of the grasslands like a border. This scene I found, where the redcaps were killed, where Henry fled, it was in sight of the tree line."

"You think he ran in here?" Robin looked around, as though expecting to see Henry waving at them from around a nearby tree trunk. Henry obviously made no such appearance. The woods were solemn and peaceful around them, the only movement in the air the soft drift of leaves, flickering in the sunbeams as they twirled, making the air in the distance twinkle like gold-dust.

"Makes sense to me," Woad said. "Open hills full of centaur everywhere, barren and featureless moors, or a good old wood to hide in. I know which one I'd choose. I'd make a bee-line for the tree-line."

"Well, that settles it then," Robin stood up decisively. "We have to find Henry, right now." The thought of him lost and alone, maybe even wounded, somewhere in this sprawling, primal expanse made Robin very uneasy. Karya grabbed him by the wrist, stopping him.

"Scion, think for a moment," she counselled. "The Elderhart is vast. I mean, *extremely* large indeed. It's the size of Wales. And Henry, for all his lanky gangliness, is comparatively small. It would be like looking for a needle in a haystack."

"Well, we can't just leave him, can we?" Robin threw his hands up. "It's Henry! I don't care if he has been a pain in the backside lately. He's not going to last out in the wild woods in a strange world on his own. You know what he's like! He'll get eaten by wolves, or starve to death, or poison himself with the wrong type of mushroom, or lose an arm to a septic splinter–"

"I'm not suggesting we abandon him!" Karya snapped, stopping Robin's worried tirade. "He's an Erlkinger. We don't abandon each other. You are not the only person here who cares about Henry." Her eyes shone angrily at Robin, who thrust his hands into his pocket, chastised.

"But," she continued, taking a deep breath, absently running her fingers over and over her dark and drained mana-stone bracelet. "There is a creature loose in these lands, at large in these very woods. It is fuelled by a Shard of the Arcania, and very bloody dangerous. *We* need to find and stop *it* before *it* finds Henry." She let go of Robin's wrist, seeing that he was visibly trying to calm himself down.

"Look," she said. "If we do what we came here to do, stick to the plan, find and kill this thing, it solves all our problems. The creature stops destroying towns and haunting the forest. The debt to the redcaps is paid and our dealings with them are done forever, and the dryads …" She pointed emphatically at their guide, "… have their king avenged. When I couldn't find Henry, and I found you two instead, I made a pact with this one. Splinterstem here was patrolling the edge of the forest, close to where I found the … remains of the redcaps." She glanced over at him. "I was lucky to find him."

"There is no luck," the dryad replied, looking over. "Only the will of the forest that brought you to me, great one."

"Great one?" Robin mouthed the words at Karya in confusion. She looked distracted.

"Don't even ask," she said dismissively. "He's been calling me that all day. Look, we do what we planned to all along, and when the beastie is dead, Splinterstem has promised that the dryads themselves will find Henry for us. They know this forest better than any of us. And they have better reason that anyone to want this monster dead."

Robin glanced at their guide. He was looking solemnly at them from between the trees. He nodded slowly. "Bring peace back to the forest," he rumbled. "And the services of my people will not disappoint you. We will locate and return this human to you."

"If he's not been eaten by the scourge before then, of course." Woad noted dutifully.

Robin walked a little way off from the others, agitated and worried, running his fingers through his messy blonde hair and lacing his hands on top of his head.

More than anything else in the world, he wanted someone to tell him what to do for the best. He would have given anything to have Aunt Irene fix things. She always seemed to know exactly what to do. Jackalope was lost to them, Hawthorn was captured, Henry wandering the Netherworlde alone. None of these people would be in this situation if it wasn't for him.

His awakening of the Shards, back on the Isle of Aeolus, had set events in motion which had put his friends in danger, as well as loosing monsters on the Netherworlde, destroying villages and harming an ancient race who wanted nothing more than to be left alone in the deepest woods.

"Saviour of the bloody Netherworlde," he muttered angrily to himself. Unbidden, he heard the voice of the banshee in his ears, echoing in his Grandmother's voice. *You walk a path of broken bones, Scion.*

Was this what it meant to be the Scion? To court disaster at every turn? How did he even begin to fix everything?

Staring up into the distant golden sea of leaves undulating far above him, watching them drift down through the sunbeams, an endless quiet rain, it was Gran's voice which rose in his head again in response. But this time, not the harsh false-Gran of the banshee. The voice of his real Gran, from memory, long ago.

"Snakes and ashes, Robin," she muttered good-naturedly in his mind. "Pick your bottom lip up off the floor before you trip over it. If things have gone wrong, don't mope and wring your hands about it. Ain't nobody in this life going to make everything better for you. When things fall down, you pick them up. And if they look too heavy and too many, then you pick them up one at a time, 'til your arms are full again."

Robin smiled a little to himself, despite his worried mood. Of course, at the time, Gran had been talking about an armful of laundry that Robin had dropped down a flight of steps at the upstairs laundromat near their house. There had been socks and underpants everywhere, strewn down the staircase in a cloth waterfall. A tangled mess. He must have been really young at the time, maybe six or seven, as he remembered being on the verge of tears about the magnitude of his disaster.

But the same applies here, he thought to himself. *Pull yourself together. One thing at a time.* Taking a deep breath, he ran a mental checklist. Find this monster, kill this monster, find and save Henry, find and save Hawthown, home in time for lashings of ginger beer and all that nonsense. He took another deep, settling breath in through his nose, breathing in the rich and spicy air of the Netherworlde forest. That's what the Scion would do. Puck it all.

He turned back to face his friends, resolved. Karya and Woad were looking at him with expectant concern. He realised, to his surprise, that they had both been waiting for him to make a decision.

In all their time together, especially in the Netherworlde, Robin had always felt like the clueless one, dragged along and protected. He'd never once thought of himself as a leader.

"Well?" Karya said. "What are you going to do?"

"I'll tell you what," Robin replied with determination. "I'm going to pick up my socks and underpants."

The girl and the faun exchanged looks of subtle concern.

SCOURGE'S WAKE

It was perhaps a testament to the strength of their friendship, or maybe it was simply that they didn't know what Robin was talking about and assumed it to be a common mortal-world saying, but neither Karya or Woad had questioned him.

They would travel onward to the dryads' haven, they would hear what the guardians of the great forest had to say about this Shard-monster, and they would take things from there.

They marched for the remainder of the afternoon, covering a great distance within the soft shade of the wood. The forest became deeper and wilder the further into its heart they delved. The autumnal trees became bigger still, the great roots a latticework over deep valleys filled with leaves like rivers of rust. Pollen hung in the air, drifting silently, countless tiny spirits, and above and around them came frequent reminders of the wild and untamed land through which they travelled. Birds, flushed from the deep undergrowth at their passing, scuttled into the air in bright clouds of complaining noise, disappearing into the tumultuous air above them. The canopy itself was a patchwork of autumnal grandeur. Blazing maple oranges, reds as dark and rusty as old blood, yellows rich as sunlight through honey, all vying for their eyes' attention, constantly changing, a shivering skin.

Robin saw wild rabbits, pale and long eared, much larger than any he'd seen back home, with bright red eyes like drops of blood. Other small, scurrying creatures, with twitching noses and long, sinuous tails, disappeared into hollow trees and bushes as the hiking company approached, climbing hills or following deep ravines along which cool clear streams cut a path.

Karya slapped the back of Robin's hand at one point. He had stopped to observe a particularly large snail which clung to a gnarled tree trunk. It was enormous, the size of a house cat, and its spiralling shell was mossy green shot with iridescent blues like the wings of a dragonfly. Robin had been about to do what any boy coming across a curious thing in the wilderness would have done, and poke it.

"What was that for?" he asked, pulling his hand back.

"Unless you want to spend the next few hours hallucinating vividly and gibbering nonsense about being one with the universe, before later succumbing to a toxin and dying in a pile of leaves, foaming at the mouth …" she said sternly. "Don't … touch … the veil-snails."

Robin shook his smarting hand a little, looking at the pretty snail with concern as she walked off again.

"In fact, don't touch anything," she said without looking back. "And definitely don't eat any berries or seeds. I'm not coming back here in a hundred years to wake you up with true love's kiss or anything ridiculous like that."

Robin was reminded on several occasions that the Netherworlde was a place most alien to him. Certain indigenous things he recognised by sight. There by the base of a tree grew a cluster of snapping foxgloves, growling softly at them as they passed and shaking their petals defensively. Over here was a cluster of Needyberry, which he remembered being told never to touch, unless he planned to spend the rest of his life touching it.

He even thought he recognised a large patch of Mobatom mushrooms, growing in long grass in a small clear space between several trees.

But there were many things, poisonous snails aside, which were utterly new to him.

Woad pointed out a cluster of red ivy clinging to a tree, which he explained was commonly known as burning-spite. Leaning close, he made a face, sticking his tongue out and screwing his eyes up. To Robin's surprise and delight, the crimson leaves shuddered and rolled together, forming themselves into a passable caricature of the faun's impish face. They mimicked his expression, sticking out a red papery tongue of leaves and returning the raspberry in a dry rattle.

Woad, however, soon grew tired of chaperoning the Scion, and eventually abandoned the rest of the party stoically stamping through the crunching undergrowth, taking instead to the branches high above them, where he kept pace like a happy blue monkey, gleefully pursuing the dark, black-furred squirrels of the Netherworlde from tree to tree. His whoops and shouts, and the loud and chittering complaints of the harassed wildlife were the loudest thing around them in the hushed endlessness of the forest.

It occurred to Robin, as his legs grew tired and his clothes matted to his back with sweat, that they were following a mysterious and unknown creature deep into a forest where no outsider ever went, or at least, never returned from. There was no path to follow back. They had not even followed a straight line. Should their guide decide to abandon them or worse, he doubted even Karya could find their way back out again from this tremendous expanse.

He didn't worry too much about it though. He was too exhausted to care by this point. It wasn't as though they really had any choice in the matter. Even if he'd had a trail of breadcrumbs to leave behind them, they probably would have been eaten by hallucinogenic snails, and at least he hadn't seen any giant spiders lurking around in the darkness of the woods, wrapping up dwarves by the baker's dozen…yet.

Thankfully, as the light in the forest began finally to dwindle, and the shadows between the trees grew richer and fuller, their guide stopped ahead of them, standing between two trees at the lip of a steep rise they had been climbing for some time.

"We will go no further here tonight," he told them. "The sun sets. It's not safe to move about the forest in the dark. Not with the scourge at large."

"How do we even know it's in this area of the forest, though?" Woad asked, swinging down out of the treetops. "I mean, it's a big place, the beastie might be nowhere near here. It could be any …"

The faun's words trailed off, and as Robin and Karya joined Splinterstem at the top of the hill, they saw why. Before them, the next valley was a wasteland. A great swathe of trees had been blasted to the ground, ancient timbers shattered to matchsticks and burnt to stumps and ash. It was a shock, to see this great empty swathe of grey and black after so much lush golden forest. The area was dead and destroyed, as burnt and levelled as if a comet had thudded into the earth, obliterating all life.

"What was this?" Robin asked quietly, scanning the large area of destruction. Beyond it, where the valley rose up again, the golden trees continued as always, but between here and there, there was nothing but grey shrivelled death. It looked like a battlefield. "A forest fire?"

The dryad shook his head. "No," he replied, sadness in his voice. He looked to Karya. "Great one, this is the work of the scourge."

"This whole area?" Karya said, her eyes roaming over the ghostly blight on the forest. "It's completely decimated."

"The creature," their guide said, slowly, keeping his voice even with some effort. "It … feeds. On the life of the forest. I have seen it with my own eyes. It takes the essence of the land into itself, like a sponge." His faceted insect eyes narrowed. "It grows in strength and size, and leaves nothing behind but ash."

He looked down at Karya. "You must stop it." Karya glanced at Robin.

He couldn't tear his eyes away from the vista of destruction. He hadn't really given a great deal of thought to what this monster was. He knew it was something infused with the Shard of Earth, a wild thing on a rampage, and he supposed he had formed some kind of blurry image in his mind, something between a troll and a wild boar or something.

Looking at the extent of the devastation before him now, this scar on the forest, it occurred to him for the first time that this could be something much much worse.

"You've seen it, you say?" he said, trying to keep his voice as light as possible. "What would you say it looks like?"

The dryad seemed to consider this for a long while, peering down with infinitely sad eyes at the destruction of the valley before them. In this area of felled trees, for the first time all day, they could clearly see the sky, open above them. Twilight was falling fast, the first bright stars of the blinking into view like diamonds on velvet.

"Like a serpent," Splinterstem said eventually, in his deep voice. "A great and terrible serpent of the earth, with many teeth."

Robin swallowed hard. "Ah," he said.

They camped there for the night, hidden in the trees on the lip of the blasted area of forest. The dryad seemed strangely intent on playing the good host to his odd guests, and by placing his hand on the earth where they set their camp, he had caused great cushions of thick and springy green moss to bloom out of the grassy ground, upon which Robin and the others fell, exhausted and grateful. It was the most comfortable they had been since leaving Erlking.

They ate a supper of cold meats and cheese, all vocally blessing Hestia to the heavens for her diligent packing, especially as Splinterstem forbade any fires to be lit.

All were too tired to talk of much, and as night fell, and the darkness under the trees began to glow with a thousand yellow fireflies, Robin drifted into an uneasy slumber.

HERE BE …

Robin stumbled through the snowfield. Icy winds lashed at his face, throwing blisteringly cold ice crystals against his frozen cheeks. The white powder tipped over the top of his winter boots, tumbling inside. It was almost as high as his knees as he pushed through it, hugging himself for warmth and desperately trying to keep his teeth from chattering.

Above him on the heartless and empty plain, stretching in white nothingness all around, the chill blackness of the night sky was dressed in billowing skirts of green and yellow light, a majestic borealis, curtains of light roaring above the wind.

I'm going to die out here, he thought to himself with perfect clarity, teeth chattering. *I'm never going to make it.*

Ahead of him, through the foggy curtain of the heavy snow, there was the shadow of a figure. Robin made his way slowly and painfully toward it, the icy gales lashing at his back with every labouring step.

The blurry figure in the snowstorm slowly resolved into a girl, standing with her arms folded, her long hair whipped away to one side.

"Nice night for it," she said cheerfully as he approached. If she felt the cold at all, she didn't show it. She was wearing a black top and jeans. The dark t-shirt whipped and cracked around her waist in the winds. She glanced around. "Really though? *This* is what you think of me?" She shook her head. "Shame on you. Come on, Blondie, I have a better place to play."

She grabbed his hand and pulled him forward as she turned and strode off through the snow. The lights faded in the sky above, the borealis winking out, and the world was plunged into total darkness. The wind died altogether.

"You know it's going to eat you alive, don't you?" Peryl said, in an unconcerned way, as though she were discussing the weather.

"The darkness?" Robin blinked, stumbling forward, still gripping her hand. Her fingers were icy, but the cold around him had disappeared altogether. Instead of snow powder around his boots, there was the rustle now of dry leaves.

"No, dummy," she laughed. "Although, that doesn't hurt as much as you would think … trust me. It's actually quite painless that. At the time anyway. Like drinking treacle."

In the darkness, he sensed her shake her purple head. "No, the hurt comes later with that one."

There was a faint golden glow ahead. It was in fact growing all around them.

"I didn't mean the darkness, although that's a distinct possibility, unless you get your act together of course. I meant the drake." She stopped in front of him suddenly. "That might hurt more of course. Not a clean business."

Robin blinked and stared around in confusion. There was enough light to see by now. They were indoors, in some kind of a golden corridor. The walls and floor were lined with odd, geometric patterns, and they seemed slightly translucent, as though carved from amber.

"I'm dreaming again, aren't I?" he said, noting that although there was enough light to see by now, she hadn't released his hand. It didn't feel as cold either, although whether her hand was becoming warmer, or his cooler, he couldn't readily tell.

"Either you are or I am," she replied. "Who knows? It's bugging me too, to be honest. But I thought while we have a moment's peace together, you ought to be prepared at least."

"Prepared to be eaten?" He wondered idly how one went about such a thing. "What's that humming?" Robin asked. There was indeed a low and persistent drone all around them. It sounded sleepy.

"Oh, I'm the queen bee these days," she replied cheekily, as though this were deliciously scandalous gossip. "Haven't you heard? Out with the old green-haired misery and in with the new?" She stopped walking and turned to face him, her purple hair falling messily over one eye. Peryl was smirking. "Power changes hands, you know. I watched him fall as I rose. It was delicious."

"I don't like it here," he decided. "This feels like a bad place. There's no air. No light either. Not real light. What did you want to tell me?"

"Only that you catch more flies with honey than vinegar, superhero of the Arcania," she said, her violet eyes roaming his. "Watch out for lies. Words are honeyed, but it isn't just bees that hide a sting. You're going to have to see past things, to the truth. I'm giving you a fighting chance, that's all."

Robin was so confused. "Penny, you're not making even a little bit of sense. Where are we?"

"The Hive, of course!" she whispered gleefully, as though they were naughty children sneaking into the cinema. "But don't tell anyone. I don't know you're coming yet, the other me, I mean. And I won't be pleased to see you when you get here, that's for sure."

"You're not pleased to see me?" Robin replied awkwardly.

She gave him a weary look, one eyebrow raised. "Well, there's me … and then there's me. And you know exactly what I mean by that, don't even pretend you don't."

Robin had no reply for this. A small part of him realised that he was talking so quietly in this dream deliberately … so as not to wake up the Puck. This made perfect sense, as dreams do at the time.

"I may have put the peppercorn of darkness in that happy-clappy rainbow soul of yours," she said. "But you threw the toaster in my bath-water, so you can't blame this mind-meld entirely on me."

"Why warn me?" Robin asked her.

"You really have no idea how clueless you are if you don't know why. That's the problem with you white-hats." She regarded him curiously. "You always assume everyone is as well-meaning and as dashed jolly decent as you are. It's a stupid and dangerous way to live. It's going to get you killed."

"I know what I'm dealing with," Robin said, strangely determined not to look weak in front of her. "I can handle the monster. I can defeat the scourge."

She clucked her tongue and let go of his hand, dropping it suddenly.

"Yeah yeah, I'm sure you can, Conan. Just don't get stuck in its throat." She tossed her purple hair. "You haven't even figured out what it is yet."

The amber light around them was suddenly fading fast, and the cold was returning.

"What is it then?" he asked. She was slipping away into shadows. It felt as though he was passing out. *Can you fall asleep in a dream?* he wondered absently to himself.

"It's a dragon, dummy," she said with wicked relish. "A flightless dragon of the forest. I saw it born. I know its secret. And you sir, are no knight."

THE BROKEN HEART OF THE FOREST

Robin's eyes shot open, and immediately squeezed shut again. Bright sunlight was stabbing down from between the treetops above him, dappled and shimmering. Disoriented, he realised with a jolt that he was moving. It felt like he was cradled in a bower of branches, a stiff hammock, and the canopy overhead was sliding by, strobing what looked like noon-time sun in and out of shadows.

"Whathebloodyhell!" he rasped, the words all tumbling out of his mouth in surprise and, wincingly, rather more high pitched than he'd intended.

Coming around more clearly, he realised that he was being carried, like a small doll in the long arms of their dryad guide. Splinterstem's long, surefooted steps a rocking rhythm that was almost lulling. The large, oddly green-tinted darkness of the dryad's face looked down at him inquisitively. Robin could see himself reflected hundreds of times over in the faceted, emerald eyes.

"Pinky! You're awake!" came Woad's carefree voice from somewhere below them. "It's about time, lazybones!"

They were walking through a deep, wooded gully, the floor in this part of the forest naked of any fallen leaves. Instead, a carpet of soft thick moss, dotted here and there with clusters of tiny bright red and yellow flowers, like splashes of paint, passed beneath them. Karya was beside Woad, and she glanced up with a smirk.

"I second that," she said. "Talk about sleeping like the dead. We couldn't wake you for a hatful of gold this morning. Would have been worried you were dead if it hadn't been for the snoring. Sounded like someone cutting down trees in the forest."

"And the drool," Woad added helpfully, his scampering feet kicking up small clouds of pollen from the springy, mossy floor, their motes shimmering in the sunbeams. "Dead boys don't drool." He made a thoughtful face. "As far as I know, anyway." He elbowed Karya. "Hey boss, that's a good name for a band, right?"

"So ... you ... carried me?!" Robin could feel his face burning red with embarrassment. He looked up to the large man hefting him through the forest like spindly-legged luggage. "Erm ... you can put me down now ... thanks," he muttered, self-consciously wiping his mouth with the back of his sleeve. "I'm fourteen, not four."

"You're only *just* fourteen," Woad said with a raised finger. "Like, one *inch* over thirteen, if you ask me."

The dryad, Robin noticed, gave Karya a questioning look, to which she replied with a nod, before releasing Robin from his grip and letting him down to the floor.

Robin had intended to leap down in a nimble and manly fashion, to prove that he didn't need carrying anywhere like a helpless child. The intended effect was somewhat ruined by the fact that one of his legs was completely asleep, so that instead he fell on his face like a sack of dropped potatoes.

Woad sniggered helplessly as Robin scrambled back to his feet, secretly thankfully for the soft carpet of moss.

"Bloody, bloody hell," he muttered as the faun passed him his satchel, which he had been carrying. He swung it onto his shoulders and looked around. "Where are we?" he asked, still a little bleary. "What time is it anyway? And what do you mean you couldn't wake me?"

Karya rolled her eyes at him and picked a small tangled branch out of his mussy blonde hair with a kind of grudging affection.

"One at a time," she said. "We're still in the forest obviously, where else would we be? But we've covered quite a lot of ground since we set off at dawn."

"It's almost dinner time," Woad said, answering Robin's second question. "You slept right through noon. I think there's only a couple of hours left before the sun goes down again, lazy Fae. We couldn't afford to waste time waiting around for you to catch up on your beauty sleep though."

They all set off walking again, passing out of the mossy clearing and back beneath the familiar repetition of the tremendously large tree trunks. Robin struggled to keep up, stamping his tingling foot to try and wake it up. He wasn't about to embarrass himself further by telling them that he couldn't walk fast yet as he had agonising pins and needles in his left buttock.

"And as for waking you up," Karya said. "Exactly like I said. We couldn't. You were sleeping so deeply. I actually wondered if you'd been enchanted." She glanced at him with narrowed golden eyes.

"You haven't, have you? Been enchanted I mean?"

Robin gave her a deadpan look. "Only by your charming personality," he quipped.

She blew air down her nose. "Good. That's something at least. Maybe you were just exhausted, I don't know. You were raised mortal. You might be Fae but the human world has still made you softer than a soft boiled egg. The point is, we tried for a good half hour and Woad even checked to make sure you hadn't licked any snails without us knowing about it. We couldn't wait around for ever. Our guide offered to carry you."

"Well … thanks for that," Robin said, grudgingly. He was trying to remember what he had dreamt about but it had slipped away to the back of his mind, the way dreams do. Tantalising glimpses on the tip of his tongue. Honey-light and whispers and cold hands?

As they marched onwards through the deepness in the late afternoon, he attempted to tell Karya about it.

"A dream about what?" she wanted to know. Robin scratched his head, noticing how dusty and grubby his hair was. A centaur chase, a run in with a banshee and being dragged hundreds of leagues underground will do that for you. He wished for nothing more than a river to clean up in.

"It's all muddled," he said, frustrated with himself. "But it felt … I don't know … important. Something about … bees? There was a humming, I think."

"Bees."

"Kind of … and a queen, and being eaten alive. I distinctly remember being told something about that."

Splinterstem and Woad had wandered a little ahead while Karya and Robin talked, and now Karya touched Robin's arm, causing him to stop a moment. She checked to make sure they were out of earshot of the others. "It might be nothing," she said. "I don't want to worry Woad, you know he thinks you belch rainbows and the sun rises and falls on your command. Also, I don't want to spook our guide if I can avoid it, but when I tried to wake you up, something odd did happen. The others didn't see it."

"Odd how?" he asked.

"Well …" She looked a little concerned. "You opened your eyes for a second, you know, how people do sometimes when they're asleep and if they're weirdos, and they … well, they weren't blue. They were green. Bright green."

Robin frowned at her. "That's only ever happened when–"

"When you become the Puck, as you call it, yes I know," she said impatiently. "Like I said, I don't want to make something out of nothing. For all I know your eyes are always like that when you're asleep. I'm hardly in the habit of sneaking into your room at night and peeping under your eyelids. But…given the situation." She shrugged, trailing off. "Also, after I saw your eyes, I looked down and your mana stone was … well … dark."

Robin automatically touched his mana stone around his neck, glancing down. It was its usual green grey, shot through with silver.

"Dark?"

She nodded. "Listen, I know you've kind of lost control a couple of times recently. Maybe it's just your age, who knows? I just think you need to keep it in mind. Focus on the mana-management techniques Calypso has been teaching you."

They set off walking again, for fear of letting the dryad and Woad get too far ahead and out of sight.

Karya was right, Robin thought. He had lost control on more than one occasion. Throwing Jackalope across the room back at Erlking, making all the stones explode when Hawthorn had been trying to teach him a basic cantrip, throwing half the wall of Briar Hill down at the centaurs. That last time had really taken it out of him. Even Hawthorn had been concerned when he had passed out. Was his fear a reality? Was the Puck really becoming stronger than he was? Rising to the surface more and more, even keeping Robin pushed to the back of his own mind during sleep? He tentatively voiced these concerns to Karya.

She gave him a thoughtful look, and didn't reply for a while, but when she did it was with a reassuring tone.

"I've said it before and I'll tell you again. You do realise there is no 'Puck' don't you, Robin?" she said. "It's a name you made up. I don't know why. Some way for you to cope with the fact that you have all this power inside you that you didn't want and didn't ask for."

She smiled at him through her frown. "It's all you, the Scion. You're just getting used to who you are, that's all. And it's not like the Puck is a bad guy anyway. You saved all of our lives last Christmas back on the Isle of Winds. Moros and Strife would have killed us all if you hadn't been the Puck. And then you beat Peryl and saved Henry from the flooding tomb this summer."

"It doesn't feel like me," Robin countered. "It feels like something else is mixed up inside me."

"You need to stop fighting yourself," she advised. "I didn't even know a Shard of the Arcania *could* shatter until it happened under that lake. We don't really understand yet what that means." She shrugged thoughtfully. "To be honest, I didn't know a Shard could summon a great big marauding forest monster either. Even I don't know everything, Robin Fellows, hard to believe as that may be."

"Maybe my using that mask fed the Puck-magic," Robin suggested. "It's ancient elemental magic after all."

"You need to come to terms with the fact that you're not normal," Karya told him bluntly. "Sorry not to sugar coat it, Scion, but you're not and you never will be. Whatever inner conflict you have going on, you need to get on top of it. You need to own this power, or it will probably tear you to bits."

Robin grudgingly nodded. "Don't I even get a break for being angsty-teen age then?"

She shook her head, smirking. "No time for that," she said. "And it wouldn't be a good look on you anyway." She must have noticed that beneath his flippant comments there was a note of genuine worry, as she looked at him calmly.

"I see things that haven't happened yet, remember?" she said. "Most of the time it doesn't make sense, but whenever I've seen you in the future, nine times out of ten, you know what I've seen?"

He shook his head questioningly.

"Not a basket-case. Not some kind of withering personality consumed by the Puck," she told him. "I see a brave and strong leader. Confident and unafraid. You're not even afraid of Eris," she added with raised eyebrows.

Robin found this quite reassuring.

"Let's catch up with Woad and the jolly green giant," he suggested, and they set off faster, hopping over a tangle of tree roots. Robin briefly wondered to himself what Karya saw the other one time out of ten, but something superstitious stopped him from asking.

The forest of the Elderhart was endless. Being told this was one thing. Seeing it on a map was another. Passing through it was another still. It became hard to imagine there was anything but the forest, in all its secretive majesty. Vistas changed, terrain changed, but the woods seemed eternal. Robin fancied that whole generations could live their whole lives within its maze-like embrace, never once seeing beyond its borders to open land and bare hills.

Karya agreed with him. People did, she told him. They were called dryads.

The last light of the setting sun was upon them before they stopped again. Robin had been walking in silence for some time, wondering where Henry was, somewhere in this endless whispering cathedral, wondering how Jackalope was, solitary somewhere in the Netherworlde once again, and trying very hard not to speculate on the fate of Hawthorn. He was gazing at the ground as he walked, mesmerised by the play of the evening light on the sea of autumn leaves, how it made everything glow like spun gold, so he only noticed the others had stopped when he walked right into the back of the dryad, getting a mouthful of leaves from his woody clothes.

"Are we stopping to camp?" he enquired, after apologising.

"No," the man replied. "We are here. The home of my people, the sanctuary of the dryads." He waved a hand before him. "Welcome, outsiders, to Rowandeepling."

Robin stepped around Splinterstem, joining Woad and Karya. The land before them stopped in a cliff, grassy moss tumbling over the rocky edge into a deep chasm that was dizzyingly precipitous. The gully was very wide, curving away from them like a horseshoe through the forest. Deep at its base, Robin could see the gold and red tops of trees, far below in the chasm, and weaving between them, the silver ribbon of a stream.

Across the canyon in the forest, which he now saw curled back in to meet itself, a huge natural empty moat, the land rose up again in a wide island, covered in the tallest trees Robin had yet seen.

There were only a dozen trees on the distant bank, growing in a rough circle, but their dimensions were beyond impressive. Robin had seen photographs back home of the giant redwoods which grew in parts of the mortal world. Some of them so tall and wide that they had tunnels carved through their bases, roads threading through them, wide enough for a car to pass easily.

These trees dwarfed them. They were titanic.

"Those are the elder trees," Karya said, with a deep respect in her voice. "So they do exist. Some say they are the oldest in all the Netherworlde, Scion."

The dryad nodded. "And beneath them, deep under the soil, we have guarded the heart of the forest. The Heart of Gaia, held in safety."

Breathtaking as the sight of the large island with its immense circle of super-trees might be, Robin was confused.

"But, there's no buildings, no people," he observed, scanning the forest island. "There's nothing over there except the trees themselves," he said curiously. "I thought you said this was your settlement. The home of the dryads?"

Woad put a blue finger under Robin's chin and pushed up, tilting the boy's head back.

Robin stared. The immense elder trees soared high into the sky, breaking through the canopy of the rest of the forest, epic natural cathedral pillars spearing into the sky, up and up, before finally erupting into their own separate roof of autumn foliage. Up there, at the very dizzying heights of the tallest branches, he could make out lights in the setting sun. Glimmers here and there. It was too far too make out any further details.

"Up there?" Robin said quietly.

"Since the time the Panthea first came to the Netherworlde," their dryad guide said. "Very few outsiders have even been permitted this deeply into our realm, and fewer still have been admitted to Rowandeepling."

"Bet there's never been a faun up there before," Woad grinned happily.

Robin felt humbled. The weight of being the Scion seemed to settle on his shoulders.

"We are honoured, however," the dryad continued, dropping respectfully to one knee before them. "To receive one such as you, and your companions."

Robin shuffled awkwardly at this act of deference. "Um…thanks so much," he said. The dryad looked up at him blankly, a tiny frown on his brow.

"I wasn't speaking to you, child of the Fae," he explained. He turned his head to Karya. "I was addressing this one."

Karya nodded respectfully as Splinterstem stood again. Robin, slightly mortified, gave her a questioning look. She shrugged at him almost imperceptibly, as if to say she didn't have a clue what the dryad was talking about either.

"Wow … embarrassing," Woad muttered under his breath with a

snigger. Robin heroically resisted the urge to push him off the cliff and into the deep chasm.

"How are supposed to get across?" he asked. "And up? I mean ... there's not even a rickety Indiana Jones rope bridge to fall off, is there?"

"We're going up in style, Robin," Karya smiled.

Two figures were drifting down out of the air before them. They had long, tangled hair and were dressed in the same organic mixture of moss skirts, woven flowers and latticed vines as Splinterstem. Their skin was lighter than his, more of a spring green than a deep moss, spotted here and there with darker mottling at the brow and neck. Females he assumed. But their eyes, like his, were large, green and insectile.

Robin didn't see at first how they were floating. They descended smoothly, arms before them gracefully. A soft purring hum accompanied them, and it was only when they finally landed, nodding in greeting to Robin and the others, that he saw they were winged.

Not feathered but long, thin gossamer affairs. They looked like dragonfly wings, almost invisible in their thinness, a mere membrane which was slightly green-tinged. As they alighted, their vast, purring wings fell still, falling down their backs like long translucent cloaks.

"I have found her," the dryad told them, quiet triumph in his voice. "Did I not tell you I would return with strength to fight this scourge? This is she. We will take her before the princess."

The two female dryads were peering at Karya in a strange mixture of awe and wonder. The girl looked a little uncomfortable under the unblinking green eyes.

"My lady," one of them said, holding out a long arm to the girl. A swirl of twined leaves and moss adorned the dryad's hand, looking like a long evening glove. "Allow us, please."

Karya allowed herself to be taken by the hand. The other dryad took her other arm, and before either Robin or Woad could say a word, the wings flicked back out, and with a rush of wind and a rolling purr, they lifted into the air once more, carrying the girl up into the sky.

They were fast, spiriting her away into the dizzyingly distant treetops far far ahead.

Robin hadn't really thought much what a dryad might be like before he'd met one. He had half-pictured something like a living tree, made from bark and twigs, but although these beings certainly clothed themselves

241

in the forest, amongst blending in with the verdant wilderness around them, he realised that with their greenish skin, their delicate wings and shimmering eyes, they were more like insects, an evolved race of fireflies.

"I shall bring her entourage," Splinterstem called up to his companions, who, holding Karya precariously between them, were already at a sickening height and climbing.

"Her what?" Woad said affronted.

Robin had no chance to speak. Their guide's long cloak parted, bisected in the middle, and great wings, identical to those of the others, flicked swiftly out and into the open air, flexing rapidly.

Without waiting for consent, the dryad reached out and grabbed Robin with one huge hand and Woad with the other, tucking each under his arm as though he were carrying luggage.

"Waitwaitwait–" Woad began, but the dryad bent his knees and sprang into the sky, the downdraft of his wings making Robin's hair flutter in his eyes.

Robin grabbed the moss-covered sleeve tightly with white knuckles as they shot upwards, leaving the forest floor far behind. They had swung out over the great chasm, making his stomach lurch alarmingly as they were carried at great speed and with very little ceremony toward the distant shimmering trees far overhead.

Robin did his best not to let out a scream. There was no time for anything like that anyway. He was far too occupied with ensuring he didn't slip out of the dragonfly-man's grip and plummet to his death.

And besides, he could hear Woad whooping with unrestrained delight as the wind rushed at his face.

ASHE AMONGST THE LEAVES

The floor fell away beneath them quite swiftly, the rough circle of the great elder trees soaring high above all else. Soon they were above the treeline, a great ocean of canopy stretching off below them in all directions, an autumn rainforest covering the world. Only the elder trees soared higher, and Splinterstem's mighty wings purred, carrying them ever upwards.

As they finally reached the dryad dwelling of Rowandeepling at the leafy summit, the structure of the place became clearer to Robin.

A spiderweb of gold hung from the branches, a large and complicated latticework of slender arching bridges, suspended like a vastly complex cat's cradle between and around the immense trunks of the trees.

These golden bridges, as well as crossing one another at every level, also led here and there, inside the trees themselves, through elegant slender openings, only to emerge elsewhere, spouting off dizzyingly again into the void to meet another. The elder trees' trunks were made up of countless separate boles, twisting and twining loosely around each other like the world's most immense weeping fig, a series of huge natural birdcage structures formed in the hollows. Many of these were encased in the same glowing golden amber as the bridges, carved out into rooms and sometimes whole dwellings. Windows, balconies, steps and stairs covered every inch of each huge tree, all hewn from the beautiful shining sap, a gorgeous city hidden in the canopy.

The web of bridges and walkways, Robin observed, were punctuated here and there with circular platforms, bowered with vines and elaborately woven flowers. It was to one of these platform that their dryad guide flew, depositing Woad and Robin, much to their relief, on the oddly translucent, golden circle.

Robin's legs felt watery as he steadied himself, gazing around. His ears had popped. There were dryads everywhere, some walking the countless pathways around, above and below them. More still flitting between on purring wings, barely visible in the falling light of evening.

Lights were coming on everywhere as the evening drew in, oddly organic circular orbs buried in every bridge and path, glimmering with soft yellow light. Jewels like dewdrops in a vast web.

There were lights glowing in the trees themselves as well, warm and welcoming, from countless windows and openings. The air smelled sweet, like honey and pollen. Robin took all this in, but in truth he was more relieved that the walkway on which they had been deposited was solid. It looked like woven brown sugar, dark glass, but it was as firm and reassuringly unyielding as stone beneath his feet.

"What a ride!" Woad grinned. "Buzzy moss-folk know how to live." He was looking around too, as their guide landed beside them, his wings folding neatly and forming a cloak once more. Of Karya, Robin noticed, there was no sign. She had been taken elsewhere.

"What is it with the Netherworlde and treetop cities?" Robin muttered, eying the edge with worry.

"Better than building on the floor, Pinky," Woad said simply. "How can you have a city in a forest if you have to rip out the forest to build it?"

"Point taken," Robin allowed. "What's this made of then?" he asked, running his hand around the elegantly woven bannister. It was smooth under his fingers and slightly warm.

"Amber," Splinterstem said simply. "The paths of Rowandeepling are the veins of the elder trees themselves. The forest provides for us."

"Tree-sap," Woad nodded knowledgable, as though he had suspected just this. He rapped his toes on the floor beneath them. "Just what I would have chosen too for a tree-top sanctuary as pretty as this. It's lovely and glowy. Very mystic. I approve."

"Where's our friend?" Robin asked, noticing several other dryads walking toward them along one of the arching walkways in the twilight.

He wanted to add 'and why did you treat her like some kind of movie star?' but he thought it might be wise to keep his mouth shut until he figured out what was going on.

"She has been taken to be more fittingly attired to be received by the princess," the dryad told them. His large green eyes looked over both of them. "As shall you."

"I'm perfectly attired, thanks," Woad said proudly. "I've got pants on and everything. That's practically formal dress for a faun, that is. Not many fauns bother with pants. I'm practically avant-garde."

Splinterstem nodded politely, "You are both perhaps a little…road weary," he rumbled tactfully. "We shall provide you with more suitable wear for the rigours of the forest."

Robin could hardly argue with the dryad's point. Since they entered the Netherworlde, between riding lions, fighting centaur, scuffling with banshee, escaping Strigoi through the earth, and then a pretty serious hike through some very unforgiving forest, his jeans and jumper were probably only fit for burning. He doubted if even Hestia could get them clean. He did not, however, relish the idea of walking around wearing what many of his dryad hosts wore, little more than moss and leaves from what he could make out.

"I don't fancy dressing up like Peter Pan meets the Lord of the Flies," he muttered to Woad in a quiet voice. "But I could do with a shower."

"Yes," Woad replied seriously, whispering back. "Yes, you could. You smell like old ham left in the sun, Pinky."

Robin rolled his eyes. "Thanks, Woad," he muttered. "You have probably enough twigs and leaves stuck in your hair for birds actually to start nesting in it. We're *all* dirty and tired."

Robin's fears of being dressed up like one of the lost boys of Neverland were thankfully allayed.

They were passed from their guide into the care of the two approaching dryads, one male, one female, both looking fairly elderly, though it was hard to judge with the species. These two dryads led the boys along the dizzyingly high lamplit routes as the sun set completely, and through a great doorway into the interior of one of the amber houses. Robin discovered that within, the word 'house' didn't really do justice. Palatial mansion, perhaps. Room after room spiralled away, hollowed and carved, with a lacework of great staircases strung between and much elaborate and delicate embellishment. Soft carpets of moss and grasses welcomed them underfoot, and the high arching roofs of the rooms and corridors through which they passed smelled sweetly of sawdust and wax. For all its great scale and soaring architecture however, it felt oddly cosy to Robin. It reminded him of those books from his childhood where badgers and moles wore waistcoats and kept pleasant warm homes in burrows beneath the roots of trees, with open fireplaces and wing-back chairs.

The rooms were furnished and appointed with all the comforts one might expect back at Erlking. Beds, woven from carved branches, lamps and tables, even a writing desk, set by a smaller archway which they discovered led out onto a semi-circular balcony, giving them tremendous views out and down through the maze of amber paths suspended in the open air. Robin stood on the balcony a moment, soaking up the sheer calm beauty of the place, watching a flock of roosting birds pass beneath the net of Rowandeepling, far below them. All around, beyond the treetop city, the canopy of the great Elderhart forest swept away, a russet ocean far beneath them, stretching to the horizon in every direction in great frozen waves as it climbed up and down the landscape.

More important than this breathtaking vista, however, there was a bath.

Robin didn't bother to question the dryad's ingenuity at drawing water so high up into the sky. Maybe they had magic plumbing. Maybe they just flew it up from a stream down below in buckets as and when they needed it. Frankly, he didn't care. He just wanted to get clean.

Woad, bored with the very idea of a bath, had gone off to explore. They had been told by the elderly dryads that they would be collected in an hour to be taken to the great hall, and he wanted to have a good look around first.

Alone for the first time since he had left Erlking, and after scrubbing what felt like a week's worth of soil and sweat away, Robin returned to the main room of the curious suite to find that clothes had been laid out on the bed for him and, to his great relief, they were not made from stringy bits of leaves. A simple rough woven shirt and dark trousers of some canvas material. There was even a pair of laced hiking boots.

He felt a little as though he was in fancy dress as a Merry Man, but at least he didn't look any longer as though he had dug himself out of a grave.

There was a mirror in the room, dark and copper-coloured, and he did his best to tame his messy hair. They were the first outsiders to visit Rowandeepling in a long time after all. As one of the few remaining free Fae in the world, he felt he should at least try and make a good impression if they were going to meet the princess.

Woad eventually returned and was convinced, after much arguing, to go and wash up while Robin hung around out on the balcony, watching the night deepen over the forest.

The sky above was a galaxy of stars, stretching cool and clear, a true nip of autumn in the air. He watched the dryads flying and walking back and forth amongst the airborne streets of their city, moving between the pinpoints of glimmering light everywhere, busy as ants. It felt oddly relaxing here. Safe and calm. He honestly couldn't remember ever feeling at ease in the Netherworlde before. Something was usually trying to kill them, or they were sleeping rough on hard ground. Here, there was comfort and shelter, and he hoped, listening to his stomach rumble…food.

His sense of peace and serenity was only slightly broken by the sound of Woad singing to himself in the bath in a very off key way, and by the fact that, try as he might, Robin couldn't help but feel guilty that he was here, in this haven of the Earth kingdom, while somewhere out there, lost in the sprawl of the woods far below, was Henry … And the scourge.

Their guides returned for them after a while, both of them politely passing no comment that Woad had ignored the clothes arranged for him, and had instead elected to wash his own faithful threadbare pants in the bath and put them back on, sitting precariously on the amber railing of their small balcony and swinging his legs until they were dried.

"The princess will receive you now, friends of the great one," the elderly female dryad told them with a crinkled smile. "A feast has been arranged in your honour, in the amber hall itself. We may be without a king, but the hospitality of the dryads will not leave you wanting. If you would like to follow us."

Woad raised his eyebrows at Robin at this mention of 'the great one' but they followed, led once more through the great tree dwelling and out onto the scaffolding of beautiful bridges. This time they headed around and up, many curious dryads, young and old, marking their passing with unblinking, green eyes. Robin noticed that the males seemed to have darker skin. The females were slightly taller and had a greater wingspan, and those he assumed to be children had light skin that was almost a soft pea green, like young shoots. It was hard for him to believe they were all Panthea, like Woad, and Phorbas and Calypso. He had to keep in mind that the Panthea were not one singular species, like the Fae, but rather a multitude of peoples, under one name, as varied as they came.

The centre of Rowandeepling was clear to see from anywhere. At the highest point of all the bridges, with only the great and interlocking autumn canopy above it, a domed and magnificent roof filled with suspended lights, the many spurs and amber pathways converged on a great structure artfully woven of wood and gold. The building hung in the net of scaffold like a jewel at the centre of a dreamcatcher. It seemed in shape like a Viking longboat upturned, a great lozenge as large as a church, resting on its large translucent platform, with lighted windows and large doors. At the foot of the steps leading up to these doors, a girl awaited them.

Robin wondered briefly if this was the princess, but the truth was much more shocking.

"Karya?" he spluttered in disbelief as they met at the steps. Woad practically boggled at his side. Their friend had also been given new clothing, but clearly a great deal more attention had been paid to her than the boys had. Even now, she was flanked on either side by two respectful-looking dryads, her own personal handmaidens.

"What have they done to you, boss?" Woad asked with unveiled curiosity.

Karya had been dressed in a long green gown, regally appointed and shot through with a swirl of tiny embroidered silver leaves. Around her bare shoulders there was a silver throw, gossamer light like spun spider silk. Her wild mane of hair had somehow been tamed, and fell down her back in copper ringlets, held in place on either side of her head with elaborate braids fastened with silver leaves. More pale threads had been woven into her hair itself.

She looked, Robin had to admit, quite unquestionably stunning. She also looked, he noted, quietly furious.

"Don't … say … a … bloody … word," she hissed, glowering at them. "Just don't dare. This was *not* my idea."

Her bad temper at least was familiar, if not her appearance. "You look …" Robin was a little lost for words. He tried to figure out whether 'amazing' or 'weird' would be more likely to get his teeth knocked out. "… Really … different," he settled for safely.

"I don't do dresses," she complained to him, keeping her voice quiet and discreet as the three of them made their way up the staircase. "They're completely impractical. But it's not like I had a choice. I haven't had a moment to myself since we got here. These dryads have been fawning all over me. Brushing my hair, bringing me drinks, dressing me up like some kind of silly doll."

"We just had a scrub," Woad shrugged. "No one brushed my hair. Good job really, I would have bitten their fingers off."

Karya gave the faun a sidelong look. "Don't think I wasn't tempted," she muttered. "But pay attention you two. This is their place, these are their customs, so let's just be polite and find out what we can about this scourge and the Shard, right?" She glanced at Robin. "You look … slightly more Netherworldey," she observed. "At least you got rid of those silly trainers. They were falling apart."

"I don't think they were really made with the Netherworlde in mind," he said, as they passed through the doorway. "And I'm not sure leather lace up boots are going to catch on back in the human world. I feel like I'm in a panto. What I want to know though, is why everyone is treating you like you're some kind of royalty? The great one?"

Karya shrugged elegantly under her shawl. She looked decidedly smaller and delicate without her habitual bulky coat of skins and furs. It was quite disconcerting.

"Don't ask me," she said. "I genuinely have no idea." She flicked her perfectly ringleted hair. "Maybe they just have excellent taste?"

The hall within was lavish, a grandly-appointed feasting space, laid out like a palace throne-room. Long tables lined the walls, crammed every inch with dishes of mouthwatering food and tall silver jugs of a sweet-smelling, golden drink. A large sunken fire-pit glowed in the centre of the room, although it seemed not to dance with flames, but instead with a rolling mist that somehow gave off heat nonetheless. Robin supposed that an open fire in a city built of and in wood would not be advisable.

The curved ceiling arched overhead, carved like whalebone and festooned with thousands of tiny lights twinkling like a Christmas tree. The surrounding walls of the great hall were curiously decorated with strange geometric patterns, an endless loop of squiggles and knots carved into solid amber. The intricate and complicated fresco, covering every inch of the wall-space, reminding Robin of the raised topography of a brain.

There were many dryads here, already feasting and talking amongst themselves, though in the absence of a king, their mutterings were subdued. The air was filled with a polite but genuine warmth. Robin's eyes were drawn to the far end of the chamber as they were ushered toward it by their guides. Here stood a dais with a long table, seated at which, beside the solemn figure of Splinterstem, was the princess herself.

"Karya of Erlking, lost ruins of the Fae, and her attendants," the old dryad at their side announced, before bowing and retreating, leaving the three of them standing before her.

The princess nodded and stood, smiling rather sadly, Robin thought, and blinking her huge green faceted eyes. Like the other dryads, her skin was a soft greenish brown and her hair was a choppy, chin-length curtain, dark against the silver flowers and thread woven through it. But unlike the majority of the dryads they had seen, she wore white. A long and close dress comprised entirely of tiny pale leaves, flowing around her like scales on a fish, each one rimmed in thin silver. At her throat, the gown was adorned with artful white flowers, blossom petals chasing up decoratively onto her throat, giving the girl the appearance of a strange forest bride.

To Robin, she looked surprisingly younger than he'd imagined. Maybe only a few years older than they were themselves.

"You are welcome to Rowandeepling, all of you," she said, very formally, motioning for them to join her at the table. "I am Ashe, daughter of the King, and I am grateful to receive such champions, here to slay the forest drake that haunts us."

Robin, Karya and Woad took their seats at the table with her. As conversations and music started up again around the feasting hall, the princess, with a gentle and delicate waft of her hand, indicated the dryad guide they were all familiar with. "You have already met Festucamossis, I know. His name is Splinterstem in the low tongue." She smiled as they nodded hello to him again. "I am aware that the high tongue of the Netherworlde is becoming a thing of the past. Pallidacinnis is my true name, but Ashe is so much simpler, don't you think? The high tongue is becoming so unfashionable."

"Did I not tell you, my princess," Splinterstem said, raising a glass to her respectfully. "That I would search the Netherworlde for one strong enough to end the reign of the beast? I have not failed you."

Ashe's soft green eyes roamed curiously over her guests. She looked very intrigued to see such exotic strangers in her court. "You have done well," she nodded to him politely. "I can always count on your diligence."

Drinks were poured for all of them. "With the loss of my father," the princess told them. "Splinterstem is currently acting steward of

Rowandeepling. He leads our people, in this time of crisis, and it is he who has been most active in finding a champion capable of ending this scourge. Something must be done. Many have died already." She looked deeply sad. "None can match the Shard."

Karya took a drink. "I'm a little confused," she said. "If you're the princess, with your father gone, why are you not ruling your people yourself?"

Ashe's smile froze a little, but she seemed to catch it on her face. "Our ways are not so simple," she said. "Power is not mine merely to take. Not without a mate. I will explain later. But first, you have all travelled far. We must eat." She reached out and took Karya's hands in her own. "We are truly honoured to have one such as yourself here in the Elderhart," she enthused. "I know you can stop this creature and bring balance back to the forest. It is almost like fate."

"Princess, take care not to overexcite yourself," Splinterstem cautioned in a low voice. "To talk of the Fates is to invite them down on our heads. Everyone knows this." He reached out and patted her shoulder a little. Robin thought he saw her stiffen slightly, although maybe the dryad girl's discomfort was just his imagination.

"Yes … yes of course," she said, nodding, "Your counsel is sounds as always, steward. Perhaps it is better to talk of other things."

"Your hall is very beautiful," Robin said, more to have something to say than for any other reason. "The carving all around, it's really detailed. You have a wonderful home here."

"It is the Labyrinth," Splinterstem said, taking a sip of his drink. Robin raised a silver goblet himself and did the same. Whatever it was, it was unfamiliar, but it tasted like honey and apples and sent a delicious comforting warmth through him right down to his toes.

"The labyrinth?" he asked, voice muffled as he spoke over the top of his glass.

"The Labyrinth has protected the heart of the forest for so long," the princess said sadly. "Although, in the end, it did not stop the heart falling into darkness, into the beast."

Karya slapped Woad's hand away from her plate. He had already cleared his own.

"I'm sorry if we seem a little ignorant, we're not really familiar with your world," she shrugged apologetically, her shimmering shawl glinting in the dancing lights of the hall. "No one is, really. Your people are quite famous for being private. Everything the rest of the Netherworlde knows about you, about the forest as well, it's all just second hand knowledge and guesswork."

"Well, there was Hammerhand," Robin pointed out. "He writes about this place in the Netherworlde Compendium, although even he doesn't say too much about it. He came here once, he claims. Is that true?"

Ashe nodded, the flowers and leaves at her throat tinkling. "Yes! I recall him," she said warmly. "The ambassador of the Fae." A tiny frown appeared in her delicate brow. "He came here in a time of great tumult. When the world changed forever, and the Arcania fell to ruin, broken and lost to the winds. I remember he was allowed here, by Father."

Splinterstem set down his goblet.

"I will tell you all of the Labyrinth," he said, bowing his head. "And the heart of the forest, the pulsing heart of the elder trees themselves. If you do not understand our history, then you will see what has happened, and why this terrible beast must be stopped."

"It must be stopped because it is a rampaging, mindless monster!" Ashe said to him firmly. She looked to the companions, her green eyes wide. "Many of our people have been killed. Hunting parties running afoul of the drake. Outer settlements scorched and withered. You have seen for yourself the destruction it brings. Death and grey decay to the very forest it touches. The Elderhart, my father's kingdom, is now riddled with just such places." She looked thoughtfully down at her hands. "And without the king to guide us…"

"It's not just your people, or your forest, in danger," Karya explained. "This thing has been roaming beyond the borders of the Elderhart. From what we've heard, it's growing more powerful all the time. More bold. It has destroyed Panthea villages, withered crops, ruined the autumn harvests. The surface town of the redcaps even, Spitrot, has been completely decimated. Many of their people were killed. Those who followed it back into the forest were also hunted and ended by this thing."

She looked past Ashe to the steward. "Anything you can tell us will be helpful. If we are to find and stop this thing. The more we understand, the better."

Splinterstem looked from the princess to Karya. "Pre-warned is pre-armed. Very well," he began.

"The dryads have always lived in the Elderhart, even since the Panthea first came to the Netherworlde. This has been ever our realm. We protect the great forest, and it protects us. We have a balance with nature. We *are* the balance of nature." He shook his great head solemnly.

"Things changed when the war came. Eris declared open war on the Fae. Panthea were split, fighting amongst themselves even. War raged all over the Netherworlde. Even here, in the deep depths of the forest, isolated from the rest of the land, we were not safe from it either. Eris' war tore our very people in two."

Robin knew that this had happened elsewhere too. The Nereids had joined Eris' cause, rebelling against their Undine masters. Had something similar happened here?

"Did some of your people? The dryads, I mean …" he asked. "Did some of them supported Eris? Went to fight for her cause, against the Fae?"

Splinterstem grunted unhappily. "They did. Not many of them, at first, but enough. Eris has a way of doubling things, whether it is dissent, unhappiness, mistrust or simply bodies. The dryads who answered her call to arms, who left the forest, abandoning our ways and swearing allegiance to Dis. They were…changed by her."

"Changed how?" Karya asked.

"Dark ways and means," Splinterstem replied grimly, setting down his plate. "Eris tampers with the fabric of order, the natural way of things. Chaos is in her very bloodstream. The dryads she toyed with, deep in the pits of Dis, well, when they returned to the forest, they had become the swarm."

Robin knew this name. Hawthorn had told him about them.

"The swarm?" he asked. "They're the ones who run the Hive, aren't they? I didn't know they were dryads like you."

"They are nothing like us!" the princess said, sounding aghast, a pale green hand fluttering to her chest, clad in white flowers. It was odd, how she managed to appear delicate and willowy, when she was in fact a good seven feet tall. "They are twisted perversions of dryads, tainted by Eris, dark and distorted reflections of everything we are." Her mouth down-turned in distaste. "The swarm are slaves to her will. She used them to great effect in the war, and afterwards, once Eris had won … Well, they made excellent guards for the prison she built."

The steward nodded in agreement. "Eris never throws away anything useful," he rumbled. "She built the Hive, far south of here, her great gaol, that dark pyramid. The swarm run the place, and all the forest around it. Their dark presence has corrupted the very trees in those parts. Dead woods, tangled thorns. It is a vile place. Avoid the dark places in the Elderhart, children. They all, every one of them lead to the swarm, and to Eris' prisoners."

"We of Rowandeepling have been at war with the swarm ever since," the princess said. "They fight us for land, and slowly we lose the forest to them, piece by piece. They will not stop, until they have what they want, what Eris wants."

"Total dominion of the Netherworlde?" Woad guessed. "She's a bugger for that. The Dark Empress doesn't like to share."

"Something more specific than that, little blue one," the steward said. "Eris desires the heart of the elder trees. She will never call the horde of the swarm off until she possesses it."

"Tell us about this heart," Karya said, drawing her chair in closer to the table with interest.

"It was the culmination of the war," Splinterstem told them, leaning back in his chair, his large hands clasped over his stomach. "The world was in confusion. The Fae King and Queen had gone, the Arcania was shattered, and then in the midst of all this upheaval, a man …" He waved a hand at them. "This outlander whom you call Hammerhand. He comes to the forest, claiming to be on a mission from the regents themselves. One last task given before they disappeared."

"What task?" Robin wanted to know, his curiosity peaked.

"Hammerhand brought an object of great, great power to my father," Ashe explained, a little breathlessly. "Tremendous power. It needed to be hidden, he told the king. Deep and safe where none would ever find it, this force of raw magic. My father accepted this burden. He commissioned the building of a great labyrinth. It lies far below us now, beneath the very roots of the elder trees themselves, and it extends for many miles beneath the forest." She looked respectfully at the steward. "Splinterstem himself was its architect. A work of genius. He is … was … very close to my father." Her glittering eyes flicked back to them. "At the centre, my father placed this object, this powerful treasure of the Fae, and named it the heart of the forest."

"It brought great protection to our people," the steward said, nodding. "It fed the elder trees. They flourished. Made Rowandeepling strong. We dryads bloomed with it, and our strength has been greater than any of Eris' swarm. But the heart of the forest must be protected. The king and I, we set a guardian within the Labyrinth, one who would surely kill any who dared enter. A fearsome thing. Half man, half beast."

This sounded oddly familiar to Robin.

"What kind of guardian?" Woad asked with interest.

"Is it ... half-person, half-bull?" Robin ventured with a frown.

Everyone at the table looked at him curiously. Splinterstem's eyes narrowed with suspicion.

"How would you know that, strange Fae?" he wanted to know. Robin's friends and the princess also peered at him closely. He felt his ears burn a little with the attention.

"Educated guess, I suppose," he said awkwardly. "It's just ... well, a labyrinth? A dangerous guardian in the centre? We have a similar myth back in the human world, where I was raised. It's called a minotaur."

The princess nodded, clearly impressed. "Yes, yes, a minotaur!" she confirmed. "Set in place to guard the heart, the relic of the Fae." Her face became concerned. "It is a very dangerous animal. None have ever dared enter. Not since the time when the Labyrinth was first built. It is a vile and bestial horror, but it has kept the heart safe all this time." She glanced away, her breath hitching.

Robin considered this. The Netherworlde seemed full of myths and legends, the Panthea in particular echoing old mythology. Mythology that didn't traditionally have any of its roots in Britain, or British folklore at all. It was very curious. The Fae, he could understand. Redcaps and banshee and ghosts, these were all things which to him seemed at home in the mists of 'ye olde Britain'. But all things Panthea...centaur, kraken, satyrs and dryads, nymphs and fauns, and now a minotaur? Things in the Netherworlde seemed so ... mixed up.

Splinterstem leaned in solicitously. "Perhaps that is enough history for now. This is not an easy topic for our people." He waved an attendant over to pour more drinks. "Now please, eat ... drink ... be merry." He poured the princess' goblet himself and placed it straight into her hand, curling her fingers around the bowl gently. He seemed to treat her like a delicate flower. Despite her regal station, she seemed resigned enough to comply with his ministrations, and relieved to escape dark talk and memories. After the feast, she promised, Splinterstem would tell them what he knew of the beast.

Robin studied the dryads as they ate. They seemed a peaceable people. Subdued perhaps, but with some terrible creature destroying their forest, they could hardly be blamed for that. He was unsure what to make of the princess too. She seemed polite enough, but distant and a little sad. No doubt, she was mourning the loss of her father. He didn't think Karya was particularly impressed with her. His friend was one of the strongest people he knew, and the princess' rather meek and ladylike bearing probably irked her sensibilities.

And as for Splinterstem, during their trek through the forest, he had been stoic and watchful, guarding them at night, leading them here on safe paths. Now they were here, Robin couldn't help but notice how attentive he was to the princess. Constantly refilling her cup, ensuring she was entertained. He spent the remainder of the evening practically doting on her, dedicated to her comfort and peace. His large green eyes attentive and respectful.

When the feasting was done, the princess, looking rather wan, declared that she was tired and needed some air. Excusing herself politely, she retreated to a balcony. As the hubbub in the great hall grew quieter, plates cleared away, and the dryads all around fell to talking amongst themselves in groups, Robin and the others gathered around Splinterstem.

"This 'heart of the forest'," Karya said in a businesslike tone, without preamble. "We all agree that what we're talking about here is clearly a Shard of the Arcania here, right? The Earth Shard."

Woad nodded enthusiastically. "I'd bet my tail on it. The Shards were hidden everywhere, right? One given to the Air priests and popped in a magic statue, one buried with Tritea the Undine at the bottom of a lake. Sneaky Fae squirrelled them all away like nuts for the winter."

"Well, I was thinking this too," Robin said in agreement. "Hammerhand was a Fae. He was a great traveller. I've read every inch of his Compendium. He was a part of the Fae high-society too. Not Sidhe-Nobilitas, but definitely a trusted member of court. It makes sense that Oberon and Titania would trust him to know a secret and safe place to hide a Shard, right?"

"We were honoured to be given such a treasure," Splinterstem told them. "Although in the end, it did not stop the swarm from forming. It has not kept our borders safe from them or from Eris."

"What I want to know is this," Karya probed. "The Shard, the heart, whatever you want to call it … If it was deep in this impassable Labyrinth, and guarded by the vicious scary minotaur for all these years, what happened? How on earth is it suddenly out in the world, embedded in a great monster? Surely someone would have had to go in to the maze? And fetch it out?"

Splinterstem looked very doubtful. "None have entered the Labyrinth," he said. "Not since it was constructed. And even if they did, they would never find the centre. I should know. I designed it. We respect the minotaur beneath the woods. The guardian of the great power. No dryad is foolish enough to attempt to pass it." He looked troubled.

"There was only ever one incident, a dryad who was foolish enough to enter, and this was long ago, when the place was very first commissioned by the king." He looked grim. "It was myself who found his body, by the doors to the maze. The poor wretch. He was … almost unrecognisable." He shook his head in distaste at the memory. "I buried him myself, his remains at least, before I even brought news back to the city. None should have had to see him in the state I found him, gored by the minotaur."

"Who was he?" Robin asked gently.

"He was a good friend of mine," Splinterstem told them. "He was also someone close to our fair princess. She has never quite recovered from the loss. It weakens her, darkens her heart even now, so many years later."

"Okay, so that rules out anyone going in there with a red rag and dodging around gorey Mr McBullface," Woad said, tactlessly. "I suppose after that, people would be extremely unlikely to try their luck, not being fauns after all."

Karya cleared her throat loudly, interrupting the faun. "But tell us about when this monster first appeared. The scourge with the Shard. Was the king its first victim?"

The steward nodded. "He was. And it is my fault," he said, looking down at his hands with a frown. "I was with him, you see, when the thing attacked. I should have guarded him, protected him. That is my job after all. My calling. The king has ever been good to me. I grew up alongside the princess, treated almost as one of his own." His green eyes narrowed. "But it happened so fast. And it was so strong. I was powerless to stop it." He looked up to them, his face grave. "I failed the king. I let him be taken by this beast, leaving our people leaderless and the princess distressed. Which is why I swore that I would find a champion strong enough to stop it. To protect Rowandeepling. To claim back the heart of the forest for us." He looked to Karya. "Then in my searchings, I came upon the redcaps at the edge of the forest. The beast had just attacked their town, this Spitrot you tell us of. I heard them speak of a great power at Erlking, one which owed them a favour." Splinterstem straightened in his chair proudly. "I can travel much faster than lowly redcaps do. So I came, and I spied for myself, to see what lay at Erlking that might assist us."

Robin realised something suddenly. "It was you then," he said. "We've been seeing odd things for months at Erlking. Woad said he saw a face at the window of my bedroom one night, made from leaves, and Jackalope swore he'd seen blossom blowing through the grounds, a tornado shaped like a walking man."

The dryad nodded. "Forgive my secrecy," he said. "I wanted to see for myself first-hand what power lay at Erlking." He looked to Karya, his eyes wide. "And then when I saw you, I knew our prayers were answered. I hastened back here to tell the princess, that I had found our champion."

He glowered slightly. "Little did I know that by the time I returned, the redcaps themselves would have already pressed you into their service, and that you and your companions were scattered through the grasslands. I was lucky to find you when I did, on the borders of the forest, by the rancid bodies of those two things." He nodded to himself. "It was the will of the Fates. The forest brought you to us, great one."

Karya looked incredibly uncomfortable. "Here's the thing," she said haltingly. "Everyone here has been very nice, but to be honest, I really don't know who you think I am." She pointed to Robin. "*He's* the Scion. That one. He's the one the redcaps came to for help. I'm just…" She shrugged. "Well, it's all rather complicated, but I suppose you could say I'm just a runaway. I have some skill with the Tower of Earth, certainly, but nothing like dryad level skills. If anyone is best placed to recover a Shard of the Arcania, it's Robin. The Shards call to him."

The dryad peered at her curiously. "There can be no mistake …" he said seriously. "It is plain for any to see who you are, surely? If you are joking at my expense, then please, forgive my ignorance, but I am outside of the joke."

Karya's face had hardened a little. She stared back firmly at the dryad, her golden eyes flashing. "I'm telling you," she said, her tones clipped. "I'm just a tracker, with some skill for prophecy. If you thought anything more than that, then I'm terribly sorry to disappoint you, but it's your error."

"Don't sell yourself short, boss," Woad piped up. "You're the best tracker there is! And your Earth Magic is strong. You're the best person I know for cooking sausages! As for knowing the past and the future, it's no wonder Eris wants you back-"

"Back?" Splinterstem asked, looking from the faun to the girl. He looked genuinely confused.

"Not that Robin isn't amazing too." Woad clapped Robin on the back. "He's the Scion after all. He's done some amazing things, and he hardly ever gets almost dismembered anymore. You did well choosing us, it's like buy one hero get one free, right?"

Woad grinned, "Plus, you get me in the bargain too, and I'm the best faun there is."

Robin had no idea what was making Karya so uncomfortable. She was more defensive than usual. He had the distinct feeling that the dryads may not react well to the knowledge that she had at one time worked for Eris, and he felt that he should help out by shifting the conversation away from the fact, back to the matter in hand.

"Sorry," he said, getting Splinterstem's attention. "You were telling us about when the beast first appeared in the forest. You were with the king; you say? Can you tell us what happened exactly?"

"It all happened so quickly," the dryad said, settling back into his storytelling. From the corner of his eye, Robin saw Karya give him a grateful look. "We had heard rumours in the forest. These were more than the usual rumblings from the swarm, and we had put out extra patrols along the borders where we normally encountered them. But there were other strange things too. Oddities in the Elderhart. Rumours of a pale man, hooded and cloaked, walking alone through the trees. Many had seen him, lurking here and there, but none had been able to catch and confront him. He was like a ghost. Our people were uneasy. I suggested to the king that it would be prudent for us to check the entrance to the Labyrinth. Ensure the safety of the heart. None had been down there for many years. It was almost a forgotten place, overgrown and abandoned. The king agreed, but he suggested that we do so discreetly, just the two of us. No entourage, no pomp or ceremony. He did not wish to cause worry amongst his people. And so we left at dawn, just the two of us . Our intention was to check that the doors were sealed. That this pale man, or anyone else, had not tampered near the minotaur's lair."

He looked troubled again. "What a fool I was. We should have taken a full guard. We might have stood a chance. I thought too much of myself. That I could handle any trouble we might encounter."

"What happened at the entrance?" Karya asked.

"The doors stood open," he told them darkly. "Someone, or something, had already been inside. We didn't enter. We didn't dare, not knowing if the minotaur was within. I had seen first hand, long ago, what that monstrous guardian could do to a dryad."

"It was there that the scourge attacked us. It came crashing out of the trees and fell upon the king. I was thrown aside." He shook his head, looking a little awed. "It was huge. Green, scaled, covered in earth and soil. It seemed like the forest itself, come alive. It came out of the trees and set upon my king. I saw the heart, the Shard, as you outlanders call it, buried in its great forehead." He tapped his own emphatically. "Like a decorative jewel … shining." He lowered his hand slowly. "And though I rushed back to try and save him, I was knocked aside again with its great tail. This time, I hit my head. When I awoke, the day had grown bright, and both the monster, and the king, they were gone."

"Definitely eaten," Woad said, rather unsympathetically. "You'll be wanting to avoid that, Pinky." Not surprisingly, this viewpoint didn't appear to make Robin or the dryad feel much better.

With his tale told, Karya and Splinterstem soon fell to the business of tracking and hunting the monster, which they both agreed should be done at first light.

There wasn't much Robin could contribute to this conversation. He could barely track his way from his bedroom to Erlking's kitchen without getting lost, and Woad lost interest in the serious minutiae business of monster-slaying when music started up, and several dryads started dancing in a slow and graceful manner, filling the great hall with movement.

The faun went off to join them enthusiastically, to 'show them how to dance properly' as he put it, and Robin, finding himself at something of a loose end, wandered out onto the balcony which fed off from the feasting hall.

He hadn't said anything to the others, but it was becoming more and more apparent that the thing they were facing was incredibly dangerous. No one seemed to have bothered to question his suitability at stopping it. He wasn't a brave knight in armour, after all. He was a skinny teenager with increasingly temperamental mana. Everyone just assumed he'd be able to pull some Shard-related trick out of his sleeve, simple as pie.

Robin was no coward. He knew he had to try, but he certainly didn't relish the idea of facing off against something which had been described as a 'giant snake with many teeth'.

It's not a snake, it's a dragon, a small voice in his head piped up, as he took in the cool autumn night air out on the balcony. The vast canopy rustled and whispered above him, the many roads and leaping bridges of Rowandeepling stretching out below, shining in the darkness amid large clouds of glimmering fireflies.

"I know," he muttered aloud. "No-one's saying the word, but it's clearly a bloody dragon." He ran his hands through his hair, sighing. "Robin Fellows, hornless wonder, dragon-slayer?"

He was trying to figure out if the voice in his head sounded more like the Puck or more like dream-Penny, when a voice beside him made him startle.

"Who are you talking to, Fae?"

Robin turned to see that the wide dark balcony was not, as he had first imagined, empty. He was not alone up here high in the trees. He'd forgotten that the Princess Ashe had come out here some time ago. She had been standing alone in the darkness, looking out over her curious kingdom. Her white leafy dress and pale wreath of flowers made her look oddly ghostly. Tiny fireflies danced in the shadows of the trees behind her, giving her a halo of flickering lights.

"Oh, sorry ... um, your majesty," he grinned sheepishly. "I didn't see you. Just talking to myself, I suppose."

He wandered over to where she stood. She still looked sad and distant, but she smiled down at him.

"Your master is brave and noble, assisting my people this way," she told him. "You must be proud to travel at her side. We are blessed to receive her."

Robin glanced back into the brightly lit glow of the hall, where Karya, still looking remarkably at home in regal settings and disturbingly unlike herself, was still in deep and serious discussion with the steward.

"Hmm," he said, looking back up at the tall, yet oddly frail, dryad. "She's not scared of anything, that's for sure," he agreed. "I think she's a bit confused as to why you are all treating her like ... well ... like she's one of you." A thought occurred to him. "Hey, she's not is she? A dryad, I mean?"

This actually elicited a laugh from Ashe, and for the first time since they had met, she looked unguarded. "You are full of jokes," she smiled. "Are all Fae so? I barely remember Hammerhand, I was only a sapling back then." She shook her soft curls. "No, she is no dryad. Would you not know, and still be her companion? What is she to you then?"

"She's a friend," he said. "That's all that matters to me." He thought of what he knew of Karya, of her past, and the strangeness with the flute, of how she had eventually escaped Eris. "I don't care about people's pasts. They're not as important as who they are now, right?"

The dryad princess gazed at him a moment, and he could tell from her expression that she didn't wholly agree. She looked away, out over the amber railing and into the deep twinkling light of Rowandeepling.

"We are all the sum of our past," she said. "It's the clay that shapes us. Every oak owes its height to the acorn it once was, and the soil before that. You cannot ignore what people once were. It is part of the very fabric of who they are now."

This made Robin think of Jackalope. Did he even believe his own words? Could Robin really say he didn't care about people's pasts? Even if those pasts included such unspeakable crimes as the murder of your own family?

He sighed, leaning on the railing beside her. "People are very complicated things."

The moon had risen above the autumn forest, a yellow harvest crescent. They watched it sail through shredded cloud for a while in surprisingly comfortable silence, listening to the muffled music and hubbub of the feasting hall behind them.

"I know my father is dead," Ashe said eventually, without prompting. Robin looked sidelong at her. Her face was composed.

"I have no illusions about that," she told him. "But until he is found, until there is proof and this drake is stopped … until the scourge is lifted, my people cannot be safe. I wish that I could offer them guidance, leadership."

"Why can't you?" Robin asked. "I mean, we all noticed … your steward, he's in charge, right? Kind of like a temporary substitute? He seems to know what he's doing, but we don't understand why you're not in charge yourself."

"It is the way of my people," Ashe explained. "Splinterstem is a strong leader. He has ever been ambitious and he was close to my father. I cannot fault him. He has been endlessly attentive to me. But even his stewardship is only temporary."

Robin smirked. "Yeah, we noticed his attentiveness too. I think he has you on a pedestal." He hoped this wasn't overstepping some mark, but if it was, she seemed not to take offence.

"I will not deny it," she said, smiling a little. "Many times, as I grew up and came of age, he has made his intentions toward me most clear. I am certain that nothing would make him happier than if I returned his affections. And then we could rule together." She sighed, lacing her fingers on the railing. "A dryad may not rule alone," she explained. "Male or female, there must always be balance. Were I to assume the throne, I must choose a mate. My father and mother ruled together for time immemorial before she died."

She leaned her hands on the railing, looking up pensively into the sky. "There are those amongst my people who believe that his refusal to take a second wife is the reason for the balance of the forest falling out of kilter now. That his ruling alone weakened the elder trees, allowing this whole calamity to happen."

Robin nodded in understanding.

"They think I do not know these things, but I know the gossip."

"So you can't be queen unless you choose a king," he said. "That explains why there's a steward, I guess." He hesitated a little. "But I'm guessing that the simple solution of you and Splinterstem is out of the question? He's not ... that is to say... I mean you don't ..." He trailed off helplessly. Robin didn't feel he was very good at talking to girls in general, and this was basically a fairy princess in a halo of fireflies. A very large one. He was a bit out of his depth.

"I don't return his affections, no," she confirmed, kindly putting him out of his misery. "He is an attentive man. He has assumed so much responsibility since the scourge took father, but I cannot give him my heart, and therefore I cannot rule my people. I lost my heart many years ago."

Robin had an inkling of what she meant. "You were in love with someone else," he said. He had an idea who that might have been. "Splinterstem told us something, about how someone was killed by the minotaur in the Labyrinth, back when it was first built. Was that ...?"

Ashe nodded. "You are far shrewder than you appear, kind Fae. Yes. That was my love. My intended. We would have ruled together one day. His name was Alder. He was not high-born, but he was a fine dryad at that. The whole of Rowandeepling was shaken by his death." The sadness had crept into her green eyes again. "Alder was a favourite of my father. He grew up with Splinterstem himself. The two were good playmates, practically brothers, rising through the ranks together." She glanced back at the feasting hall. "It was not only my heart which was broken the day Alder died. I lost my love. Splinterstem, a brother in arms, and my father lost the man he already thought of as son and, one day, heir."

"I'm sorry," Robin said. There didn't seem to be anything else he could say, so he didn't.

The princess looked back out over Rowandeepling. "My selfishness, my refusal to betray my heart, is leaving my people without a queen. I wonder sometimes…if I should reconsider my options." She looked painfully conflicted as she looked back to him. "But could I betray my own heart that way? Betray my memories? When Alder died, I told myself I would never love again, and I never will. My heart is a cold ember. Perhaps that is cruel of me, selfish. Splinterstem tells me not to trouble myself with worries. He fears my constitution is weak." She sighed. "Is love more important that duty? What would you say, child of the Fae. I would hear your counsel."

Robin honestly didn't know what to say. The princess was looking at him in earnest. He got the distinct impression that, shepherded by Splinterstem, surrounded at all times by handmaidens, she very rarely had anyone to talk to, candidly at least. He considered her dilemma.

"I think …" he said eventually. "I don't know much about being in love. But I think your father would want you to be true to your heart … not to your throne." He looked over at her. "He never remarried, did he? After your mother died." He shrugged. "Maybe there is only one perfect person for all of us? It sounds like he thought so. If you're lonely, maybe you should consider taking a new mate, I don't know. But if you feel the same way your father did, I think you have to trust that you know, deep down, what's more important."

She returned his look for an uncomfortably long time. "You are wise, I think," she said eventually. "And you have a good and honest heart. I can see why she would keep you as her trusted counsellor." She smiled a little more warmly. "And worry not for your part. I am fairly certain that with your heart and that Fae face, you will know plenty of love in your life, child of Erlking. Amor est vitae essentia," she sighed. "*Sine amor, nihil est vita.*"

264

Robin blushed and turned back to the hall. "Now you're just teasing me," he muttered. "I don't speak a word of the Netherworlde high tongue."

Karya and Splinterstem were standing in the archway, evidently having come to fetch them. Robin thought Splinterstem looked a little suspicious, seeing him out here alone with the princess. He glanced over at the girl rather possessively.

"We have a plan, Scion," Karya said, her arms folded under her silky shawl against the cool night air. "Tomorrow, at dawn, the beast of the Elderhart will be tracked and found, and we'll do what we came here to do."

Robin nodded. Splinterstem crossed to the princess, guiding her back inside with a respectful hand at her elbow. "And you should rest, Princess," he told her softly. "This is wearying. Soon, there will be an end to this darkness over our forest, I promise you that."

Ashe nodded a polite farewell to Robin as the two of them disappeared inside, and Karya, once they were gone, looked at her friend, smirking. "I think he thinks you're the competition," she said, rather playfully. "What are you doing out here alone with pretty girls in the night anyway? Sweet-talking the princess, eh?"

Robin felt his face grow hot again. "Oh shut up," he said. "We were just talking. I know you're only winding me up for fun."

She laughed. "Yeah, I know. I can't imagine you being comfortable enough to talk with a pretty girl under the moon, surrounded by fireflies and magic treetops."

"I'm talking to you quite competently, aren't I?" Robin countered, defensively, slumping on the balcony.

Karya stopped, looking a little surprised. She opened her mouth as if to say something, but seemed to change her mind, pulling her shawl closer around her shoulders instead and looking rather self-conscious. Fireflies danced silently between them in the shadows, a cool wind ruffling her curled hair.

"You'd better get some sleep, Robin Fellows," she said eventually, with a small frown. "We all had. After all, we're hunting beasties at first light."

DARKNESS IN THE HOLLOW

Robin thought he would not sleep well, despite the cosy comforts of the treetop palace and soft moss beds in their suite, which were a blessed heaven after sleeping on the rough and root-filled forest ground. He thought he would be too worried. It's bad enough trying to get to sleep the night before an exam. Surely dropping off knowing that, in the morning, you were off to face a dragon was worse.

There was so much else to worry about as well. His missing friends, Hawthorn, Henry and even Jackalope, the sad story of the princess and her lost love, the terrible shame carried by the steward at the death of the king. But astonishingly, even with all these things whirling around his mind, and the insistent chainsaw buzz of Woad's snoring from the balcony, Robin fell asleep almost as soon as his head hit the pillow.

Perhaps it was the comforting honey elixir of the dryads he had been drinking all night, perhaps the lulling, constant susurrus of the autumn leaves below their lofty eyrie in their endless whispering sea, or maybe it was just sheer exhaustion. But he slept like a babe.

The following morning, as the sun's first light was rising above the tree line, Robin, Woad and Karya left Rowandeepling and found themselves back on the forest floor at the base of the great elder trees. The journey down from the sky, carried once again by helpful and strong dryads on their purring iridescent wings, had been no less alarming than their ascent. Karya looked almost as green as their guides.

The princess had bid them farewell up in the hidden city, and almost every dryad of the haven had turned out to watch the three companions leave on their mission, with only Splinterstem himself remaining with them now back on ground level.

He insisted on helping to track and hunt the scourge. To avenge the king.

He stood with Karya, who had dressed herself once more in her familiar travelling garb and was infinitely more normal-looking to Robin and Woad, buried in her huge coat of animal skins. She seemed far more comfortable, more herself. The two of them were examining tracks on the floor near the base of the chasm, while Robin and Woad stamped their feet in the cold morning mist, listening to the autumn leaves fall endlessly around them. Robin was rolling his mana stone over and over between his fingers, trying to remember every single combat cantrip he knew from the Towers of Air, Water and Earth. Woad was simply stretching and looking a little bleary-eyed.

"Hey look, Pinky," he nudged Robin, pointing across the great gully back to the island of the elder trees. Robin followed his gaze. "That must be the entrance to the Labyrinth over there."

Robin could indeed make out, nestled amongst the gargantuan roots, what looked to be a great stone archway. It was covered with vines and tangled roots, looking dark and disused, reminding Robin of pictures he had seen of Angkor Wat back in the human world, old stones completely overgrown. On either side of the dark stone doorway, there were hanging cages, man-sized, slung from the trees themselves.

"I was chatting to some of the dancers last night about the Labyrinth," the faun went on. "That one who was feeding me grapes. She said those cages over there are where they used to imprison criminals. Bad dryads." He sniggered. "Didn't leave them there long or anything, just a day or two to teach them a lesson. She said the punishment of being so near to the horror of the minotaur and hearing its bellows was bad enough for most. Even if it couldn't come out and get them."

Robin thought this was a grisly idea, but he could see from the look of the empty, rusted cages, even from this distance, that they were clearly empty. No one had used them in a long time. Maybe just the threat of being put into one as punishment was deterrent enough.

"Why *doesn't* it ever come out?" Robin wondered. It hadn't occurred to him until now, why the creature wouldn't just escape into the forest given half the chance. He couldn't imagine it was a very nice life, guarding a dank and lightless underground maze.

"It can't," Woad said. "I asked that too. It's chained up, see. Really long chain, mind, so it can move about, up and down the corridors, but not long enough for it to get anywhere near the entrance. It's a prisoner there." He wiggled his fingers in a playfully spooky way. "The dryads told me that those who spent the night in those cages came back with tales of hearing the horrible howls and bellows of the minotaur, and the dragging, constant clank of the chains as it lumbered around endlessly in the tunnels." He grinned evilly. "A bone-chilling clank, a terrible clatter, the constant haunting music of the chains of the beast!"

Robin punched Woad lightly on the arm. "Cut it out, you moron," he grinned.

"If you two have finished sightseeing," Karya called. "We have found the freshest tracks, and I have cast a finding spell." She kicked dirt over a pile of twigs on the floor which were still spinning lightly with her imbued mana. "The scourge is this way, I'm sure of it, and Splinterstem agrees. Let's go slay a drake."

The dryad led them deep into the primal woodland. They walked for hours through hills and valleys under an unbroken canopy of leaves, papery underbrush thick as snowdrifts through which they ploughed, sometimes thigh deep. The day was warm and bright for autumn and the sun, rising high as the day wore on, burned away the mist and fell here and there through the branches high ahead in slender bright beams. The forest was constantly in slumbering motion, filled with the endless drift of pollen, lending the quiet solitude of the wood a magical, dreamlike air. Robin found it difficult to believe that anything bad could be stalking these woods, whether a Shard-maddened monster or the swarm. It was a fairytale space, deep and wild and untamed.

It was also, he remembered, as they left Rowandeepling many miles behind, knackering.

The constant slog up and down hills, between the trees, clambering over knotted roots and under straggling ivy and vines, took its toll even on the seasoned hikers. By midday, Karya called a halt to their exploring.

"It's nearby," she said, in a low and careful voice.

"Really?" Robin said worriedly. "That was quicker than I expected."

Karya scowled at him. "I'm never wrong," she said, her golden eyes glimmering like the leaves around her. "Well, nearly never wrong. And any tracker could tell you that. Some of these trees are gouged, bark flaked, moss nearby flattened, and don't tell me you haven't noticed the smell."

As they made a camp for lunch, sharing the now meagre rations they had left from Erlking, Robin couldn't help but agree. The air in this part of the great forest was somehow richer, earthier, the petrichor freshness of newly-turned soil, the mulch of leaves, and the sharp, almost acidic tang of new cut grass. It smelled…alive.

"Anything?" she asked him, as they sat on the leaves in the hollow of a great trees roots, passing a waterskin between them. Robin's hiking boots, much better for this terrain than his old battered trainers, had nevertheless begun to rub, as all new shoes do, and he was glad of the rest. He had taken one of them off and was shaking it upside down, getting rid of tiny stones from inside.

"Anything what?" he asked, confused.

"She wants to know if your Shard-senses are tingling," Woad explained. "You are the Scion after all. Are you not getting a tingle in your waters, or whatever happens?"

Robin had to admit, he did have a strange sensation. It was nothing to do with his 'waters' or whatever the faun was blithering about, but the hairs on the back of his neck had been standing on end for the last couple of miles. He'd thought this might just be nerves.

"Maybe," he said uncertainly. "Look, what is the actual plan when we find this thing? Do we even have one? I've never slain anything before. I mean, I know a few combat moves, but I think going in blind is a bad idea. We only have a sketchy idea what we're up against."

Karya nodded sagely. "Keep it simple, I thought," she said. "Splinterstem and I will use Earth magic to try and hamper it as much as possible, maybe root it to the floor if we can, try and keep it in one place," She pointed at the faun. "Woad, you do what you do best and cause a distraction." Woad nodded eagerly, cracking his knuckles. "And then you, Scion, rush in and take the Shard from it."

"How do you expect me to do that?" Robin wanted to know. Karya shrugged.

"We'll have to play it by ear," she admitted. "In the past, the Arcania has wanted to come to you, it's almost like it yearns for you. On the floating island, the Shard shot over the room and literally stabbed into you, right? And in the sunken tomb, the second Shard sucked you into its watery tornado so you could get it. I'm hoping the same thing will happen here. Thought there might be more of a struggle as it's already been claimed."

Robin didn't feel this was a very solid plan for them all to risk their lives over, and said so. Karya pointed out that no one else had any better ideas, and he couldn't really argue with that.

"Do you think we should be concerned about this 'pale hooded man'?" he asked, as they set off again. "Splinterstem said there were strange things in the Elderhart, before the beast ever showed up. Not only trouble with the swarm, increased skirmishes or whatever, but this oddball wandering around. He might have been the one who went into the minotaur's lair and got the Shard out. The one who woke up the monster we're hunting right now."

Karya agreed this pale wanderer was an unknown factor, and they should certainly be on the lookout for anyone of that description, but they had so little to go on, it wasn't something they could devote much time to worrying about.

At mid-afternoon, they reached a part of the forest which was reasonably level, a deep and wide bowl of a valley which cut between high wooded hills on either side. The tall dryad suddenly stopped dead, hand raised to halt the others.

"What is it?" Karya whispered. The woods around them were quiet and hushed. The occasional falling leaf the only movement.

"Listen," the dryad said. "Do you hear?"

Robin, like the others, strained to hear anything. There seemed only the rhythmic rush of the wind, high above them in the trees, and he looked at his companions in confusion.

"I hear it," Woad whispered excitedly. And a moment later, Robin did too.

Hiding beneath the sound of the wind, matching it in waves, rising and falling, there was a deep and distant breathing, some great creature.

"And look," Karya pointed away between the tree trunks. Some way off to their right, there was a natural break in the valley wall, where the crumbling mossy hill was broken and a gorge of sorts, half hidden by leaves and tangled branches, made a form of tunnel. Bare jagged limestone poked through the earth like old bone through green flesh, and the grass and leaves around it seemed withered and grey.

"The mark of the scourge," the dryad said. "It sucks the life from the forest wherever it goes."

Robin listened to the loud, heavy breathing. He knew, without a shadow of doubt, that beyond that narrow pass between the wooded cliffs, the creature they hunted lay. He felt it in every quivering fibre of his being.

Karya raised cupped hands to her mouth and whispered something to herself. When she opened her hands, dozens of tiny green fireflies fluttered from her palms, little guiding lights. They watched as this slim, glinting tide weaved away through the trees, disappearing into the crevasse of gnarled trees.

"We've found it," she hissed to her companions. "Finding spell. Basic Earth mana. Come on."

They advanced cautiously through the trees toward the gap, taking care not to step in deep leaves that may rustle and give them away. As they closed in, and the grass beneath their feet became dry and coarse, sucked clean of life and vitality, the sound of the heavy breathing became clearer, long and slow, and huge.

"The heart of the forest *must* be retrieved," Splinterstem told them, grabbing Karya by the arm. His green eyes were bright and hard. "It must not be damaged or hurt. It must be taken back to Rowandeepling. All depends on it."

"Understood." Karya shook him off rather impatiently. "That's what we're here for."

They passed cautiously into the hollow, Robin somehow finding himself in the lead. His heart was pounding, his mana stone pulsing against his chest, matching it with a second beat. The autumn day was golden but had grown cold. Yet even so, he felt sweat trickle between his shoulder blades with nerves.

Beyond the gap, through a screen of tree branches which were completely dead, white and petrified, the forest opened up into a sunken glade. Everything here in this low bowl of land was dead. The ground was grey and bare, what grass there remained was crisp and dry. The leafless trees were pale and blasted, or blackened and scorched. All seemed ash and dust and desolation. Deep in the blighted hollow, where the ground rose up in a high rugged hump, there was a cave, wide, jagged and dark, and filling its mouth was the beast itself.

"It *is* a bloody dragon," Robin found himself whispering urgently, almost against his will. "I *knew* it would be a bloody dragon. It's a big bloody *dragon*."

Only the head of the enormous drake was visible, the rest of the great

271

creature evidently lost in the darkness of the cave behind it. This vast, lizardlike countenance rested on the forest floor, amidst the dry and withered grass, and it was truly immense. A skull easily the size of a large car, draconian and wild. The drake was a deep, sage green, scaled and rough looking, and along its face, in ridges beneath its eyes, and in great curls above its strangely equine brow, long grey horns sprouted. It seemed positively vibrant against the grey of its surroundings, a thick beard of tangled green moss cushioning its snout on the dead, dusty earth. Stones seemed embedded between its scales, riverbed-round and flecked with sparkling mica. It was the forest incarnate.

Like the earth-lions they had rode, out on the grasslands, the scourge of the Elderhart was made, it seemed, of earth and tree and soil and leaf. Only on a far greater scale.

A wild and dangerous spirit of the woods, abundant with life and fertility, resting amidst the desolation it had wrought.

Of primary interest to all of them however, was the shining diamond-shaped glow which emanated from the drake's huge forehead. It was emerald green, a jewel as sharp and long as a sword blade, and embedded in the forest-dragon like a third eye. It shimmered and pulsed with such a raw energy that to look directly at it made their eyes water, made them feel as though they were being pulled slightly from their sockets.

Robin had been so entranced by the sight, feeling oddly mesmerised by it, that he felt the Puck stir deep within him, curiosity raised, and he was clear of the trees and halfway down the slope of the deadly hollow before he realised it. Stopped only by the frantic hisses of his companions.

"Scion!" Karya snapped from the bushes, desperately keeping her voice low. "What are you doing?! Get back here, you idiot!"

"Pinky, you'll be eaten!" Woad agreed, peering from behind the skeletal branches at the top of the rise.

Robin blinked in confusion, feeling as though he had been sleepwalking. He had no real memory of leaving the others and walking slowly down the slope. The Puck had risen and taken over. His eyes were drawn by the Shard, that great glimmering emerald in the skull of the nightmarish beast before them. His own eyes itched, and he blinked rapidly, determined to regain control. He had no doubt that the Puck had moved him. It wanted the Shard, and the Shard wanted him. There was no question of danger. He would as readily have walked blindly into a hungry lion's cage.

Robin shook his head forcefully, squeezing his eyes closed. He had no doubt that they were as green and bright as the Shard. His hair probably white as milk. The Puck rose like gorge in his throat and Robin forced himself to swallow mentally, pushing the power back down. He would *not* lose control, he told himself. It was as Karya had said. *He* was the Puck. It was a part of him. He could control it. He had to learn how.

It was insanity, walking down into the hollow, into the mouth of the great sleeping drake, but the draw of the Shard was so strong. It sang in his bones, a vibrating music, impossible to resist.

Karya motioned frantically for him to return "You're going to–"

A blast of hot air from the nostrils of the huge animal rolled over Robin, blowing his hair back from his forehead, and he halted, shocked. With a gargantuan rumble of motion, the large head ponderously lifted from the ground, shaking loose a small avalanche of scree, which fell to the ground with a clatter. Its head turned to the side, an ancient dinosaur built from bark and earth, and its hoary, snake-like eye, as large as Robin himself, flicked open.

"… wake it," Karya finished weakly.

The eye was orange, as bright and fiery as a setting autumn sun. The vertical pupil took in Robin, a milky inner lid sliding over its jewelled surface, and it contracted to a thin slit. As Robin stumbled backwards, the great drake opened its mouth wide, revealing an alarmingly large red maw, filled with teeth as long as swords, and it roared.

The noise deafened them all, shaking the trees, causing a flurry of leaves to dislodge from the forest canopy above and rain down on the hollow in a snow of red and yellow flakes. Stones and pebbles jumped and danced like popping corn kernels in a hot pan, and the great scourge lumbered out of the cave, dragging its moss-covered body thunderously across the ground.

Robin scrambled quickly to his feet, his hands scuffed with mud. He was dimly aware of Karya and Woad leaping down into the depression to join him, both slipping and sliding on a small wave of leaves. Woad was shouting something. Karya's mana stone bracelet flashed like amber lightning as she built her mana, preparing to cast. But Robin was transfixed by the huge and commanding creature in front of him.

It wasn't a snake, as some had said, though its body, emerging from the cave in long coils was snakelike, long and scaled and sinuous. Its sides and flanks were covered with moss and patchy grass, and along its long back there grew a spine of sharp and jagged rocks, a stegosaurus. But this long snake had legs, powerful claws digging into the soft earth beneath as it dragged itself forward, tearing up the ground as it reared above Robin, never once taking its fury-filled eye off the boy.

It looked to him like a Chinese dragon. There had been parades, back when he had lived in the city with Gran, every Chinese New Year, and people would dress up, forming a conga line of sorts under a long and curious dragon body of silk panels, weaving and undulating through the streets to cheers of the crowds which lined the pavements, dancing along to powerful banging drums and the clash of cymbals. Robin had a clear memory of going to see the spectacle as a young boy and he had found the street dragon terrifying and mesmeric at the same time, with its bobbing, wide-mawed head and large wild eyes. This was the same. The creature in the grove coiled and weaved sinuously, leaves falling from its sides in flurries. It filled his immediate future.

"Don't just stand there like a lemon!" Karya yelled, suddenly at his side. She dropped to the ground and thrust her arms into the soil, coat flying out behind her. Beneath the beast, the floor bucked and writhed, and suddenly, from a hundred points, the earth erupted. Strong vines, thicker than a man's waist, shot out from the ground, green and snaking. With a shower of soil, the countless tendrils coursed up into the air around the drake, cracking like powerful whips as they arced through the sunbeams. Waving green tentacles, they flew in every direction, wrapping around the huge creature, falling over its bucking sides and plunging back into the earth, burrowing deep. Karya's eyes glowed, golden fire, and sweat was standing on her forehead, arms still thrust into the soil to her elbows, as she drew the net of creaking vines tighter. A binding spell. She was trying to pin the beast to the ground, to catch it in a net of vegetation.

Robin saw Woad spring over the mass of vines, clambering up them even as they grew and thickened, and the monster bucked and strained against their weight. The faun scampered up the sides, leaping from creeper to creeper with dizzying agility and a manic bellowing war cry. His own mana stone flashed, a white storm, and wisps of alarming firecracker light began to pop and burst in mid-air around the beast, disorienting and distracting. The faun fearlessly made his way to the top of the scourge's back, scaling the stones of its spine like a cat up a tree.

It seemed to be working. The vines were thick ropes, tangling the forest dragon, pulling its squirming, writhing body to the ground. The immense animal bellowed again, shaking the forest.

Robin grabbed for his mana stone too. He had to help. But where on earth was the dryad? Why wasn't he helping? In the confusion, he glanced around and saw Splinterstem, still high at the lip of the hollow, half-obscured by the branches which had marked their entrance. He was just standing there, watching them, as still as the trees all around them. Perhaps he was paralysed by fear.

There was no time to worry about him. Robin knew his mana had been hard to control lately, but he had to get it in hand. His friends were depending on him, and this close to a Shard of the Arcania, he could feel the Puck bubbling just beneath the surface of his mind. He had to let it out, to relinquish control, to trust that he could direct the power of the Scion inside him.

There was a cry of pain from Karya. Something had gone wrong with her spell. The vines around the drake were withering, turning grey and papery. The scourge was absorbing the life from them, feeding on Karya's Earth mana. As he watched, they were dying one by one, crumbling into dust. The creature reared, snapping hundreds of them with deafening cracks. Untethered vines lashed out and fell everywhere, thudding into the hillsides of the hollow with great speed and force. Robin leapt aside to avoid being crushed by one which landed where he had been standing only a moment before, gouging the ground even as it disintegrated.

The drake shook itself violently. A cry came from Woad as the faun lost his footing, tossed high in the air as the monster worked angrily to free itself. The blue boy fell and slid head over heels down the creature's long and scaly back, out of their sight.

With an almighty roar, the drake broke free of the petrifying net, and with a lightening quick buck of its coiled flanks, it lashed out with its great tail, catching Karya full force, sending her flying through the air. Her body was catapulted across the clearing to land in a rolling heap amongst a deep drift of dry dead leaves.

"Karya!" Robin shouted. She had been hit and thrown with such force that Robin's blood ran cold. She might have been killed. He started to turn, to look for Woad. Where had the faun fallen? Had he been crushed by the weight of the monster? But as he turned, the drake reached out and, with a swipe of its great claws, caught Robin hard, lifting him high into the air as well.

Winded, Robin tumbled over and over, hitting the ground several times as he rolled to a halt, leaves in his hair and face. He was half-buried in mud and dirt, gasping into the ground. His arm felt like it was on fire. Had he broken it? His vision was blurry where his head had bounced along the floor, and there was a high pitched keening in the back of his skull.

Get up! he shouted at himself, feeling the ground thunder and shake as the forest drake lumbered swiftly after him, bearing down on the boy like an avalanche. *Get up get up get up, it's going to kill you!*

Forcing himself groggily to his knees, Robin raised a shaking arm and with a flash of mana let forth a barrage of Galestrikes in the dragon's direction. They were powerful blasts of Air magic, invisible javelins of wind. He saw them tear the forest floor into tornados as they roared across the ground, scattering leaves, but watched in horror as they hit the great, serpentine head of the creature like nothing more than a strong breeze, ruffling its long beard of moss. The drake shook its gargantuan head, casting off the winds, its grassy flanks fluttering and flowing in the slipstream of the attack. It roared again, seemingly only angered by Robin's barrage.

He stood, arm throbbing and teeth clenched, refocussing his mana, remembering his stances from every combat lesson he'd had at Erlking. Robin dug his heels into the soft earth, dropping low and threw with all his might a flurry of Needlepoint spells. Daggers of ice, a thick maelstrom erupting from his open arms. They glittered in the sunlight, flickering through the air, and buried themselves in the monster's approaching hide, as efficient as toothpicks. Almost immediately on impact they began to melt, simply sinking into the nightmarish creature's skin.

Yes, well done, Robin, he told himself slightly hysterically. *Water the great big plant dragon, good plan, that'll help.*

Nothing was working. It was simply too strong. It had a Shard of the Arcania fuelling its anger.

With nowhere behind him to dodge, the steep sides of the hollow at his back, Robin ran straight at the drake as it bore down on him, diving at the last moment to avoid its dangerously snapping jaws. Throwing himself onto his stomach between its clawed legs, he rolled under the belly of the enormous creature, covering himself in a flurry of crumbling dead leaves and dirt, and scrambled out the other side, back to his feet, trying to get behind it, away from the end with the jaws. He knew that much about dragons. Stay away from the pointy end. Dragon-slaying 101.

With a crash like a falling oak, the scourge's tail hit the ground, inches from his face, forcing him to leap to the right to avoid being crushed.

The beast hissed, a loud sound of pure fury, as it began to turn to follow its elusive quarry.

Robin stared around the hollow, wild-eyed and panting, seeking out the others. Karya, he saw lay some way off, still unconscious …or worse. And there was something else wrong with her. The girl was covered in vines, tethering her to the ground, keeping her body firmly prisoner against the forest floor. How had this happened? Was this the beast? Could it control the earth too? Tying her in a net just as surely as she had tried to with it?

A flash of blue in the grey and blasted ground nearby drew Robin's eye as he ran around the monster's powerfully lashing tail, and he saw with horror that the same fate had befallen Woad. A humped pile of tangled vines, as thick as a nest of snakes, made a green and mossy grave-hump, tight and inescapable, from which there stuck a single limp blue hand.

His friends were out of action. It was just him alone in the hollow. Robin and the scourge.

A deep rumbling growl immediately behind him made Robin spin. He stumbled as he saw that the dragon had turned fully while he had been momentarily distracted, seeking out his companions. Its huge face was mere inches from his. It was all that he could see. Before he could react or think, its massive jaws opened wide, and Robin was staring into the deep and deadly throat of the monster.

This is it, he thought, in a strangely detached way, as fear rooted him to the spot. *This is how I die? Eaten by the forest.*

He raised his arms in instinctive defence, but there was no time for anything else. Nowhere to dodge to, left or right, hemmed in by coils on both sides. Robin squeezed his eyes closed, grimacing.

A force, invisible and strong, gripped Robin around the waist like a great ghostly hand. It was cold and it lifted him swiftly into the air like a rag doll. Dragged upwards, wind whipping past his face and blowing leaves from his hair, Robin let out a cry as the dragon snapped, just missing taking off his leg.

He soared high over its head, flying like a terrified Peter Pan, arms and legs flailing. A puppet on unseen strings as he rose higher still.

From his dizzying vantage point in mid-air, he saw a sight so unexpected, that for a moment, even amidst the confusion and the panic of being forcibly hurled through the air, he goggled in shock.

A large figure had entered the hollow, making its way down the slope hurriedly, crashing through the leaves. It was clad in black armour, looking like a shadow amongst the sunbeams. In one hand, a long, cruel sword was drawn, the point dragging in the hillside behind it as it descended. The other arm was outstretched toward Robin, holding the boy aloft effortlessly with the sheer force of mana alone. Behind the shining figure, a dark knight come to face the dragon, a long cloak of black feathers rushed.

Strigoi?

Robin had only a moment to process this. Strigoi, the Wolf of Eris, who had been hunting him relentlessly, had just saved him? Had used his mana to throw Robin clear of the monster's jaws?

"You, Faespawn …" the wolf-headed man hissed coldly, his metal mask trained not on Robin, but solely on the scourge, "… are in my way! This Shard is mine!"

Without breaking stride, Strigoi flicked his hand as he reached the bottom of the hollow, sending the giddily-suspended boy careening through the air and away from the thrashing danger of the dragon. Cast aside like a brushed leaf, Robin hit the high slopes of the glade hard, lightening pain shooting up through his injured arm, as he rolled back down the steep slope, end over end.

Bewildered and disoriented, he struggled woozily back to his feet, shaking mulch out of his hair. What the hell was Strigoi doing here?

He watched as the armoured man rushed headlong at the drake, which had turned to face this new threat, rearing up its long green neck and hissing in anger. The creature swiped at the dark figure with its claws, but Strigoi ducked easily beneath the huge talons, a flurry of ebony feathers, rolling beneath the monster's grasp and leaping back to his feet with an agile spring which Robin would have thought impossible in such cumbersome and clanking armour. A black metal hand waved, slashing the air, and even from across the hollow, Robin felt the pulse of mana erupt, flying toward the drake in a shimmering wave of heat-haze.

Remarkably, Strigoi's mana unbalanced the forest dragon, knocking it backward, stumbling and roaring in surprise. Without giving it time to recover, the Wolf of Eris lunged onwards viciously, swinging his huge sword over his head in a practised arc and bringing it down with a great slash across the exposed throat of the beast.

The dark jewels set in the sword's grip flashed as the blow landed, Strigoi pushing even more mana into the blow, and a deep wound opened on the mossy neck of his enemy.

It was not blood which spurted from this wound, Robin saw, but a deep green ichor. It landed on the dead grass in splatters. Where the liquid fell, the forest immediately revived, flourishing into life here and there in sudden patches, wild green grass thrusting up urgently through the dead soil and springing wildflowers uncurling, red and white.

The Scourge countered his aggressive blows, lunging with snapping jaws for the man. Strigoi leapt back nimbly, just in time, a grunt echoing in his fearsome visage.

He must have tracked them to the forest, followed their path all this way, to Rowandeepling. Strigoi knew that following the Scion would eventually lead him to the beast, and the prize he sought for his mistress.

The dark knight ran around the drake, swift and sure-footed, his long cloak whipping noisily behind him, a flurry of black wings. He was constantly moving, forcing the creature to turn, coil into coil, to follow him, never giving it a moment to centre itself and lunge.

The wound on its great neck however, Robin saw, was already beginning to heal, the Shard embedded in its forehead blazing as the gory slash crept over with moss and bark and rolling stone, knitting it back together slowly. But Strigoi was giving it no quarter. Blast after blast of relentless mana poured from him, thrown like invisible spears at flank and claw and tail, slapping away the scourge's swipes and lunges, connecting each time with a thunderclap of force that sent ripples of power rolling out through the hollow.

Robin had to stop him. Strigoi could not be allowed to claim the Shard. He *had* to get it first. He was furious at being cast aside like a bothersome fly and worried sick about his friends. Every part of him ached, and the battle between the dark champion of Dis and the great beast was ranging all over the hollow, perilously close to where Karya and Woad lay immobilised. They were helpless. It was only a matter of time until the scourge brought down one of its huge feet, crushing them.

"Stop!" he yelled, finding himself rushing, against all reason, back down into the fray, headed straight toward the battling duo. "The Shard is mine! You won't have it!"

Strigoi ignored Robin completely, his entire focus on his relentless barrage on the snapping, roaring dragon. With each slap of dark mana, the sword sliced the air, finding its mark more often than not. Cuts and wounds were appearing all over the drake. The ground in which the two fought, dancing around one another, slowly becoming a verdant carpet where the green blood fell, vegetation creeping further up the dead hillsides with every blow and each passing moment.

Robin dodged a great sweep of the beast's tail, ducking under it as it soared overhead. He was full of anger and fear, but he had to admit, also a little awed. Strigoi simply would not tire. He was fast, much faster than Robin thought possible, and he was either fearless or completely mad, throwing himself in leaps and lunges over and between the violently thrashing coils.

The metal mask, with its fierce expression of frozen cruelty, flicked toward Robin, who sensed anger pouring from it in waves. Clouds of breath escaped it.

"Get back, you useless wretch!" Strigoi hissed. "Not yet! I have no use for you until it is weakened!"

Strigoi raised a hand toward Robin while slicing at the dragon's flank, and the boy found himself hit once again full force in the chest with an invisible fist. It knocked him flat on his back and sent him skittering away once more, out of range of the battle.

Robin swiftly leapt back to his feet, his temper snapping completely. He was being pushed aside as though he were nothing! He would *not* let his friends fall. He would *not* let this whirlwind of dark violence steal the Shard from him.

The familiar anger which had been bubbling up inside him all summer rose to the surface, and Robin closed his eyes, taking a deep breath and feeling his mana stone blaze like a hot coal on his chest. He was afraid of the drake, yes. It would be bloody stupid not to be. He was afraid of Strigoi too. His worst and most powerful enemy, battling right before him and seemingly not even close to tiring. But of one thing, Robin was sure. He was no longer afraid of the Puck. Of himself.

Come on, he thought angrily. *I need you now.*

From deep within him, like a roaring tide, he felt his mana rise, happy to be willingly summoned in full force for the first time.

The power of it roared through his veins, consuming him from within, a dark storm, and for the first time he could remember, Robin didn't fight it. He welcomed it.

The drake roared again, lashing out with its great tail, this time catching Strigoi on the back of the legs, knocking the armoured demon onto his back amidst the newly-grown grass and flowers, crushing them and sending up great sprays of pollen.

Across the hollow, Robin opened his bright green eyes, and the Puck stared out at the scene before him. Wind and water raged within his mind, the forces of the Arcania, unbridled and unfettered. Atop his head, he could feel the autumn wind rushing through invisible horns.

Strigoi was scrambling back to his feet, but Robin saw that the beast was bearing down on him, one great claw descending like a hammer. It was going to crush him, skilled a fighter as he was, the Wolf of Eris wouldn't get clear in time.

Robin cast a Galestrike, a sonic boom of mana thundering around the hollow, shaking the trees and the earth, leaves whipping everywhere. The Galestrike hit the huge claw full force, blasting it apart in an explosion of moss, soil and rock.

The drake reared back, howling deafeningly in pain and anger. Its severed claw, blasted to smithereens, rained down on the forest floor, clumps of living matter. Thick grass and small, pale saplings wormed swiftly out of the earth where the blasted chunks fell.

Strigoi was back on his feet and his dark visage glared across the hollow to where Robin stood with the force of the Arcania flowing through him. Wind crackling around the boy's bunched fists. Wind tinged with a flurry of shadow.

"Interesting," the dark man whispered, regarding the Puck in person for the first time. "The worm has teeth it seems."

He took advantage of the reeling drake, throwing himself forward into its bucking body. Strigoi leapt and ran up the exposed arch of its throat as it reared backward in agony, thrusting his sword deeply into its rocky green side. The blade disappeared to the hilt and the man hung from it, slicing the flesh in a long swoop as he fell back to the ground.

"More!" he growled in fierce command. "It is weakened! It is almost time!"

Robin had no time to consider the strangeness of this unlikely combat team. Puck was steering and Puck did not care who helped and who failed.

Puck wanted only the Shard, by any means. Through the chaos and the noise of the fight, it called to him, a high clear note, a musical saw cutting through the fury of battle.

Robin ran toward the drake, fearless and filled with power, a fury equal to Strigoi, throwing out Needlepoints before him. Shards of ice as long as his arm and thicker than spears formed in mid air, sailing toward the dragon and thudding into its side, peppering it with heavy attacks, over and over, until the scourge resembled a long, snakelike porcupine. This ice was permafrost, harder than iron, and it hissed and steamed in the creature's flanks as it tried to right itself. The dragon's orange eyes were filled with dark murderous fury.

In the increasingly verdant glade, Strigoi and Robin lashed out together at the beast, caught between them, attacked from both sides. Sword and Galestrike, Strigoi's walls of mana and Robin's blasts of furious wind.

The beast was beginning to buckle. It shook its great head in animal confusion, snapping at Robin with its huge mouth, a deadly blow which the Puck avoided by using Featherbreath almost unconsciously to lift Robin out of the way, a leaping, horned fury in a tornado of leaves.

"It is time, Fae-thing!" Strigoi said, triumphantly, circling the dragon toward the boy. "The beast is weak. The Shard is mine for the taking … but I cannot take it."

He grabbed Robin by the wrist, cold metal tight around his skin. Robin, even with the power of Puck flooding through him, felt the bones of his arm grate under the grasp, and he cried out in pain.

"The Oracle told me! Only you can claim the Shard from the monster," Strigoi hissed, his carved animal face inches from Robin's. "Even dogs have their uses. Once *you* have it, then *I* have it. Now, be an obedient dog…and fetch!"

Without warning, Strigoi launched Robin bodily into the air, throwing him at the ailing dragon.

Robin, yelping in pain and shock, flew across the glade, a vision of the hollow spinning before him as he hurtled toward the scourge's head and the Shard embedded there.

In that last moment of confusion, Robin saw Strigoi below him, standing amidst the coils of the beast, knee deep in grass and crushed flowers, his black armour glinting, his demonic wolf face grinning up at the Fae he had just thrown like bait to a shark. He was panting, his cloak tattered from the battle, his heavy sword at his side. And then the tail of the injured dragon lashed out and struck him.

Eris' wolf was smashed through the air, a swatted fly. He soared across the hollow, hitting the steep banks with a great thud, and rolling bonelessly back down the slope to the floor, where he lay facedown and motionless.

Robin had no time to react to this. Puck turned his head toward the dragon, the hunger for the Shard all consuming.

He had been flung at the creature's face, propelled by Strigoi's mana, but it was not the glowing prize of the Shard embedded in its forehead which Robin now saw awaiting him. It was the mouth of the dragon, open wide, deep and red. And into its immense throat, brimming with the forces of the Arcania and helpless to stop himself, Robin fell, hearing the jaws slam shut behind him with a snap, as his world was plunged into darkness.

DUO REGIS

Robin floated in a featureless sea of peaceful green light. Weightless, still and calm.

He slowly began to feel his body around him, arms and legs outstretched, his white hair flowing straight upward from his head, curling and tangling softly against horns, tall antlers of white ivory which were as strong as solid oak. It was like being in the ocean, submerged in a soft warm place, bobbed along by unseen and gentle tides which flowed around and against him from every direction.

He felt peaceful, sure of himself. He was not afraid. He was the Puck, and the silent majesty of the greatest forests, with their deep and secret places, filled every cell of his body like a resonant song.

If I'm dead, he thought oddly to himself, *then this isn't so bad after all. It doesn't even hurt.*

His aches and pains were gone. His damaged arm did not burn, his battered head did not smart. He simply let himself flow through the endless green light, feeling it fall across his face, dappled and warm as the sun.

I'm not dead, he realised, with the same strange certainty one has in dreams. *I'm in the drake. Somehow. Not mashed into a pulp, not in its stomach, but within it, at one with it. With the Shard, with the Arcania.*

There was no up or down here on this primordial plane, no real sense of direction at all, but almost simply because he wished for it, he felt his feet touch a solid surface, found himself standing, the gentle, strong flow of the forest heartbeat still pushing gently all around him.

And I'm not alone, he decided with certainly.

In the shimmering emerald glow, Robin found himself turning in this silent prismatic space. Behind him, there was another figure, on its knees, shoulders slumped, head down. Robin, through the crystal clear eyes of the Puck, regarded it solemnly.

It was a man before him, a dryad. His clothing was, as with all dryads, an artful patchwork of the trees and woods themselves, woven moss and leaves, a great cloak of russet autumn foliage spilling around him. Atop his bowed head, there rested a silver crown, carved in the shape of many entwined leaves.

"You are the king," Puck said. He hadn't been certain, before he spoke, whether his voice would carry in this strange, dreamlike space. It didn't seem real after all. Not a physical realm, more ... a meeting place for minds. But the words echoed around him. It was still Robin's voice, but it rustled like the susurrus of the forest canopy too.

"The king of the dryads. We are ... within you," Robin confirmed, quite sure of himself. He looked around, at the endless shining power of the Shard about them. And realisation dawned.

"You were not killed by the beast, by this dragon of the forest," the Puck said curiously, walking slowly toward the huddled figure, power flowed around him in eddying currents as he moved. "You *are* the beast."

The dryad king slowly raised his head as Robin approached. His face was old and lined, but not unkind. He wore a long mossy beard, and his faceted, insectile eyes looked tired. Wearier than any eyes Robin had ever seen.

"I am," he said in reply. "The Shard ... the Shard has made me so. The Shard has made me the scourge of my own kingdom."

The king, still kneeling, opened his large cupped hands, and Robin saw that he cradled something. A shifting, prismatic nebula, flickering and blazing silently. It rolled over and over on itself, enchanting and beautiful, throwing its light up onto their faces. Power, raw and overwhelming, poured from it. Robin felt it tingle in his horns and stab hungrily into his eyes.

"The Earth Shard," Puck said in quiet wonder. "The heart of the forest."

He knew then what had happened. The beast had not come out of the shadows, emerging from the forest, attacking and killing the king of the dryads. That hadn't been true at all. The king had taken the Shard, somehow. It had been too powerful for him to control. Its power had engulfed him.

"You could not contain it," Puck said, hovering his hand above the Shard, feeling its warmth as the weary king, still kneeling, held it out before him like an offering. "Too much power, even for a ruler of the forest. It consumed you…devolved you…built the forest around your body. You have become the drake."

The king looked up at Robin, his lined face grave. "I am dead," he said simply. "But the Shard … it will not let me go. It has such hunger, for life. I roam the forest, taking more of it into myself. I grow, become more terrible. I take the life of the land into myself. It will not stop."

He blinked at Robin, his old eyes roaming over the primal force of the teenage boy standing before him in this unreal place, horned and shining like a fierce young god.

"I know who you are," the king said. "You are Fae. You are the Scion of the Arcania. How is it that you are you here?"

"My enemy," the Puck explained simply. "He threw me to the beast, to you. He knew the Shard would take me too. I think he counts on my strength to control it. To take the Shard back from you."

"And can you?" the king asked hopefully. He seemed so withered and weary. "Can you take it? I am so tired, Scion of the Arcania. I wish for the everafter. I wish to see my wife."

"Then give it to me," Robin said calmly, the voice of the Puck rolling from him with quiet command. "There is no power I cannot bear. I cannot take it from you however. Power stolen from a king can never last. It must be given freely."

The king of the dryads nodded, and in that peaceful place, glimmering green and bright, he passed the Shard of the Arcania into Robin's hands.

Robin felt the weight of it. Its energy poured up his arms like twisting roots and vines in his bloodstream. The sheer, intoxicating power of it.

The warm and comforting green light, in this odd, unreal dimension, was beginning to fade. The king stooped, exhausted, lowering his head but looking relieved to be free of the terrible burden of the Shard. He sank back to his knees, sighing, as though a great weight had been lifted from his shoulders.

"Thank you," he whispered. "You have saved me, Scion. You have… released me."

He was sinking into shadows, the green light plummeting fast now all around Robin, so that he could barely see the spirit of the dryad king at all. The only remaining light was the Shard itself, flickering and pulsing in his hands, throwing its illumination and power back onto him in silent pulses.

"But why?" he asked, his voice more Robin than Puck. He had to know, before this place disappeared. "Why did you take the Shard from the Labyrinth? Why did you tear out the heart of the elder trees?"

In the near darkness, he thought he saw the king raise his head, a glimmer of faceted green eyes in the shadows.

"I did not ..." came the reply. "Not I. Do not ... trust him."

The endless green void was gone. The Shard pulsed once more in Robin's hands, and with the hands of the Puck, he raised it before him and stared into its swirling depths. The twinkling lights at its core, fireflies in dark treetops, flickered out one by one, and then there was nothing.

Robin opened his eyes, gasping. Light flooded into his face, harsh and bright after the soft and dreamlike space of the Shard. And with the light came pain. His arm screamed, his head throbbed, and his ribs felt bruised and scraped. He was lying on his back, under some kind of tight and smothering blanket. Whatever it was, it covered half his face as well.

Coughing and spluttering, he forced himself to sit up, shedding the heaviness above him as he realised it was not a blanket at all. It was moss and grass and soil. It had grown right over him.

Dizzy and shaking, he tore the moss cocoon from his legs and chest, digging himself out of the ground. Everything was very quiet and still around him.

I'm in the hollow, he thought to himself, disjointedly. *I'm back.*

Looking around blearily through watering eyes, he saw that the drake, the transformed scourge that had been the dryad king, was gone. Its huge draconian body, made from the forest made solid, willed together by the power of the Shard, had crumbled. It lay around him in chunks. Boulders, swathes of moss, great lattice heaps of twigs and branches. The green lifeblood of the beast had spilled all over the once dead floor of the empty hollow and, feeding back the energy it had stolen, it had created a sweeping carpet of lush vegetation. Ivy was growing everywhere, fast enough that Robin could watch its questing, quiet fingers, curling around the rocks and wood that had made the body of the great monster, tearing it apart bit by bit. The dead leaves of the ground were covered in thick fresh moss and grass. Robin had been buried under it where he had fallen.

Staggering to his feet, he gingerly felt the top of his head. There were no horns. Evidently, Puck had retreated. But he felt...different. His vision swam. There was no quiet inner voice at the back of his head as there had always been before. Noticing its absence was like noticing the soft ticking of a clock only when it stops.

He had accepted the Puck, had ceased to fight against his own power, tinged as it was with a dash of darkness. The conflict which he had felt raging just below the surface for months was gone. Despite his aching and bruised body, he felt strangely calm. At peace.

Looking down, Robin saw something resting in his hand. He was gripping it so tightly his bloodied knuckles were white, but he hadn't even realised he was holding it.

It looked like a large jewel, as big as a fist. An emerald, rough and uncut. Deep in its shining heart, golden sunlight flowed.

"I have the Shard," he said, shocked by how hoarse and broken his voice sounded.

He stared around the freshly verdant hollow, desperately seeking his friends. Where were Woad and Karya? Were they still trapped under vines? Had the creeping carpet of moss and grass, in its eagerness to spread, grown over them too? He had to find them, free them.

He looked around. The glade, transformed utterly by the death of the drake, was unrecognisable. Even now he could hear the creaking of small saplings as they pushed their way up into the air between the mossy boulders, rustling as their new leaves opened to the sky. All around his feet, bushy grass shook and grew, and flowers folded back their petals. The whole place was in quiet, lively motion.

Robin took a few stumbling steps, feeling dreadfully unsteady, turning in a circle and trying to get his bearings. He could see the mouth of the cave where they had first sighted the drake, although now he saw its dark opening was covered in a thick curtain of trailing creepers, even now blooming with pale buds.

"Karya? Woad?" he yelled. "Where are you?"

He made his unsteady way across the floor of the hollow, between the new trees and behind a fallen tangle of twigs and scree, scanning the ground for friend-shaped lumps. Where had Woad been lying? He was sure it was here. His eyes fell on a small hillock, lumpily distorted. *Oh thank God!* He lurched towards it, nausea spiking with each lumbering step. He dropped next to the form, vision swimming as he tore the growth from the body.

There, lying motionless in the grass before him, looking up at the sun, like a shining, overturned beetle, was Strigoi.

Robin's blood ran cold. The Wolf of Eris wasn't moving. He was either unconscious or dead, lying incongruously on the lush ground with the soft sunbeams falling on his dark cruelly-shaped armour. Tiny vines and plants twined around his legs and his still, gloved fingers.

Strigoi's sword had been thrown clear when the beast had launched him violently across the glade. It lay some way off, blade embedded deep in the soil. Thin curls of twining vine were creeping up the black hilt, odd white flowers opening and shivering here and there across its length. It reminded Robin of the old Arthurian legends, of the sword in the stone.

Gripping the Earth Shard tightly, Robin stooped over the wolf, staring down at his fallen enemy. He listened, and in the stillness of the forest, from within the metal mask, he heard quiet, laboured breathing.

"Not dead then," Robin said to himself, a little shakily. A dark part of Robin toyed with the fact that they were out in the middle of nowhere. No one was around for countless miles, and a very heavy Shard of the Arcania was in his hand. A blunt instrument of the highest order.

Would anyone blame him? Really?

He dismissed the idea at once. He may have a little darkness in him, but he couldn't strike down a helpless, unconscious person, even one as loathsome as this.

Instead, summoning his courage, he inched closer to Strigoi's head. The breathing was regular. He wasn't hurt then, not badly. Just knocked out when the drake had caught him. Just after he had thrown Robin like a human sacrifice into its mouth.

"Thanks for that," Robin said coldly. He reached out tentatively and gave the prone figure a quick poke in the arm. When Strigoi failed to retaliate, he inspected the man more closely.

A curious part of him wanted to lean forward and lift off the mask, to see face-to-face this Wolf of Eris. This powerful creature whom even the Grimms feared. Would he appear as a Grimm did? Ghastly while, old and reptilian, a pallid ghoul? Or something worse? The twisted face of a demon, hidden from view by mercy by this strange animal mask.

A worrying thought occurred to Robin. Maybe he really was a wolf. Dark fur and bared, grinning teeth, cold, hungry yellow eyes grinning in the darkness behind the metal, drooling and waiting to bite.

This is what happens when you stray from the forest path, he thought chillingly. *You meet wolves in the shadowy places between the trees. All the better to eat you with.*

The train of thought made Robin shiver.

He had more pressing concerns. Strigoi was powerful and dangerous. He had to find Woad and Karya, and get away from this place, far away, before their enemy awoke. They had to get the Shard back to Rowandeepling.

A shadow fell over his crouched form, making Robin jump in alarm and spin around, his vision taking a few seconds to catch up.

Splinterstem the dryad stood over him, looking down curiously.

"You have it," he said simply.

Robin staggered to his feet, furious, glaring up at the enormous dryad. "Where the *hell* were you?" he yelled, completely forgetting any notions of not waking the wolf. He stared at Splinterstem. "Where were you when the battle started? Eh? Woad and Karya? They didn't think twice about fighting! Even when this nightmare turned up and started throwing me around the place? Where were you then? What? Were you hiding under a rock somewhere?"

If the dryad was ashamed, he didn't show it. "You really must be the Scion of the Arcania," he said, not talking his eyes from the Shard, the glittering green jewel in Robin's hands. "You defeated the monster, the scourge is ended. You retrieved the heart of the forest."

"Bugger the heart of the bloody forest!" Robin snapped angrily. "You're a coward! Hiding in the bloody trees. Is that what you really did when the king was taken, eh? Where are Woad and Karya?"

The dryad pointed across the clearing. "They are perfectly safe. Look," he said reassuringly.

Robin turned, staring off in the direction the dryad was pointing, unable to make out anything but the tangle of the newly lush forest glade.

"Where? I don't see anything," he said. Something itched in his mind. Something he had just said had sounded wrong.

Wait, Robin thought. *This doesn't make sense at all. If the king was the drake, then how could Splinterstem have seen the king attacked and taken by it?*

He turned back to the dryad, confused. Splinterstem was looking down at him with his large, calm green eyes. Robin noticed he held a rock in his hand.

The dryad brought the rock up full force. The crack against the side of Robin's skull was sharp and hard. His legs buckled and he fell bonelessly to the ground, thudding gracelessly onto the carpet of thick moss beside Strigoi. The Shard of the Arcania tumbling from his fingers and rolling away in the grass.

Amidst the sickening pain, as Robin's vision disappeared down a long black tunnel, he saw the hand of the dryad stoop calmly to claim the Shard.

FRENEMIES

It was some time later when Robin clawed his way painfully back to consciousness.

He felt as though his head was splitting in two. Every bone in his body ached, and his mouth was dry. He became aware that he was lying, curled in a foetal position, hugging his knees, and that the surface beneath him was not deep moss, but cold bare iron with a light coating of old rotten straw.

Shakily, he looked around, every movement of his head agonising. His vision was blurred. The light stabbed his eyes, darkening though it was. Sunset? He laid his head back down carefully. There was silence all around him, only soft noises of the Elderhart. And he was alone.

Splinterstem, he thought groggily, struggling to focus. Splinterstem had hit him. With a rock. With a bloody great big rock.

Memories flooding back, he struggled to sit up, unable to do so without crying out in pain. His head hurt so much it felt like a cracked egg. With tentative fingers and eyes screwed closed, he gingerly felt the side of his head. It felt tacky and tender. Dried blood.

Dried though, he thought to himself. *That's good, right? It would be worse if it was still bleeding. What had happened? What had the dryad done to him?*

Opening his eyes properly, fighting the almost overwhelming urge to retch, he blearily took in his surroundings. He was in a cage, circular and suspended just above the forest floor on a long chain, his small prison hovering only a few feet above the grass. The bars were close set together and flecked with rust. There was room to stand, but he didn't dare try to. He felt quite certain that if he tried, he would most definitely throw up or pass out, probably both.

Beyond the cage, the forest stretched away. There were other swinging enclosures, two or three, all looking long-disused and empty.

I know where I am, Robin realised, hanging onto the bars for balance. Behind him were the great roots of one of the elder trees, vast and wide like a knotted cliff face, and only a few paces away was the dark and overgrown stone archway that marked the entrance to the Labyrinth.

I'm back at Rowandeepling, he thought. *The dryad brought me back here. But why?*

Robin looked upwards carefully. Through the roof, he could see the great circle of the elder tree's trunk stretching up and away into the sunset crimson sky. High, far above, he could just make out the glimmering latticework of amber bridges, the treetop city of the dryads.

He tried to call out, but his voice was nothing but a dry croak. He coughed and spluttered, each spasm making his head creak.

Why would Splinterstem do this? Why were the other dryads allowing it? And why were none of them flying down here to see who was in the cage?

Robin peered desperately around the forest. He had no answers. He was utterly alone. He didn't know where Karya was, where Woad was, and though it worried him to admit it, he was badly hurt.

"And the Shard's gone, don't forget that," he muttered to himself. "Great job. Perfect."

The sun slowly set while Robin rested, waiting for enough strength to return to be able to stand. Gloom and twilight slowly descended on the wood, and still no one came. Not a single noise or movement was in deep darkness of the forest. The autumn air grew chill.

Come to think of it, something else was very wrong, he realised after a time. He looked up again toward the distant settlement of the dryads far ahead. It was dark above. There were no glimmering distant lights, no lanterns making the bridges beneath the canopy of the elder trees glow. The sanctuary of the dryads seemed still and silent. Robin felt it in his bones. Something very bad had happened.

When he eventually felt he could safely stand, feeling watery and tired with the cold of the growing night, Robin gave the bars an experimental shake. They rattled noisily, but didn't budge, of course. The only thing he achieved was to set the cage lazily rocking, which made him feel nauseous again. He hadn't expected much.

He would have to use magic, he decided. Featherbreath perhaps, or a Waterwhip directed at the chain holding the cage aloft. It might be enough to break an old link? Or he could use the Golem cantrip, summon a few rocks and boulders. Maybe if he got them to pile up next to his swinging prison, he could roll one up this slope beside the cage and into his hand. He had an idea he might be able to bash at the bars with such a rudimentary weapon, bend them out of shape somehow. It might be enough to slip through and escape.

His heart almost stopped when he reached for his mana stone with trembling fingers and found it gone.

The dryad had taken it. In blind horror, Robin searched the dark floor of the cage and the grass that he could see beyond the bars in the fading light, hoping against hope that maybe it had just fallen, that he might see his seraphinite shining in the darkness nearby. He knew, deep down however, that his stone hadn't merely fallen off. It was gone. Stolen. He was utterly without magic.

He spent some time listing inventive curse words.

"Okay," he said, forcing his voice to be calm. "Don't panic. Panicking won't help anything. You just ... you just have to think this through. You recently defeated a king who was enthralled to the power of a Shard and turned himself into a dragon. If you can fight a dragon, you can think your way out of a cage."

But it was easy to say, and harder to feel. More than ever, stripped of his mana, he felt like nothing more than a teenager way out of his depth. Without weapons, lost and alone in a great strange forest in an alien world. His friends were gone, the Shard was gone, his magic was gone, and he was really seriously hurt. As far as he knew, no one in this world or the next knew where he was, and no one was coming to help him.

"This is really, extremely bad," he muttered, clamping down on the rising panic.

Splinterstem's betrayal was unfathomable to him. He had to get out of here. He didn't want to rot here, forgotten and alone at the mouth of the Labyrinth. Or else, even worse, to sit and wait for Strigoi to awaken and track him back here. He didn't fancy coming upon the wolf here in the deep woods, without even a smidgen of mana to defend himself.

"This is what happens ..." he said aloud, to no one in particular, "... when fairy tales are right. There's always a wolf hunting you, and even the bloody trees want you dead."

After a while, the moon rose, shimmering down through the silent canopy in grey beams. The forest seemed a large and lonely place around him. Time wore on, Robin nursed his wounds as best he could, and the air grew colder.

Miserable and trapped, he would have given anything, anything in the world to have been back at Erlking. Arguing around the dining table with Henry and Karya and Woad. Even Jackalope, murderer or not.

He wanted Aunt Irene, stoking the fires with her poker and complaining about doors being left open everywhere. He wanted Mr Drover, snoozing in a high-backed chair under a newspaper, his snores as commonplace as the ticking clocks. He wanted Calypso, sitting knees tucked up on a deep window-seat, reading her obscure poetry. He even wanted Hestia, fussing around like a clucking hen and accusing them of tremendous crimes against the household.

Robin wanted Erlking. He wanted home. So badly it ached.

After a while, he lay in the thin straw, listening to the endless, uncaring forest going about its night business, and buried his aching head in his hands. He was glad of the dark then, and that there was no one around to hear him. The great saviour of the Netherworlde surely should not sniffle.

He was roused from the straw some time later, deep in the night, by a noise.

It was very dark in the forest. The moon was hidden now above by the canopy and thick cloud, and the shadows were deep. Robin could barely see beyond the bars. But there had definitely been a noise. Something other than the occasional scurry of some small woodland creature going about its invisible business in the unseen undergrowth.

He tensed, suddenly alert, straining to hear. In his mind's eye, he thought he imagined the clanking of chains and the heavy footfalls of the minotaur, dreaded guardian of the Labyrinth. He was sure there had been footsteps, out there in the deep grass, close by.

This was just his imagination, he knew. It wasn't the minotaur, come to claim him from his cage. Woad had already told him that the beast was chained, unable to leave the underground maze.

But still, *something* was out there. A forest animal perhaps, coming closer out of curiosity to see the odd spectacle of a Fae caged like a songbird in the night? The treacherous dryad come back to finish him off? He scanned the darkness warily, straining to make out a shape in the trees. Maybe it was Strigoi, having tracked him down at last, following their path from the hollow of the forest drake, back to

Rowandeepling. He imagined that dark grinning wolf face, looming silent and unseen in the shadows, watching him hungrily, and shivered with goosebumps.

"Who's out there?" he asked, striving not to sound afraid. In truth, he was so weary that his voice, if anything, sounded irritated.

This time he definitely did see a shape, something detached from the darkness in front of him. Coming not from the direction of the Labyrinth but from the depths of the trees, back toward the deep ravine which separated the island of the elder trees from the rest of the forest.

He wasn't imagining things. There *was* someone there. Someone approaching in the dark. All the hairs stood up on Robin's neck. He could hear the quiet footsteps in the grass. He was painfully aware that without his mana stone, he was utterly defenceless. The shadowy figure drew closer in the dark.

"Bloody hell," the stranger said breathlessly. "It really *is* you!"

Robin blinked in utter confusion. The voice was so familiar, but so unexpected here in this dark place in the misty night. He hardly dared to believe his own ears.

"Wh ... who ...?"

The shadowy stranger rushed forward, running across the grass.

"Robin!" Henry cried, grinning.

Robin stared down through the bars at his friend. It was Henry. It couldn't be, surely? It seemed impossible, and yet here he was. The boy's tangled and tousled brown hair was matted to his head. His face was smeared with dirt, but it really was Henry, wide-eyed and grinning up through the darkness. He reached in through the bars and Robin grabbed his arms, feeling a desperate urge to check he was real, that this wasn't just some fevered dream brought on by one too many knocks to the head.

"Henry! You're here!" he croaked, staring. "You're really here? How are you here?"

Henry, Robin noticed, was in his white school shirt, though it was filthy, tattered and torn along the arm. His school tie, he noticed, was rather surreally tied around his head like a bandana, keeping his messy mop of hair out of his eyes. The gangly boy looked practically feral.

"And why do you look like you just stepped out of Lord of the Flies!?"

"You're one to talk, mate!" Henry laughed. "You look like something ate you up and spat you out!"

"Something did!" Robin replied a little hysterically, unable to stop himself from grinning.

"And you're all hung up like a Christmas decoration," Henry babbled. "God, it's good to see you, mate! Where's everyone else? I didn't believe him when he said he could find you. This bloody forest." He shook his head in disbelief "I swear, Rob, it's endless!"

"Who?" Robin asked urgently. "Henry, how on earth did you find me? Where have you bloody been all this time?"

Henry's initial manic elation was becoming tinged with a look of serious concern as he noticed how badly beaten up Robin was.

"Wow, you really have been in the wars, haven't you?" he muttered, his eyes roaming over Robin, clearly making a catalogue of injuries. "Can't leave you alone for two minutes, can I? And here I thought *I'd* been having a rough time. I got a splinter, and I fell in some sort of poison ivy yesterday. Not a laughing matter, honestly, you should see this rash–"

"Henry," Robin interrupted. "Focus, you blithering idiot." He couldn't stop grinning, although it was making his injured head pound terribly.

"Oh, right, yeah," Henry nodded. He really did look trail-beaten. But Robin didn't care. He was alive, and he was here, against all the odds. "Rob, you're gonna have to let go of my arms, mate. I feel like I should be serenading you or something."

"Sorry." Robin released Henry. He hadn't been aware that his grip had been so tight. "Can you get me out of this thing?"

"'Course," Henry nodded seriously. "Then I want to know what's been going on with you."

"You too," Robin agreed wholeheartedly. He had so many questions. "How have you survived alone in the forest? Where the hell have you been?"

"I've not been alone," Henry said, and something cautious in his tone made Robin pay attention. "And listen … when I tell you, right? You're going to freak out, but don't freak out, okay." He shook his head a little. "It's just too weird for words, but you're goin' to have to trust me."

"Trust you about what?" Robin asked, scooting back while Henry pulled and fiddled with the heavy lock on the outside of the cage.

"Wow, this thing is bolted fast," Henry grunted. "Why didn't you just blast your way out with magic?"

"My mana stone is gone," Robin replied, looking at his friend with open curiosity. "Henry, trust you about what?" he asked again, insistently.

"I can't open this," Henry decided. He looked back over his shoulder into the darkness. "Hey, can you do anything about this, old man? Could use a little help here."

Robin peered into the gloom in confusion, unsure who Henry was talking to. He'd said he hadn't been alone. Who was he with? For the first time, in the shadows, keeping its silent distance, Robin made out a second shape, much taller than Henry. It was a man, wrapped in a long dark and hooded cloak which was mud splattered and threadbare. Robin jumped in surprise.

"Henry, who is that?" he asked. "Who are you with?"

Henry looked up at Robin, as the figure behind him began to walk forward toward the hanging cage.

"*Promise* you won't freak out," Henry implored him. "I mean it, Rob. Seriously, I've had the *weirdest* few days."

Robin looked up warily as the tall stranger approached. He remembered what the dryads had said. That there had been rumours of an odd man, a pale and hooded wanderer, haunting the forest of late. A strange and oddly portentous chill ran down Robin's back.

"Good evening, Master Fellows," the stranger said. His voice was cold and crisp, and horribly familiar. It sounded amused. "How is it ..." the man mused from beneath his deep hood, "... that whenever we meet, you seem to be in a cage? The amusement of the Fates, perhaps?"

Robin stared from the man to Henry with wide, unbelieving eyes, his mind refusing to process what his ears were hearing. Henry gave him a wan, almost apologetic smile.

The stranger leaned close to the bars, and with white hands and long, spiderlike fingers, he lowered his hood. There, in the darkness of the forest, floating in the shadows like a pale will o' the wisp, was the cold, lined face of Mr Strife.

In shock, Robin instinctively fell backwards from the bars, scooting away and making the cage rock.

"Strife!" he shouted. He stared at Henry in alarm. "Strife?" he repeated. His eyes flicked back to the green-haired ghoul leering in at the bars. The old man wore a tight, humourless smile, and his eyes were as black and cold as space.

"*Mr* Strife, if you please," he said politely. "One must observe manners, Master Fellows. Or else one is nothing more than an animal."

This made no sense to Robin at all. He glared at Henry, wide-eyed. "Why are you with Strife?!" he gasped. "You do know … you *know* who this is?!"

"Yes, yes I know," Henry had his hands raised, trying to calm Robin down. "I knew you'd freak out!" He looked sidelong at the Grimm looming at his side. "I told you he'd freak out."

Strife did not acknowledge Henry. His beetle black eyes were fixed entirely on Robin.

"Calm yourself, Scion of the Arcania," he said, in a rather bored tone. "At this present time … things being as they are … I can assure you that you have little to fear from me." His lip curled. "More's the pity."

"Like hell!" Robin said. "Henry? What the hell is going on?"

Henry looked at Robin seriously. "Look, Rob. I know it's beyond weird. Trust me, I *know*, okay? But really. He's not here to do damage. Just … let's just get you out and I'll explain. I wouldn't even have been able to find you if it wasn't for him. I'd still be wondering the forest like an idiot."

"My skrikers are keen trackers, Master Fellows," Strife said to Robin, in cool but conversational tones. "We found this human boy, we found the site of the dragon's death - congratulations on that by the way. Excellent work. And we found you." He held something up in the darkness beyond the bars. It was Robin's pack, the satchel he had been given by Aunt Irene for his birthday. It dangled from Mr Strife's long fingers by its strap. "My skrikers got the scent from this. You left it at the drake's corpse, buried under moss and earth. Very careless of you really."

Robin gritted his teeth. "I was busy being eaten alive at the time, and then hit with rocks," he countered. "And if you expect me to believe for one second that you're not here to do harm, then you must think I'm stupid!"

Strife narrowed his eyes, dark slits in powdery white paper. "Oh, I mean to do harm," he admitted freely, dark relish in his tone. "There is plenty of harm coming your way from me, Robin Fellows. Make no mistake about that." He leaned back from the bars a little. "But not today, however. You are lucky. I have other, far more important fish to fry than you at present. And lamentably, I require you alive in order to fry them." Admitting this seemed to revolt the Grimm. He made a face as though he had smelled something vile.

The old man's free hand passed in a wave over the lock of the swinging cage, and with a flash of shadows, there was a metallic pop, and the bolts fell broken to the grassy floor. The cage door swung ponderously open with a loud grinding creak.

"For the present time at least," Strife said, stepping back from the cage. "You and your little human friend have nothing to fear from me. You and I have a common enemy. You have my word."

Robin stared at the Grimm, disbelieving.

"Your word?" he asked. "You have to be kidding me."

"A gentleman is nothing but the strength of his word, young man," Strife hissed. "Had you even the slightest modicum of breeding you would know better than to question mine."

"It's true, Rob," Henry said. "Look, I've been with old ghoul-face the whole time since I got to this bloody wood, he could have killed me a hundred times over by now. He's telling the truth. Come out. Let me explain everything. I know you don't trust him, I don't trust him either." He glanced at Strife. "No offence."

"None taken," Strife replied dryly.

"But … you trust me, right?" He held out his hand to Robin.

Robin decided that things were so strange, so beyond the natural order of things, that he had no choice but to give up and go with the flow. "Of course I do," he admitted. "You're my best mate."

"Then get out of the bloody canary cage," Henry said impatiently.

Robin did so. Every part of him aching and complaining as Henry helped him down out of the swinging prison. Not for a single second did he take his eye from the looming and ghastly figure of Mr Strife. Robin noticed that the Grimm's bright green hair, usually so perfectly oiled, looked mussed and out of place, and that beneath his long and unusual battered cloak, the pinstripe suit he always wore seemed creased, dirty and damaged. It was spattered with dried mud and threadbare. Strife, Robin thought curiously, usually so perfectly presented, looked unkempt, frayed around the edges. He looked like a man who had fallen on hard times.

"You really are hurt," Henry noted with concern, helping the wavering Robin to stand. "Rob, it looks like your arm is broken. And you have a lot of blood on you. You look in a bad way."

"I can fix that," Strife said simply. Robin shot him a warning look, filled with violent mistrust, which the old man noted.

"Listen to me, you tiresome child," he said quietly. "This will be a lot smoother if you stop expecting me to lunge at you. I have told you already. I am not…currently…your enemy. And believe me when I say that this statement is as repulsive and abhorrent to me as it no doubt is to you. But you are of absolutely no use to me, or to your snivelling friend, if you are broken beyond repair."

He reached into his robe and extracted a small black bottle.

"I'm not snivelling," Henry argued quietly.

Strife held out the small bottle to Robin in the dark. "Drink this," he instructed firmly.

"What is it?" he asked suspiciously. "Poison?"

Mr Strife sighed, his lip curling again in irritation. "Yes of course, Lord of Erlking," he spat. "I have tracked you through the forest to the cage where you lie, wounded and bleeding out, trapped and helpless. A place where you would have been dead of exposure and your wounds had you been left but a single day longer … all for the sheer giddy joy of setting you free only to poison you." He snorted. "I have better things to do with my time than to slip dark drinks to ungrateful Fae. It is powdered tartarus. Mixed in the juices of the firedrake, and it will heal your ills."

Robin took the proffered bottle, this simple task taking an alarming number of attempts due to his wavering vision, and uncorked it, sniffing the contents. It smelled peppery and bitter. He stared at Strife with open distrust.

"Or if you prefer …" Strife spread his long white hands beneath his ragged cloak. "You can just stand here for the next few moments until you pass out from your terrible injuries, and fall down dead and helpless. I shall not force your hand, Scion. The latter choice, while of much less practical use to me at present, would at least provide me with some amusement."

Robin considered his options. Realistically, he admitted, he didn't have any. His legs were already feeling watery, and his head was hurting so badly. Strife was right. He was more injured that he had admitted, even to himself.

"It is the most powerful healing draught in the Netherworlde," Strife explained in cold tones. "My own, personal supply. Incredibly difficult to come by and impossibly rare." He snorted unpleasantly. "Not to mention outrageously expensive. To think the day would come when I would share it with a Fae. This is what I am reduced to."

"Bottoms up, Rob," Henry said encouragingly.

Robin screwed up his eyes and took a drink. The liquid was peppery and warm. No sooner had he swallowed than a heat began to flow through his body. An odd sensation like pins and needles. It was strange but not unpleasant, and he felt almost immediately better. His arms and legs were tingling, as was his scalp. He waited a moment to see if he was going to drop down dead.

When it was evident that he wasn't, he corked the bottle and passed it back to Strife, who took it silently. "Aunt Irene *never* finds out I did that," he said to Henry.

Henry nodded in earnest understanding.

"The sensation you are feeling will pass in moments," Strife told him. He passed Robin his satchel. "Your bones and body are knitting back together. Soon, you will be a fresh and loathsomely healthy Fae once more."

"Right." Robin, who could actually feel the strange draught at work inside him, wiped his mouth with the back of his hand and looked from one unlikely companion to the other. "I think you had better tell me, Henry, what *on earth* is going on."

Henry and Robin sat on the ground, only a few paces from the hanging cages. Strife remained standing, silent, his long bony arms folded under his robe, staring darkly out at the forest. Henry wanted to know where Woad was, where Karya was, and why Robin was in a cage, but Robin insisted on hearing his side of things first. "And don't leave *anything* out," he warned. "I want to know how my best friend ended up on a nature hike with one of the bloody Grimms."

He'd come home after school, he explained, meaning to get changed and then come up to Erlking for the planned Halloween feast, but his cottage, with his father gone, had been full of danger.

"Bloody redcaps," he told Robin. "Out of nowhere, lurking in my own house!" He shook his head in disbelief. "They attacked me. I mean, I fought back, but redcaps are stronger than they look, and there were two of them. They were going on about how you had a job to do, and I was going to be their safety net. They overpowered me, said they were taking me to the Netherworlde, a hostage you see. Just in case you didn't keep up your end of the bargain."

Henry indicated his tattered clothes. "I hadn't even had time to get changed," he complained. He looked around at the dark wood. "I seem doomed to spend all my time in the Netherworlde in my bloody school uniform. Dad's going to go mental when he sees the state of it."

Robin dragged Henry back to his story. He'd been spirited away by the redcaps, over the moors and through Janus to the Netherworlde. He told how they had marched through the grasslands with him as their prisoner, headed for some place called Spitrot. The town was a wreck, destroyed by this dangerous dragon they kept going on about, but there was an entrance to their underground world there.

"I didn't have a single chance to escape," Henry told Robin grimly. "They had my hands tied up tight behind my back, marching me along like bloody cattle. And they were always watching me, one or the other, little red demons. I thought maybe if I could get my hands free somehow, I could at least send you a hex-message, let you know what had happened, where I was? But as it turns out, my scrap of enchanted parchment wasn't even with me."

Robin nodded to this. "Yes, Karya found it at the cottage, in the mess. She took it back to Erlking. I think it's still there now, with Calypso or Hestia." So far, Henry's story was tallying with Karya's earlier guesswork. "So, did you manage to escape the redcaps when the centaurs attacked you?"

Henry frowned at his friend in confusion. "Centaurs?" I don't know anything about centaurs. I never saw any."

This took Robin by surprise. "But ..." he started, confused. "Karya saw their heads on spikes. And the ground was all messed up, trampled? We thought you'd been ambushed by centaurs."

"No mate, that's not what happened," Henry argued. "We were attacked, yeah, right by the edge of the forest, my friendly little kidnappers and me. But it wasn't any centaurs. It was this big green bloke, all leaves and twigs. Massive guy. He killed the redcaps, barely noticed me. I'd legged it as soon as he burst out of the trees and they all started fighting. Saw my chance. The way I figured it, I didn't owe the redcaps any help, evil little monsters. They were on their own." He sniffed. "Serves them right to get attacked by some manic forest man. I ran for the trees and didn't look back."

The effects of Strife's healing elixir were fading by now, and Robin felt the warmth in his mended body replaced with a foreboding chill.

"Splinterstem ..." he said, pieces falling into place. "He must have used Earth mana to churn the ground, make it look like a centaur attack ...

and then he waited for Karya to arrive, knowing full well that she was tracking you. He's been playing us all for idiots from the start."

Henry clearly had no idea who Splinterstem was.

"He needed us in the forest," Robin told him. "He wanted us at Rowandeepling, to hunt the drake and retrieve the Shard so he could take it. He must have known that there was no way any of us would have left the grasslands if we thought you might still be out there somewhere, travelling with the redcaps. Karya, Woad and I would have kept you our first priority. So he killed the redcaps, eliminating their inconvenient kidnapping, giving us no reason not to go with him into the woods. That manipulative liar. Promising his people would help find you, once the scourge was dead."

"The only person who found me," Henry said. "Was old skin-and-bones over there." He nodded towards Strife.

Henry leaned in close to Robin. "Look, I know what he is, and who he is. Believe me, I'd been lost in the woods almost a full day at this point. Running blind, it had taken me hours just to find a sharp enough rock to cut through the ropes at my wrists and free my hands. Believe me when I tell you, Robin, I was as terrified as you were when I stumbled onto him."

"But why is he helping us?" Robin asked, equally surreptitious.

"Strife was already in the forest," Henry told Robin. "He's been here for some time. He has his own mission in the Elderhart, which I'm sure he'll fill you in on shortly. When he stumbled upon me, I barely even recognised him. He looks a bit…threadbare…right?" Henry shivered. "I thought I was done for. Dead for sure. But as it turns out, Strife wanted me alive." He nodded at Robin. "Or you, to be more accurate, and thought that saving me might convince you that, for once, he doesn't actually want you dead."

"You're what? A show of good will then? Strife's peace offering?" Robin raised his eyebrows doubtfully. "I don't like any of this, Henry."

"Neither did I!" Henry said emphatically. "Believe me, I'd have rather been with anyone else in the world. It was hardly like I'd stumbled on to some well-meaning ents here in the woods. But, I will say this for the evil old ghoul. He knows his way around this forest. He knew what was safe to eat. Where springs were that you could drink from. If it wasn't for him, I'd be dead by now." Henry shook his own head. "Never thought I'd say that. But he's having troubles of his own, you see. Bit of a fall from grace, and from what I understand, you're the ladder he's going to use to climb back up."

"I can hear each and every word the two of you say," Strife's voice carried over, crisp and cool. He didn't bother turning around. He was still staring watchfully out into the night.

"He said that you were in the forest and that his skrikers could find you," Henry said, ignoring the old man. "I didn't really believe him. Couldn't figure out what on earth you'd be doing here but, well ... here you are."

Robin digested all of this. And then, at Henry's insistence, he filled his friend in on his side of things. There was a lot to tell. The centaurs and Briar Hill, Hawthorn and the Mask of Gaia, the dark revelations from Jackalope and his sudden departure.

Robin had expected Henry to leap on this particular bit of information, to triumphantly scream 'I told you so' or 'aha!', or some other loud and annoying way show how vindicated he was for not liking the hornless Fae. But at the news of Jackalope's dark history, Henry merely paled, looking shocked.

When Robin was describing the battle with the drake and his unlikely alliance with Strigoi, Strife's ears perked up and he actually glanced toward the two boys. "The Wolf? Here in the forest?" he sounded surprised.

Robin nodded at him. "Trying to capture the Shard, of course," he said. "For your bloody dark Empress."

Strife looked thoughtful. "No," he said slowly. "The Wolf has no orders regarding this Shard. I can assure you of that. He is stationed far to the north at present, on the Gravis. If he is here, roaming the grasslands and stalking the forest, it is not on the orders of Eris. I doubt the empress even knows he is here. Under his own steam?" Strife glared thoughtfully at them. "This is of great interest to me. This could prove to be very valuable knowledge to have."

Robin was not the least bit surprised that the servants of Eris kept secrets from one another. The last time he had seen them all together in the war camp in the far north, there had been three Grimms and Strigoi, and they had done nothing but bicker and snipe at one another the entire time.

"... Anyway, the dragon was the king of the dryads and it was this Splinterstem who betrayed him. He's also the one who koshed me over the head and left me in the cage," Robin went on. Henry dutifully growled some very choice names, making Robin smile.

"He wanted the Shard for himself, the whole time," Robin guessed. "There's no other explanation for it. He knew he couldn't defeat the scourge himself, so he used us to get it for him. It was all planned." He thought back to the battle in the hollow. "I'm pretty sure, now that I come to think of it, that it was him, not the drake, who tied up Woad and Karya with Earth magic. He took them out of the equation, then stood back and let me fight the monster for him. But why? If the king himself couldn't control the Shard, surely he knows he can't either? It doesn't make sense."

Strife walked over to them. "It only doesn't make sense to you," he snapped with disdain and irritation, "… because you are clueless idiots, with only half a story."

Both boys looked up at the Grimm. He was staring at them with open distaste.

"You think this pathetic, treacherous dryad of yours is the big bad villain in your tale? You are hopeless. A worm he was, certainly," he allowed. "A traitor, with his eye on the throne and the princess, yes. But the master-mind behind all of this chaos in the forest?" Strife sneered. "Hardly."

"Then who?" Robin asked.

"The same person, blundering and blind little Fae, who has wanted the Earth Shard all along," Strife said through gritted teeth. "The same person who, even now, as we squat in the mud like animals, sits on a throne in the Hive, miles from here, making schemes." He pushed his bony hands together, popping his knuckles loudly. "Directing puppets like this dryad as though they were helpless chess pieces on a board. The same person who dethroned me in the eyes of our Empress and reduced me to wandering in ignominy, the lowest of the Grimms! Forcing me to make … decidedly unpalatable … alliances with the likes of you, in order to restore myself to my rightful station."

In the darkness, Mr Strife looked away, his cruel black eyes roaming the forest until he lighted upon the dark stone archway which marked the entrance to the underground Labyrinth.

"My dearest little sister, of course," he spat bitterly. "Agent of chaos and a blacker heart than my own. Peryl."

THE MAN WHO WOULD BE KING

Robin demanded an explanation, but Mr Strife dismissed the boy utterly, motioning for them to follow him as he stalked away from the cages, through the dark grass toward the overgrown and crumbling entrance to the maze.

"There is little that I could explain to you that you could not learn more readily and easily from this 'Splinterstem' yourself," he snapped. "I don't have the patience to guide your baby steps and join your dots for you. The truth is better shown than told, and your answers, Robin Fellows, lie just within this doorway."

"In the Labyrinth?" Robin peered into the darkness dubiously. His arm, as he tentatively flexed his fingers, felt fine, not even bruised. He reached up and gingerly felt his head, but beneath the crusted blood that had stuck in the short hair at his temples, there was neither a cut or a bruise. It wasn't even tender. Strife's potion really had healed him utterly. He would feel almost his own self, were it not for his lack of a mana-stone.

"You expect us to go into the Labyrinth?" Robin looked up at Strife. "So you are trying to kill us after all then? I've heard the stories. Only one person ever went in there and they were killed by the minotaur."

Strife looked down at Robin for several silent seconds. Robin had the distinct impression that the ugly old man was mentally counting to ten.

"Is that so?" he said eventually.

"Yes," Robin insisted. "It is … .so."

"And who … pray, told you this?" Strife asked, his voice withering, raising his thin arched eyebrows expectantly.

Robin faltered. "Well … Splintertstem, the steward did … actually," he admitted. "But that doesn't mean it isn't true. Lots of other dryads knew about the death. It was the princess' true love who was killed. It's not a made-up story. The princess herself told me it had happened."

"Hmm," Strife sounded extremely unconvinced. "And tell me, did your princess, or indeed any other dryad actually *see* this body?"

Robin paused. Henry was looking from the old man to his friend, clearly lost in the conversation.

"Well … no … not exactly … Splinterstem said it was so horrific … he disposed of the remains himself, to spare them …" Robin said uncertainly.

"Hmm," Strife said again with feeling, still peering down at Robin. "And who, please enlighten me, was the *only* person to see this death, to actually discover this unfortunate body?"

Robin swallowed.

"Splinterstem," he said quietly, beginning to feel foolish.

Strife cocked his pale head to one side, rather sarcastically. He rubbed gently at his green-haired temples as though developing a migraine. "The same person who claimed to have seen the king attacked by this dragon-scourge of the forest, even though, knowing now as you do, that the dragon was the king, that this is highly unlikely to be true?"

Robin stared into the black opening of the Labyrinth.

"Are we beginning to see a pattern here, Master Robin?" Strife sighed. "You witless child."

"He's a psychopath, isn't he?" Robin muttered. "I'm going to find Splinterstem, and I'm going to make him pay."

"Oh, I'm afraid you're far too late for anything of the sort," Strife said lightly, as he stepped into the shadowy tunnel under the archway. "Your scheming dryad friend was the pawn of my sister after all, a minnow playing games with a shark. Out of his league. I think you will find he has already 'paid' his dues." He glanced back at them over his shoulder, his pale face lost in the folds of his hood. "Miss Peryl rarely keeps her toys once their use has expired. She bores very easily. But with that mask you carry in your little bag, you may find that your treacherous dryad still has sights to show you yet."

Against every sensible instinct in his body, Robin followed Mr Strife into the dark tunnel, Henry close behind.

It had been dark out in the forest, but here, at the mouth of the maze, it was pitch black. The air smelled stale and damp. Close and earthy. Robin was acutely aware of the huge weight of the elder trees above them, the soaring heights of Rowandeepling, dark and silent.

They had walked maybe only ten paces into the blackness when Mr Strife muttered something under his breath and a dull, purplish light bloomed before him. He had conjured a ball of softly glowing mana, which he held aloft before him like a candle.

By its dim light, Robin and Henry saw the tunnel through which they moved. It was ancient, hewn from crumbling, damp stone. The floor was packed earth littered with rocks and stones, a forgotten dungeon. Here and there on the roof above them and trailing down the walls were roots, pushing through the stones, making the surface bumpy and irregular, cobwebs and trapped dry leaves stringing between them. The tunnel flickered and leapt about them, eerily animated by the dim luminance.

"I didn't know you could make light," Robin whispered. He felt uncomfortable speaking in anything louder here, in this bleak and silent place. It felt like any noise might make it crumble and collapse on them. "I thought your Tower was Darkness."

"You cannot have darkness without light, you idiot child," Mr Strife replied, not turning around. "They are two halves of the same thing. Now come ... look at your answers, and the handiwork of my sister."

Robin moved closer, his skin crawling at his proximity to the tall Grimm. By the light of his mana, the boy saw what lay before them in the long dark tunnel.

Splinterstem lay on the ground on his back, utterly motionless. His green eyes were wide, his strange face frozen in an expression of shock. His large body was splayed, laid out on his wings, half extended and crumpled around him like a collapsed parachute, brushing the wall either side.

He was quite dead.

"How?" Robin stared at the body, its green eyes oddly dull and empty of the usual glittering light.

"Dark mana," Strife shrugged, unconcerned by the details. "Maybe a blade. Who knows? Or for that matter, cares? My sister is difficult to predict. Look at him, Scion of the Arcania."

Robin peered down at the frozen corpse in the flickering shadows, horrified. "I am looking."

"No." Strife indicated his backpack. "I mean ... *look* ... at him."

Robin realised what Strife intended. He slung his pack from his shoulders and rummaged around inside it, his fingers finally closing around the hard wooden edges of the Mask of Gaia. He pulled it out and regarded it in the purplish light.

"What's that thing?" Henry asked, interested.

"A powerful object indeed," Strife said, looking at it hungrily. "The Mask of Gaia."

"Who's Gaia?" Henry asked Robin.

"An elemental," Robin replied absently, turning the mask over in his hands and looking down at the dead body. "They're all gone now."

"What's an elemental when it's at home?" Henry sounded more confused than ever. "Just how much did I miss?"

Mr Strife interrupted Henry, peering at Robin. "It will not work the same as when you look at the living," he said. "Disjointed memories, fragments, may be all you glean. But it should shed some light into the darkness."

Robin nodded. He knew what he had to do. He raised the mask to his eyes, feeling its smooth warmth mould to his skin. He felt the branches above the empty eye sockets twine in his hair as the flow of mana stored in the mask seeped into him. Looking down at the sad and sombre sight of the dryad before him, he blinked, and was engulfed by light.

The world fell away.

A series of visions danced across Robin's mind, like a broken movie. The forest, sun dappled, a great rain falling on the canopy, and next moment, bright sunshine. He saw an acorn falling, a woodland stream filled with silvery fish. The images in turn were replaced by another. The glowing lights of Rowandeepling. All flashing through his mind, frozen snapshots. These, he knew, were the memories of Splinterstem. He could feel the dryad's mind.

Through the shifting images, Robin saw the court of the dryads, the king on his throne and the Princess Ashe seated beside him. Robin was an invisible presence in the great feasting hall, and all around him were dryads. Away to one side he saw Splinterstem, seated at a table with others of his kind. The dryad was looking up thoughtfully at the royals, and Robin could feel his hunger. Hunger to possess the throne, hunger to win the heart of the princess. His mind was filled with lofty dreams and ambitions. A determined and all-consuming want.

Images blurred, and another memory surfaced like a dream. Here, Robin saw Splinterstem walked along the amber bridges of the city, on some soft summer night in Rowandeepling, looking down to the similar pathways which crisscrossed here and there below him. He was watching a couple walk together, unaware they were being observed. It was the Princess Ashe, smiling and laughing, and by her side a tall and relaxed-looking male dryad. The two looked comfortable in each other's company, talking softly as they walked the lamplit paths. Robin knew from Splinterstem's emotions that this other man was Alder, and that the watchful dryad whose mind he inhabited was conflicted. Alder was his friend, almost a brother to him. But there was no mistaking the princess' laughter, the easy and private smiles passing between the two of them down below. And Splinterstem was feeling the throne slip away, his dreams of courting the princess too. Everything he wanted, everything that should be his, was being pulled from his grasp.

Another shifting blur, making Robin dizzy, and now he felt, years had passed. The forest was not autumnal but rich and leafy, a riot of greens in the height of a long ago summer. The Fae had come to their city, the one who called himself Hammerhand, bringing his treasure, this green and glimmering Shard of power. Outside the peaceful and isolated kingdom of the dryads' lands, he had told them, war was raging across the Netherworlde. A terrible war that would soon send echoes even here, in the deepest parts of the forest. The Fae King and Queen were gone, the Arcania itself had been shattered, and it looked as though Lady Eris would win her war.

Through Splinterstem's memory, Robin saw the king solemnly accept the burden of the Shard from a surprisingly short and bearded Fae bearing twin sets of pale horns, twining around each other. This man was Hammerhand. Robin knew this because Splinterstem had known it, but the boy was curious nonetheless. He had never seen a portrait of the great Fae explorer and this was the first time he had seen what the man looked like.

The king of the dryads, with great ceremony, exchanged a gift with the Fae, a great treasure of Rowandeepling. A mask, to return to Erlking with, the Mask of Gaia, he told Hammerhand, which he hoped may prove to show a clearer way to troubled Fae during the dark times. Hammerhand accepted this gift, leaving the dryads with the Shard of Earth, with what would become the heart of the elder trees.

Time and vision blurred once more and Robin, thrust forward again through the haze of the dead memories, now found himself standing with many other dryads at the foot of the trees. The great Labyrinth was newly completed. The Shard had been set at its heart, never to be touched again. The king was giving a great speech to his gathered people, reassuring them about the growing menace of the swarm, their own lost kin, now growing far off in the south forest. He swore that the Shard would protect them, and he commended Splinterstem, standing at his side, on his genius contribution, at placing a guardian of his own creation and design at the centre, ever to keep the heart of the forest safe.

Pride poured through Robin, Splinterstem's emotions, as he ascended in importance through the king's court to sit at his right hand on his council, the respected genius of the labyrinth, the dutiful protector of the kingdom. But underlying this feeling was a terrible dark guilt, spreading like ink, burrowing troublesomely through what should have been a bright moment. Robin could not understand.

Robin closed his eyes within the jumbled haze of visions and memory, and focused his will. He knew this had all happened. What he needed was to see closer to the present, to understand how the Shard had been loosed in the first place.

Mentally forcing his way forward through the jagged slices of Splinterstem's memories, he found years had now passed. The war had been won and Lady Eris ruled the Netherworlde, Empress of all. Much of the southern Elderhart forest had fallen to the swarm, and internal war loomed in the woods, no matter how hard the dryads had fought to remain separate from the troubles of the wider world. Alder was long gone, and Splinterstem had felt sure that in time, the princess would manage her grief, as he had himself, and see past her pain to the promise of the good mate who stood before her. He had been sure that in time, he would claim her hand. But she had not seen past her pain and loss. She remained polite but cold to him.

She would never marry. And by now the queen was dead, and the king ruled alone. The position of the dryads in the world was weakened further still.

Splinterstem was filled with injustice and bitterness. He would never have the throne. He would never marry the princess. After all he had sacrificed and done to engineer his future. Still power and happiness were forever beyond his reach.

He began to resent them. The time of the dryads was coming to an

end, he decided. They were insular, hiding in their haven, wilfully ignorant of the world beyond, of where the true power of the world now lay.
They had become irrelevant in the new world order, a relic, doomed to
dwindle. The swarm at least had strength, Splinterstem knew. They were
organised, powerful. They were part of something larger than themselves.
The victorious reign of the Empress.

Robin suddenly saw a slice of memory then which made him stop. It
had been as though he were sliding along a reel of microfilm, scan-reading
old articles. But here, he sensed a tipping point, a moment of importance.
He dropped right into the memory.

A forest glade, not far from the island of the elder trees, resolved before
his eyes. Splinterstem had been walking alone, troubled and embittered,
tired of the constant struggle to maintain a respectable face at the dryad
court, tired of being so close to glory and never able to taste it. The dryad
had been lost in a cloud of dark thoughts when he had met the girl.
Wandering alone amongst the trees, carefree and relaxed, as though she
owned the whole wood. Young, she had seemed to him. Smiling, and
dripping with power.

It had been Miss Peryl.

Robin saw the dryad's wariness. And the girl's relaxed air. She seemed
at once dangerous and friendly, like a playful cat that might tire of toying
with its mouse with soft paws at any moment and fall upon it.

They talked, the two of them, isolated and secret out here in the woods.

She was from the Hive, she told the dryad. Things were better there,
for people of his ambition. People of his strength were not ignored or cast
aside. She, unlike his precious king, recognised, and rewarded potential.

They spoke at length of the Shard, buried deep beneath the elder trees,
hidden and closely guarded in its impenetrable maze. It served no real
purpose to the dryads, she had told him. They had been here long before
it, and they would be here long after it was gone. No one had laid eyes
on the artefact in years anyway. Who would know if it was gone or not?

No one knew their way safely through the maze, no one but him,
its architect.

In the shadows beneath the trees, a dark deal was struck, a simple one.
If he would fetch the Shard and give it to her. He would have proved
himself worthy of the Hive. He would finally be rewarded with the power
he craved, the status he knew he deserved. The status that she could see he

313

was worthy of. The king of the dryads was an ailing fool. His daughter a cold-hearted brat. Neither of them deserved his loyalty. Had he not given his entire life to serving the dryads, she told him, and they repaid him with what? A seat on the council to quiet his grumbles, an appeasement to keep him happy. It was an insult. They cared nothing for his leadership, nothing for his strength. They were blind to it.

She, the girl with shining black eyes assured him, was not.

For the first time, in his darkest moments, here was someone who recognised his greatness, who confirmed for him everything he had always believed. That he was worthy, that he deserved better. She was right, the Shard was a trinket. And he the only one who could enter the Labyrinth and retrieve it. None would ever know it was gone. The Shards of the Arcania may recently have awakened, but what did it matter to the insular and remote dryads? It meant little to him. And if he brought the Shard to this girl who was no girl, he would reign in the Hive anyway, finally recognised. Finally, for once, on the side of power.

Robin didn't want to believe any of it. That Peryl had been given the run of Eris' dark jail, that she had tempted this dryad away from his own people with empty, honey-laced promises of power. Making all his ambitious lifelong wishes finally come true. She wanted only the Shard. And she would have it from him however she could.

Once more, time and vision blurred, and now it was dark, and Robin was back at the Labyrinth entrance.

He watched as Splinterstem emerged from the doorway in the silent shadows, a stealthy thief unharmed by the minotaur. He was the only one that knew its secrets. Retrieving the Shard has been simpler than even his new, purple-haired patron would ever know.

In his gnarled mossy hands, he carried the Shard of the Arcania, an emerald jewel shaped like an arrowhead.

But, Robin observed from the periphery of the vision, someone had been waiting for him at the entrance.

Long suspecting something wrong with his most trusted counsellor, the king himself, concerned with Splinterstem's behaviour, had secretly followed him down from Rowandeepling in the pre-dawn mists.

Confronting the dryad now at the doors to the minotaur's lair, the king demanded to know what was happening. What was his advisor, his trusted friend, doing with the heart of the forest? Was this treason?

They argued back and forth as Robin watched, helpless to intervene. He felt the king's sting of betrayal. He felt Splinterstem's overpowering mixture of shame and anger, bubbling into furious resentment. And finally, the king lunged forward, trying to take the Shard from Splinterstem by force. Robin stared in horror as the traitor pushed him away, furious beyond measure that once again, his final chance at power was in danger of being crushed, snatched away by his own people. Robin saw Splinterstem raise the Shard high, teeth clenched in rage, and bring it down with great force, burying it into the chest of the king like a green dagger.

The king staggered backward, staring down in disbelief at the glowing Shard protruding obscenely from his body. Splinterstem's face was a mask of frozen emotion, his arms limp at his sides with shock, at the enormity of what he had just done. And then a great shockwave erupted from the king, a flash of green light which stripped the leaves from trees and shook their trunks, which sent Splinterstem flying, cannoned backward to land against the Labyrinth wall in a heap and a rain of stones.

Robin wanted to rush forward and help the fallen monarch, but of course, his legs would not move. He wasn't really here. This had already happened and he was helpless to do anything but bear witness. The king crawled along the floor, bellowing in agony, as the grass roared up from the floor beneath him, tangling around his arms. Twigs and shoots wrapped around his body, stones rolling from all over the clearing to cover him as he struggled to get away, headed blindly for the trees. By the time he was out of sight, Robin could no longer make out the shape of the king at all, only a writhing mass of living forest, entombing and encasing him even as it moved and fought against it. The great and untamed power of the Earth Shard, thrust unwillingly straight into his heart, was lashing out, keeping him alive the only way it knew how … by devouring him, making him one with the living breathing forest. As he disappeared from sight, Splinterstem got shakily to his knees.

Miss Peryl stepped out from the shadows of the trees. She had her arms folded and her purple head on one side, looking mildly irritated.

"What have I done?" Splinterstem was whispering, and Robin felt his fear, his numb horror.

"You have lost me my Shard, that's what you've done," Peryl replied. She sighed, cupping the stunned dryad's face in her hands. "And you had better get it back," she said sweetly. "This is your mess, tree-boy. Clean it up. By any means necessary, or every one of those fluttering insects you have just betrayed will know *exactly* what you are. Exactly what you have done. I don't think that will go well for you, do you?"

The dryad dragged his wide green eyes away from where the king had disappeared, and stared at Peryl in horror. She was smiling at him, as though he were a naughty child she were indulging.

"I … I can get it back for you," he spluttered. "I'll find a way."

"Darn tootin'," she agreed, releasing his chin and clapping him warmly on the shoulder. "Bring it back to me here. And quickly. You won't be able to take it from the king. Not now that he's claimed it. Or rather, it claimed him." She looked off into the forest thoughtfully, biting her own cheek. "There's only one who can. You probably want to go search at Erlking. Find yourself a champion."

"Erlking? The old Fae palace?" the dryad stuttered, clearly confused. "But it's just a ruin. All the Fae are gone."

She shook her head. "Not on the human-world side of the coin," she assured him. "You can find a patsy there, trust me. They're all over the Shards like white on rice. But if I were you, I wouldn't waste too much time." She looked up at the trees, hands on her hips, expression thoughtful. "Fires start so easily in the forest, don't they?" she said breezily. "You'd be amazed how quickly they catch. I like to play with matches sometimes, you know, if I get bored, or if I'm kept waiting too long."

In the morning mist, she grinned warmly at him, purple lips beneath dark eyes.

"Now, you'd better think up a convincing story to tell your fluttering friends. Cover up your dark deeds, eh?" she smirked. "I mean; it wouldn't be the first time."

Robin staggered backwards, pulling the mask from his face. In a flash, he was back in the dank and dark tunnel, Henry and Strife both staring at him as he caught his breath.

He stared down at the rather sad, ambitious and treacherous body of Splinterstem. "Power," he said, a little breathlessly, reeling from all that he had seen. "He wanted power. It ate him away. And he lied, stole and murdered for it."

"Power promised by my wretch of a sister," Strife nodded, looking down also, but with considerably less humanity. "As if she'd share it. She's not the type. I should know, look what she's reduced me to. But I will give her this much, she always knows what people want. It is one of her few talents, the manipulation of others. She must not have this Shard."

"I don't understand you at all," Robin said, still holding the mask in his hands. "Eris wants all the Shards, doesn't she? Isn't that your end goal? I don't understand why you're not working *with* Peryl. Why instead you're creeping around the forest like some homeless wanderer?"

"Zombie Aragorn," Henry muttered to himself, and then, under his breath with a slight snigger. "Araghoul."

Strife bared his teeth at Robin, looking fearsome in the purplish gloom.

"Because I rule the Grimms!" he snapped. "*Me! Strife!*" Robin and Henry actually took a step backwards in the face of his sudden anger.

"Our cataclysmic failure at Hieronarbos was bad enough!" the old man hissed. "We failed to capture the valley, we failed to subdue the Undine. The only thing we achieved was that half of the Peacekeeper army was blown free of their husks! Even now, months later, Brother Ker still labours to rebuild his forces, to channel his mana into new soldiers and flesh out our decimated ranks. We were … disgraced!"

He calmed himself with some effort, leaning back and smoothing down his green hair with the palms of his long white hands, fingers splayed.

"But little Peryl, the runt of the litter?" he growled. "*She* returns to Dis with half a Shard. Holding the power of the Arcania proudly before her, filled with it, flowing with it, and with the blood of fallen Fae-scum on her hands. Suddenly, she is the toast of the court. My lady's new favourite. And I?" He smoothed his lapels. "Well, I was lucky not to be thrown into the pits with dear Moros. Reduced instead to border patrols? This is my punishment. The great Strife, tasked to the hunting of stray and unimportant outlaws. Me!"

Robin and Henry nodded to show that, they too, found this clearly unacceptable. It seemed the safest thing to do, alone as they were in this underground place with the simmering Grimm.

"I *need* my station," Strife explained. "I need the freedom to act which is afforded to the leader of the Grimms, in order to pursue my own … interests. And while Peryl lords it over all, reigning Queen of the Hive, I cannot do that."

Robin wondered what Strife meant by 'his own interests'. He thought it safer not to ask.

"Imagine how much worse it will be," Strife continued bitterly, actually grinding his teeth against each other. "Should the loathsome, idiotic girl deliver the Earth Shard to Eris too. I daresay she would surpass even Strigoi himself in our lady's favour. It cannot be borne! It must not come to pass."

"So what you're saying is," Henry said carefully. "You'll happily backstab your own kind, and actually risk losing a Shard of the Arcania to the likes of us, just in order to spite your own sister?"

"It is more important to me that Peryl fail than it is that the empress gain a Shard," Strife hissed. His voice was incredibly low, as though he dared not say this louder. Robin could guess why. For his own personal reasons, Strife was willing to deprive Eris of a Shard? That seemed like a very dangerous move to make against a ruler who, by all accounts, was not famed for her powers of forgiveness or mercy. It was not the kind of plan you voiced openly.

"So ... you'll help us get the Shard, and our friends, back from Peryl?" Robin asked, still finding it difficult to swallow the fact that, at least temporarily, he and Strife were on the same side.

"I will do nothing of the sort," Strife told them dismissively. "But your little friends, if they are still alive, will have been taken with the Shard to the Hive. There are no doors or windows in the great pyramid of the south. The Hive is an impenetrable fortress." He smiled humourlessly in the dark. "Unless of course, you are me. What I will do, is open the door and leave it ajar. What you do next is entirely up to you. I myself must make myself as distant from this place as I can." A cunning, scheming expression filled the old man's harsh face. "It would be wise for me to be in Dis perhaps, when the Hive is infiltrated by rebel Fae scum. I must place myself as far from the incident, and as visible to Eris as possible. The only skirts stained by this will be my sister's, I assure you of that. And her fall from grace ... will be my ascent."

"We should go up to Rowandeepling," Robin said. "Tell the princess and the others what has happened, with the scourge, with Splinterstem."

"You really are without the remotest modicum of intelligence," Mr Strife sneered. "They are gone, you imbecile. There are no dryads in their treetop city. The princess and the rest have all been taken to the Hive. They are its prisoners now. The swarm has won. The forest is theirs for the taking. My sister with the Earth Shard in her possession? A force to be reckoned with, I assure you. The sacking of Rowandeepling, while you slept in a pool of your own blood and a cage of your own foolishness, was swift and brutal."

Robin didn't want to believe it but it made a dark kind of sense. It explained why no one had come down while he was in the cage. Why there had been no lights in the city high above. The only dryad remaining in Rowandeepling was the dead one lying at his feet. The turncoat who had betrayed them all and doomed his own people to slavery and destruction.

"So, how do we get to this Hive then?" Henry asked. "It sounds like such a charming, welcoming place."

Strife's mana-light bobbed ahead. "The only way into the Hive is through the Janus station which lies at its inner chambers."

"Is there a Janus station in the forest we can use? Do you know how to open it?"

"Of a sort. And of course I can use it. We aren't all helpless ignorant scum," he sneered. "It is in here." He gestured to the cavern.

"What? In the Labyrinth? You want us to go in here?" Robin gawped. "What about the minotaur?"

"Whoa, hold on, mate," Henry butted in. "Minotaur? As in, *minotaur* minotaur?"

Strife took a long-suffering breath. "We can, of course, go to the other nearest Janus station if you wish," he said, to which Henry fervently nodded his approval. "It's far beyond the borders of the forest, across the grasslands where the hills meet the ocean. There are countless centaur between here and there, and it would take weeks to reach on foot. Eris would have the Shard by then, and all your friends would be dead."

He turned on his heel without a further word and walked off into the gloom. Robin and Henry looked at each other.

"Bugger," said Henry emphatically.

"I'd have to be really unlucky to get eaten twice in the same week, wouldn't I?" Robin asked.

Henry raised an eyebrow. "Just like I'd have to be really unlucky to get kidnapped twice in my school uniform?"

Robin groaned, turning to follow Strife. "Bugger."

THE CHAINS OF GAIA

The entrance was soon lost far behind them, the cool open night air of the great Elderhart forest nothing but a distant memory. The two boys followed their ghoulish guide, stalking ahead of them, mana flame flickering in his spidery hand and dark ragged cloak billowing out behind him with every long loping step. Robin felt like he was following the grim reaper into the claustrophobic pits of hell.

"I think I remember something about mazes," Henry whispered behind him, as Strife led them along the dank and twisting corridors, their footfalls echoing. They had made many a left and right turn by this point, and by Robin's reckoning, had been ploughing into the darkness for at least half an hour before any of them had spoken. So far, despite straining to, he had not heard the sound of chains clanking nor any other sign of the legendary minotaur.

"About labyrinths?" Robin asked. "Really? Henry, you get frustrated with the wordsearches in your dad's newspaper. I have seen you swearing at the Sunday edition at the breakfast table."

"No, really," Henry insisted. "It's something like, always turn left, and you'll get to the middle." He frowned in the dark. Both of them were constantly hurrying to keep up with Strife, who set a brisk pace and had not once looked back to check if they were following. "Or maybe it's left always and you'll find your way out?" Henry sounded uncertain.

"Well, we don't want to find our way out, we want to find our way in," Robin replied.

"And what about this bull-man then? Any plans? I didn't think to pack a matador costume when I was so thoughtfully dragged out of my house by redcaps. Did you bring one?"

"No," Robin admitted distractedly. "I didn't. I don't know. We'll deal with that when we have to. That's the way to deal with this whole thing … Socks and underpants … Just pick up one thing at a time."

"What on earth are you babbling about?" Henry asked. "Are you sure your head isn't still cracked?"

"Never mind," Robin said, dismissively. "Just … keep an eye on Strife. I know he's not done anything yet, but I don't trust him one inch. If he can turn on us and get away with it, I know he will."

"Oh, don't you worry, mate," Henry agreed. "I'm not actually stupid, you know. I've been alone with the guy in the forest remember. Have you ever slept with one eye open? It's harder than it sounds, and bloody exhausting. I kept thinking I was going to wake up dead."

"Henry, that doesn't even begin to make any sense," Robin smirked, despite their grim situation. He hadn't realised how much he'd missed Henry's company until now.

Strife led them onwards into the twisting dark. The corridors were endless. The only varying feature was the pattern of fallen blocks, here and there, and the spiderweb tracery of roots and vines clinging randomly to the walls, pale tubers following the lines of mortar like fingers following braille. It was as though the trees above were feeling their way through the silent maze in the absolute darkness. Slowly questing themselves toward the centre, towards the Shard's former resting place.

"You're such a goon," Robin told Henry, not unpleasantly. "But I'm glad you're not kidnapped or dead."

"Yeah yeah, love you too," Henry muttered gruffly. "Can we save the hugs until we're not being buried alive? Honestly, I think I prefer the redcaps. And that's saying something. You wouldn't believe what those guys eat."

Robin slipped on some scree, banging into the wall. "Ow … You would never have *been* kidnapped at all, you know, if you had just come straight up to the house after school, like you used to do. You've been avoiding the place, avoiding all of us, since Jackalope came. And yes, you get to say 'I told you so' about that."

Henry stopped dead in the corridor behind Robin, his feet scuffling. "What are you on about?" he asked.

Robin stopped too, turning in the darkness. "Look, *everyone* noticed you've been coming up to Erlking less and less. You're always busy, making excuses or having to leave early. It's painfully obvious you didn't want to be around the guy." Robin shrugged a little awkwardly. "Or me. I figured you'd kind of fallen out with me…a bit."

Henry actually rolled his eyes. "Is that really what you think?" he asked.

Robin frowned. What other explanation could there be.

Henry actually laughed, shaking his matted mop of hair. "Robin Fellows, you might be the son of a Fae lord, practically a superhero and deliverer of the galaxy or whatever, but honestly … you can be such a fussy old woman sometimes." He held his hands up. "Yeah, I admit, I had my reservations about taking in Jackalope after he split with us and went over to Team Evil." He paused, peering past Robin to Strife, who had stopped, turning to see what the hold-up was. "Of course, after this, I realise there's some irony in that. I might have to readjust my thinking a bit. But yeah, if my instincts were right and he did turn out to be a bad penny, murdering his big brother and all, I can't say I'm happy about it." He sniffed a little. "I would have been happy to have been proved wrong."

"Yeah," Robin said quietly.

"But that's not why I wasn't coming around as much!" Henry insisted. "Sulking? Really?" He shook his head. "No, I was busy…" He halted, as though unsure of how to continue.

"Busy doing what?" Robin asked. "You've been so cagey about it."

"'Cause I reckoned you'd all laugh at me," Henry said. "But what the hell now," he sighed. "I've been taking classes."

"Classes?"

Henry nodded. "Archery. Two hours a day, *every weekday*. Learning to use that bow you got me for my birthday." He looked awkward. "And you know, self-defence stuff too. Bit of martial arts, bit of boxing, learning to fight."

Robin peered at his squirming friend in disbelief. "Archery? Self-defence? What for?"

"So I could be *useful*, moron," Henry blurted out hotly. He glared at Robin, almost defying him to say something. "So I could be part of the group."

"Henry," Robin stammered, utterly confused. "You *are* part of the group. Have you lost your mind completely?"

"No but … yeah … I know we're friends," Henry tried to explain. "But you, and Karya and Woad, I mean, look at you, you're like the magical triangle or something. You're the bloody Power Rangers. You have all your Scion powers. You've mastered two and a half elements. You've just

322

killed a dragon from the inside, for pete's sake! And Karya? She's such a badass. She speaks like a hundred languages. She's stronger than anyone I know and she can tear between worlds. And Woad, well, he's a bloody force of nature isn't he, little acrobatic firework." He threw his hands up. "What am *I*?"

Robin stared at his friend, totally taken aback by this outburst.

"I felt like …" Henry scratched at his head a little, trying to find the right words. "I don't know, like that, in the great orchestra or Erlking, I'm the kid at the end of the row with no talent who gets given the triangle to play."

Robin raised his eyebrows, trying very hard to keep a straight face. It was clear this was something that had been bothering Henry for some time.

"So, your solution was … to become a … ninja?" he managed.

"Har-di-har" Henry narrowed his eyes sarcastically. "I dunno, I thought, if I could at least fight well, I could be more useful. Feel like something more than just the one human in the band of merry Netherworlders." He stuck his hands in his pockets. "Then when silver top woke up and started lording it around, showing off with his throwing knives and bloody scissor kicks, well…it's like I could see my replacement right there in front of my eyes. I knew I had to step up my game." He studied Robin's face in the gloom for a moment. Silence passed between them.

"Rob, if you start humming 'eye of the tiger', I swear to God I'm going to lamp you," he growled.

Robin shook his head. "You, Henry Drover, are a prize idiot," he said eventually. "Like we could ever replace *you*. You're not the triangle player. How do you think *I* feel? I'm like the guy handed the conducting stick but without a damned clue what the hell I'm supposed to do with it. I'm just waving it about and hoping for the best."

Robin sighed heavily, raking his hands through his hair. "But you … you're loyal and brave and confident. *Nothing* knocks you off your stride. You drank kraken venom and jumped into a bottomless well without a second thought. Just so I didn't have to do it on my own. You dressed as a Peacekeeper and threw a spear at Strigoi. At Strigoi!" He shook his head in amazement. "And I've been worried you're dead in the forest some-where, choking on poisoned berries or tripping over your own shoelaces, and what have you been doing instead? Teaming up with a Grimm and turning into Bear Grylls of the Netherworlde." Robin shook his head.

"I'm the one who was locked in a cage bleeding out of my skull like a helpless numpty, remember. You're tough as old boots."

Henry looked at his feet a little bashfully. "S'pose," he muttered. He looked up again, grinning a little. "Plus, I guess one of us in our ragtag group has to be the rakishly handsome one, right?"

Robin patted his friend's shoulder. "Henry," he said. "With the best will in the world, you look like someone dropped a sack of old potatoes, and right now, you smell like old cabbage."

"Thanks," Henry said. "Sorry if I gave the wrong impression."

Robin shook his head, "Forgotten. I shouldn't have assumed–"

A dramatic and drawn-out wheezing sigh came from Strife in the darkness ahead. "If you two are going to kiss, I may vomit," he rasped dryly, boredom dripping from his words. "I cannot bear affection. Are we quite, quite done with the man-hugging and happy families? Only, there is something of the pressing issue of a Shard and a familial betrayal to avenge."

"We are working through some stuff!" Robin glared at Strife sharply.

The old man returned the boy's stare with an absolute lack of humour or indulgence, his face a mask of bitterness. "*Te odeo*," he muttered under his breath murderously, in his crisp low tones. "*Interface te cochleare*."

"I have got quite good, actually," Henry said, in much lighter tones, as they began to follow their dark guide once more, ignoring his dark mutterings. "With the bow, I mean, and with fighting. I've been doing MMA"

"I'm sure you have, Xena," Robin said. "You're still naff at following orders though. Come on."

They started off again, turning yet another corner, weaving deeper into the Labyrinth. Something occurring to Robin. "Anyway, you *do* have your own special talent you bring to the group already, something you're better at than any one of us."

"What's that then?" Henry wanted to know.

"You're really, really good at getting kidnapped," the blonde boy teased.

Henry, muttering in the darkness, suggested that Robin go away and do something anatomically impossible, using some very colourful language.

"How do we know we're on the right track?" Robin asked, calling ahead to Mr Strife. It felt that they had been stumbling in the gloom for an eternity. Surely an hour, maybe more, had passed since they first entered the maze, turning endless lefts and rights along the cobwebbed corridors. For all he knew, they could be going in endless circles. The tunnels were designed to look identical, confusing. He was beginning to suspect that they had passed the same clump of moss more than a few times now. He voiced the opinion that maybe Henry was right about always turning left.

"Netherworlde mazes all have one thing in common," Strife told them. "They have checkpoints. Markers of progress. Traditionally, there will be two of these. Usually where the way is blocked, and this is usually bypassed only by a test."

"A test?" Henry asked dubiously. "What, like sums?"

"A test of *wits*," Strife sneered. "Between you two, that would be two halves."

"We haven't seen any checkpoints though," Robin argued. Strife had stopped dead ahead of them, and as they caught up, they saw they had come to a dead end.

"Until now," the old man said, his dry voice rich with satisfaction. He raised his flickering purplish mana-light to the stone wall before them. It was carved with lettering.

"What does that say?" Robin asked. "It's in the high tongue, isn't it?"

"It is," Strife agreed, running his fingers over the carved words on the stonework before him. It seemed to be an etched tablet, covered in script. Below it, set into the wall there were three smaller carved squares, each with a rough and primitive design. One looked like a rudimentary tree, a fir, Robin thought. The next was three waving lines atop another, a flowing wave, and the last of the three, a primitive sun. A circle with carved lines radiating.

In the hushed and enclosed darkness, Strife translated aloud. "It is a riddle," he confirmed. "Always runs, never walks. Often murmurs, never talks. Has a bed, never sleeps. Has a mouth, never eats."

Robin and Henry exchanged a look. "Hopefully the answer's not 'the minotaur'," Henry said. "I don't like the idea of a massive bull-headed man that runs all the time instead of walking. Imagine it charging towards us down these corridors."

"Murmurs without talking?" Robin pondered. The image which rose in his mind's eye was a witch, bent double and muttering incantations into a bubbling cauldron. The three sinister sisters who had spent time at Erlking recently. But that didn't seem right.

He stared past Mr Strife at the three symbols. Suddenly, the answer was obvious. As clear as day.

"Got it!" he said, reaching past the old man. His fingers touched the carved square which contained the three wavy lines, and he pushed, feeling the cube of stone slide backwards with a grating rumble.

"It's a river," Robin declared.

There was a loud, worrying rumble around them, the walls, floor and ceiling of the tunnel shaking, dislodging a cloud of dust. The wall before them slowly sunk into the ground, revealing behind it tight stairs curving away downwards.

"Onward, to the lower levels," Strife said, matter-of-factly when the noise and movement had subsided. "Further to the centre." His eyes, black and shining like pools of tar, bore into Robin. "You are lucky, hasty Fae-child, that your guess was correct."

"Why?" Henry asked, as they followed the narrow steps down, descending even further into the earth and darkness. "What would have happened if we'd guessed wrong?"

"Booby traps most likely," Strife said. "The tunnels are usually designed to collapse and crush those who fail."

"Oh," came the quiet reply in the shadows.

The next level of the sprawling Labyrinth was much the same, only the walls here were less weathered, fewer roots penetrated this deeply, and most of the stones were unbroken. It was a long time of walking, turning corner after corner, left and right and left again, before they came at last to a second barrier. It occurred to both Robin and Henry that, were Strife to simply vanish, to extinguish his light and slip off into the darkness, the chances of them ever finding their way out again were extremely slim. There was no going back.

"I still can't believe we're 'allies' with Strife," Robin whispered to Henry at one point, stumbling along in the dark after the stalking Grimm.

Henry nodded sympathetically. "I know, mate. I feel like I need to have the hottest shower in the world to stop my skin from crawling too. But the enemy of my enemy is my less enemyish enemy, or whatever the saying is, right?"

"We are not allies," Strife hissed angrily without turning around, once more reminding them of his supernatural powers of hearing. "Make no mistake. The pitiful human is only alive because he was my offering to you, to ensure your compliance. And *you* are only here in the form of my tool. I do not ally with the rebellious wretches of Erlking. This leaves as vile a taste in my mouth as it does yours, Robin Fellows, mark my words. If you were not useful to me at the present time, I would be serving you up to my Lady Eris in a series of boxes … extremely small boxes."

There was a curious smell down on this level, and it was getting stronger with every twist they took and every corner they chose. A bestial, animal smell. Rank damp fur, rotting meat … and something darker.

Robin and Henry both noticed this, and neither of them spoke of it. The minotaur was at the front of both their minds, but it seemed superstitiously perilous to mention it, as though it could be summoned just by thinking of it.

Robin was still holding the Mask of Gaia lightly in his fingers, and as he followed the Grimm, it suddenly occurred to him that he might be able to use it to check that Strife's true intention was not to lead them to their deaths. Staring at the back of the Grimm, he lifted the mask to his eyes.

A flash as the power of the mask rolled through him, and a grainy, silent image rose swiftly before his eyes. But it was one that made no sense to Robin at all. He was in a long room filled with beds either side in rows. They looked sparse and utilitarian, the kind you saw in old hospitals or boarding school in old black and white movies from long ago. A high, arched ceiling rose above him timbered and shadowy, and a long set of tall windows across one wall divided the room into slices of shadow and light.

The air smelled of floor polish and dust, chalk and ink, and before he had a moment to properly take in his surroundings, he noticed that in this quiet, bare place, there was a tremendous atmosphere of sorrow. A deep sadness rolling through him. It was emanating from two hunched figures, who sat together, side by side on one of the slender beds.

They had their backs to him, but he saw they were boys, their legs dangling from the edge of the bed, crisp black school shoes not quite reaching the floor.

One of the boys was crying softly, his back rocking as he buried his head in his hands. The other, sitting close by, had an arm protectively around his shoulders, trying to comfort and quiet him.

"Hush, William," Robin heard, softly, cajoling. "It will be fine, you'll see. Chin up, old boy, eh?" It was almost a whisper.

The sobbing boy's voice was broken when it replied. "We're never going to leave here, are we?"

Robin made to take a step forward towards them. They couldn't have been more than nine or ten years old. But as he moved, a great terrible shadow seemed to rush up at him, flooding the room like an ink blot as it roared towards him, obliterating the scene.

Robin felt a slap, hard against his face. The mask was knocked loose, falling clattering to the floor of the dark Labyrinth corridor, bouncing off the wall with a noise that echoed up and down its length.

He staggered back, blinking and disoriented. Strife was standing before him, hand still raised and shaking. Robin had never seen such fury in his face.

The Grimm looked manic, eyes bulging, lips drawn back across his skeletal face.

"How dare you!" he hissed angrily. His cold voice shook.

Robin stumbled. "I … I'm sorry, I just …"

Strife gripped the boy roughly by the front of his shirt, almost lifting him off the ground as he shook him angrily.

"If you ever dare … ever … to point that foul thing in my direction again," he spat, his face inches from Robin's. "Ever! It will be the very last thing you do. Is that quite understood?" Robin nodded urgently, trying to twist out of the old man's grip, but Strife, still shaking with indignation and fury, held him in a vice of steel.

"My mind is no place for someone like you!" he growled.

"Who … who's William?" Robin stuttered.

Strife dropped him as though he had just burned his fingers. Robin fell to the floor, onto the dark dusty stone, Henry rushing to help him up.

"Bloody hell, steady on!" Henry said. "He said he was sorry, didn't he?"

Strife straightened up, composing himself, but his hard black eyes still filled with fury. "Unless you wish for our distasteful arrangement to come to an end," he said, razor blades in the darkness. "A very swift and bloody end, you will do well to keep your business out of mine, Robin Fellows."

Robin nodded, getting to his feet. Not taking his eyes from the old man, whose fists were clenching and unclenching, he picked up the mask and put it carefully away.

He felt horrible, as though he had crossed some impassable line, committed some terrible crime of privacy. He wanted to apologise, even if it was Mr Strife, but staring into the old man's hard and hate-filled face, he couldn't find a single word.

"Anger me again, Scion," Strife said, drawing his cloak around him. "And I shall cut out your heart. Are we perfectly clear?"

"Crystal," Robin said hoarsely.

"Good." Strife's tone was deliberately businesslike. "Because our wanderings are almost at an end."

He set off again, and they followed. Henry gave Robin a questioning look, but Robin, with a vile taste in his throat, merely shook his head, still smelling floor polish and chalk.

"We are soon to part ways," Strife told them not long after, as they turned yet another left and he stopped before them. "Here is the second marker. The second challenge."

"If nobody but this dead dryad guy who designed the place knows the way to the centre and back, how come you've been able to lead us so well?" Henry asked, the thought suddenly occurring to him.

"Because I am a hunter," the old man growled, with a menacing pride. "I can track the shadow of an eagle across the moonless moor, human brat. I have been chasing your elusive and troublesome golden-eyed girl for some time before your treasured Fae friend even came to Erlking. I found you in the forest, did I not?" He pointed to Robin. "And him. I have been following the dryad's tracks, and his scent. Both are still fresh from when he retrieved the Shard."

Robin looked beyond Mr Strife to the wall ahead. For the first time, they had reached a part of the maze which did not, in its crumbling, stone-hewn way, resemble every other part. Before them was a large arch of stone bricks, and filling its centre, solid rock, upon which more words in the high tongue were carved.

Beneath these words, this time there were two carved images. The one on the left, within a circle of carved stone ivy, seemed to be a depiction of a bull's-head, surrounded by curling, spirals and whorls, reminding Robin of old, organic-looking Viking carvings. The one on the right, in a stone frame of holly was identical, another bull's head, only here the pattern in its backdrop was not curved and twining, but instead geometric, all lines and edges, corners and squares.

Strife read aloud, translating for the others.

"Rivers with no water. Forests with no trees. Cities with no buildings."

He stared for a moment. "That's it. That is all that is written."

They all pondered this for a while, quiet in the flickering purple glow of Strife's bobbing mana-light.

"Sounds like some dead place to me," Henry suggested tentatively. "You know, post-apocalypse kind of thing? A river without water, like it's dried up long ago. Forests that have been cut down, an abandoned town?"

Robin shrugged. "Maybe," he said. "But what does that have to do with either of these two carvings then?"

Henry had no answer to that. Apart from the differing decorative backdrops, the stone bulls seemed identical.

"A dream of a place?" Mr Strife offered, almost speaking to himself. "That would fit the riddle. What except the mind can create things that are real, but that are not there? A waterless river can exist in your imagination. You can picture a city without building it …"

Robin didn't think this sounded quite right either. He was lost in thought, his fingertips tracing the carvings, following the swirls on one, and the angular lines on the other, careful not to put any pressure on either until they knew which one to safely choose.

He rolled the strange riddle around in his head as his fingers moved. The pattern on his left was quite hypnotic, circles and whorls, his fingers tracing the route in one long and unbroken line. The one on his right was less so. Every couple of inches, the carved lines changed angle, so that his finger was forced to move in a different direction, up down, right, right again, left. It reminded him of being in …

"It's this one," he said suddenly, his hand dropping away from the swirling design. He pointed to the other, the bull's head in a geometric backdrop. "This is the right one. I'm sure of it."

"You should ensure that you are indeed *sure*, Scion," Strife cautioned darkly. "Your blundering haste last time was half luck. I have little wish to be buried alive in a collapsing corridor with the likes of you."

"I am." Robin said. "I'm sure. This angular one."

"How do you know?" Henry asked.

"Because it's the Labyrinth," Robin explained, looking at his friend in the gloom, his blue eyes shining. "Look. Left and right turns … it's a picture of a maze, with the minotaur in the centre here. It's a schematic of the Splinterstem's Labyrinth we're looking at here."

His companions both examined the stone carving carefully their eyes narrowed.

"The other one, that's just pretty curls, but there hasn't *been* a single curved corridor since we came into this place. It's always been straight edges, ninety degree turns, just like this."

"That may well be a drawing of the Labyrinth," Mr Strife agreed, rather grudgingly. "But even if so, how would you know that is what we are meant to be looking for here?"

"Because the riddle tells us what we're looking for," Robin said, very sure of himself. "What's got forests without trees, cities without buildings, and rivers without any water?" He grinned. "A *map* has. A map has all of those things. That's what the riddle is telling us to find, and of these two carvings here, only *this* one is a map."

Henry nodded, supporting Robin's choice, still looking a little baffled.

"Beyond this doorway," Strife counselled. "Lies the centre. There may well be the legendary guardian of the Shard within. Although it is no longer guarding anything, which I imagine may have put it in rather a sour mood."

Robin's hand hovered over the stone tablet. "Well," he reasoned. "We didn't come all this way for nothing, did we?" He didn't relish the thought of meeting a giant monster, if he was being honest, especially without his mana stone, but as his gran used to tell him, very little was ever achieved by those who stay at home safe and warm. He might well be deep underground in questionable company and considerable danger, but Karya and Woad were counting on him, and the Shard was waiting.

"What's life without a little terrifying hazard, eh?" Henry agreed.

For once Mr Strife seemed to agree with them, nodding.

"Dulce periculum." He placed his pale hand, fingers spread wide on the tablet and pushed. It sank into a recess with a grating rumble, and again, with a shaking of the world around them, the entire carved wall filling the archway descended smoothly into the ground. In the dust cloud that filled the corridor, Robin and the others moved forwards.

The chamber beyond was a wide open space of flagged, spiralling tiles, a circular high stone wall meeting in a root-covered dome above them.

All of their attention however was drawn to the centre of the room. Here, there was a circle of stones, each as tall as a man, thin and black as polished jet. They circled a deep black pit, lining its edge. Suspended above this hole, strung from the arms by long thick chains, silver-grey lengths stretching away either side to the periphery of the large space, there hung the minotaur.

"Bloody hell," said Henry breathlessly, staring up at the great figure strung up and spread-eagled over the pit. "That's ... big."

The straining monster had the body of a man, enormously proportioned and covered in coarse, short black fur. It wore a chained belt around its waist, beneath which long legs dangled, ending in huge hooves hovering over the deep pit below it. Both of its massive arms were stretched out either side, held fast and taut by the thick chains that held it aloft, and its great head was the dark and horned face of a monstrous bull, lolling on its chest.

The rank smell of wild animal filled the chamber. The minotaur raised its head as the three entered its domain, staring at them from where it hung with small, glowing red eyes like hot embers. It loosed a deafening bellow, the noise bouncing off the walls, amplified in the harsh acoustics of the room and rolling around the circular space, echoing up from the deep pit beneath it. The huge chains rattled, clanked and strained.

Robin's heart was hammering.

"Why ... why is it strung up like that?" he asked, as they stepped warily into the chamber. It was clear at least that the huge animal was not about to charge them. It could not move an inch. "It looks like a prisoner here."

"Well, of course," Strife glanced at the commanding creature with only the barest hint of interest, as though he saw terrifying mythological beasts every day of his life. "Do you honestly think any sane creature would stay in this place of its own volition? Of course it's restrained."

The minotaur rolled its large head angrily, casting huge shadows on the spiral flagstones at their feet with its long, wickedly pointed horns. To Robin it looked more like a demon than any natural animal, sinews and veins bulging on its neck and furred temples. Chained and secured here for so long, deep underground, away from the light. It bellowed again, deafening. Loose soil and dust fell in showers from between the cracks of the roof above, raining down softly on them. Henry had instinctively covered his ears with his hands.

"But, I thought it walked the passageways ... scaring people off, attacking anyone who entered," Robin frowned, unable to tear his eyes from the straining beast as they cautiously approached. "It can't move at all. It's completely bound."

His eyes followed the long chains, the links of which were each as thick as his arm. He noticed that the tree roots which covered the ceiling, worming in from the earth above, had grown along these metal cords over time. They twined in and out of the metal links, using them as a trellis. Woody vines and pale, questing roots threaded up and over the hands of the minotaur itself, wrapping around its thick and hairy forearms.

"The elder trees roots have grown all along ... the chains I mean," Robin observed. "This creature can't have moved for *ages*. I mean, a seriously long time. It's just been left hanging here."

"Too right!" Henry said with feeling, staring up at the bellowing creature with wide eyes. "It'd kill us in a second if it wasn't. Look at it Rob, it's just pure rage. Talk about mad cow disease! We should be grateful it's not loose to gore us!"

"One imagines ..." Strife said thoughtfully, contemplating the dangling, straining beast as though it were an installation of modern art. "That perhaps the creature is rather put out that its sacred charge, the Shard of the Arcania, has been removed from the chamber. It is now, in every sense, a useless thing. Dangerous to the extreme of course, but it has no purpose now."

He frowned down at the circle of stones and the deep black pit which formed the prison of the bound minotaur. "Rather vexingly, whilst I do enjoy seeing a being suffer so, it is also entirely in my way. This is the Janus station of which I spoke. It is unlikely we can get close enough to activate it without being gored to death by this rabid creature. Its arms may be bound, but a flick of that head will still run anyone of us through."

The old man looked around thoughtfully. "I suggest we throw it the human boy," he said to Robin. "It may distract the minotaur long enough for us to activate the doorway. Although it would be horribly messy of course."

"Oi!" Henry protested. "No one's throwing me anywhere!"

Robin ignored them both. He was staring, transfixed at the minotaur. It was a thing of pure anger, every muscle and bunched sinew straining uselessly against its chains, head tossing back and forth, mad red eyes rolling, filled with bloodlust. Danger rolled from it in waves. It exuded pure menace ... and something, he decided, was wrong about it.

"This isn't right," Robin said quietly. His companions didn't hear him immediately. They were bickering amongst themselves.

To Robin's eye, the minotaur, held fast in mid-air, crucified above the deep pit, seemed ... well ... *too* scary. Too violent and large and feral. It was almost as though it was overblown in its efforts to convince them of its danger. Insisting a little too hard on its own great terribleness.

"It's too pantomime," he muttered to himself. "It's like those houses with the fake dogs."

Henry had broken off with Strife and now looked at his friend curiously. "What are you on about, Rob?"

Robin glanced at him briefly, then looked back up to the thrashing, violent ton of murderous man-bull above them.

"You know, back home ... in the human world, I mean. Mr Burrows, Gran's neighbour, he had one of them."

Henry looked puzzled. "A ... minotaur?" he hazarded.

"No," Robin shook his head. "A fake dog. It's like a gadget, just a novelty item really," he explained. "It's a little voicebox thing and you leave it in the hall, near the front door. It's got a motion sensor, and when people get near it, it lets out a recording of an angry dog barking." He looked at Henry and Strife. "You know, scary, but fake. Mr Burrows had one of those stickers in his window too, the ones that show an angry dog, usually looking vicious and foaming with 'warning; I live here' written underneath. He didn't have a dog at all though. He had a parakeet."

"Why would anyone have such a ridiculous thing?" Strife asked him spitefully.

"A parakeet?" Henry asked. Strike glanced at him sidelong.

"A fake dog."

"It's supposed to warn off robbers and burglars," Robin explained. "To put people off breaking in. A deterrent. It's supposed to make you think, hang on, there's a big scary dog in there, no thanks. I like my arms attached, not chewed off. I'll go rob a different house today."

Henry was looking bewildered. "Mate, you have totally lost me. What's your old neighbour's fake dog alarm got to do with anything? My dad went through a phase of having one of those plastic fish on the wall that sing reggae songs. He thought it was hilarious. It wasn't. So what? Bad taste isn't going to help us fight Señor Steroids here."

"My point is, it was never convincing, the fake dog alarm," Robin explained testily. "The recording, see? It was way too vicious. It sounded like a hellhound or something. Gran and I used to have a right old laugh about it every time we heard it going off through the walls of the bungalow. It wouldn't fool anyone. It was…well, it was trying too hard."

Above them, the great beast, fur matted with sweat, let out another enormous bellow, shaking the floor beneath them. It clanked and writhed in its chains, threatening to break free at any given moment. Just looking at it gave them all the urge to flee, while they still had a few seconds head start. It radiated a powerful wave of imminent danger. One more second in here with me, it seemed to scream to every cell of their bodies, and you'll be dead. Run now!

"Just like this," Robin looked at the minotaur. He shook his head. "This isn't *real*. I know it. I don't know how I know it, I just feel it."

"Your Scion-senses tingling, are they?" Henry looked up at the monster from Robin's side, although from a wise couple of steps further back. "'Cause it seems pretty real to me, mate. I don't think I've ever seen anything realer than those horns!"

Robin nodded. "It's all greasepaint and stage-decoration. Someone wants us to feel this place is full of anger, full of bloodlust and danger," he said, looking around the room. "But it isn't. It's full of pain … and suffering."

He turned and looked directly at Strife.

"This is a glamour," he said firmly. "Illusion magic, Tower of Light stuff. Do you know how to dispel it? We don't have any glam juice with us. Unless you have some in your cloak as well as that healing draught."

The Grimm curled his lip in an ugly way. "I am Strife of Dis. I do not need tinctures and vials to dispel a simple glamour, foolish brat," he said, his voice full of scornful pride. "I am a Grimm. The true leader of the Grimms, no less. Light and illusion is no match for my darkness."

He rubbed his hands together, and then cast them wide at the floor, as though scattering seeds. Dark, inky shadow flowed from his fingertips. Coiling black smoke, which rolled around before him on the floor, growing into two great nebulous lumps. As Robin and Henry watched, and the chained minotaur roared above them, ferocious but unheeded, the shapes resolved themselves into two extremely large black dogs.

Mr Burrows, Robin's old neighbour of the unconvincing novelty alarm system, would have been impressed. These were true hellhounds. Formed

335

of smoke, greasy and impenetrable, solid masses of ever-shifting shadow. Yellow eyes glowed, thin cruel slits, staring at the boys, and sharp, wolfish teeth shone wetly as they growled and grinned.

"Spitak, Siaw," Mr Strife said, with something almost close to repellent affection for his creations. They were his totems, Robin knew. All the Grimms could make them. It was their mana made solid, and Mr Strife's huge hunting dogs, the skrikers, were the worst of them all.

For a frozen, horrible moment, Robin was convinced that this was it. That for reasons unknown, perhaps only for his own amusement, Strife had faked this unlikely truce, luring the two boys here, deep underground and far from help or escape, only to let loose his beasts upon them. He and Henry wouldn't stand a chance. Not without magic, without mana. They would be torn to shreds in seconds.

But Strife did not set his skrikers at their throats. With a gesture, each of the two dogs set off around the circular chamber at full pelt, one in each direction, so that they met on the far side and passed one another, circling the room and returning to their master. They made another lap, fleet paws slapping on the ground, hulking shadows blurring, and then another. Robin and Henry saw that they were leaving shadows behind them, great black trails of smoke. With each lap of the speeding hounds, the black shadows grew thicker, climbing the walls, encasing the room, its inhabitants, the Janus station and the writhing suspended minotaur, in a thick black ring. Soon, there was nothing but darkness around them, a solid circling wall.

Strife closed his eyes, and, head bent low, he clapped his hands together sharply. A small red gem just visible in the pocket-watch of his suit beneath his ragged travelling robe glimmered, and the wall of smoke collapsed inward on them, a tidal wave from all sides, smothering and blocking out the light and everything else as surely as volcanic ash.

Robin and Henry spluttered, and in the darkness, the anger of the chained minotaur let out one final bellow.

Then, as quickly as it had formed, the smoke was gone, dissipating swiftly and the skrikers with it. The air cleared and they were alone once more.

"What …" Henry asked, staring in wonder, "… is that?"

Robin stared too. The stones of the Janus station remained, although the deep black pit was gone, now merely stone floor, swirling tiles like the rest of the room. The minotaur too was gone. In its place, kneeling on the stones in the centre of the circle, still chained at the wrist with sagging metal and twining roots, there was a man.

His body was painfully emaciated. Thin shoulders slumped, ribcage agonisingly visible through dark green skin. His wasted arms were splayed on the floor before him, and covering his head was a ragged sackcloth mask, to which two horns had been clumsily affixed, crudely sown. The mask, without eyeholes or any other feature, was tied on firmly at the throat with a thick rope. The cloth billowing and sucking back at the bony man panted with exhaustion.

"It would appear to be a dryad," Strife observed, with some degree of detached curiosity. "Or the tattered remains of one, at least. So, *this* is the real centre of the Labyrinth then."

Robin rushed forward toward the stooping figure and dropped to its side. It was horribly weak, its arms still wound all about with roots as tight as the chains.

"Help me," he said to the others. "Help me get this off."

Henry joined him, and together, with no resistance from the prisoner who was clearly too feeble to respond, they fumbled with the rope, loosening the sackcloth mask with some effort.

Robin pulled off the horrible hood, casting it aside with revulsion. The dryad beneath was shivering, feverish and hollow-cheeked.

"Give me your cloak," Robin snapped at Strife. "Hurry."

Strife peered at Robin with interest, and the man almost collapsing by his side. The dryad's eyes were bleary and confused, blinking in the sudden light after who knew how long, a prisoner under the glamour of the minotaur.

"I said, give it to me!" Robin yelled.

To Henry's surprise, Strife complied, unhooking his tattered travelling cloak and tossing it gracelessly over to Robin, who quickly placed it around the shoulders of the dryad, covering his shivering form. "Can you open these chains?" Robin asked.

Strife did not step toward them, but he raised a hand lazily and made a simple gesture in the air. Black shadows flickered around the dryad's wrists, and with a clatter, the manacles fell open with a clunk. The green skin of his wrists was raw and sore, badly abraded and scarred.

"It's okay," Robin told the dryad reassuringly. "You're free now. You're going to be alright."

"Rob," Henry was staring at his friend. "What is going on? Who is this? You're acting like you know the guy."

Robin looked up at Henry. "I do know who it is," he said grimly. "I've seen his face before. In someone else's memory."

It was clear to Robin suddenly. All of it. The extent of Splinterstem's ambition, his deception. This was Alder.

"Alder?" Robin asked, kneeling before the huddled form. The dryad was rubbing his wrists weakly, still looking confused and shell-shocked, as though waking from a long and terrible dream. "Alder, my name is Robin. We freed you. It's alright now."

He instructed Henry to fetch some water from his satchel, and after a few gulps, the dryad stopping shivering and began to look around. His faceted green eyes looked dulled and dazed.

"Where … am I?" he said eventually, in a shaky voice.

"Don't talk, just keep sipping that," Robin told him. At his insistence, Strife provided more of the same healing draught he had shared with Robin. The boy took the potion from the Grimm and forced the dryad to drink it.

"Slowly," he instructed, "Don't gulp. This will bring you back. Well, this and about a hundred decent meals."

While the prisoner drank, Robin looked to the others.

"Splinterstem was more dangerous than we knew," he said, feeling a little sick. "He was willing to do anything to get what he wanted. This is Alder. He's a dryad. He was presumed dead years ago, back when the Labyrinth was constructed. The story was that he wandered inside and was killed by the minotaur. But, obviously, that's not what happened."

He remembered, when searching Splinterstem's memories, the day of the Labyrinth's completion, while the king gave his ceremonial speech and Splinterstem had felt such conflicting feelings of pride, and shame. Robin now understood why.

"Alder, here, was the lover of the Princess Ashe, and therefore an obstacle in Splinterstem's way. They were clearly in love, and he couldn't have that. He wanted the princess, and the throne she came with, for himself," Robin explained to the others. "When Hammerhand brought the Shard here and the Labyrinth was built, clearly he saw his chance. A way to get rid of Alder for good. Get him out of the way."

Alder nodded weakly, confirming this. His thin hands were still shaking, but to Robin's amazement, the healing potion of the Grimm already seemed to be at work. His skin looked slightly less dull, and his eyes were beginning to clear.

"Ambition can make a man do terrible things," Strife observed. "How ingenious. Lure your rival to the Labyrinth. Overpower him and shackle him deep within, and then cast a glamour, turning him for all intents and purposes into a terrifying monster. One that no one would ever dare seek out. Better than being buried alive." He sounded full of quiet approval. "I feel I may have gotten along well with this Splinterstem, had my sister not gotten her claws into his dark and hungry little heart first."

"But why?" Henry wanted to know. "I mean, if this guy was his rival for the princess, why didn't he just, you know…kill him? The old fashioned way? Why fake his death and go to all this trouble, making up a story about a minotaur?"

"Because a dryad cannot kill a dryad," Alder croaked, surprising the boys. "Not without it showing. A dryad who kills one of its own kind … it shows on the skin, a sickening. It's against the laws of the forest …"

Alder rubbed at his eyes, exhausted.

"So instead, he imprisoned you here," Robin said. "Returned to the treetop city crying minotaur, claiming to have already disposed of your body. No one ever checked, and no one ever dared entering the Labyrinth again. A perfect plan to keep the crime hidden and keep the Shard safe."

Henry looked down at the dryad. "But … how is it that you're not dead? How have you not starved? Or died of thirst? You've been down here a prisoner for years."

Alder held up his arms. They saw that although the shackles of steel had fallen away, the twining roots which had fed down from the ceiling were still wrapped around his forearms. Only now, as Strife's potion seemed at last to be bringing the man some strength back, were they beginning to slowly uncurl, to release him from their living grip.

"The roots," Strife surmised. "They have nourished him." He looked upward at the tangled ceiling vaulting above. "We are directly below the elder trees themselves here, Scion. They are part of the dryads, and the dryads are part of them. Do not forget, this man has been in this chamber all this time alone with the Earth Shard. Clearly, it has kept him alive, feeding him through these woody bindings, an intravenous drip from the forest itself. Your friend Alder here has been save by these chains of Gaia."

"This certainly explains how Splinterstem was the only one who could retrieve the Shard for Peryl," Robin realised. "He would have been the only one *not* afraid to enter the Labyrinth, because he alone knew there was no minotaur. Just his own eternal prisoner."

He thought of the steward, guiding them through the forest to Rowandeepling, how he had gently carried Robin when he was trapped in sleep. He thought of how noble and attentive he had seemed at the feast, doting on the princess, so dutiful and honourable in his concern for her wellbeing. And all the time, he had been hiding this dark secret, knowing that far below them all, this injustice had been playing out, wrought by his own hand.

"No one is ever what they seem, are they?" Robin said quietly.

Strife look thoroughly unsympathetic. "When you have truly learned that, perhaps you will be less of an annoying boy and more of a man," he snarled. "I care nothing for this sad little dryad, or whatever tiresome courtly intrigues led him here. We are wasting my time."

To Alder, Strife now turned. "Your enemy is dead. The one who imprisoned you here. You should be happy to know that. His corpse lies still cooling not far from here. Your torment is of no interest to me, but I can understand all too well the sweet release of revenge. The bad news I'm afraid, is that your lady-love, the princess, as well as every other one of you sorry little tree-folk, man, woman and snot-nosed child, is currently in mortal danger and in the less than gentle hands of my sister."

He leaned closer to Alder, tilting his head to one side. "And might I add, if you think *your* captor was cruel, my sister makes him look like a child playing in the sand. So you … are in our way. The only hope for your people lies with this yellow headed Fae." His cold black eyes narrowed, pointing at Robin. "Stop shaking on the floor like a fallen leaf, and stand up."

"Give him a minute!" Robin complained, but Strife's less than genial bedside manner seemed to have had some effect. Unsteadily, Alder got to his feet. He stumbled a little, and he looked at Robin.

"Thank you," he said hoarsely. "For freeing me."

"Well, technically, *he* did," Robin nodded at Strife. "But don't tell him that, it will probably make him feel terrible or bring him out in a rash or something. Take it easy, okay. You need serious rest."

Strife strode away into the circle and began to walk from stone to stone in a seemingly random order, placing his hand at the centre as he passed each one.

"Are you dialling Hive HQ?" Henry asked, watching the man.

The stones Strife touched were beginning to glow softly from within as the old man stalked back and forth between them, over and over in a complicated pattern.

"That's certainly one crude and rather dull way of putting it." he hissed. "I am opening the way now."

Robin looked to the dryad while Strife was busy and distracted. "Listen," he said. "Do you know how to use one of these? Can you operate a Janus station?"

Alder nodded weakly.

"Good. Once we're gone, open the Janus station again, immediately. Use it to get away from here. Somewhere safe, where you can rest, get your strength back. It's the only way you'll get out of the maze." He lowered his voice further. "Don't stay here with the old man," he whispered. "I can't guarantee he won't kill you just for the cruel fun of it. You can't trust him. Get clear, find aid, and then, when you can, return to Rowandeepling overland."

"The princess ..." Alder coughed.

"Don't worry about her," he assured him. "Henry and I are going to get her back. We're going to get *all* of the dryads back. Wait for us there. I promise we will get them back to you. We'll undo what Splinterstem did."

He hoped desperately this wasn't an empty promise.

Behind him was a rush of cold air. Robin turned, to see Strife and Henry standing outside of the circle. The centre of the Janus station had now filled with gold mist.

"The way is open, Scion of the Arcania," Strife said. "I have done my part. I have let you into the Hive. The rest is up to you. I don't care *how* you do it, but Peryl *must* fail. She must not present my Lady Eris with another Shard. Disgrace! Ignomy! Failure! They will be her bitter fruits to taste. No longer mine."

Robin regarded the Grimm. Without his travelling cloak, he looked much his old, sinister self. But his usually smart tailcoat and suit were horribly worn and tattered, dirty and threadbare. His dilapidated state was only slightly less alarming than the manic, cold gleam in his black-on-black eyes.

"I know what needs doing," Robin said, shouldering his pack. "I'm

341

doing it for my friends, not for you." He nodded to Alder, ensuring that the healing dryad understood to use the station after them. To get somewhere safe, somewhere away from this dark underground prison.

"Your motivations are irrelevant to me. It is only results that concern me, boy. Ensure you do not fail," Mr Strife said. "You will find I am most unforgiving of failure. A trait no doubt inherited from my glorious mistress."

"Well," Henry clapped Robin gamely on the shoulder. "This has been a horrible, horrible, truly icky truce. So long, Grimm."

As he and Robin stepped into the mists, feeling the tingling of the Janus station begin to work, Robin glanced back at Strife. The old man reached his long arm into the glimmering haze and dropped a small bottle unceremoniously into Robin's hand.

"Nyctophil," he explained. "It may hide even you two bumbling dolts from sight. At least long enough to do what I need to be done." His eyes narrowed. "Have no illusions, Robin Fellows," he said quietly. "Our ceasefire is at an end from this moment. When next we meet, power will be mine once more, and you...you will merely be my quarry. I shall have your scalp."

"Lovely doing business with you too," Robin muttered. He gripped the bottle tightly as the golden mist of the Janus station transported them away, far across the immense forest of the Elderhart, and into a different kind of darkness altogether.

A TWISTED REFLECTION

As always when Robin had used a station, Janus gave no real sense of motion or travelling at all. The golden mist merely settled around them, thinning and dropping away to the floor as it faded, and Robin and Henry looked around warily to see where they had arrived.

After the gloomy cold and damp of the minotaur's maze, Robin hadn't been sure what to expect. All he knew of the Hive was what Ashe had told him. It was a great stepped pyramid, hidden deep in the south of the forest, where the trees were sickly and withered. He had pictures something like the old Mayan pyramids he had learned about in school, the kind you were always told people ended up getting sacrificed on top of. He hadn't given much thought to what the prison might look like on the inside. Whatever he might have imagined, it wasn't this.

He and Henry were standing in the centre of another Janus station, this time a neat circle of pure white stones, squat and flat, neatly squared at the edges and none higher than his hip. The room they had arrived in was circular and domed, like the one they had just left, but much smaller. There the similarities ended.

It was bright here, a sickly golden light that seemed to drain the vitality out of their skin. The walls were yellowish, and curved upwards into the dome above in a smooth and seamless arc, devoid of any feature. They seemed to glow from within, as though they were slightly translucent. Deeply coloured glass perhaps. The floor beneath their feet, Robin saw, was tiled, perfect interlocking hexagons, and it appeared to be of the same material. There was no obvious source of the draining yellow light. No flaming torches, no light-wells or windows. It seemed to exude, insipid and jaundiced, from the warm, soft-looking walls themselves.

"Well, this is horrible," Henry whispered queasily, looking around.

They were, blessedly, alone in the still and silent Janus chamber. There was only one door to the room, a slim oval, presumably leading out to the prison proper. From what they could make out, another luminous corridor stretched away from it.

The air smelled and tasted thick, somehow stale. It was unpleasant to breathe.

"At least we're alone," Robin noted quietly, as the two stepped out of the circle. "I was expecting guards. Surely you guard the only entrance and exit from a prison?"

"Maybe there's just no need to," Henry said. "If it's the only way in here, and the only people who can set a path from another Janus station to this one are the jailers. Your worry with prisons isn't really about people breaking in, right?"

Robin couldn't argue with this logic. He looked down with interest at the small black bottle in his hand.

"What is that?" Henry asked.

"Nyctophil," Robin answered, without a clue what that meant. "A parting gift from our least favourite Grimm. He said it might be useful for us."

Henry made a face. "It's probably poison," he reasoned flatly. "Or some horrible concoction that makes bits of you fall off. I know he healed you, Rob, but we both know why. I wouldn't trust that creepy old cadaver to put a sugar lump in my tea, never mind down a bottle of Dis brewery's finest ale."

Robin tiptoed towards the doorway stealthily. The floor felt warm under his feet, even through his boots. It was slightly sticky. An altogether unpleasant sensation. "I know what you mean," he said. "But I don't think even that charmless nightmare would go to all this trouble, swallowing his pride and admitting he needed *us* to do something *he* couldn't, just for the cheap laughs of tricking now. He's the sort who wouldn't poison a person unless he could be there to watch you drink it. It would spoil the fun."

Something moved beyond the doorway, a shadow. Robin froze, heart beating fast, motioning silently for Henry to halt too.

Cautiously he crept closer and peered carefully around the edge of the door.

Beyond was a long corridor, with another oval opening at the far end. It too was sickly yellow and slightly transparent. A creature stood in it, leaning idly against the wall.

Robin had never seen a member of the swarm before. He knew that they were dryads once, so his mental image of them was quite vague. He had been imagining them to look the same as those he had met at Rowandeepling, only maybe sterner looking, and more heavily armed.

This being however was something quite monstrously different.

Much taller and thinner than a dryad, its skin was a sickly pale and jaundiced hue, like old custard. *Dryad killing*, Robin observed. Its stringy body was clad in rust-red and black armour, sharp, sectioned edges folding over one another like the interlocking thorax of an insect exoskeleton, giving the thing a wasp-like appearance. Its wings, folded along its armoured back, were not wholly unlike the dragonfly wings of the dryads, though they looked duller, and a little ragged and grey. But the major difference was the head. The hive-guard's head was utterly bald, like a boiled egg. Its face was a mystery to Robin, covered as it was entirely by a mask of metal, the same colours as its armour. The mask had large, round, tinted glass eyes like portholes in studded metal, and a long nozzle where the nose and mouth should have been, concertinaed like an elephant's trunk. This metallic tube fed down and around and connected somehow into the armour on the creature's back. There were several protruding wires and tubes. It looked to Robin exactly like an old gas mask from the world wars, only glinting gold and red.

With its large round eyes and long snout, the swarm-creature looked even more insect-like, a steampunk mosquito from a nightmare. It was with faint disgust that Robin noticed that the many tubes and nozzles fixed here and there on its armoured body seemed to feed directly into the creature's bald skull, burrowing into it like worms. The gas-mask face piece was not merely decoration. It was fused at every edge directly and permanently to the creature's face.

From within the helmet there came a constant, low chitinous clicking.

"I think we've just met some more of Eris' handiwork," Robin whispered as Henry cautiously joined him and peered around his shoulder. "Now I'm wishing we'd brought weapons." He thought for a moment. "Maybe a really big can of fly-spray."

"I didn't know there would be bee-people," Henry sounded agitated. "Did you know about this? Why didn't you tell me about the beeple?"

"More important than what it is, how in the world are we supposed to get past it?" Robin murmured worriedly. If he'd had magic, a well-placed

Needlepoint would have done the trick. But without his mana stone he had about as much magical ability as Henry. They were just two boys armed with nothing but their wits and Henry's ninja skills.

"Wits … and a potion," Robin remembered, holding up the vial. He uncorked it, giving it a sniff. "Any better ideas?" he asked Henry, who looked dubious. "Half each?" He raised the bottle to his lips and was about to take a drink when Henry snatched it out of his hands and glugged from the bottle instead.

"What did you do that for?" Robin hissed, as loudly as he dared.

Henry stood very still, holding the bottle with an expectant look on his face, clearly waiting anxiously to see if he was about to explode or if anything of importance was going to drop off.

"Me first," he said. "If it *is* poison, well, then we'll know. You're more important. You're the Scion, you have all the Shards to collect and a world to save remember? We can't risk you. I'm just Henry. I've never even managed to collect a full sticker album."

But Henry didn't drop dead. In fact, as he was speaking, shadows were growing in the air around him. They shimmered, encasing him in a nebulous cloud. When it faded, the changes wrought to the boy were abundantly clear …as was Henry. He was hardly there at all. Nothing but a thin, almost invisible sketch of him remained, extremely faintly in the air. To Robin, the bottle seemed to float of its own accord.

"Henry," Robin said. "Firstly, you're insane, and don't ever do something like that again. But second, and maybe more importantly, you're invisible!"

"I am?" Henry exclaimed. Robin assumed he looked surprised. To Robin, he didn't look anything.

"Cloaked in shadow," Robin thought. "Strife is quite the alchemist. He's practically a walking Boots the Chemist. I bet you anything he does a lot of his snooping around the Court of Dis with this stuff. Here, pass it over."

"What if it's permanent?" Henry mused, as Robin took a deep swig, draining the remaining contents of the bottle. It tasted like aniseed and nettle soup.

"Then look on the bright side," Robin shrugged, as he watched his own hands fading away to almost nothing. "We'll never need to bother about a haircut again. Come on. I've no idea how long this stuff lasts. We have to find my mana stone, the Shard and our friends, and we have to do it really *really* quietly."

Sneaking past the hideous swarm-guard was nerve-wracking. It clearly didn't see them, and the corridor was wide enough for the two boys to creep along on the golden, glowing floor without coming too close to the insectile, metal face. But they had no way of knowing if the thing might sense them another way. It could have feelers for all they knew, checking for disturbances in the air, or ultrasound, with that ceaseless, chirping clicking.

Robin and Henry inched along the corridor, painfully slowly, backs brushing against the soft, unpleasantly warm walls. Both kept their eyes fixed on the circles of polished glass that made up the creature's inhuman eyes. It was difficult to believe that it had ever been anything like a dryad. They were part of nature, practically offshoots of the forest itself. This thing was a metal hornet. It couldn't look less natural if it tried.

Thankfully they reached the other end of the corridor without issue, slipping through the far doorway with relief.

The space they had entered now was an open area, and it was so vast, it took their breath away.

Robin had seen a documentary once about a shipyard, where the largest ocean liner of its time had been built, put together piece by piece in a massive building, erected for this purpose alone. It had been the most enormous indoor space he had ever seen, a vast warehouse, many stories high, larger than the largest aircraft hangar. The ship has sat, immense in its own right, but looking dwarfed, tiny and lost amidst the city of scaffolding and gantries surrounding it.

This place was the same. If the Hive was indeed a great pyramid, then it was totally hollow within. Scaffolding soared into the sky like a spider's web, supporting suspended rooms and buildings, soft golden walls, rounded edges. Crooked walkways criss-crossed the open air in a mad hatchwork, leading to and from everywhere. They looked as though they had been thrown in from above to settle wherever they landed, slanted and precarious.

Everything here was made from the same strange substance as the Janus room, the glassy yellow bridges and catwalks like spun sticky sugar. Above it all, a huge, sickly amber light shone down, washing scattered and spiky shadows over everything.

To Robin, the walkways were like Rowandeepling, the whole arrange-ment was built along the same lines, but whereas the treetop city of the dryads, resting peacefully under the open sky, with its elegantly carved and sweeping bridges had been a joy, lit everywhere with softly glimmering lights, a magical and enchanting space, this was anything but.

The Hive was a nightmarish perversion. Enclosed, dark, and claustrophobic despite the dizzying open space. Wan insipid light bleached through the plain ugly spikes of the crazed scaffold. It looked chaotic and uneven, sickly, unfriendly and utilitarian. And with the humid, sticky heat and softly glowing walls all around, close and oppressive.

There were no carved and beautiful facades surrounding the intersections here, no grand woodland palaces with welcoming windows and brightly lit doors. Instead, the four vast sloping inner walls of the pyramid looming up on all sides of them, were covered and lined with row upon row of identical cells, each a hexagonal opening, covered with spiky looking bars. There were thousands, levels upon levels of them. Henry and Robin seemed to have emerged about halfway up, their corridor spitting them out directly onto one of the countless yellow spokes. The tiers of cells coating the walls rose high up above them to the distant apex, and down below, far beyond the full reach of the great yellow light. It descended into misty, rolling shadows, a great abyss below.

"I can see why they call it the Hive then," Henry whispered, invisible at Robin's side. The cells made the place resemble a giant honeycomb. "It's huge," he said. "I mean, really really big. If you took out all these creepy funhouse bridges everywhere, I bet you could fly a helicopter around this place and never even notice you're not outside."

Robin looked up at the spokes criss-crossing the air around him. "I feel like I'm inside a giant game of Kerplunk," he said. "How on earth are we going to find Karya and the others? We can't search every one of these cells. And it's hardly like we're alone here anyway."

He was right. The great Hive was filled with the swarm. They rushed along the bridges. They hovered in mid-air in the dark spaces between. They marched here and there along every perimeter balcony, adjoining the cells. There must have been more than two thousand creatures, buzzing and clicking and scurrying around. Each one identical to the one past which they had so carefully crept. Oversized insects, armed with long and barbed spears.

"That's a lot of beeple." Henry agreed. "I reckon though, all the important stuff is going to be up near that."

Robin, unable to see Henry at all due to his current invisibility, could only assume his friend was pointing upwards, and followed his gaze. There in the centre of the pyramid, just beneath the ill-looking sun was a large circular platform, on which a building stood suspended, a domed and windowless bubble. It looked like a fat spider sitting in the centre of its web. From that platform, he realised, it would be possible to look out at all four inner walls, to see directly down into each and every one of the countless softly phosphorescent cells below.

"Command centre?" Robin guessed. "Think that's the heart of the Hive up there?"

"Well, it doesn't look like the work's canteen," Henry replied. "Come on, before we become visible again. It's going to be tricky enough clambering through that maze of nonsense as it is, without having to swat mecha-mosquitos on the way."

The climb up through the scaffold of the Hive was dizzying and treacherous. Unlike the pleasant leaping and linking paths of Rowandeepling, these walkways were without any form of handrail, carved or otherwise. Mere slender spits of amber sliding out against one another into the void, barely wide enough for Robin and Henry to pick across.

Robin did his best not to look down as they zig-zagged across these promontories. The yawning chasm below, falling away into immense darkness, was vertigo-inducing. The countless spikes of the interlacing roads making up the space would serve, if one were to fall, as nothing more than a lot of interesting things to hit and bounce off on the way down to certain death.

Not being able to see one's own feet didn't make things any easier either. Robin knew where he was standing by touch of course, but without being able to see his own invisible appendages, it was like trying to walk around with his eyes closed. His judgment and balance were all off.

"I know …" Henry muttered sarcastically behind him as they made their way back and forth across the countless bridges, slowly and steadily picking paths that took them ever upwards. "Let's build a great big pit of death, and let's make the paths really slippy and gross too. That'll be fun!" He sniffed. "There's no bloody health and safety in the Netherworlde, that's the problem right there."

Despite his grumbling, Robin had to admit, Henry had a point. Here in this giant honeycomb prison, the walkways were slightly damp from the oppressive humidity and treacherous going. He had a queasy feeling that the swarm may well have built the place the same way other insects do, with their bodily secretions, but he was trying very hard not to think about that. Certainly, he might be currently invisible, but he was sure that barfing over the edge of the chasm might give away their location.

"I'm … never … touching … honey … again," he replied. "Now shush."

The swarm milled around them, alien and deadly, flitting here and there, but mercifully oblivious to the presence of the two interlopers. It was nerve-racking, being surrounded on all sides by enemies, stealing their way silently between them. More than once, the two were forced to hastily backtrack and choose another route, when one of the hideous, tall grotesques fluttered down onto a walkway in front of them and began scurrying forward, glass-eyes flashing, thinking the way clear.

Unlike the boys, the swarm-guards moved along fast and without fear on the slender scaffold. Robin reasoned that you had little to worry about falling when you had wings.

It seemed a tense and painful age before they began to reach the top of the pyramid's inner core, the large platform with its nest-like structure becoming larger and closer with every twist and turn. Whenever their careful and stealthy exploration reached the outer walls, Robin saw up close the cells lining the walls. Each one was squat and featureless, their walls yellow, and the horrible light left no shadows at all, bleaching the life and form from them. And almost every one of these cramped cells contained a despondent dryad, peering out through the bars with worried or fearful eyes of glittering faceted green.

Robin shivered, wondering what fate awaited these people if he didn't free them. Would they be left here to rot? Or would they be shipped off to Dis, to Eris' dark workrooms to be made into more of the ever-swelling ranks of the swarm? How could Splinterstem have ever thought he wanted this? Would he had felt the same, to still be willing to betray his people for a moment of glory and power, had he even once seen inside this hellish place? Seen what became of its occupants?

Robin pictured the Elderhart, that vast and majestic forest, finally conquered. Withered and dead, poisoned from end to end and filled, league upon endless league, with the countless stinging hordes of Eris. Perverted creations, victorious under the unstoppable power of the Earth Shard. He couldn't let that happen. Robin had come here to save his friends, but he knew the Puck had come here to save everyone. He would find a way to keep his promise to Alder. He would free all of the dryads here. He would tear the Hive to the ground if he had to.

"This … is … the … last … level," Henry gasped and panted. Robin glanced over at him, as they stepped off the final bridge and onto the long gallery which encircled the final high floor. His friend looked exhausted.

Robin's heart froze. He realised with horror that he could *see* his friend looking exhausted.

"Henry!" he hissed, "You're not invisible anymore. Well, not completely anyway. It must be wearing off."

Henry stared back in alarm. "You too," he confirmed. "I can still see right through you, like a hologram, but I can make you out. Strife and his cut-price potions! Last time I take a drink off that guy."

Robin made a face at Henry's sarcasm. "Well, I think that was a given," he agreed, beckoning Henry to hurry off the bridge and join him by the cells. The light did not shine as strongly at the sides of the immense space. They were less likely to be spotted. "The point is, if *we* can see each other, *they* can see us too."

Luckily, there didn't appear to be any of the swarm up this high, they flittered and marched about below, crawling like ants over everything. Up here, apart from the control room, there was nothing but the last and highest row of cells.

A voice behind Robin made him jump so much that he almost fell off the narrow ledge and into the open air.

"I've seen everything now," the voice said. "I must be finally losing my mind, ahahaha. Yes. That's it. Ghost boys. Two ghosts come to keep me company, is that it? I wonder if they have anything to eat? Ahaha."

Robin turned, staring into the cell at his back.

It contained, not a dryad, but a man. He had a bushy, dirty-looking beard, sticking out in all directions. His head was bald and shiny, and his clothes, once a fine suit covered in elaborate brocade, seemed filthy and torn, like an antique sofa left on a garbage heap in the rain.

The pitiful-looking man was huddled in the corner of his cell, hugging his knees. His bright orange eyes were staring a little wildly at Robin, looking tired and ringed with dark bags.

"You look a little like someone I know, little ghost," the man said. "Has he died, then? The little boy in the big house? Terrible shame if so, really. Wouldn't be surprised though, ahaha. Dangerous place for children, that old Fae place. Shouldn't be allowed … bound to happen …" he trailed off, mumbling into his beard.

"Ffoulkes?" Robin said, incredulously. He stared in disbelief. The poor creature rocking slightly in the cell was almost unrecognisable. But the voice was the same. It was the last person Robin had been expecting to see.

He gripped the bars, dropping his voice to a whisper. "Mr Ffoulkes? It is you! It's me, Robin Fellows! I'm not a ghost. I'm not dead. It's … well it's a long story. What on earth are you doing *here*? In the Hive?"

Ffloukes' eyes focused sharply and he stared at Robin clearly. "The Hive?" he repeated. "Aha. Is that where I am then? I see. They didn't tell me, you understand. Quite rude really, utterly unacceptable. I could have been anywhere. Anywhere at all."

"Ffloukes, why are you a prisoner here? What happened to you?" Robin tested the bars, but despite them looking like crystallised sugar, they felt as strong and sturdy as iron under his hands. The man looked haunted, as though his mind was more than a little baffled. Robin wondered how long he had been a prisoner here. He and Henry had been in the Hive less than an hour, and already he felt it was getting under his own skin.

"Is that the guy who was staying at Erlking?" Henry asked, peering through the bars at Robin's side. "Bloody hell. He looks like he's been through the wringer."

Robin explained briefly. Henry hadn't been there at Halloween. He hadn't witnessed Ffoulkes shameful attempt at theft, or his inglorious exit from Erlking. Henry made an aghast face as he was filled in on the details.

"Knew there was something shifty about him! Sounds like an idiot to me. Serves him right, ending up here. We should just leave him."

The man scuttled across the small space of the cell on his knees with surprising speed, reaching out and grasping Robin's still-translucent hands urgently when he heard this, his brocade and lace cuffs in tatters.

"Nonono," he said quickly. "Don't leave me here. Terribly sorry about all that bad business…really. No hard feelings, eh? Water under the bridge and all that? Just a…misunderstanding. Business is all it was. One does always have one eye on the value of things, doesn't one? Aha." His eyes were wide and desperate, his grip firm and shaking.

"You deserve to be locked up, you do," Henry argued righteously.

"No he doesn't!" Robin said, making his friend glare at him in surprise. "No one deserves to be here in this place, not even him. He got what he deserved when he got a kraken to the face and Hestia and Calypso shooting both barrels. He's a light-fingered, conniving coward, yes, but it doesn't mean we can leave him to waste away in Eris' dungeon because of it."

"Yes! Quite!" Ffoulkes said eagerly, a little desperately. "Well said, young man. Well said. You are a good soul, Robin Fellows, a kind and warm-hearted one. I knew that the moment we met. It's written all over your face ... which ... aha ... I can see through at present. Did I mention that ... that is odd, isn't it?"

Robin suspected Ffoulkes had gone quite some time with no-one to talk to, or rather in his case 'at'. He wrenched his hands free of the fire Panthea's hands, asking again how he came to be here.

"Set upon by centaur," Ffoulkes told him. "Not long after I ... well ... left your company, shall we say? I got to the Netherworlde, the sisters, my travelling companions, they had gone on without me. They are a strange flock. Always so secretive with their business." His bright eyes crinkled. "Between you and me, my boy, I was rather glad to be rid of the burden of escorting them. Terribly unfashionable. I've never seen three drabber hags, have you? Rather brings one down. Aha."

"The centaur?" Robin pressed.

"They're all over the grasslands," Ffoulkes replied, sounding indignant. "I've never known the like. So many patrols. Impossible not to be seen, you see. Thing is, I'm not very popular here. None of the Panthea who escaped the war, refusing to take sides and hiding in the mortal world are. They all think we're the lowest of the low. Cowards, refusing to take a side, refusing to fight for or against."

"You are a coward," Henry nodded flatly. Ffoulkes glanced through Robin at the boy. "And look where it got you."

"Perhaps I am," Ffoulkes agreed shamelessly, not sounding remotely offended by the accusation. "But I think you will find, young man, that I have lived a great deal longer than many heroes have."

He looked back to Robin. "The penalty for deserting the Netherworlde, under Eris' law, is imprisonment eternal," He said. "The centaurs had me as soon as I stepped onto the hills. They could smell Erlking all over me. Brought me here. Where I've been ever since."

He looked thoughtful. "I suppose that deal I was supposed to close in the agora town has probably fallen through by now. That's a terrible shame."

"We'll get you out," Robin promised.

"Robin, he's pondslime!" Henry argued.

"It might be a crime according to Eris to be a coward," Robin told him. "But in my book, there's no crime in being afraid. Granted, he might not be the bravest person, or indeed … even remotely trustworthy, but that doesn't mean he deserves to rot in hell." Robin's semi-transparent stare was so stern that Henry closed his protesting mouth, and after a moment, nodded.

"There's nowhere for me to go outside this place," Ffoulkes said. "I never should have come back to the Netherworlde. If it wasn't for me trying to steal that ridiculous mask. Nowhere left for me now."

"There's Erlking," Robin said. He noticed that his hands, resting on the bars, were almost fully solid again now. "There's always Erlking. We don't turn anyone away. Even wastrels like you."

Ffoulkes looked at Robin with something close to wonder. "You really are a remarkable young man," he said, for once seemingly forgetting to add an affected laugh to his words. "After everything I did, you would still offer me sanctuary?"

"Let's not get too far ahead of ourselves, eh?" Robin said. "We have to find some other people too first. Then we have to figure out how to open these cages."

"Other people?" Ffoulkes tilted his head to one side. "It's mainly forest folk here. We had a heck of a lot of new arrivals yesterday. But there are some others too. An old man, a little girl and a very valuable-looking, mint-condition faun perhaps?"

Robin and Henry both stared at the bedraggled prisoner.

"You've seen them?" Henry cried, completely forgetting to keep his voice down.

"Well, yes," Ffoulkes nodded. "There's very little to do here other than watch. The swarm are terrible conversationalists. It's all chitter-chitter buzz buzz. And the food here is terrible." He lowered his voice to a gossipy whisper. "Personally, I suspect it's already been eaten once by the time they bring it to-"

"Where are they?" Robin interrupted the man's rambling.

"They're in the next cell along," Ffoulkes told them, blinking.

Robin leapt to his feet, but the man grabbed him urgently by the wrist, making him stop and look back.

"You will … you will come back for me?" he asked, his voice trembling, though he was clearly attempting to keep his tone as light and conversational as possible. "If you find a way to escape. You and your lovely friends? You won't leave me here?"

Robin shook his head. "I promise," he said.

Ffoulkes searched the boy's face. "I would leave you," he admitted. "In your position. I would get myself away and not give the rest of you a second thought. I am, in many ways, a wretched person."

"Yes, I know you are," Robin shook his hand free. "But we're not. We will get you out of here, I swear it." He looked at Henry. "We're getting everyone out of here."

They left Ffoulkes gripping the bars, his bushy tangled beard poking between them like a madman, and hurried along to the next hexagonal opening, both scanning the Hive warily for signs of any high-flying swarm.

Robin's heart leapt when he reached the bars and saw inside the tiny cell.

"Well, *there* you are," said Karya, sounding completely unsurprised to see him. "I knew you weren't dead." She was sitting cross-legged in the centre of the cell, her bulky coat pulled around her. She didn't look desperate or ragged as Ffoulkes had. She just looked inconvenienced.

"I told you he wouldn't be dead," she called out behind her. "Doesn't matter if we saw him eaten by a dragon. As if something like that is going to keep our hornless wonder down for long."

"Pinky!" came a happy squeal. Woad, who had been sitting back to back with the girl, both leaning against one another, rolled into sight and scampered up to the bars. His face was a beaming grin from ear to ear. "And Henryboy! Look, boss! Henryboy is here too! He didn't fall down a hole in the forest or get eaten by a bear at all. You were wrong about that!"

"I only said it would be *just like him* too," Karya sniffed, getting to her feet. "Not that he *had*."

"You're both alright?" Robin grinned at them, gripping the bars. He was so relieved to see them. "They didn't hurt you?"

"Other than that two-faced dryad traitor strapping us to the ground with vines and delivering us like two tightly wrapped gifts to Miss Peryl, Queen of the Hive, no. We're otherwise fine," Karya smiled. She was doing her serious and businesslike frown, but was not entirely successful in her attempts to hide how clearly happy she was to see them both.

"We thought between the dragon and Strigoi, you might have been a bit delayed, but we never doubted you'd come for us." She looked past Robin to Henry, who was grinning sheepishly at her. "Good to see you in one piece too," she nodded. Her golden eyes took in the dark haired boy's appearance. "You look like the forest ate you up and spat you out as much as it did Robin, but at least you're alive."

"Don't go getting too mushy," Henry said. "You'll only make me blush."

"How are you here?" Woad asked. "How are you both here?"

"Henry rescued me," Robin said. "I was left at Rowandeepling, I don't know why Peryl didn't just bring me along with the rest of you."

"It wasn't just me doing the rescuing," Henry said honestly. "I had some help."

"What help?" Karya looked from one boy to the other. Her eyes were suspicious.

"You wouldn't believe me if I told you," Robin said. "Trust me on that. Time for that later."

"I could not agree more," came a voice from the furthest corner of the cell. What Robin had taken to be a pile of rags unfurled itself. It was Hawthorn, who had clearly been sleeping. The old Fae nodded in greeting to Robin, dipping his horns. He looked oddly proud.

"Never leave a fellow Fae behind, eh?" he said. "Unless he wants you to."

"Hawthorn! You're here too." Relief rushed through Robin. "I'm glad you're alive. Back on the hill, we didn't mean to leave you, we-"

Hawthorn raised a hand, silencing him. "Yes yes, no need to explain. Your friend the girl here has told me everything. You were right to be whisked away from under my feet. I am indeed grateful that you were. Otherwise, you would have been left with the impressive sight of me taking out seven or eight centaur, before finally being subdued. It was a sight to behold my young friend, you would have been quite intimidated."

Woad gave the old Fae a glance. "It was *two or three* centaurs the first time you told us that story. They're multiplying every time you tell it."

Robin began to introduce Henry to Hawthorn, realising this was the first time the two had met. Hawthorn eyed the boy curiously with his long eyes, admitting he had never met a human child before, and what curious creatures they seemed.

Karya interrupted them all.

"This is all well and good," she said. "But can we all catch up and shake hands later on please? Preferably far away from here?" She looked to Robin through the bars.

"Peryl is here, Scion. She's the overseer in this misery factory. And she has both the Earth Shard and the Princess Ashe in her custody. I believe she means to make a gift of both to Eris, and very soon." She pointed behind his shoulder, out across the void, where the large suspended platform stood with its windowless building.

"She's in there, lady of the manor. And more importantly, so is all of our stuff. Mana stones, weapons." She shook her head, irritated. "There's nothing any of us can do about getting out of here if we don't have magic."

Robin nodded. "Understood," he said. "I'll get it back." He wasn't sure how yet, he was pretty much making it up as he went along, but his voice sounded assured and confident, even to his own ears, and this seemed good enough for his imprisoned friends.

"Henry, I need you to stay here, with the others," he said. Henry looked shocked.

"Are you mad?" he asked. "No way, you need my help."

"Exactly!" Robin said. He asked Karya if she still had her hex-message parchment, and after some fumbling in the pockets of her coat, she produced it. Robin gave it to Henry. "You have a clear view of the entire Hive from out here on the ledge," he told him. "I need you to be my lookout. Tell me if anyone moves who shouldn't. If anyone comes up here, or if you see anyone headed towards that place where I'm headed." He tapped his own pocket. "I have mine here. Message me if you do. I'm visible now, so I'm going to have to go flat across the bridges to that platform, I'll have no line of sight at all."

Henry took the paper and nodded. "I still don't like the idea of you going in there alone," he said.

Robin glanced at them all. "It's only one Grimm," he said, as lightly as possible. "How hard can it be?"

SCRYGLASS

Leaving his friends and setting off alone, Robin scrambled from the gallery and set off cautiously across the highest bridge, crouched so low as he crept along the narrow yellow ledge that he was almost on his hands and knees. He felt terribly alone and horribly exposed. The scrap of enchanted parchment was clutched in his fist. He could hear the purr of insect wings below him, as countless members of the swarm flitted to and fro beneath his precipitously slender walkway.

Part of him wished he still thought of the Puck as a separate entity. The one good thing about having another person living inside you, Robin thought, was that you never truly felt completely alone. But after the business with the dragon, after willing the force of the Arcania to life down in the hollow in order to fight the beast, accepting and owning his own mana willingly, he no longer felt that was the case. He was the Puck, and the Puck was him. Whether that made him feel bolder or more vulnerable, he had yet to decide.

He made it all the way across across the walkway without being spotted. The parchment in his hand had not vibrated, no urgent warning had come from Henry, his lookout. The odd suspended building stood before him, a squat yellowish dome, strung here in the cat's-cradle of spokes above the yawning abyss. There a single opening leading inside, through which Robin slipped, as stealthy as possible.

Inside, the chamber was the first furnished space he had seen within the Hive. The floor, as elsewhere, was an interlacing pattern of hexagonal tiles, and the walls the same softly glowing amber, glassy and smooth, reaching up to a domed and organic-looking ceiling, but some attempts had been made to make the place more fitting for non-insect life.

Expensive-looking and heavily patterned rugs were strewn across the floor. There were long tables here and there, many piled with tottering old books. There were maps of the Netherworlde rolled out flat on workspaces, full of pins and flags, rolled scrolls by their sides. Several large and ornate bookcases stood against the walls, all packed to the brim, and there were even stuffed wingback chairs, ornate and claw-footed. Robin half expected to see a roaring open fireplace and a drinks table shaped like an antique globe. It seemed as though someone had raided the contents of an old gentleman's study and vomited them into the hive.

The humanity of it looked all the more surreal against the alien walls.

Standing at the far end of the room, back turned as she leaned over a table, studying something there, was a Miss Peryl, slender and spiky, dressed in a crisp tailored suit which was as black as midnight. Long purple hair fell down in waves across the dark fabric.

Silently, Robin glanced around the room. On a table to the left, there was a pile of junk, dropped haphazardly amidst old leatherbound books. A few closed candle-lamps, something resembling a large circular bronze shield, and also, rather incongruously, a dish filled to the brim with a selection of chocolate M&M's. To his relief, he also saw a pile of mana stones, gathered reverently in a rough circle on the tabletop. Karya's bracelet, Woad's stone, Hawthorn's bow and his own seraphinite teardrop, slung in its leather thong. He hadn't realised how much he had missed it until he saw it, sitting there innocently on the table like nothing more than cast off jewellery atop a dresser. He had never been more happy to see a lump of rock before in his life.

"If you're thinking of tiptoeing around like some cartoon character, I shouldn't bother," Miss Peryl said lightly, without looking up or turning around. "I already know you're there, I practically heard your heroic theme music as you came in."

Robin froze. Behind him, the oval door slammed shut, sealing him in the large and windowless room.

The Grimm turned lazily, tucking a lock of purple hair behind her ear. Unlike when he had seen her in his dreams recently, where she had appeared almost human, here, in her dark midnight suit, with skin as white as glowing chalk, she looked quite otherworldly. Every inch a Grimm. She smiled at Robin, dark lips on a powdered face, and leaned back against the table in a relaxed and familiar manner, as though they were old friends.

Miss Peryl's eyes were as black as tar from edge to edge.

"Scion of the Arcania," she said, with relish. "Do you know, I had a dream you were coming? Honestly, I'm not even kidding. I haven't dreamed in *years*, how weird is that, right?"

Robin's eyes flicked to his mana stone on the table and back to her. This did not go unnoticed.

"Oh geez! Where are my manners?" she said, flapping a hand at the table near the boy. "Go right ahead and get your stone, yes of course. I won't stop you. It wasn't *my* idea to take them off you all anyway. It was his. He's so particular about disarming enemies, everything's always by the book with old dogface." She sighed. "But where's the fun in that? That's what I say. I like a good scuffle, keeps the blood moving. And besides …" She reached behind her and produced something, the object she had been studying when he had entered.

"I have a bigger rock!" she said in a playful sing-song voice.

In her hand, she held a canister. It looked like an old closed gas lantern case, hexagonal brass with glass panels all around. Suspended within this protective case, glowing and turning softly over and over, was the Earth Shard of the Arcania. Its flickering green light reflected up onto her smirking face.

"Isn't it just peachy?" she said proudly. "Green is such a difficult colour to carry off, don't you think?" She gazed in at the stone through the glass. "And so pretty too."

"Sure it is," Robin replied, moving slowly towards the table with the mana stones, keeping both eyes firmly on the smiling Grimm. "It really brings out the murderous psychopath in your eyes."

"Now that's just flirting," Peryl replied. "Shame on you." She was still glancing down at the Shard. "Don't you listen to the mean old Fae, Shardy," she said in cooing baby voice. "You're beautiful. He's just jealous because we got you before he did."

Robin scooped up his mana stone, quickly slipping it around his neck. Peryl made no move to stop him, though her eyes did flick up at him, narrowing approvingly.

"There … that's better," she said. "See, now we're all properly dressed for dinner." She placed the Shard-lantern back on the table next to her, as though suddenly bored with it. "And you don't seem very pleased to see me," she scolded. "A little gratitude wouldn't go amiss, you know. You owe me big time."

"I ... *owe* ... you?" Robin replied, spluttering in disbelief. "You kidnapped my friends. You've enslaved an entire colony of people. You've ... you've ... shamelessly manipulated a dangerously unstable dryad into giving you the Shard, and then killed him. You're a walking trail of destruction And you think I ... owe you?"

Peryl rolled her dark eyes. "Oh blah blah, all that's just business," she said dismissively. "You can't really blame me for Splinterstem, be fair. He was pretty unhinged to begin with. All I did was give him a little nudge. One that he wanted already. I'm a Grimm, remember? I was doing my job. Which I happen to be very *very* good at, by the way."

"Yeah, I heard from someone that you got a promotion," Robin said dryly, trying to buy for time while he figured out a way to get past the girl to the Shard on the table behind her.

"Queen of the Grimms!" she grinned, as though she had been pronounced high school valedictorian. "And it's a role with benefits, let me tell you. I like the view from the top, blondie. It's *fun* up here." Her grin widened, her dark eyes flashing. "Lady Eris has given me a whole bunch of evil wasp-fairies to play with, all of my very own! I have minions, actual honest to heck minions! How neat is that? Plus, I get to boss around all my horrible brothers and sisters too. After so long at the bottom of the food chain, let me tell you something, that ... is just not getting old." She laughed.

"Why do I owe you?" Robin asked again. He was cautiously, slowly, moving forward into the room. Peryl was like an asp. She seemed calm and relaxed, but he had no doubt she could strike at any moment, without warning. He was trying to think of a way to catch her off guard, what cantrip might be best, now that she had bizarrely allowed him to arm himself. What would be the best way to knock her off balance, giving him a chance to get to the Shard?

"Because I left you hanging in a cage, dumbnuts," she replied. "Everyone else was brought here, when I sacked Rowandeepling. Now, *that* was satisfying. Those tree folk are annoying. I've been lurking around this forest like a bog hag for *months* controlling that idiot Splinterstem. Not fun. I think I have allergies."

She waved a hand airily.

"I brought your little ragtag entourage here. They're going to be a present for the Empress, a little amuse-bouche before the main course of the Shard itself. But you? I thought I'd give you a break for once. At least give you fighting chance." She shrugged aimlessly. "I figured it was fifty fifty. You'd either escape the cage eventually and go running back to Grandma Silverbun at Crinkle Manor with your tail between your legs, or you'd come over all heroic and square-jawed and try to get to me, to stop my schemes most dastardly." She regarded him thoughtfully, her glittering eyes lost in a sea of dark kohl. "I suppose I wanted to see which."

"Why?"

"I guess I just wanted to see what kind of person you were, when it comes to it. Take away a person's magic, leave them in a cage with nothing but broken bones. That's when you see what they're really made of."

"And what are you made of Peryl?" he challenged. "You say you dreamt I was coming here. I've been dreaming about you too."

Peryl looked thoughtful at this. "Really? Oh wow. That's kind of neat. A bit…icky, but still, neat." Her brows knitted. "I hope we weren't riding a romantic ferris-wheel or running along a beach or anything like that. So, I'm in your little fluffy head, am I?"

"Uninvited, but yes," Robin admitted. "But you're not like this." He indicated her with a gesture.

"Not stylish?" she asked, glancing down with concern at her crisp, tailored suit. A look of mock horror came over her face. "Oh gods. I'm not … I'm not blonde, am I?" She gave him a genuinely worried look. "In your dreams I mean, because you can pull off the whole choirboy angel look, but on me? With this skin tone? Just … wan."

"When I've dreamt about you … you're a person," he said flatly. "Not a …"

"Grimm?" she finished for him, her dark eyes very direct. "Wishful thinking on the part of your Arcania-addled adolescent mind, I'm afraid, Scion. Slice me down the middle and you won't find happy fluffy feelings. All you will find is power and-*stop moving*! *Do you think I'm utterly stupid? I can see you trying to inch towards me!*"

She shouted this last sentence so loudly, Robin was startled.

"You're all talk. There's more than just cold Grimm in you," Robin said. "I know there is, because I put it there. I didn't mean to, but I did anyway. Back in the tomb under the lake. You know full well what happened between us. Don't even try to deny it."

Peryl stared at him, still looking her unique combination of faintly amused and bored. She flicked her hair.

"You make it sound so lovely," she said. "I think I remember it quite differently, as we tore the Arcania Shard apart between us. The way I recall, you gave me nothing but *pain*. I don't know that I'll ever find it in my black little heart to forgive you."

"You're lying," Robin said. "There's some of you in me, Peryl, in my head. I know there is. I've been angry, I've had darkness rising in my mana, colouring my magic with shadow like ... like some kind of bad flu I can't shake off. You didn't mean to, but you put some Grimm in my soul, or my mana, or whatever, and I *know* the same thing happened to you."

"Nonsense," she countered, dismissively. "I don't share my grimness. What a stupid notion."

"Some of my humanity went into you," Robin pressed, ignoring her protestations. "Even just a peppercorn's worth. You can deny it all you want, but that's why you saved Jackalope, that's why you delivered him to Erlking. Because you felt guilt, you felt ... *something*."

"So what if I did, for a second?" she shrugged, folding her arms. "A fleeting sneeze, that's all it was. I'm all better now. Nothing says 'look-how-grimm-I-am' like backstabbing a dryad in a dark labyrinth."

Robin knew she was lying. This ghoulish, dangerous creature, as black-hearted as Strife perhaps, and with a very skewed sense of what was acceptable fun. But whatever she was, she was lying. Either to him or herself.

"I was told that the seed of darkness in me would only grow, if I resisted it," he said. "If I didn't accept everything I was fighting, everything I was angry about. The Puck, being the Scion, never being normal like other people. It would grow and consume me. And it almost did." He held his hands up. "I've accepted who I am. Dark parts and all. You? You haven't. If you keep denying what the Arcania did to you ... It will consume you." He shook his head, pleased to see that she seemed to bristle a little. He had her on the back foot. "You're going to lose your grimness, bit by bit, Peryl. There's nothing you can do to stop it. And when it comes crashing down, all you're going to be left with is the guilt of all the things you are doing now. Every crime you are committing, every dryad you're dooming here. There'll be no getting away from what you've done."

Peryl stared at Robin for several silent seconds, her eyes growing large and soulful. He watched uneasily with a frown as her bottom lip actually began to quiver.

"I'm ... I'm just such a ... bad egg," she confessed, her voice hitching. "Maybe if I reach deep down ... perhaps you're right...maybe I can find the warm tingly light and power of friendship."

Her eyes narrowed suddenly, mouth turning up into a smile. All affectation of true emotion falling away. "Oh please," she sneered. "Don't come at me with the emo teenage nonsense, blondie. One cannot do soul searching, when one doesn't have a soul."

She raised her hands towards him. Darkness flickered around her fingers like shadowy worms, smoky in the air. "I'm bored of talking now. Let's play instead. I'll even be a good sport and let you go fi–"

Robin threw out his hand and let loose a Galestrike with all his might, not waiting for her to finish her sentence. It shot across the room with a roar, fluttering pages and throwing scrolls into the air in its wake. Peryl balked in shock and alarm, but she deftly dodged out of its way, the powerful wind ruffling her purple hair as it shot past her, slamming into the strange yellow walls. The surface cracked and splintered like eggshell behind her, shaking with the impact.

"My *my*," she grinned. "Dirty fighter. You *have* been learning from a nymph, haven't you?" From her crouch, black whips of darkness flew, snaking through the air and wrapping around Robin's legs below the knee. As she stood, the shadowy coils pulled back, tugging him off his feet and onto the rug-covered floor with a heavy thud.

Winded, Robin shook the dark mana loose, rolling to the side behind a table just as a shower of black and wicked-looking darts hailed down from above, thudding into the spot where he had been lying and burying themselves deep into the floor.

He leapt up from behind the table, feeling his mana stone glowing as he built his next cantrip.

Peryl had stepped to one side, away from the broken wall and in front of one of the large bookcases, rolling her neck on her shoulders. Robin made a fist, pulling his arm back in towards him, using Featherbreath to pull the bookcase forward. It scooted across the floor with a sharp squeal, slamming into the Grimm's back and then toppling down on top of her, showering her with books with an almighty crash.

"If you want to fight, that's fine with me!" he shouted.

The bookcase shuddered and exploded in a flurry of splintered wood. Peryl erupting from the wreckage. She leapt clear like a feral cat, her hair in disarray and a snarl on her face. A flicked hand as she shot through the air sent a bolt of shadow hurtling across the room. Robin ducked at the last second, hearing it explode behind him, shaking the room. Several of the large candlesticks exploded, and the huge bronze dish he had seen earlier, bonged loudly like a gong.

"Oh ... I *always* want to fight," she gasped, getting her breath back. "I just rarely find anyone worth fighting."

She raised her hand again, preparing to follow up with another strike, but Robin sent a Waterwhip flying from his palm, a long thin ribbon of white water. It snagged around the girl's wrist and he heaved, dragging her into the air. With a flash of mana that left him dizzy, he threw her across the room, sending her flying with a crash into the long table where the Earth Shard lay, rocking in its capsule container.

He could feel the anger rising in him, the darkness that was now forever a part of the Puck. But he was in control. The two energies had twined around each other inside him. He'd accepted his power, and he wasn't afraid to use it anymore.

"You're not taking that to Eris," he scowled. "No more apples for the teacher, Peryl. I have more mana than you do, you lunatic Grimm, I can do this all day."

Peryl kicked herself up off her back, standing on the table and scattering books. Her suit jacket was torn, but she was grinning wildly, as though she were having a whale of a time. She looked decidedly lunatic. "Promises, promises!" she said. "Maybe you do, but I'm *better at this* than you. I've been doing it for a long time." She threw her arms wide and thousands of pitch black moths erupted from her, flowing out from the blackness of her clothing like a dark cloud, their wings beating and fluttering like ticker tape.

Robin stepped back as the countless insects filled the room, more and more every second, a dense fog of confusing movement, blocking out the light. The moths plunged the room into darkness. Robin staggered blindly, beating at the moving air with his hands, as their tiny, dusty bodies battered at his face and body, a sea of living dark mana brimming in the chamber. He was completely blinded, suffocated.

"Plus, of course," he heard Peryl say from somewhere in the impenetrable smokescreen of moths. "I have the advantage ... *You're* not actually trying to *hurt* me."

Something shot out of the black cloud. Peryl was right in front of him and her fist had just lashed out, a hard punch catching Robin in the stomach. She was much stronger than she looked, and he doubled over, wheezing, as she disappeared back into the shifting, confusing darkness.

"What … makes … you … think … that?" he gasped angrily, lashing out blindly, his questing blows meeting nothing but papery darkness, fluttering against his fingertips like black confetti. He heard her sniggering, somewhere behind him. She was circling him like a wolf in the dark. The only light he could see was the flickering of his own mana stone, a tiny pulsing light in the confusion. A sharp kick came without warning to his back, sending him sprawling forward, clattering to the floor onto a heap of unseen obstacles.

"Because if you were," her voice came, sounding playful. "You would have shot a needle of ice into my heart by now. But you're not a killer, Robin Fellows. You don't have the taste for it … *not yet*, anyway."

Robin spun on the floor, aiming himself in the direction he thought her voice was coming from. Gathering all of his mana and focus, he span a Galestorm around himself, whipping the air into a circular, roaring tornado. The storm scattered the moths, sending them swirling around and around him, caught in the powerful cyclone, forming a clear space in a moving wall of ceaseless shadowy motion.

"Neither do you," he argued, alone in the clear eye of his own storm. "You're all talk, Peryl. You couldn't kill me before, back when you took the Shard from Splinterstem. Left me hanging in a cage instead. That's practically affectionate for you."

The girl stepped suddenly from the shadows, walking out of the circular wall of spinning moths, the whipping tornado of fluttering shadow and into Robin's open clear space. She had her hands on her hips.

"You were unconscious. It was pathetic," she argued. "Would have been like kicking a puppy. Where's the fun in that?" She looked manic, her hair flying upwards in the wind, the gloomoths a spinning black wall at her back. Wind roared around them both as Robin scrambled to his feet, concentrating hard to keep the Galestorm going, to stop the cloud of the Grimm's mana from closing in around him again. With all his effort he kept them at bay, trapped in his cyclone, he and the Grimm at its core.

"This is much more fun," Peryl said, smirking, looking around. They could hear the sounds of furniture breaking, being torn to pieces in the mixture of their mana, buffeting darkness around every corner of the room destructively. "You have to admit. Besides …"

She blew a fast cloud of darkness across the space, a billowing inky smoke, leaving her mouth like black dragon's fire. It hit Robin full in the face, knocking him backwards. His spine slammed into an unseen table-top, sending a jolt of pain jarring up his spine.

In this second of disorientation, Peryl had crossed the empty space, quick as a striking snake. She was suddenly right before him, her forearm held up before her and pressing against his chest, forcing him back against the table. Her other hand held a wickedly sharp knife close at his throat. The blade was very cold.

"You enjoy sparring as much as I do … You're just not ready to admit it yet, are you?" she whispered gleefully. "It's nice to have a dance partner who isn't all left feet for once."

Her face was inches from his. He could see his own reflection in her wide, black eyes. The edge of the blade dug against the skin of his throat dangerously. Robin noted, rather surprisingly given the urgency of the situation, that just as in his dream, the manic girl smelled faintly of liquorice.

"Call … off … the … wind," she instructed firmly.

"Call off the moths," he counted stubbornly, glaring defiantly. He was trying to talk without moving or bobbing his adam's apple. "You're not going to slit my throat."

"Are you sure?" she said in a sing song voice. "I mean, would ya bet the farm on it?" She looked him up and down. "You got taller too … huh," she added lightly, as though they were old friends chatting over coffee.

"Eris would slit yours," Robin insisted, hoping this was true.

They stood a moment longer, face to face across the blade, cocooned in the whirlwind of air and shadow, rolling over and around them. He searched her eyes, and she stared into his. Robin could feel the darkness deep inside him, beating away. He knew, however much she denied it, that his humanity was doing the same inside her chest, even if it was no bigger than a grain of sand in a dark ocean. They were both breathing heavily with the effort of the fight.

Peryl smirked at him eventually, her face thoughtful.

"If you were going to kiss me," she said. "That was the moment, you just missed."

She took a step back, taking the knife away from his throat and dropping her arm. With a lazy flick of her free hand, the countless moths dissipated, flickering away like blown smoke, bringing the room suddenly back into sickly amber light.

Robin's hand went to his throat automatically, checking if he was cut, but it came away clean. He dropped the Galestrike, the spinning wind roaring around the chamber dying away.

The room was utterly destroyed, furniture overturned, books and scattered chairs flooding the floor. Loose pages fluttered slowly down to the ground around them like errant yellow leaves.

"Besides, roughhousing is great fun and all, but I'm afraid I'm just killing time really," she admitted. "Until *he* got here." She winked at Robin, turning her head to indicate the doorway he had entered by. It was open once again, and Robin stared at the figures stepping through it.

The Princess Ashe, hands bound before her, and by her side, Henry, looking shaken. The two were shoved roughly into the large chamber by a third figure, who followed them inside. Tall and broad, clad in dark armour, cloak flowing out behind him with a whispering rustle of feathers.

"My Lord Strigoi," Peryl said respectfully, running her fingers through her hair to neaten it. "You join us at last."

Henry stared wild-eyed at Robin. "He came out of nowhere, Rob!" he babbled. "Right out of the shadows! He was too quick for me!"

Panic rose in Robin. He was already exhausted from fighting Peryl. He had used more mana than he cared to admit. Seeing the grinning wolf-face of Strigoi roughly shoving his two prisoners before him filled him with dread. There was only one way in and out of this room, and Strigoi was firmly between them and it.

The Wolf of Eris surveyed the total carnage of Peryl's chamber in silence, his head turning this way and that. He levelled his dark gaze at the Grimm. "You are a tiresome fool," he said lowly. "Stop your toying with the Fae-brat. He is not your entertainment. The princess is prepared for transportation." He pushed Henry and the princess before him, knocking them both to the ground like so much useless garbage. The princess looked utterly despondent.

"What are *you* doing here?" Robin asked, trying not to pant. Peryl looked a little chastised.

"Our dear Lord Strigoi here has come to convey the princess to Dis,"

Peryl explained. "A little birdie told me he was in the forest, you see. I have eyes all over the place. Or moths, rather. The rest of the dryads, well, they're my toys now. But I thought the great and noble Princess Ashe, this delicate little flower, would benefit from a trip to the capital." She smiled down at the princess, who Henry was helping to her knees. "The Empress is going to be very happy to have you to visit," she said. "And who better than the Empress' favourite lord to bring you there in style! Don't want you slipping away on route, do we? Very little chance of that with Lord Strigoi. He has quite the firm grip."

Strigoi had noticed the Shard of Earth, still somehow standing on the table, encased in its capsule lantern and oddly untouched by the storm which had wrecked the rest of the room.

"I came when you called, Hive-queen. You told me only of a prisoner. A prize for the good Lady Eris." His masked face turned to Peryl slowly. "And yet I see you have the Earth Shard, Grimm," he noted in his cold whisper.

Peryl looked darkly pleased with herself. "I do indeed," she smiled. "So, we both have gifts for our lady, Lord Strigoi. You have the princess, and I will bring her the Shard … And now, the Scion. Won't she just be elated?"

"I should take all three," the wolf turned his head thoughtfully towards Robin. "I am headed to Dis with this dryad prisoner of war. If the Earth Shard is won, what does it matter *who* brings it to the Empress? All that matters is that she gets it."

Peryl's face fell into a dark scowl. "It matters to me," she said. Robin didn't think she would dare defy Strigoi, but he could see the sudden anger flicker in her eyes.

Robin, still leaning back against the broken table, was trying to figure out the power play here. Clearly, Peryl didn't know that Strigoi had been on his own hunt for the Shard, or that he had used Robin to retrieve it and to defeat the drake. The dark man would no doubt have made away with it there and then, had he not been unconscious at the time. Clearly, he now saw an opportunity to pick up his plan.

Robin got the distinct impression that Peryl only knew that the Wolf had been in the woods. She had seen an opportunity to use him to ferry the princess south to Dis for her. She had been enjoying lording her new status over everyone. Perhaps she was realising this was not something she could do to the likes of Strigoi.

For his part, Robin guessed, Strigoi had no doubt awoken in the hollow in a less than perfect mood and had come here on sufferance. He seemed surprised to see both Robin and the Shard here in the Hive.

Not a one of these servants of Eris trust each other, he thought. They're all a bunch of backstabbing conspirators. A nest of vipers. Karya had told him once that Dis and its inhabitants were less of a family tree and more of a knotted clump of thorns.

"The swarm are bringing up the others from the cells," Strigoi said, ignoring Peryl's protestations. "This Fae-creature's companions. Traitorous Panthea, one and all. They shall all be transported together … *with* the Shard. I will take them now. There is no discussion to be had."

"Then I should take them all myself," the girl countered quickly.

"Our Empress has set you to watch over the Hive and to war with the dryads," Strigoi hissed dangerously. "A task you have risen to admirably. She has instructed you to be here. This is your place … know it. I shall take them to Dis … immediately."

Peryl's fists were white, clenched knuckles shaking as Strigoi overruled her utterly. Robin knew why. She wanted the glory. Eris had already rewarded her richly for delivering half of the Water Shard. He could only imagine the praise heaped on the one who delivered another full Shard, along with the Scion himself and those who aided him.

Beyond Strigoi and the doorway, Robin could see, with a sinking heart, Karya and Woad being marched up the long slender walkway to the Grimm's chamber. Hawthorn was with them too, as was Ffoulkes, evidently scooped into the mix.

"Why haven't you used the Shard?" Robin asked, suddenly realising that during their battle, Peryl had not once attempted to use the power of the Earth Shard against him. It made no sense not to. Not when she was one who so craved power. It was such a monumental weapon.

She glanced over at him, her fury at Strigoi still evident on her white face. "I know what it did to the dryad king," she said. "I was there, remember? Do I look stupid? I don't fancy 'communing myself' with something that's going to cover me in forest and turn me into a monster."

"You're already a monster, you mad witch!" Henry spat from his spot on the floor at Strigoi's feet.

The Wolf of Eris reached out swiftly and caught Henry hard across the head with the back of his hand, sending the boy crashing onto his back amid the scattered debris. "You do not speak, human animal," he hissed. "You are not amongst equals here. You are less than an insect."

"Don't hurt him!" Robin yelled, raising his hands, feeling his mana build to a cantrip. "I'll kill you! If you harm *any* of them–"

Strigoi looked up at him sharply. Without even raising his own hand against the boy, Robin felt the invisible wall of the dark creature's will shoot out and hit him fully, slamming him back against the table, forcing his own arms down against his will. Robin couldn't move a muscle. He strained furiously, but the grinning wolf merely regarded him with its inscrutable, frozen face, like a cat looking down at a trapped and struggling mouse.

"If I harm any of your lackeys, Scion of the Arcania," he whispered dangerously. "It will be because it is my pleasure and whim to do so. And if I so wish it, you will watch. If I so wish it, you will dance a merry jig while I do it, even if my mana must break every bone in your arms and legs to make this so."

The black eye-slits of the wolf mask glared. "Speak again to me, and the human dies. It matters nothing more to me than scraping centaur dung from my boot. Does it matter to you, I wonder?"

Robin glared back in silence, his jaw working. Hatred poured out from him. He said nothing.

"I thought as much," Strigoi sneered, tilting his head back. "You are *weakened* by your need for these creatures."

Karya, Woad and the others were bundled into the room, Robin seeing that their hands were similarly bound. Hawthorn was glaring at Strigoi with a look that was murderous. Robin had rarely seen such hatred on the old Fae's face.

"And you, traitors …" Strigoi addressed them as the swarm guards ushered them into the sickly yellow room. "Why do you insist, against sense and reason, on rebelling against your ruler?" He pointed a gnarled black hand across to Robin. "Look. Feast your eyes on your saviour … a frightened, helpless boy. Even with his mana-stone, he cannot lift a finger to save himself … or any of you. Not against my might. Not against the unbreakable will of Dis. Why do you follow this Fae?"

Karya, hands bound and hair falling across her face, glared up hard at Strigoi. Despite his fierce appearance and evident power, there was no fear in her bright golden eyes. They were ruthless and defiant. "We follow him because he can lead us out of darkness," she grimaced through

371

gritted teeth. "We follow him because there is nothing he will not do to stop Eris, and the rest of you. Nothing he will not sacrifice. He would die for us, and we would die for him."

She looked over at Robin, and the sheer, determined strength in her eyes seemed to kindle courage in his own.

"Some of us *will* die for him," she continued. "Before this war is won. We have no illusions. But it is better to die free, you yapping dog, than to live a slave."

"Oh, can we *please* just gag them all?" Peryl said dramatically, rubbing her temples. "I'm going to get a headache." Something seemed to occur to her. "Or we could kill them, I suppose?" Eris only needs the Shard and the Scion right? Double trouble. These other losers, they're all just side dishes."

"Their fate is for the empress to decide, not you, little Grimm," Strigoi growled. "You have enough playthings to take to pieces with the dryads here. But silencing them is a good idea."

Peryl waved a hand airily, the red gem on the lapel of her dark suit flashing. Bands of shadow appeared around the mouths of all of Robin's friends, tied as tightly as cloth.

"I will prepare the Janus station for travel to Dis. I will return for these whelps," Strigoi told his sulking companion. "Keep them here, keep them quiet, and no more of your foolish games." He glanced at the gaggle of muted prisoners. "If any of them move, kill them." He looked at Robin, and the boy felt the dark mana which had been holding him in place disappear as he was released from the man's iron will. "And if the troublesome Fae-spawn makes any move … kill them again."

He glanced at Peryl. "This son of the old relics might risk his own life stupidly to escape. But he will not risk theirs. They are his weakness. Find the weakness of a creature, and it is easy to control it."

Strigoi left the room without a second glance, striding out over the bridge, sending the swarm guard scattering where they hovered, eager to be out of his path.

When he had gone, two of the tall, yellow insectile creature returned, blocking the exit, stopping any hope of escape there.

Peryl folded her arms, crossing over to the Shard in its casing. She drummed her fingers on her inner elbows testily.

Robin's mind raced. He looked to Woad, Karya and Henry, all of whom were looking back, silenced by their gags of shadow and bound at the hands. They knelt in a line of the floor, incapacitated along with Hawthorn and Ffoulkes.

Only the princess was not gagged. She sat a little way off, knees drawn up and eyes to the floor. She looked utterly despondent, destroyed by the enslavement of her people and the betrayal of the steward.

He had to think of something. Their situation had gone from bad to worse. If they didn't get out of this, they were all going to end up in Eris' throne room in Dis.

Robin had no illusions there would be any coming back from that. He looked around desperately. The two creepy looking swarm-creatures were standing at the door, watchful, long wicked-looking spears clutched in their hands, their glassy eyes trained on the prisoners.

Robin didn't dare use magic. Strigoi wasn't bluffing, and he didn't doubt for a moment that Peryl would harm his friends given half an excuse. She was clearly furious. He turned his attention to her desperately.

"Looks like you're not going to get your glory after all then," he said, hoping to play on her anger. "Must be frustrating, for you to have done all the legwork, put in all this effort, sowing all your seeds in the forest all this time, only to have Strigoi waltz in here and take it out from under your feet."

"What's that annoying buzzing noise?" Peryl replied. "Kind of like a whine?" She glared witheringly at Robin. "Oh … it's just you. Be quiet."

"It must have been satisfying, being the one to deliver the Water Shard, right?" he pressed. "After spending so long practically invisible, being ignored at court, bossed around. No power of your own. I can only imagine old Strife's face when you toppled him from his golden pedestal. I would have paid to see that."

Peryl turned, and actually smirked, despite herself. "Well … I'm not going to pretend *that* wasn't fun," she admitted. "The old, dried up sour-puss has been lording it over the rest of us for so long. I think it came as a bit of shock to see me rise through the ranks like a Valkyrie. Victory is sweet, Scion." She sneered, glancing around at the prisoners. "You should try it yourself some time."

Robin ignored this barb. "Strife will probably find *this* quite funny, I guess. Strigoi being the delivery boy, not you. Metal-muzzle is already Eris' darling golden boy, isn't he? From what I hear. It's not like he *needs* the extra credit. Whereas you? Well," Robin shrugged. "You're only just proving your worth, aren't you? This would have been a permanent notch in your belt. Proving Eris' faith in you was not unfounded? Secured your position for good, eh?"

She walked over to him, putting her hands in her trouser pockets, looking casual and relaxed. "Do you think I'm *completely stupid*, blondie?" she asked. "You are so painfully transparent. Trying to turn me against the Wolf of Eris? Appealing to my ego? Do you honestly think I'm foolish enough to defy *him*, no matter how gorram galling this might be?"

Robin shrugged. "I don't think you're stupid," he admitted honestly. "Dangerously insane perhaps, incurably sociopathic, but not stupid. I suppose…I just thought you were not the kind of person to let someone else come into your kingdom and walk all over you, that's all. Maybe I was wrong."

Peryl sneered. "This is a long game we play, Scion," she said. "Kind of like a dance, and I know every step. Strigoi may take the glory here, but I don't forgive or forget. I can wait a long time for revenge on those who undercut me."

"I bet Strife can too," Robin reasoned. Peryl's face darkened.

"You're all so scared of Strigoi," the boy said, folding his arms. "Every one of you. He doesn't seem so scary to me. At least he talks straight, not round and round in circles like the rest of you. I think I'd rather be *his* prisoner than *yours* anyway. Maybe there's some honour in being captured by someone like him, as opposed to someone like you, who skulks in shadows and uses clueless puppets to do all her dirty work so she doesn't get her own hands dirty."

Peryl's eyes blazed. Robin seemed to have managed to find a nerve.

"Not so scary?" she asked thoughtfully. "You'd rather be with him than with me, eh? An honourable adversary?" She barked a humourless laugh, shaking her head slightly. "Oh my *my*, Robin Fellows. You really are the *most* clueless creature ever to walk the Netherworlde, aren't you? You know nothing about what he is … what he has done."

She strolled over to the prisoners, walking behind them until she came to Hawthorn. "This old man here …" she said, whispering as though sharing darkly delicious secrets. "He could tell you a tale or two about old Strigoi, couldn't you mister?" She ruffled Hawthorn's hair playfully. The Fae jerked his head away, muttering muffled curses through his gag of shadow. If Peryl even noticed, she ignored his anger. "Hawthorn here was one of the great and good, wasn't he? One of the best and brightest of Oberon and Titania's knights in shining armour, back in the day?" She circled the prisoners, making her way back to Robin. "Sidhe-Nobilitas, that was the name, wasn't it? The order of Fae knights. Noble and righteous and good as butter? Your dear old daddy was one of them too, right?"

Robin frowned at Peryl, flicking his eyes to Hawthorn, who was glowering darkly, and then back to the girl. "What about it?"

"Oh," she sounded mock-surprised, actually raising a pale hand to her mouth. "You mean, you don't *know*? About the *end* of the Sidhe-Nobilitas? No one's told you what actually happened to them?" She glanced back at Hawthorn, tutting. "Shame on you, old man. Keeping the boy in the dark like this. Don't you think he has a right to know?"

"To know what?" Robin asked angrily, annoyed by her teasing.

"At the end of the war, my dear, constantly baffled Scion," she explained, flicking an imaginary piece of lint from her pitch black suit. "After your mighty and all-powerful King and Queen had gone 'poof', disappearing into thin air, and leaving your entire race alone in the world, just when they were needed the most. Well, let's just say it was a rather … chaotic time."

She folder her arms, tilting her head to one side. "The Arcania shattered, the great and wonderful palace of Erlking reduced to ruins. The Sidhe-Nobilitas was lost and leaderless. They did the only sensible thing they knew to do." She leaned in toward him. "They went into hiding," she whispered. "Yes, I'm sure they had noble plans to regroup and strategise, to rally their forces and strike back at Eris. Your kind always has these noble ideas. You just never realise when you've lost, even in a war. It's incredibly tiresome."

Hawthorn was glaring at the back of Peryl's head murderously.

"Of course, you won't know anything about this yourself," she said. "You were only a babe in arms at the time. Mewling and helpless. Spirited away out of the Netherworlde to be hidden under a gooseberry bush or whatever." She waved her hand dismissively. "Mummy and daddy wanted to keep you safe after all, from all the mean old nasty Panthea. I remember it. I might not be much older than you are, but I've been not much older than you are for quite a long time now. Mom and pops and all the knights, they had a secret place, where they were safe…or…they thought they did anyway."

"What are you saying?" Robin asked.

"We hunted all over for them," Peryl said. "The Grimms that is, the other forces of Eris too. Turned the Netherworlde upside down. The empress was hell-bent on finding all the Sidhe-Nobilitas, wiping them out, erasing them from the face of the earth, those who had led the opposition." Her eyes narrowed to thin slits.

"We're all good hunters, Scion. We can all track. But in the end … it was Strigoi." Her voice darkened. "It was the big bad wolf who blew your house down. Though he wasn't much of a wolf back then. A mere pup. Strigoi who flushed your family and the other tattered remains of the Nobilitas out from their hidden burrow. Strigoi who led the forces of Eris right … to … their … door."

Robin's face felt cold and numb.

"He found them … Eris found them." She shook her head. "It was a bloodbath. Like shooting fish in a barrel, from what I hear."

With a pale hand she reached out and gently, almost consolingly, stroked Robin's cheek. Her touch was like ice, but her dark and glittering eyes looked odd, almost sad. "He killed your parents, Robin Fellows," she confessed.

Robin was shaking. He didn't want to believe this. He stared past Peryl to Hawthorn, who was looking at him with hooded eyes filled with anger and sadness. The old Fae clearly saw the question on the boy's face, and, resigned, he nodded.

"Is it really any wonder why Eris made him her best-friend-forever after that?" Peryl said suddenly bright and breezy again. "Wow. Talk about hitting the jackpot. It's a shame for him that a couple of the critters managed to get away. Peaseblossom, that old man cowering in the corner over there, running for their lives like rats up drainpipes. But still, we round them up, one by one." She glanced at Hawthorn. "You're one of the last aren't you, old timer?"

"Strigoi killed my parents?" Robin's voice was shaking. All he could see before him was the looming dark image of that cruel wolf mask, endlessly grinning, a taunting demon.

"They died, and the glory was all his," Peryl confirmed. "Guess he got a taste for it after that. It's easy to let power go to your head when the empress makes you her favoured dark knight. Your dear mother and father died like rats in a hole, Robin. Alone and afraid on a dark and moonless night, and you have the Wolf of Dis to thank for that."

She straightened up, hands clasped behind her back. "So maybe, before you start talking about honour and reason, you should get your facts straight, huh? People here in the Netherworlde are just like people anywhere else. They are rarely how they appear."

Robin didn't argue with this. His jaw was clenching, his knuckles white. He had known, of course, that his parents had died in the war. But he hadn't known how. He hadn't known that more than once now, he had been up close and personal with their murderer.

"I'm going to kill him," he whispered, his voice low and trembling. Karya and the others were looking up at him, their faces unreadable behind their gags of shadow.

"Oh, don't bother getting all avengy, you would die trying," Peryl said dismissively. "Trust me. You can't even get close to that one. And neither can I. Strigoi is untouchable."

She picked up the Shard in its case on the table, sighing a little sadly, as though she had been enjoying a fun game but now it was over, and it was time to tidy up the toys. "This sport is done," she declared, turning it over and over in her hands. "You're all going to Dis, whether I like it or not. Me? I will choose another battle to fight. I guess I should look on the bright side. At least it isn't the old man Strife taking my glory away. One must be pragmatic about these things…if you want to keep your head on your shoulders, that is."

She turned suddenly, utterly unprovoked and lashed out across the room with a bolt of dark mana. It hit Robin squarely, sending him skittering across the floor, to land in a heap with the others, alongside the Princess Ashe.

"You're so stupid! Coming here. You could have run home, safe in your silly mansion. Now look where you've ended up. Now behave and … just … be quiet," Peryl suggested. "I'm done talking to you."

Robin lay on the floor, winded for a moment, hating the Grimms, hating Eris, but hating Strigoi most of all. The anger and bitterness coursing through him was more powerful than he had ever imagined, even in his darkest moments.

There was truth in Peryl's words. No-one was as they seemed. Look at Ffoulkes, a complete sham of a showman, a lowly thief and coward disguising himself as a preening peacock. Look at Jackalope, darker and more damaged than any of them had ever guessed, with the blood of his own brother on his hands. Splinterstem, on the outside a noble and dutiful steward of the dryad court, while inside, a seething mass of selfish ambition, willing to imprison his friends, to murder his own king and sell his own people to the enemy, just for a chance at the power he craved.

Even the Grimms and Strigoi, playing their vile games, plotting against one another, sneaking around with their own secret agendas. Their pasts filled with darkness and murder and horrible, unforgivable deeds. Who could Robin be expected to trust, in a world like this?

He was surprised to find, as he pulled himself up off the floor, that the Princess Ashe had taken his hand in hers. She squeezed his fingers gently, and he looked up questioningly into her sad, green eyes.

"Don't blame yourself, Scion of the Arcania," she whispered softly. "All has come to ruin. Perhaps even with the most noble of intentions, you could not have prevented it."

He stared at her, his own eyes feeling hot and dry. Her face was resigned, sad and dignified, even as she knelt on the floor of her enemy's domain.

"I lost my love," she said. "Then my father, and now my kingdom." She blinked slowly, long eyelashes brushing her cheeks sadly. "You and your friends. You tried to help. But what is there left to fight for? When all is lost? We go to our deaths. Let us go with dignity."

Robin looked over at his friends. Woad was struggling quietly and persistently against his bonds. He was clad in iron, a struggle even for a faun. Robin had no doubt he would get free eventually, but they didn't have the luxury of time.

Karya and Henry were close together, both watching Peryl closely.

His helplessness overwhelmed him, but stronger than that, much stronger, was his anger. That they had fallen to this, overpowered by the enemy. After everything they had been through, they were trapped here in this prison. No way out, no hope of escape, no help coming from the outside world. Even now, far below them, the monster who had destroyed the Sidhe-Nobilitas, who had wiped his parents from the face of the earth, was preparing a gateway to Eris herself, while here they waited, trapped by a Grimm and her dangerous, buzzing guards, powerless to act. It infuriated Robin. The sheer injustice of it.

"What is there left to fight for?" he wondered aloud, under his breath. A poem his grandmother had been fond of came into his mind, unbidden. She had liked poetry from time to time. Sometimes, she had read aloud to Robin, though he had been very young at the time and seldom interested, unless it had been something hilarious or outlandish like the Jabberwocky. The line that came to him now was not hilarious, but it whispered in the back of his mind, in a memory of his gran's warm and scratchy voice, as darkness seemed to be falling all around their best efforts. 'Do not go gentle into that good night …' he heard her say softly. 'Rage. Rage … against the dying of the light.'

"I know what there is to fight for," he told the princess, squeezing her hand. "Hope. Even in this vile prison they can't take that away from us." Karya had looked up at him as he whispered, and he caught her golden eyes. "You're right, Karya," he nodded to her. "I would die for any of you. I probably *will*." He nodded. "But not *today*. We're not lost yet, any of us."

He turned to the princess. "You haven't lost everything," he told her. "You're wrong. And you're not weak and feeble. Splinterstem spent years convincing you that you're some kind of delicate flower that needed his strength and his protection. But Princess, you're a queen. Your people need you now. You can't give up. There is something worth fighting for." He squeezed her hand. "Your Alder is *not* dead."

She stared at him in confusion, dropping his hand.

"He's alive. We found him. He's waiting for you at Rowandeepling," Robin insisted. "Ashe, you're stronger than you think. There's a life and a world outside these dark walls still waiting for you. Your people need you to lead them. To rule." He forced a smile. "Love and duty, you asked me how you could ever choose between them?" She stared at him. "They're one and the same thing."

She looked as though she didn't dare believe him. She couldn't. Her eyes searched his for long moments. He could see her caution, and beneath it, a desperate, terrified longing to believe that what he was saying was true. He stared back at her steadily.

"Free my people," she whispered softly. "And we will destroy this swarm from within."

Robin nodded. Keeping one eye closely on Peryl, who had turned away to place the Shard back on the table, he reached into his back pocket and drew out the crumpled slip of magical parchment. He wasn't sure if this would do any good. But he knew that, however much trouble they were in, they were not truly alone in the world, not ever.

The Grimms just had a way of making you *feel* as though you were.

Fear and despair was their power. But there were still others in the world who did not fear Eris.

Robin had no pen. He searched the littered floor until he saw a sharp sliver of pottery, a fragment of a smashed vase, debris from his battle with Peryl. Picking it up slowly and carefully, one eye on Peryl as she contemplated the Shard, he jabbed the sharp, ragged end into the tip of his finger, wincing slightly at the pain.

As a droplet of blood began to well, he lowered his bleeding finger to the parchment and with a shaking hand wrote a message.

Trapped in the Hive. Strigoi here. Grimms. Need help.

He watched anxiously as the blood settled into the parchment, the red and blotchy lettering smeared like a child's finger painting and darkening like old rust. After a moment, the words disappeared, dissolving away and leaving the paper blank.

It was a long shot, but he was out of options.

Peryl had picked something else up from the table. It was the curious disc. The metallic gong he had noticed earlier, a large bronze shield or a mirror, burnished and golden. He had thought it only a decoration like the rest of the affected room, but now he suspected it was something else altogether. It was glowing, illuminated from within by soft pulses of light. They were bathing Peryl's face in silent flashes of golden light. Whatever the curious object was, she looked extremely concerned as she held it in both hands, staring down at the polished surface.

Robin crumpled the parchment and stuffed it back into his pocket.

"What's going on?" he asked her. "What is that thing?"

Peryl looked at him over her shoulder as she cleared a space on the table, pushing aside tottering books and propping the large disc against the wall, so that it stood facing her. "Not that it's any of your business at all," she said tartly. "But it's a scryglass. It's how we keep in touch with the capital." She sounded concerned. Very concerned. "It's a direct line to the empress. All Grimms have one, wherever we're stationed."

A magic mirror? He thought. The glowing intensified, the mirror pulsing warmly and silently. For some reason Robin couldn't explain, it seemed quietly menacing, and its flashes of light were becoming more rapid and urgent.

"Aren't you going to answer it?" he said, as lightly as he could. "Seems pretty insistent to me."

Peryl glared at him. "Be quiet," she said. She stared back at the mirror, her hand stroking her lapels in a nervous way. "There's no reason for the Empress to be contacting me," she muttered to herself. Robin could plainly hear the unease in her voice. "Why would the Empress be contacting me? She doesn't know I have the Shard yet. I've sent no message. I–"

"Maybe not the wisest idea to keep the boss hanging on the line," Robin said, needling her on purpose. His eyes fell on the floor by the Grimm's feet. There, to his surprise, amidst the fallen books and other rubbish, he suddenly saw Karya's mana stone bracelet and Woad's opal nearby. Clearly they had been tossed around in the storm like everything else. He shot a glance at the insect guards. It was hard to tell, with their large round, mirrored eyes, but they seemed to be watching the prisoners at their feet, not him.

With Peryl distracted by the strange golden mirror, this might be his best chance. As stealthily and carefully as he could, summoning every ounce of mana-management he had ever learned, he silently cast Featherbreath across the room, seeing the two mana-stones lift, an inch from the floor. They revolved in mid-air, glittering, behind the Grimm's heel, floating like tiny planets in zero gravity. Robin began, slowly and extremely carefully, to drift them silently across the room, praying that they didn't drop and clatter.

Karya and Woad had both seen this, and they stared at him with wide and hopeful eyes, Woad nodding encouragingly, Karya practically glaring caution at him, as Robin delicately guided the stones across the yellow tiled floor. Beads of sweat began to form on his forehead. The first time he had used Featherbreath, he had sent an sheet of paper hurtling through the air, sticking it to the ceiling in the atrium at Erlking where, to this day, it still remained. He focused, harder than he ever had before. Remembering every single tedious lecture and lesson, every hour of whale song and introspection he'd been forced to endure in the blue parlour.

It was one thing to topple a bookcase onto someone with Featherbreath. That was a great angry push of mana. Anyone could throw a clumsy punch. But this, this was like delicate open-heart surgery.

Peryl reached out tentatively toward the mirror, still wholly distracted by its insistent and foreboding pulsing. If this was the Empress' way of contacting her servants in the field, then she most certainly was not giving up.

"This is not good," Peryl muttered. "I swear, blondie, whenever you're involved, things never go to plan. You're like a curse on me. I don't know why I put up with you at all."

Robin ignored her. She had such an odd way of talking, as though they were good friends and all of this, life and death and war, it was all just a silly game to her. None of it real, no consequences. Karya's bracelet and Woad's opal were all the way across the room now. He floated them behind their respective owners, drawing on every ounce of skill he had, sending them off in different orbits around the bodies of his friends. Eventually, and with great relief, he dropped them silently into their open hands, still bound behind them. Robin saw Karya's fingers close slowly and carefully around her bracelet, and she looked at him with her fierce eyes. Still bound and silent, she nodded ever so slightly. He could only see half of her face above the shadow, but she seemed full of pride.

"Maybe you should have installed voicemail in your glowy dish," Robin said to Peryl. "Then you could have screened your calls from the evil queen of the world. Sloppy planning that."

"I told you to be quiet!" Peryl said angrily, practically stamping her foot. "Am I going to have to gag you as well? Speak out of turn again and I will end one of your little buddies here." She glanced around. "Maybe that bald guy shaking next to the old Fae. He looks like he's going to cry anyway. It's irritating."

Ffoulkes, to whom she was referring, huddled down, trying to make himself less visible, hiding behind Henry and Hawthorn. He was shaking with fear.

The Grimm seemed to reach a decision. She took a moment to straighten her black suit and smooth her hair, then, after taking and releasing a deep breath, she cracked her knuckles, and waved a hand across the surface of the mirror.

It made a keening noise, like a musical saw, and the glowing became a steady light, growing in intensity until it was so bright, it shone out into the room like a golden spotlight. Too fierce for Robin or any other the others to look directly at.

Peryl however, her face thrown into sharp contrast by the illumination blazing on her face, stared unblinking into the disc. The surface of the mirror looked formless now, liquid or smoke or somewhere between the two, rippling and shimmering.

"My Lady," she said, in a soft and respectful tone which Robin had never heard her use before. She bowed her head dutifully. "Praise to Dis, and praise to the Empire."

From the shimmering and blazing mirror, throwing ripples of light around the room, there came a low and hushed whispering. It was barely loud enough for Robin to make out. He could hear no words, but the sound of it seemed to crawl on his skin like ants.

The Grimms were menacing and dangerous. Strigoi was worse, frightening and intimidating. But this noise, this…presence…flowing out of the disc, was something altogether different. A cold power so intense, it seemed to waken a primal instinct in Robin. The urge to flee, at any cost. Whatever animal instincts remained in his consciousness, after millennia of evolution, they were screaming danger at him, flooding his body with adrenalin. The faint whispering made his heart pound, his head ache with the sudden rush of blood brought on by panic, and every bone in his body screamed at him to get away. To get as far from this thing as possible, put as much distance as he could between himself and the owner of this near-silent whisper.

He was aware that the others seemed to be experiencing the same overwhelming reaction. The princess at his side had drawn her knees up and had buried her head in her hands, refusing to look up into the room. Henry looked ashen and slack, as though he might pass out at any moment from the waves of power flowing from the disc. Even Karya and Woad had their heads bowed, as though to shield themselves from a great blast of cold. Hawthorn alone was glaring at the mirror over Peryl's shoulder, his old face set in a hard line. His eyes blazing defiantly. By his side, Ffoulkes lolled helplessly, having passed out immediately as soon as the horrible, insidious whispering had begun to fill the room like a poison gas.

Peryl nodded at the lens, clearly able to hear what was being said.

"Yes, my Lady," she said haltingly. "It … it *is* true. I have obtained the Earth Shard of the Arcania. Even now, I prepare it for transport to you. Lord Strigoi himself is–" She faltered as the whispering resumed.

"Yes … of course … I should have made you aware immediately … I only wanted …"

Peryl halted again as the mirror blazed even brighter, molten gold before her. The whispering grew in volume, making Robin feel as though the ant were beneath his skin now, crawling inside his skull.

"Of course, my Lady. A … a … thousand apologies … I can only…"

More hushed conversation. The presence in the mirror continued to seep into the room, making it difficult to breathe. Even the two swarm guards had stepped backwards, outwards through the door. Still guarding their prisoners from the vantage of the slender bridge, but either unwilling or unable to remain in the overwhelming presence of the Lady of Dis.

"The Scion?" Peryl said, and Robin heard her struggling to keep her voice light. "Well yes … as it happens, I *have* captured him too … How did my Lady …?"

She bowed her head apologetically, cowed as the mirror shone even brighter, a solar flare of anger. Robin saw the Grimm's knees actually buckle a little, as though she had been landed an invisible blow. She remained upright only with a great will of effort.

"Yes … of course … at once." Peryl turned to face Robin across the room. "Come here," she commanded, a controlled tremble lurking under her words. "She wants to see you."

Robin was filled with bald horror at the thought. He would rather claw his way out of the wall behind him than take a single step toward the shimmering golden disc blazing malignantly on the table. It was pure danger. He shook his head, unable to form any words.

Peryl's eyes widened in a kind of blank desperation. "You don't get to say no, idiot. None of us do," she hissed at him. "Here. Now. Or it will be far worse."

Her expression was wild and somehow seemed to be pleading. She looked as terrified as he was.

Robin swallowed hard, forcing himself to stand up. He was the Scion of the Arcania, he told himself firmly, summoning all of his inner Puck. The world's last changeling. He imagined if Aunt Irene saw him cowering on the floor like a scared child. He imagined if Gran could. Neither of them would have stood for it. He was the son of Lord Wolfsbane and Lady Dannae. They would *not* have died on their knees, whatever Peryl had said. He *knew it.* He knew it in his heart. And neither would the last Lord of Erlking.

Robin walked slowly towards Peryl and the blazing golden mirror, every step a struggle. It felt like walking toward an explosion. Every instinct he had screaming at him to turn and run.

I don't run, he told himself firmly. *Especially* from things that scare me.

He felt the Puck rise inside him, coming gratefully to his aid. He felt, rather than saw, his own hair whiten as he drew close to the mirror, knew that his blue eyes were bleeding into green as hard and bright as emeralds. It was as though the sheer power radiating from the lens was drawing his own power to the surface in self-defence.

Peryl regarded him with something between fear and wonder as he stepped up to her side, unblinking. He glanced over at her, managing to drag his eyes away from the mirror for a second, and saw her pale face with its dark, made up eyes and tight mouth. She looked washed out in the brightness from the mirror, and Robin couldn't help but feel a smattering of pity for her.

If this was what she answered to. If this malevolent, powerful being was the price of her power. Robin turned to the golden disc, and stared defiantly into it, his heart hammering but his face set.

The surface was polished metal. It showed him no clear reflection, only a smoky outline. But it was not his own. The blurred form shifted a little, smoky and indistinct. What Robin could make out, with perfect clarity, was a pair of eyes. They were gold, solid gold, as brilliant as twin suns, as beautiful as the dawn and as regal as a lions. They stared hungrily out of the glass, burning into him, peering past his flesh and blood and penetrating deep into his core, searching his very essence.

They were the most beautiful, terrible eyes he had ever seen, and he could not look away. They held him fixed, and he would have stood there forever if they had commanded it. The eyes of Eris fell on him like sunlight and fire.

"Robin Fellows. The favoured child," a whisper from the mirror. He heard it quite distinctly. A female voice, soft, whispering, almost warm. "At last," it breathed.

Robin stared helplessly, his own eyes watering, wondering absently if he was going to pass out, or throw up.

The eyes disappeared into the mist, the shadowy silhouette shifting slightly, and Robin, released from their grip, fell backwards, stumbling and blinking. He became aware that he hadn't been breathing for several seconds, and gasped painfully. His green eyes felt scorched. He could feel his mana racing through his bloodstream, raw energy as he blinked furiously trying to shake the after images of the eyes of Eris from his vision.

Robin heard the shape in the mirror whisper something else to Peryl, and then, without warning, the light dimmed, and in seconds, the glow had gone altogether.

The light dimmed in the room, reverting back to the wan sickliness of the Hive, and the circle of burnished bronze was once more nothing more than a disc of metal, reflecting nothing.

Peryl turned on Robin. "Great!" she yelled, sounding shaky and panicked. "Wonderful! Fantastic! How did he know? How did he know? That conniving, vicious old–"

"How did who know what?" Robin shook his head, pressing the heels of his hands against his eyes. The oppressive and overpowering presence of Eris had gone from the room, but he could not shake the image of those eyes, peering right through him.

"Strife!" Peryl slapped at the mirror furiously, knocking it flat onto the table in anger. It fell noisily with a metallic clatter. "Strife! That poisoned dart! That crooked blade of a man! He knows I'm here with the Shard! That spying wretch! And…" She pointed a finger at Robin, shaking slightly. "He knows *you're* here too!" She glared at him. "He has told the empress that you have infiltrated the Hive, meaning to steal the Shard which I have obtained and which I had 'not bothered' to inform her of right away." She was grinding her teeth in anger. "He has 'concerns' about my ability to keep the Shard safe, and about the dangers of a rogue Scion at loose in the Hive," she spat furiously. "Eris is *not* pleased. Not *one little bit*! She is coming here. For the Shard, for you. She is coming *herself*, blondie!"

Robin glanced at Henry. *Strife*. That double, double, double crossing snake. He had high-tailed it back to Dis, ratting out his sister and her procurement of the Shard. He had placed Robin in the Hive, a place from which there is no escape, and then revealed his exact whereabouts to the empress. Robin didn't even know why he was surprised. Strife had trapped them all, put them under the glowing lens of the empress.

"Did you even hear what I said?" Peryl cried, her voice shrill. "Eris. Lady Eris. She is coming here, to the Hive. Right now. For the Shard. For you." The Grimm looked terrified herself. She clearly didn't want her mistress here in her Hive-kingdom. Robin didn't either. He didn't want to be anywhere near the force that had shone through that golden mist.

"You understand nothing," Peryl said, turning away, running her hands through her long hair. "Eris won't show mercy. She isn't like me. You should have stayed in your stupid cage in the forest. She's going to destroy you."

"Peryl, I'm sorry," Robin said, reaching out behind him, fingers searching the table, brushing past the fallen mirror.

The Grimm turned to face him, confusion clouding her stricken face. "Sorry? For what?" she snapped.

Robin's hands found what he was looking for and closed around it. With a great swing of his arm, he brought the lantern capsule containing the Earth Shard up in a swift wide arc, cracking it hard against the side of her head.

The capsule shattered, the force of the blow knocking the Grimm to the floor. Peryl fell in a crumpled heap, splayed and motionless on the yellow tiled floor.

"For that," he said hoarsely.

With a shrieking hiss, the two swarm-creatures swooped furiously back in through the doorway, spears raised in retaliation, but the air around them was suddenly filled with loud crack and pops and flashes of light. Their wings fluttered in panic, battering the walls and the doorway. Their bodies colliding in confusion as they crashed into one another, disoriented by the blinding fireworks exploding in front of their lens-eyes.

Robin dropped the shattered lantern case to the floor, dimly aware that the Shard of the Arcania had rolled, clattering like a glass paperweight, across the floor to land at the feet of the Princess Ashe.

Robin flung out both hands, casting twin Galestrikes, swift and deadly. They hit each of the dazzled guards full force, sending the swarm creatures spinning out through the doorway into the great void, tumbling over the slender bridge. Their wings twisted and beating uselessly as they fell, far out of sight below.

With a popping hiss, the shadowy gags which had muffled his friends disappeared, the dark mana which had held them in place clearly gone with Peryl unconscious.

"Bloody hell, Robin!" Henry gasped loudly, eyes wide. He stared at Peryl, lying motionless on the floor, her face covered by her hair. "Did you kill her?"

"Grimms don't die from blows to the head," Karya said urgently, getting to her feet. "She's out for the count though. Well done, Scion."

"Thanks for the light show, Woad," Robin said, stepping hurriedly over the fallen Grimm and untying the faun's metal bindings, freeing his friend's outstretched hands.

The faun was grinning. He flipped his opal mana stone in the air and caught it again as soon as his hands were free. "Figured you could do with a little help," he said, slipping his stone back around his neck. Together they quickly freed the others, the princess leaping up and helping them untie Hawthorn, Henry and Karya.

"Someone should wake the pile of soft pudding," Hawthorn said, prodding the unconscious form of Ffoulkes with his toe. "Or I can just carry him."

Karya stared from Robin to Peryl to the doorway urgently, slipping her mana stone bracelet over her wrist. "Right. We have to get the hell out of here, and now, right now," she said briskly. "I can flip us to the human world, but not here. We're at the top of a very tall pyramid. If we appear in the human world at this height above the ground, it's going to be a long drop and a sudden stop. Plus, I need wood or earth to tear through. There isn't either here. We have to get to ground level first."

"We're not running," Robin said firmly. The girl stared at him, dumbfounded.

"What are you talking about?" she gasped. "We have the Shard, we have the princess, and in case you weren't paying attention, *Eris is coming*." She stared at him wildly. "*Eris!*" she repeated for emphasis.

"I know!" Robin argued. "But we can't leave them all. How many could you flip? All the dryads here?" He glared at her, knowing full well she couldn't. "Can you imagine Eris' fury? If she arrives here and we're gone with the Shard?"

"I'd quite *like* to imagine her fury," Woad said, raising his hand. "If we're taking a vote. Imagine it from a great distance rather than, you know, being *here* when it's happening."

Robin was adamant. "No. She'll kill every dryad here." He looked to the princess. "All of your people. We can't just leave them all here to die."

"Such is sometimes the price of war, Master Robin," Hawthorn counselled grimly. "*You* are more important to the cause. You and the Shard. Our priority has to be to get you away."

"I cannot leave my people here to die," Ashe argued desperately. "I won't!"

"They're not going to die!" Robin raised his hands, trying to stop everyone from arguing. He stared at Hawthorn. "I'm not more important. The cause? What cause? What are we trying to even save if we run and leave these people behind?"

Hawthorn glared at him. "You can't save everyone, Robin Fellows."

"I can bloody well try!" Robin argued hotly, his green eyes flashing. "Save the Netherworlde from Eris, right? The Scion's duty? These people *are* the Netherworlde. I'm not leaving them behind."

"Robin, I can't flip that many people over," Karya said. "And we can't free them all. The swarm is filling this place. There isn't time. Eris is coming, right now. She'll be through the Janus station any minute."

"I don't mean to leave anyone behind in the Hive," Robin said firmly. "Because there isn't going to *be* a Hive."

They all stared at him.

"Whatever you're going to do," Henry said desperately. "You need to do it quick, before sleeping-crazy there wakes up or metal-muzzle comes back."

QUICKENING

Robin crossed swiftly to the princess. He knew they only had seconds to spare. The two guards he had sent tumbling through the void would surely not have gone unnoticed. He could already hear the low rumble of a thousand angry buzzing creature, rising like a tide from beneath them.

"Ashe, I need the Shard," he said. She had picked it up in the confusion, and it shone and flickered, cradled in her pale green hands. She looked at him, seeing him as the Puck for the first time.

"It wants to come to you," she said. "It doesn't want me. I can feel it. It remembers you I think, from earlier. You took it from the drake, didn't you? Strigoi told me it killed my father. But you took it. It's already yours as far as its concerned."

Robin held out his hands, nodding, and she placed the Shard in his cupped palms. It was hot, and Robin felt its great power flowing into him.

A warm, flooding sensation. Sunlight on forests, the rippling of cool grass between shadowy trunks. The endless furling and unfurling of leaves, more than a galaxy of them, rolling through the endless forest of the Elderhart, more numerous than the stars in the heavens.

The Shard shone in his hands, flickering from a glimmer to blaze with light, and he closed his eyes, letting it take him, feeling it flow over and through, filling him with the knowledge of the Tower of Earth. With the deep and dark secret majesty of nature. Robin's veins felt golden, flowing with the sap of a thousand trees. His breath was the wind in leaves. Between his tousled white hair, he felt the shining white spikes of his horns, tall and solid, the proud antlers of the strongest stag.

When his eyes opened, his companions were all watching him closely.

"So," said Henry carefully. "Who are we looking at now, then? Are you Robin right now? Or are you the Puck?"

Robin smiled. "There's no difference," he said. "Not anymore."

"How are you planning on using Earth magic?" Karya asked. "There's nothing natural here to manipulate. Everything's made from this disgusting waxy swarm-stuff." She kicked at some of the broken boards of the collapsed bookcase Robin had earlier thrown onto Peryl. "Even *this* isn't really wood. It's just glamoured to look that way. Peryl is so strange."

Robin looked to the princess. "A leaf from your dress?" he asked, holding out his hand.

Confused, Ashe nodded. She tore one of the silver leaves from her long dress and handed it to him.

Robin closed his cupped hands around it, dropping into a crouch close to the floor.

"What was it you told me back in Rowandeepling, your Highness?" he asked, his tall white horns bowed low as he put his mouth to his cupped hands, as though about to blow into a conch shell. "Even the mightiest oak owes its power to the memory of the smallest acorn?"

He put his lips to his fingers holding the leaf between them. "Time to wake up," he whispered to the small dead thing, and he pressed it flat against the yellow waxy floor. His hands, he noticed for the first time, were tinted slightly green by the power of the Earth Shard.

Beneath his splayed palm there was a rumble, and the floor shook. The noise intensified, making the walls buckle and tremble. Robin looked up at everyone.

"Get ready to hold on tight," he told them. Hawthorn had picked up the unconscious body of Ffoulkes, heaving him onto his bony shoulders in a fireman's lift. He nodded, regarding the Scion with a curious expression.

"Tight to what?" Henry asked, struggling to keep his balance as the room shuddered around them as though in an earthquake.

Cracks appeared in the ground at Robin's feet, spiderwebbing in every direction through the cracking tiles. As the roaring, creaking rumble intensified, the floor suddenly erupted, great shoots and vines bursting forth from the soft yellow wax. They spilled into the room, spreading everywhere at a tremendous pace, thickening and growing ever larger as they flashed out around the chamber. Leaves were already unfurling along their length as the powerful, thickening tendrils crashed into the walls, splintering them. They roared upwards, still growing, as thick as trees now, as Robin and the others backed away. They pushed woody roots down through the floor which splintered and began to fall away in great chunks, revealing the dizzying void of the Hive beneath. The great, shaking vines and creepers burst through the ceiling, smashing through the yellow surface with ease, breaking it apart like smashed sugar. It rained down on them in pattering chunks, as the great and unstoppable creepers continued their relentless growth, thrashing around the disintegrating room.

"Grab onto the plant!" Karya yelled above the deafening cacophony. "The room is coming to pieces!"

They all leapt onto the thick creepers as they shot here and there, twirling and growing, thrusting out, powerful battering rams. Robin leapt onto one great green offshoot, his arms wrapped tightly around its stem, feeling absurdly like Jack clambering the beanstalk. In the confusion of the twisting jungle, growing larger and denser by the second, a writhing mass of lush vegetation in constant motion, he glimpsed the others. Karya and Henry were wrapped around a similar huge vine, clinging on for dear life as it shot upwards through the ceiling of the crumbling room, out into the void of the central Hive, questing for space to grow and taking them with it. He saw Hawthorn and Ffoulkes, wrapped in an embrace of twining leaves and creepers, hoisted into the air at great speed, and Woad, clinging tenuously to a great leaf, still in the process of unfurling, which was as big as he was. The faun was a blue smear as the tendril crashed outwards through the crumbling walls.

Between the thrusting, thrashing shoots, the Princess Ashe darted on her swift dragonfly wings, a pale shape, dwarfed by the expanding vegetation.

As Robin's creeper thrust upwards, rocketing him out of Peryl's chamber as the last of its crumbling walls and destroyed floor fell away into darkness, he looked down in time to see the Grimm's limp body rolled into a great leaf, curling and growing around her unconscious form, bringing her along for the ride. Her books, scrolls and broken furniture tumbled down into the great dark void of the pyramid beneath them. Heaps of detritus, crashing down and bouncing off the latticework of criss-crossing walkways below. Robin glimpsed the bright golden mirror tumbling away, over and over, as it fell, flashing as it caught the light before falling into darkness and mist far below.

The swarm was everywhere in the immense cavern of the pyramid's interior, hundreds of their yellow armoured bodies filling the pallid air. An angry wasp's nest that had just been kicked. They flitted around in panic as the power of the Earth Shard swelled, and the great, unstoppable plant expanded, sending out great green tentacles like some immense sea beast, thrashing in every direction. Its immense arms and branches wrapped around the yellow paths, covering the brittle maze of bridges, squeezing the walkways with questing vegetable strength until they began to shatter, one by one, under the relentless pressure. Robin's creation was tearing the Hive apart from within. Amidst the roar of growth and the musical explosion of walkway after walkway, it twisted and branched, spreading like wildfire, crisscrossing the monumental space with an ever growing net of green life and newborn vitality. Road after road fell to its tangled mass, bridge after bridge torn apart by weaving fingers. Everywhere, it knocked the swarm out of the air with whips of fury.

Robin heard Woad whooping somewhere in the confusing maelstrom like a maniac. He held on for dear life. He was still Robin, he could feel his arms wrapped tightly around the tuber and his knees gripping it as it shot through the dark space, but he was also the vine. He could feel every questing root as though they were his own toes, thundering downwards, shooting into the deep mist at the bottom of the darkness, questing for ground, for soil. He could feel the countless climbers and ivy-covered creepers lashing against the outer walls, dressing them in a knotted skin of vegetation, piling up layer upon layer of tangled, living tissue, fibrous shoots and vital tuber, the weight and the insistence of his living creation straining and groaning against the strong outer walls. The power of the Tower of Earth filled this cloying place, flushing dizzying oxygen into its nauseating stale air, and through it all, Robin and his friends swooped and dived, riding the twisting plant like long green dragons, threading acrobatically through the fog.

"Are you doing this?!" Henry's voice came, bellowing across the space as his vine swept past Robin's own swiftly-moving perch, the two like funhouse rollercoasters thundering in the dark.

Robin wasn't entirely sure. He felt at one with it all, but not remotely in control. He didn't think anyone could ever really be in control of something this. It was too primal, too fierce. The stuff of life itself, it grew, and expanded. It filled the great pyramid, and it pushed against the walls, yearning to be free, wanting the open air.

All over the Hive, now more a green maze than an empty space, there came an endless chorus beneath the constant rumble of growth. The ceaseless musical tinkling as countless slender whips of greenery smashed the bars of the cells, freeing dryads everywhere. Cell after cell was broken, popping and shattering in the sea of churning forest.

Soon, the air was filled with dryads, swooping free, furious at their imprisonment and, led by the Princess Ashe, fighting with the swarm. A great and furious buzzing was everywhere.

The swarm were at a disadvantage. They were used to the darkness, the silence. This green and vibrant confusion was anathema to them. The dryads however, were in their element.

Quite literally, Robin thought.

The branch on which he rode appeared to have stopped moving. It had wedged firmly against the outer wall of the pyramid. Finding itself unable to go any further, it was now sending out further vines and shoots, covering the inner surface of the great wall in a thick carpet of tangled ivy. It was beginning to flower here and there, the wall of the pyramid no longer visible at all. The woody stem with Robin on, however, was still growing, thickening all along its length. In moments, it was wide enough to stand on, a natural horizontal bridge in the leafy maelstrom.

Robin searched the great hissing and rustling forest, trying to make sense of what was going on. There were dryads everywhere, sweeping and diving between the giant leaves and through the enormous knots of vines. They soared with ease and precision like fighter planes, chasing desperate and disoriented swarm-guards, half hidden by the giant leaves still unfurling everywhere.

After a moment he saw, to his relief, Karya, Woad and Henry, picking their way toward him, jumping from root to shoot and clambering over leaves.

"This is just like one of those jungle gyms!" Henry shouted. "Or, you know, those forest activity places, where you get to zipwire through the treetops. Except we don't have any safety harnesses on, and there's a billion foot drop to certain death everywhere." He sounded full of adrenalin and more than a little hysterical.

Karya on the other hand, seemed practically elated. Earth was her Tower and she was loving every minute of it. The destruction of the Hive, the ever moving nest of giant green blades. He saw her bracelet flash time and time again as she and the others moved towards him. She was directing pathways, making connections, bending the huge mass to her will to forge them a clear path.

"Now *this* is the kind of showboating I can completely get on board with," she yelled, as they finally made their way onto Robin's wide and barky bridge. They ran along it towards him. "Eris is still coming though," she cried urgently. "I think I passed the Janus station chamber a moment ago. It was kind of hard to tell, as there were about eight thousand leaves slapping me in the face at the time, but I swear I saw the circle of stones and mist. Someone was coming through it, and I doubt very much it was your Father Christmas. We have to get out of here *now*."

"We're still halfway up the pyramid," Robin said. "Nowhere near the ground. You can't tear us through to the human world from here."

"We should bust out of here then!" Woad suggested.

"The wall is too thick," Robin replied. "I can feel it, through the vines. It's bending, but our little new Eden isn't strong enough yet."

From above them, sliding down a long tube of passing greenery as though it were a waterslide, Hawthorn appeared, landing at their feet and still carrying Ffoulkes. Robin noticed that the Fire Panthea appeared to have woken up from his faint, but he was still clinging to the wiry old Fae for dear life, staring around wild-eyed at the primal jungle.

"I think the pyramid is stone, on the outside at least," Robin told them all, his green eyes sparkling. "I can feel it creaking, but it will take time for even these huge things to break through."

"We don't have time!" Henry cried. Several of the swarm had spotted their group and were descending on them rapidly, darting between the knots and loops of vegetation, their spears held high. Robin threw a Galestrike upwards, knocking them off course and sending them spinning away, crashing into the darkness, lost in the sea of leaves.

"More are coming," Woad said, as they all turned to the outer wall, now deep in a thick carpet of living plant life. "We need an out!"

"There is no *out*!" a voice behind them called, sounding furious.

They turned away from the wall. Staggering toward them, looking battered and dazed, making her way carefully along the thick woody bridge, was Miss Peryl. The Grimm looked dazed and dishevelled, but her eyes blazed like a fury. She was flanked on either side by an insectile guard, swarms hovering in midair, their ghastly gas-mask faces flashing. Both of them had their spears raised, hoisted over their shoulders and ready to throw.

"Don't you numbskulls *get it*?" Peryl shouted. "Eris is *here*! You're not getting away from her. And …" She raised a shaking finger, pointing at Robin as she stalked towards them out of the chaos "… *I want my Shard back!*"

Robin could feel the wall at his back, heaving but holding. The ancient skin of the pyramid, heavy and well built, was moving, cracking under the pressure of the insistent life blooming within it. But painfully slowly. There was no way they would escape in time. They had destroyed the inner Hive. The dryads were free. The swarm were falling everywhere, dropping out of the air like flies as they were overwhelmed by the combined efforts of their enemies and the colossal living landscape. But Robin and the others had nowhere to go.

"The Shard is *mine!*" Robin shouted back.

Peryl grimaced, baring her teeth. "Oh for the love of everything, learn how to *lose*, will you?" she shouted at the top of her lungs. "You are all going to surrender, or you are going … to … *die!*"

As she yelled this final word, one of her guards, skittish and hovering uncertainly as it dodged the ever-growing plants, seemed to startle. In its confusion and nerves, it threw its spear, full force overarm, clearly mistaking Peryl's sharply bellowed warning for a command.

The spear was swift. The long barb shot through the air, a lance of metal as sure as a lightning bolt. Robin stood in dumb shock. He didn't have time to react. The deadly missile hurtled towards him, unstoppable, aiming directly for his chest.

Time slowed.

He saw the barb, whistling through the air toward him, a flying metal needle of death.

He saw the rage drop from Peryl's face as the spear hurtled towards him, replaced with shock, and something close to fear. He heard her shout wordlessly. It sounded like a warning, and saw her thrust her out desperately, loosing a coil of dark mana, a swift snake of shadow, which chased the shaft through the air as it flew towards its mark. She was trying to knock it off course. Trying, for reasons he couldn't understand, to save his life.

Her shadow bolt crashed into the hurtling spear, knocking its trajectory aside, the Grimm's mana dissipating with the impact.

It flew past Robin harmlessly, mere inches from his stomach, and landed instead, with an embedded thud, deep in Karya's chest, lifting the girl clean off her feet and throwing her backwards with the impact.

Someone shouted. Robin wasn't sure who. It might have been Woad.

The faun rushed to Karya's side where she lay, crushed against the wall. Her face a mask of shock. The spear buried deep in her, an obscene and horrible barb, pinning her to the vines like a butterfly.

Robin felt the blood drain from his face as he stared. Peryl was frozen in place, out-thrust arms still raised towards him, her fingers shaking uncontrollably. The Grimm's eyes were wide and horrified as Robin stared from his fallen friend to her. She shook her head frantically.

"No ... I ..."

"What have you done?" he whispered, lips feeling numb, his voice shaking.

Shadows lashed out from behind Peryl, thrashing in the air like dark tentacles growing from her back. Her mana spilling out unconsciously. The ribbons of darkness shot up and twisted around the two swarm guards either side of her, grappling them, twining around their necks and pinning their arms. With great force, she flung the insect-like creatures away into the void, sending them spinning away helplessly with panicked buzzing squeals. Both ricocheted off vines and thick walls of woody vegetation, tumbling away into the deep void below.

Woad and Henry had both dropped to Karya's side. Woad was cradling the girl's head, looking horrified. Henry had one hand on the cruel shaft, his other pressed to Karya's chest, lost in the folds of her coat.

"Rob ... she's hurt," he said shakily. "*Really* hurt." His hand came away red and wet, his fingers shaking.

Even over the sound of the raging battle and the ever moving vines and branches, Robin could hear Karya's breath coming in ragged, irregular gasps. The noise was nightmarish.

Before him, amidst the gloom and confusion of the writhing mass of greenery, Peryl stood, looking lost and appalled. Staring at Robin, she opened her mouth to speak, her eyes, dark and wide, ringed with violet. Before she could form words, a shape descended on her from behind. The Princess Ashe had swooped out of the battle above, her pale leafy dress fluttering, wings humming. She fell on Peryl, shoving her hard as she landed on the great root-bridge, and the Grimm was thrown from her feet with the impact.

Tumbling off the wide creeper and away into the darkness below, Peryl fell without a scream, head over heels, until she was lost in the shadows.

Robin turned, ashen, to his fallen comrade as the princess, her wings folding along her back, rushed towards them all.

Karya's face was deathly white, her golden eyes wide and shocked. She looked up at Robin. Her own hands were wrapped around the spear, closed over Henry's.

"Ow," she said with feeling and some difficulty. "I got … a little bit … stabbed."

"The blade must come out," Hawthorn said firmly in a frank tone.

"That could *kill* her!" Robin snapped. It felt as though the bottom had dropped out of the world. The snaking vines around them, the aerial battle between the dryads and the swarm. They all seemed distant, irrelevant, as though they were happening somewhere else, to someone else.

"Do it," Karya coughed, her voice shaky but still managing, in her own way, to sound bossy and irritable. "Just … be quick about it."

Robin and Henry grabbed the spear and pulled. It came free, the girl grimacing in agony. Henry looked at the cruelly barbed thing in disgust. It was dark and slick with blood. He threw it away with a clatter.

Karya's shirt below her coat was dark and wet, and the stain was blossoming quickly through the weave.

Henry pressed his hands down hard on the wound, making her grit her teeth and groan.

"Keep pressure on it!" Hawthorn instructed. He looked to Robin, grabbing him by the upper arm and dragging him to one side. "We have to get out," he hissed in a low voice. "Right now. The girl will die here."

"I'm not … dying … in this … bloody … place," Karya said stubbornly. She managed to force her face into a smile. She looked as white as a Grimm, her lips tinged with blue, making the brightness of her gold irises stand out more than ever. "I mean … I would have … seen it coming … right?" She coughed, the movement making her wince in pain. Henry grabbed her hand, looking stricken. "Don't be dramatic," she muttered. "Just a scratch …"

Robin stared helplessly at the wall. It was bucking and groaning, but showing no sign of collapsing.

A sudden chill fell over them all.

The air in the Hive had grown arctic all at once, as though a great wind had ripped through it, rattling every vine. Robin felt an enormous shudder through every one of the countless huge branches. A shockwave like an earthquake as the whole plant seemed to shudder and tense.

Somewhere in the Hive, Lady Eris had arrived. Her presence seeped through everything, a surge of solid power, the same as had blazed from the mirror but magnified a hundredfold. The swarm and the dryads seemed to hang everywhere in mid-air, their battle momentarily forgotten as the menace rolled through the great space like invisible fog, chilling all.

From above Robin, over the pounding of his own heart, he heard someone shout his name.

Looking up, dragging his eyes away from Karya, he saw, standing above them on another branch, the silhouette of Strigoi. His bestial face grinned demonically down at them, taking in the scene.

"Fae!" he called, his voice its usually hissing whisper. "How? How have you done this? You bring destruction to order. You and your *creatures*."

Robin glared up with a rising surge of hatred, bile in his throat. His green eyes blazed at the murderous creature looming above them. His parents' killer.

"You were wrong," he shouted up to him. "You said my friends were my weakness." He gritted his teeth. "But every bit of strength I have comes from them. Every bit of power. It's a power someone like you will never know!"

Strigoi raised his dark clawed hand, holding it out towards Robin, and the boy felt the man's mana building in his palm like the electric charge before a thunderstorm.

"The empress is here, stupid Fae. Death fills the Hive, and it comes for you," he answered. "Tell me, slippery prisoner. Are you as *swift* as you are strong?"

The Wolf of Eris let loose a great blast of mana. His own personal Tower of the Arcania, sheer will alone. It blasted down toward Robin, deadly and unstoppable, crashing through leaves and boughs, tearing them to shreds.

Robin *was* swift, as it turned out. At the last second, shaking off Hawthorn and shoving him out of the way, the boy dodged aside from the blast, throwing himself protectively over his friends, his arms covering Karya. Woad and Henry ducked as the wall of deadly mana blasted angrily right over their heads.

The force smashed into the wall, making the pyramid shudder. The creeping vines and carpet of vegetation covering it were smashed apart like tooth-picks. It was like a bomb going off above their heads. With a cacophonous noise, a great hole tore in the skin of the pyramid, blocks of dark stone, coated in the sickly honeycomb surface of the inner Hive, exploded outward, flying off into the sky beyond.

Daylight streamed in, bright and dazzling, thrusting light into the dark interior of the Hive for the first time since the hellish place had been constructed long ago. Dust rose everywhere in huge clouds, blocks of masonry larger than Robin himself crumbling outwards, rolling away like boulders as fresh, cold air rushed in to greet them all.

Robin looked up, blocks falling all around him, smashing heavily into the thick tubers on which they all balanced. There was no time to think. The presence of Eris loomed all around them. This was their chance. He slammed the palm of his hand onto their vast green vine, throwing all of his remaining mana into it, injecting it with every ounce of the Earth Shard he still controlled. He felt the last of his power flood into it, quickening and vitalising it.

The great creeper shuddered beneath them, and then, no longer encumbered by the barrier of the still crumbling wall, it quested forward, breaking out of the pyramid through the huge ragged hole like a green, unfurling tongue.

Robin held on for dear life, Henry and Woad gripping onto his arms, the three of them forming a rough circle around the fallen form of Karya. The great shoot waved in the blinding daylight of the outside air, growing fast and roaring as it careened down the slope of the outer pyramid. Other huge shoots following it, pushing out alongside and behind, widening the hole, striving for the sky. The weakened structure of the pyramid cracked and buckled, struggling to contain the force of nature striving inside it.

Robin saw the sky, high above them, cool and clear, filled with sunlight and wispy high clouds. It was the most welcome sight he had ever seen.

The forest lay around them on all sides but it was dead and withered, a great, petrified expanse of sickly trees, tainted by the poison of the swarm. The draconian pyramid of the Hive, seen from the outside for the first time, was dark grey stone, stepped and huge. It dominated a great open clearing of bare and lifeless grey earth, commanding the forest around it from a bald and flat hilltop. The grey ground around the structure was blasted and bare, dead grey soil threaded with white and powdery vines like raised veins on skin.

The Hive was crumbling behind them, cracks and holes appearing all over its surface. Immense blocks of stone burst free, rolling with thuds down the countless steps. Through every hole, green life thruster, writhing and growing, desperate to be free.

The dead space atop the hill, Robin saw as their huge questing root barrelled down out of the air, was not empty. The entire hilltop was full of moving figures. Centaurs, hundreds of them. Robin had never seen so many in one place. They covered the grounds outside the Hive, rearing up as the ground shook beneath them. Roaring and whinnying, stamping back and forth in agitation. Strigoi's forces, his entire mounted horde, clearly stationed outside the Hive while their master attended to business within. They milled around, glaring up as one with their long masked faces, at the pyramid erupting above them like a volcano.

Robin's vine carried them relentlessly down towards this great horde, crashing into the ground and scattering the huge beasts in every direction as the giant shoot of life burrowed into the dry, cracked earth. Robin and the others tumbled clear in a heap, rolling in the dead and dry dust, finally back on solid ground.

Robin scrambled to his feet, looking around wildly, still blinking in the bright daylight. Woad had Karya in his arms and Henry was crouched defensively beside them. Hawthorn had thrown Ffoulkes clear before jumping nimbly to safety. Robin turned to the amassing centaurs. The last of his mana had gone into their escape, and he felt that his horns were gone, his blurry eyes blue. His own mana stone was heavy around his neck.

The centaurs were everywhere, rampaging back and forth around him in panic. They reared up on their hind legs and came crashing back to the ground, giant vines and shoots landed everywhere amongst them, bombarding the horde as they erupted from the collapsing Hive behind them. The prison itself shook and buckled. Beyond the crowds of centaur, Robin could see huge portions of its walls collapsing, a thunderous noise rolling away across the forest, shaking the trees and making the ground under his feet tremble. From every new opening, the dryads were escaping, streaming out in a large cloud of bodies, making for the air … and freedom.

"Pinky!" Woad yelled above the chaos, oblivious to the hordes of Strigoi around them. He was kneeling by Karya in the grey earth. She looked small and vulnerable. Centaurs hooves crashed down all around them. "It's boss. She's not moving. I don't know what to do!"

The Earth Shard was drained, leaving Robin dizzy and weak. Blearily, he blinked at them both, his legs like water.

Karya looked dead. *She can't be dead*, he told himself. That was a ridiculous idea. His mind reeled from even the thought of it. Henry and

Hawthorn, he saw, were defending the girl, back to back, trying to move in a circle, protected her from the stamping hordes. The centaur had spotted them, and despite the destruction of the Hive and the bucking, trembling of the earth all around them, they were closing in on them from all sides.

Above them in the sky, the daylight was darkened with the mingled bodies of escaping dryads and fleeing swarm, fighting and flying, turning it to an unnatural, flickering twilight.

Robin tried to take a step towards his friends, but his legs felt like lead and there was a high pitched ringing in his ears. He didn't know how they could get away. What chance did they have?

"Scion!" Hawthorn bellowed from nearby, a cry of warning. "Behind you!"

Something hit Robin in the back before he could turn, sending him flying onto his face in the dirt. He rolled painfully onto his back, blinking up into the sky in agony. A centaur had come up behind and kicked him to the ground with its powerful hooves.

Unable to move, Robin stared blearily up at it, as the ugly creature stamped its feet, rearing up again above him. He stared into its strange bone mask, its red, mad eyes glimmering mercilessly down at him, great jets of breath issuing in a snort from its long snout.

There was nothing he could do, destroying the Hive had taken the last of his strength. He watched the hooves descending, heavy and deadly. *I got them out*, he thought. *The dryads are free. The sky is filled with them.* But Karya…would she live? Would any of them? How long would the rest of them last, out here on this battlefield?

A second before impact, a figure darted from the side. A shape barrelled into the centaur, leaping onto its back. A boy. His arm held high, a silver knife shining and flashing as it caught the sun.

The assailant's other arm wrapped around the beast's neck, twisting it violently, and he brought down his arm, driving the knife deeply into the centaur's pale flank.

The beast roared, thrown off balance, crashing away, its deadly hooves missing Robin's head by inches as it tumbled to its side, shaking the ground as it fell dead.

Robin forced his head up, fighting grogginess and exhaustion, trying to focus on his rescuer.

The ash-haired boy emerged from behind the fallen body of the centaur, silver eyes flashing, wiping the long shining dagger clean on his trousers.

"Jackalope," Robin said woozily. "How ... how are you here?"

The hornless Fae dropped to Robin's side, gripping his outstretched arm and lifting him roughly up into a sitting position with very little grace.

His face was stern and cold. "Blame your stupid knife," he said to Robin, brandishing Phorbas. "It's been trying to get back to you ever since I left you on the hill. Thing's like a blasted dowsing rod. Led me here." The pale boy took in the chaos around them. The centaur, the vines and creepers and the tumbling Hive. "What in all the *Netherworde* have you done?"

"You came back," Robin said, wonderingly. He shook his head. "The Hive ... got the Shard ... Karya ... we're injured."

Jackalope glanced over at Robin's friends, taking in the sight of the fallen girl and her circle of protectors. "You idiots can't do *anything* right, can you," he muttered, still clasping Robin's arm firmly.

"Jackalope," Robin said seriously. "You should run. Don't stay in this place ... Eris is coming."

"No," the older Fae said, staring across the field of roots and centaur to the crumbling edifice of the pyramid. His voice was grim "Eris is *here*. Running is done."

LUX

Robin followed the other boy's gaze. He could see a figure standing in a gaping opening in the side of the pyramid. All around it was chaos, but this figure, cloaked and hooded, almost lost to view in the destruction, was perfectly still. He could feel its eyes.

"We can't get away," Robin said, unable to tear his gaze away from the distant figure. It seemed to be searching the hilltop, hooded head slowly roaming across the battle of dryad and swarm, scanning the mess of thrashing vines and piles of tumbled masonry, searching through the crowds of centaur. It was looking for him, he knew.

It was only a matter of moments, Robin realised. Eris would see them. The centaurs would close in again. There was nowhere left to run for any of them. He became vaguely aware that he was still clutching the Shard of the Arcania, the green stone still and silent in his hand. Hope seemed to fail them all.

And then, from the far border of the long hilltop, someone emerged from the forest. A solitary figure, clad in a long pale dress. She strode onto the battlefield without hesitation, calm and commanding, stepping into the mass of centaur without the slightest hint of fear or concern. Robin glimpsed her blearily. An old woman, tall as a spire, back ramrod straight, long silver-grey hair flying out behind her loose and long in the wind, a shining, spider web curtain reaching well below her waist.

It was impossible. He wondered if he was hallucinating. Some fevered wishful thinking brought on by the desperation of their situation. She couldn't really be here. She seemed so out of context, out of place.

But his aunt was no illusion. She was here in the Netherworlde, alone and unarmed, and seemingly undaunted by the massed ranks of her enemy. Aunt Irene stopped after she had walked a few steps into the chaos of the raging centaur army.

Her sharp, eagle eyes quickly roamed the field, finding Robin and Jackalope immediately. He saw her swiftly take in the scene. See Karya fallen, see Hawthorn, Henry and Woad surrounded, and Ffoulkes unconscious nearby, face down in the dirt.

Her expression was calm but stern. Her eyes as hard and glinting as diamond. Her hair blew loose around her shoulders.

The old woman slowly raised her hand, holding it out towards the distant pyramid, across the minefield of danger, levelling her palm directly at the shadowy, barely glimpsed form of Lady Eris. Robin saw the shadowy figure in the ruins turn its head to contemplate her.

The two faced one another a moment, both still and silent across the battlefield. Two queens on either side of a great gameboard.

There was a flash from Irene's hand, silent and bright. As powerful and blinding as lightning frozen in a great nebulous storm cloud. It rolled out from the old woman in a wave, a torrent of light, flowing over everything in a tidal wave. Centaurs fell before it, hundreds of them, knocked to the ground like toys, their ranks toppling.

Giant roots in the path of the beam snapped and blasted apart, torn to shreds by the advancing wall of silent destruction. It flew through and over Robin and the others, bathing them in an eerie calm. A warm tingle of power like pins and needles as the shockwave washed over them harmlessly, its touch as light as a feather, while all around them, centaur were blown from their hooves like leaves in the wind, and high above, the swarm were blinded and dashed out of the air.

The wave hit the pyramid. Bathed in light, the crumbling rocks trembled and shook.

The shadow of Eris, after a moment, was lost in the darkness, retreating silently from the light into the shadows within.

Irene walked forward, arm held before her. The fallen forces of Eris rolled out of her way, debris and bodies scattering as though driven aside by an invisible snowplough, clearing a path through which Irene walked swiftly and calmly, the long hem of her pale dress swishing around her ankles.

She did not look at the creatures surrounding her. She paid no heed to the swarm above, nor did she glance at Robin or the others as she walked.

Never once, as she made her way to them, did she take her bright eyes from the pyramid.

She stopped by the companions, standing amongst them like a lighthouse in a choppy sea.

"Karya," Robin stuttered, staring up at his aunt. She seemed so tall. Strength and silent power blazing from her like a phoenix.

"Hush, Robin," she said softly, her voice firm, but not unkind. "Karya. Daughter of Dis. Wake up. You're needed now." Her voice was commanding and no-nonsense, as though Karya were being a silly girl for having the temerity to bleed to death on a battlefield while there was work to be done.

Robin heard a shallow gasp from nearby. The light around them was blinding, the silence absolute. As nothing more than a faint outline, sketchy in the brilliance, he saw Karya move, her chest rising in a hitch.

"Can you take us home please?" Irene asked politely, her eyes still trained on the pyramid, lost in a blaze of white light.

Robin faintly heard Karya reply.

"Good," Irene said, the slightest strain in her voice. "Quickly now, girl, to the mortal world. All of us."

Henry and Woad were staring at Jackalope, still clutching Robin's arm. They both seemed to have only just noticed his arrival in all the chaos.

"He's a killer," Henry said softly.

Robin gripped Jackalope's forearm tightly, staring up at Irene. She glanced down at him, taking her eyes from the pyramid for a split second. Long enough to read her nephew's expression. She nodded. To Karya she said again, "all of us."

Robin felt the world twist as Karya tore between the worlds. Everything fell away. The light around him died, and exhausted, he sank gratefully and helplessly into utter blackness.

A MATTER OF DEATH AND LIFE

Robin later remembered the journey back to Erlking only in fragments. His communion with the Shard had left him weakened and disoriented. He'd wanted to black out, but he fought it, clinging to consciousness by sheer willpower alone. He couldn't leave Karya, not in the state she was in. He had a terrible fear that if he did, she wouldn't be there when he woke up.

And so he stayed awake, drifting in and out of his senses and remembering events like a jumbled and disjointed dream.

They had flipped back to the human world. He remembered that. The chaos of the Elderhart, the threat of Eris, the centaur and the swarm, and nature reclaiming the broken stone bones of the Hive itself, dragging it to the ground with strong green fingers. All were gone.

It had been cold when they arrived on the mortal side. Late afternoon and sleety rain. Slivers of slush were falling on his face. They were somewhere in the wilderness. A high and bristling hill, but there were signs of the mortal world everywhere. The vapour trail of an aeroplane, high overhead, a line of electricity pylons stalking away over the hills, metal skeletons strung with wire.

Hawthorn had woken Ffoulkes. Woad carried Karya, cradled carefully in his thin but strong arms. Robin thought he remembered Henry and Irene either side of himself, propping him up, helping him to walk, but in truth the memory was unclear and confused.

There had been patches of snow on the ground, he had noticed, melting in the grass. The blazing firework autumn of the Netherworlde was gone. The colours here seemed by contrast muted and quiet.

There had been a country road, Robin remembered that much quite clearly, a ribbon of tarmac edged by an old drystone wall. And cars were parked there, two of them. One was Henry's father's. Mr Drover's beaten up and ancient old rustbucket. The other had been a classic car, a Phantom, he recalled with odd clarity. Ffoulkes' car, which he had gifted to Irene.

The next memory was of driving, the countryside rushing past the windows of the car. Sleet was hitting it thickly and the sky was dark outside now. Some time had passed. He didn't know who was in this car with him, and who was in the other which followed. He knew that he was in the Rolls Royce though. It smelled of expensive leather and polish. Irene was driving, her hair was back in a tight silver bun. She looked just like an old woman again. It seemed funny to see her at the wheel. He had never imagined she knew how to drive. She always seemed the kind of person to be driven. He was half-way across the seats, his head resting on the shoulder of the person next to him, who had their arm protectively around his shoulders, occasionally giving him a soft pat. It made him feeling strangely, but not unpleasantly, like a young child. He vaguely remembered it being Hawthorn who held him. To Irene he said, rather slurred, "you got my message then."

The old lady hadn't turned around. She kept her eyes on the road, the headlights of the car cutting through the rain in the darkness. "It is lucky for you, my young ward …" she had said. "That Hestia is prompt with the post as always. Whether it's a letter in the post or a cry for help on enchanted parchment, written in blood."

"Hush now," Hawthorn told him. "Rest, son. Home sooner than you think."

The next jagged slice of memory was the iron gates of Erlking, open in the dark as the convoy passed through it, rolling up the long avenue of trees which led up the hill. And then, as Robin's senses seemed to finally return, there was much confusion within the great entrance hall.

They had all come inside at once. The place was dimly lit, and Robin had the sense that it was sometime in the very dead of night. Everyone was talking at once. Irene barked orders over the top of the clamour as they all dripped November rainwater onto the hall floor in great puddles. Karya was carried in, limp and silent, and given over immediately to the care of Hestia, who had been waiting attentively, Calypso by her side with folded arms, looking vaguely interested. Their faces were both serious and businesslike. The girl had been whisked immediately away, despite loud protestations from Woad. The faun was instructed by Calypso to stay out in no uncertain terms. And to let the housekeeper do what she could. They had disappeared behind closed doors.

Robin remembered seeing Jackalope standing slightly off to one side on his own, looking lost and awkward, and Irene taking him by the wrist and leading him gently but firmly into her study. In her other hand, he saw, she had carried Robin's satchel.

The overwhelming relief of being home, of having Erlking's warm and welcoming walls surrounding him, listening to the rain beat against the leaded window panes as autumn slid away like a thief in the night and winter rapped its first icy tattoo on the glass, washed over Robin. The others were all talking amongst themselves, and he caught his own reflection in the long, age-spotted mirror which stood in the hallway.

When he had first come to Erlking, what seemed like a lifetime ago, a twelve-year-old boy on the cusp of turning thirteen and with no one to share it, he had done the same thing. Looking at himself appraisingly before he had gone through to meet his Great Aunt for the first time.

Now he looked curiously at himself again in the dark glass. He looked so odd, taller, wilder, still dressed in Netherworlde clothes. His face looked tired, his hair a little crazier than usual. But it was his eyes that had changed the most. One of them was blue, the same as always, but the other, he saw, was green. What he had come to think of as the colour of the Puck.

It hadn't reverted when the power of the Shard had left him, as it had done before.

Henry appeared, dragging him away from his strange reflection, the glass in which he barely recognised himself. Ffoulkes was asking fussily about a shower, he said. Everyone should get cleaned up, get some rest, maybe some sleep.

No one did of course.

They made some effort to still themselves, allowing themselves to be herded by Mr Drover into a side parlour, where a warming fire was blazing in the shadows, despite the lateness of the hour. They allowed themselves to be forced into chairs, soft and comfortable. Robin, Henry, Woad and Hawthorn. Drover pressed drinks into their hands. Something strong and bitter and, Robin suspected, quite 'medicinal', as Drover himself would have put it.

But aside from Ffoulkes, who fell into a deep, exhausted slumber almost immediately, his plans to bathe forgotten, none of them could relax.

They sat in silence in the quiet night-time parlour, perched on the edge of their seats. Wrapped in blankets Mr Drover had fetched, they waited. For news of Karya.

The clock ticked on the mantle in the dimly lit room. The rain beat softly on the window as the night rolled onwards, and the fire crackled and popped in its grate.

It seemed hours, painfully long hours, surely close to sunrise, when the parlour doors finally opened, and Hestia entered. She was holding a towel, cleaning her hands, and her grave little face with its dark small eyes fixed on them all as they stared at her as one, expectantly.

"I have never seen a wound like it," she said, rather tremulously. "It was all I could do to dress it." She shook her head in disbelief. "There was nothing I could do."

Robin almost felt the glass slipping out of his fingers. Woad had gotten to his feet.

"Nothing *for me* to do," Hestia continued. She sounded bewildered. "That girl ... I don't know what ... the wound was *already* knitting. Healing *itself*. There was nothing for Hestia to do ... but watch and wonder."

"She lives?" Hawthorn asked.

The housekeeper nodded emphatically. "She is not yet out of the woods," she told them. "And she needs rest, lots of it, and time too. But her body is ... putting itself back together." She shook her head in quiet disbelief. "She will live. She is too hard-headed to die, that one, whatever manner of *thing* she is."

Relief rushed through Robin, more powerful a force than any mana he had felt of late. Henry and Woad were hugging each other tightly. Mr Drover shaking his head in wonder and relief.

Robin barely noticed any of this celebration. The only important thing were Hestia's words, ringing in his ears. *She will live.*

As though as one, the tiredness seemed to have caught up with everyone. A soft bed seemed like a promise of paradise. Robin felt he would be able to sleep for a week, maybe longer.

Hestia firmly rejected Woad and Henry's pleadings to see Karya immediately. The girl was resting, the housekeeper told them firmly. Sleeping herself, and the nymph was watching over her, seemingly rather gruesomely fascinated by her wounds. The last thing she needed was idiot boys clamouring and shouting in her sickroom.

They should all go to bed, she insisted. Sleep before they all dropped down dead on the spot and she would have to hoover around their corpses in the morning. She glanced over at Robin. "Except you," she said. "Your aunt wants you first. In her study, if you please."

Robin followed Hestia out of the parlour and along the corridors of Erlking, leaving the others to celebrate, to rest. The housekeeper's flat, polished shoes clacked on the floorboards as she hurried along, Robin in her wake.

He wanted to thank Hestia. If she hadn't seen the message … if she had locked Henry's hex message parchment away peevishly in some drawer somewhere, instead of keeping it on her person … they would all be dead. Eris had almost taken them all.

As they stopped outside of Irene's study door however, he couldn't think of a thing to say to the small woman. She looked him over critically.

"You look as though you have been dragged backwards through a hedge," she said sharply. "A mess of a boy, that is what Hestia thinks!" She shook her head. "Supposed to be the young master of Erlking and here you are, a half-drowned chimney sweep. It is shameful." She glanced down. "And you have left footprints on my floor I see. Tracking your filthy boots. Dragging half the soil of the Netherworlde over the floors. What peace I have had while you horrible children have been gone." She sniffed a little, not looking directly at him.

"I have had no cleaning up after your messes to do. And now? You all come back in pieces and chunks! And I suppose those two, the old Fae and the fiery thief, they will want rooms made up for the night too." She tutted angrily as though this were all too much to bear.

"Sorry we're such a bother, Hestia." Robin said, a little listlessly.

She made a face, as though he were the most irritating child she had ever known. "You will be wanting a fire in your room I imagine. Little lord of the manor." She nodded. "Hestia knows what is what. It is already set. And a bath is drawn, and clean sheets laid out."

Robin blinked at her, lost for words.

"Do not bleed on them, or I shall give you cause to fear old Hestia more than Eris!" she grumbled. "Now go to your aunt, foolish boy."

And with that she walked off, busy as an irritated hedgehog, to tend to the others.

* * *

411

Irene was standing by the fire in her study. Jackalope sitting opposite her on the edge of a high-backed chair. The knife Phorbas was resting innocently on a side table, and his aunt held in her hand the Mask of Gaia, dangling loosely from her fingers.

Robin closed the door softly behind him as he entered, looking from one to the other curiously.

Irene looked … normal. Stately and calm and perfectly turned out as she always did. If he hadn't seen her in the Netherworlde with his own eyes, he would have sworn her most exerting activity recently had been a game of bridge.

"Firstly," she said to him, fixing him with her sharp eyes over the top of her half-moon spectacles. "I may *never* let you out of my sight again. I step outside of these walls, and you step outside of this reality and into danger it seems." She raised a hand to silence him as he made to speak. "I am aware you were under the geas of the redcaps," she allowed. "And as it happens, I do agree that you had no choice but to go, given the circumstances." She raised her eyebrows. "A debt to those people must *always* be repaid, and repaid in *full*. You have retained the honour of Erlking, as foolish as it may have been to rush off chasing dragons. We will speak of this matter later … of the Earth Shard … in depth." She sounded stern about this, making it plain that Robin was not off the hook.

"Secondly, I have spoken at length with this boy." She looked to Jackalope. "He has told me everything. Where you went. Why he left you."

Robin's eyes flicked to Jackalope, whose silvery eyes shone in the firelight. Irene seemed to read the question on Robin's face. "Yes, he has been perfectly candid with me about his past deeds." She glanced down at the mask in her hand. "I could not truly believe it. And so he consented for me to view him with this curious device you have unearthed. This relic of the elementals."

She looked back up to Robin, beckoning him away from the door and into the room. "I have seen his past with my own eyes. He believes himself a murderer," she said. Her face was unreadable. "He is wrong," she concluded simply after a second.

Robin was confused. Jackalope wasn't looking at either of them.

"He believes he killed his brother," Irene said. "With all of his heart. But he did not."

Robin stared at Jackalope. "I *knew* you couldn't have killed your own brother," he said, almost accusingly.

The hornless Fae glared at Robin. "This old woman is wrong," he said. "Whatever you saw through your magical mask. I know what I did. He is dead, and it is because of me."

"Be quiet please," Irene commanded. "Erlking does not accept cold-hearted killers to its bosom. This matter must be settled here and now."

She took off her glasses, letting them rest on their long chain around her neck. "You left my nephew, and the others, on Briar Hill, consumed by shame. They had seen what the banshee revealed. The dark secrets you hold in your heart. You left not because you wanted to, but because you felt you did not *deserve* to stay. You blame yourself that much. To live a life of isolation and penance? That much is perfectly clear. You left to protect them from yourself." She sighed, as though the boy were exasperating. "You are not the monster you fear you are, Jackalope. Hardly any people truly are. In many ways, you are ... broken. But things can mend, eventually. Few things in this world or the next are ever truly beyond repair."

"Why *did* you come back?" Robin asked. "You're no coward, Jack. That much is obvious. You saved my life from that centaur. I would have been ground to a pulp."

"I told you already, and I have told your guardian the same," Jackalope said defensively. "Your knife! Your stupid dagger. It is haunted. Always it was dragging me in circles, straining to get back to you. It was like a dowsing rod. I'm tired of it. I thought if I followed where it led ... well ..." He shrugged. "It would lead me to you eventually, and I could return it. Be done with it, and the rest of you. How was I to know you'd be in the middle of a battle with nearly every centaur in the Netherworlde?" he scowled. "I should have learned my lesson back when I followed you into the Undine's hidden valley. Wherever you step, trouble follows, Robin Fellows."

Robin eyed the seated Fae carefully.

"You could have just thrown it away," he said.

Jackalope glared at him.

"It would seem," Irene said quietly, "that your old tutor, Mr Phorbas, does not like to lose a student. He is still, in many ways, very much still with us."

She looked at the grey headed Fae, her face softening somewhat ... not with pity, Irene was not the kind of person to whom pity was a useful emotion. With kindness perhaps, Robin thought.

"Shall you tell Robin how your brother died?" she asked him. "Or would you prefer me to say what I saw in your memories? Which is easiest for you?" She placed the mask gently on the table by the knife.

Jackalope said nothing. He stared away from them, into the fire. Rain thrummed on the windows behind the thick curtains.

"Very well," Irene said softly, clasping her hands before her. "The camps of Dis are a place of misery beyond understanding, Robin. Jackalope here knows that all too well. He grew up in their desolation and hopelessness." She looked over to Robin. "Many lived and died in those camps. Fae and rebellious Panthea alike. Robbed of their dignity, of their humanity." She glanced at the tattoo on Jackalope's forearm, the branded numerals. "Robbed of their names even. Reduced to numbers, reduced to … things. This is how Eris and her kind win a war. They take away everything worth fighting for. Freedom, love, even, eventually, hope itself. It is how they break you."

She sat slowly, opposite Jackalope, in her own chair, still looking at Robin. "It is not enough for the overseers of the camps that Fae are simply captured and held. They must be broken, body and mind, and most importantly…will. So that this race can never again rise up in rebellion against Eris.

This is the purpose of the camps of Dis, the hills of blood and bone, as they are known. They are factories for destroying hope. For taking apart your soul piece by piece. The jailers are cruel, and they are most … inventive … are they not, Jackalope?"

The boy did not reply. He stared still into the flames, his jaw working.

"Any camaraderie amongst the prisoners is stamped out, Robin," she explained. "Familial bonds, love? It is worked on and worn down, destroyed, bit by bit. The jailers hate it. You see, love makes people strong. People, when they care about each other, are a dangerous force, and Eris knows this all too well." She sighed.

"You and your brother, you kept each other sane, in that place, didn't you?" she said to Jackalope. "All the years you were there. All the inhumanities thrown at you, you could always bear them … just. Because you had one another. Strength they could not break, no matter how hard they tried."

"*He* was strong," Jackalope whispered hoarsely, still looking at the fire. "I was not. He protected me. I needed him. I was nothing but a burden around his neck, a snot nosed kid to worry about, as though he didn't have problems of his own. He never showed that though, not once."

"No doubt because he needed you too," Irene said. "Keeping you safe, having someone to worry about. I do not doubt that it gave him strength, and the determination not to be broken like so many of the other prisoners."

"But he died," Robin said, his own voice barely a whisper. "What happened in there, that makes you think you are a murderer?"

Jackalope still said nothing. His hands were on his knees, bunched and his pale knuckles were tight as cords. He still did not look at either of them.

"As I have said," Irene told Robin. "The jailers of the camp were ... are ... inventive in their cruelty. There was one tradition, Robin, a vile sport for their own entertainment, known as the wild hunt."

Jackalope stiffened a little.

"What's that?" Robin asked.

"A simple enough concept," Irene explained "Designed with the sole aim to pit prisoner against prisoner, to break down any friendships suspected of forming, any bonds in the camps which needed pinching in the bud." Irene sighed. "Two prisoners would be loosed into the wild. Like animals. Given a shot at freedom, or at least the illusion of one. The jailers would then give chase, hunting them down for fun, and the cruellest part was this ... whichever of the two prisoners was captured first would be killed on the spot as punishment. The other, the one who evaded capture longer, would merely be cast back into the camps. They would even receive preferential treatment as a kind of reward for winning the game. Extra food rations." Her eyes were narrowed and thoughtful. "Though even this was designed to cause resentment amongst their peers of course."

She looked at Robin. "Do you see the wickedness in it?" she asked. "However fake the chance of freedom may have been, no one ever actually escaped during these hunts. One was always killed, the other always recaptured. But still ... there remained the slimmest possibility, the smallest sliver of faint hope. Maybe this time they would be the one who got away."

Robin imagined two prisoners who had become friends in that dark and fearful place, drawing comfort from one another, strength, their companionship making the hell of the camps bearable. Suddenly pitted against one another. Competing for the impossible.

"Fear and desperation make people do such questionable things, Robin. People who, in other circumstances, might be good," Irene said. "It was not

415

uncommon, during these hunts, for the friends to turn on one another, to hobble or incapacitate the other, so desperate were they to escape. Even knowing their ally would be killed when caught first."

Her mouth was a hard line. "This is the world Eris creates for her enemies. She casts down her apple between friends and sets them at one another's throats like mad dogs. There was never any winner in these games. The loser dies, brought down like a wild animal in the dark wilderness. The winner is dragged back to hell, and now, instead of having a companion to make it bearable, they must live with the guilt of what they did to their only friend. Only the jailers win. It is almost certain that prisoner will never form a bond with another again. They would not dare or want it."

Robin stared at Jackalope, beginning at last to realise what must had happened. "You were chosen for the hunt, weren't you?" he said. "You … and your brother."

Jackalope looked at him. "Yes," he said thickly.

"When you were loosed," Irene said, glancing at the Mask of Gaia, its smooth wooden surface flickering in the firelight, memories fresh in her mind. "Your brother told you that you were both going to escape, that you could both make it. He'd been planning it all for weeks, since he'd found out you were the next offerings. And you believed him. He was trying to make you feel less afraid. To give you the hope you needed to run so fast and so far."

"They caught him instead of you, didn't they?" Robin asked, his voice cold with the horror of it.

"No," Jackalope said flatly. "Not right away. *He* caught *them*."

"His brother was a strong and determined Fae," Irene said to Robin. "The mask showed me the events of that night. How far they both ran, deep into the woods beyond the camp, how desperately. And how their pursuers followed, faster, on horseback." She leaned forward to Jackalope. "It showed me where you stopped running, where an ambush was laid. Your brother took out two of them before you both ran again. And in the confusion and the darkness, from one he felled, he tore away the creature's mana stone."

Robin knew it was a terrible thing in the Netherworlde for anyone, friend or foe to touch another mana stone. They were the most personal objects one could imagine. Almost a part of yourself. To steal one from a corpse and run with it was clearly an act of the boldest desperation.

"Your brother was an Earth Panthea," Irene said to Jackalope. "He hadn't used mana in years, not since you were first taken to the camps, stripped of your own stones, when your horns and your names were taken from you. But he remembered one trick. He hid you. He hid you in the trees, wrapped in leaves, masked in a disguise so perfect none would see you, no matter how hard they searched. You were part of the forest. He told you he would lead them off. That he was going to draw them away. A wild goose chase. Isn't that right?" she nodded. "You were to stay put, a whole day and night, before daring to move. To wait for him to return. He told you that he would circle back eventually for you." She sighed deeply down her nose. "He also told you that if anything happened, if he didn't return by that time, you were to leave. Continue north, keep off roads and in the trees wherever you could. That he would find you. You were to put as much distance as you could between yourself and Dis."

"He didn't get far," Jackalope said bitterly. "He'd hidden me, like you say. He'd thrown the mana stone deep into the forest. They would only track its trail of power. But they were closer on our trail than we knew. They passed through the clearing only minutes after he had left … minutes." The boy's silver eyes were distant. "They headed straight after my big brother. They could follow his tracks, anyone could have." He looked down at his own knees. At his clenched fists. "There were so many of them, on their horses, whooping and cheering like this was the best game in the world. Like … we didn't matter. I knew they would catch him. I … I *heard* them catch him." His mouth was taut in the dark room. "He was still so close, he never stood a chance, not really. I could have jumped down from the tree, I could have run and helped him. I know … I was just a child, but he had done *everything* for me, to get me safe and free, and … I didn't."

He shook his head, as though to dislodge the thoughts. "I didn't move a muscle. I froze. I was so afraid. I sat in the tree, wrapped in his illusion, and listened to them kill him. I listened to my brother die, and I did nothing to stop it." His voice had grown very quiet. "Nothing."

The fire popped and hissed in the shadows of the study.

"I think he might have called my name, at the end," Jackalope said. "I couldn't bear it. Couldn't bear to hear it. I don't remember it now, that's funny, right? That's why I took his. I left that child in the tree when

417

I finally came down, and that wasn't until a full day later. The hunters had long gone, searching for me elsewhere in the woods. I didn't dare move until I knew they were far away."

He looked directly at Robin and, for the first time, Robin noticed that the boy looked extremely tired. "They hadn't taken him away, you know. I found him just where they had left him, cast aside on the floor of the woods beyond the camps of Dis, like garbage. They hadn't even closed his eyes." He looked up, at Irene. "You saw the rest," he said bitterly. "Did I avenge him? Nothing so noble. I ran. Ran north, just as he said I should. I hid in shadows and every night I was sure they would find me, convinced they were still hunting me, that I was still part of their game." He gave a bitter half-laugh. "I'd covered half of the Netherworlde, a skulking, cowardly shadow, a traitor to my own brother, before I let myself believe the truth, that they had given up on me. That I really was the one who got away."

"And that's where I was when you found me, Scion," he said to Robin. "'Go north', my brother had said. 'Put as much distance as you can between yourself and Dis, and stay out of sight'. That's exactly what I did, hiding in the snow, in the wilderness of the Gravis Glaciem. Alone, for years, with what I had done."

Robin stared at Jackalope. "You didn't do anything," he said.

"That's the point," Jackalope smiled coldly. "I didn't do anything. I let them kill him. To save my own skin."

Robin shook his head, as though irritated. "No. You were a frightened kid. And you were doing exactly what he had told you to do."

"His death was my fault," Jackalope insisted. "I could have intervened. I could have stopped it. He was dead because of me."

"His death was the fault only of the creatures who killed him," Irene told the boy. "Not yours. And yes, you are quite right, you could have intervened, but you could *not* have stopped it. He would still have died, and you would have been dragged, captured again, back to the camps, their pitiful 'victor'." She was peering at the Fae very closely. "Then, and *only* then, would his death have meant nothing."

"He knew he didn't stand a chance," Robin said. "That's obvious, even without looking into your memories with the mask. He knew, even when he was hiding you that he wasn't coming back for you at all. That's why he gave you instructions. He knew how long to tell you to wait, how long it would take for them to tire of looking for you. That's why he told you where to go, and how to get there on your own."

Jackalope stared at Robin, his eyes liquid mercury. His expression was unfathomable.

"Jack, you *didn't* kill your brother," Robin told him. "Any more that I killed my Gran or Phorbas. He died *for* you. He sacrificed himself to give you a chance. You didn't fail him. He wanted you to live."

Jackalope stood up slowly. His face was whiter than ever, even in the flickering light.

Robin noticed he still had centaur blood flickering his cheek and neck.

"I'm a bad person," he said. "I should have saved him. I should have tried."

Robin was aware that Irene was watching him closely, as though waiting on his judgement, offering none of her own. He nodded to the other Fae.

"You were a kid. And he would never have forgiven you if you'd come after him," he said. "No, you didn't save his life, but he saved yours. You're not a bad person, Jack. You saved my life ... twice. You're just ..." He searched for the right words, casting about with his hands.

"...You're just an idiot," he finished with feeling, giving a weak smile.

"Running and hiding does not solve problems, my boy," Irene said softly, a tiny smile touching the corners of her mouth at Robin's exasperated words. "Believe me, it never has, not for anyone. They always find you. You can't run away forever, certainly not from yourself. You may as well try to outrun your own shadow." She folded her arms thoughtfully. "You wish for my advice? Make a stand. Here at Erlking."

Jackalope looked to her. Robin knew what the boy was thinking. He had been invisible to the world for so long, hiding in shadows, alone with his terrible burden of guilt and loathing. The world didn't see him. But here this old lady was looking right at him, and there was no judgement in her eyes, even after he had laid his soul bare. There was nothing in her eyes except firelight.

"You think I want forgiveness?" he asked quietly. "Is that it?"

"I think that's *all* you want," Robin said. "I just wish it was mine to give you. That's something you'll have to work on yourself, I suppose. But it doesn't mean you have to do it on your own."

"Erlking welcomes the lost, Jackalope," Irene said. "I trust Robin's judgement. You don't have to run anymore."

Jackalope ran his fingers through his pale hair. His permanent scowl

419

was still in place, but he seemed to Robin more than ever not a wild and feral thing, not a seasoned survivor, fiercely independent and proud. He seemed just a boy. He appeared to be struggling.

"You told me, back at Briar Hill …" Robin said, putting his hands in his pockets. "About the night when the Peacekeepers came to your town. How they took you and your brother. How no one helped, no one raised a hand to stop them. They didn't even look, they turned away."

The hornless Fae nodded.

"You've got a home here, Jack," Robin said firmly. "A family even … if you want it. We see you, okay?" he swallowed. "We won't turn away. No matter what happens."

The rain pattered softly on the dark windowpanes of Irene's study. The sleet had melted away, the first bite of winter softening as outside dawn approached, and a new day, quiet and uncertain, approached Erlking. And with a silent nod of his head, that was that.

Jackalope would remain at Erlking.

INTERESTED PARTIES

The following week was a busy one at the hall. A lot seemed to happen in a short space of time. They all rested, they all healed.

Hawthorn announced, to Robin's disappointment, two days after their return, that he was leaving. He was headed back into the Netherworlde, he told them. He was part of the Fae resistance there, after all. And he had to seek out their leader, Peaseblossom, and relay to him what had happened, with the Shard, with the Hive.

"He will be most interested to hear about you, young Master Robin," he told the boy, as they all stood saying their farewells on Erlking's steps, bright morning sunshine baking the stones. "You are quite the Fae."

Robin had been fairly unsuccessful in hiding his disappointment at Hawthorn leaving. Who would teach him the Tower of Earth, if he wasn't here? But the old Fae narrowed his long eyes, clearly amused. "I think you have mastered that Tower all on your own," he told him. "Earth is about will and determination, and you have proved that you have plenty of both."

He promised he would return when he could, and Robin instructed him to be careful out there, to stay off the grid.

Hawthorn took with him the Mask of Gaia when he left. Irene had decided that now the Shard of Earth was in Erlking's possession, the mask, with all its dangerous power, may be better suited to others elsewhere. She had told Robin that the Princess Ashe and her people had returned victorious to Rowandeepling. The swarm had been decimated and driven from the forest. The dryads were rebuilding their empire. She was planning to marry, apparently. Preparing to rule alongside a love she had once thought long lost.

"Love is never really lost though," his aunt had told him, with a small wry smile. "It is a fire which can always be rekindled. The mask may serve the dryads well, as once it did before. Offer the princess guidance to rule and guard the Elderhart. She will not be duped by the likes of Splinterstem again."

Robin learned that although the Hive had been destroyed and Eris' forces driven from the great forest like a cancer purged, no one seemed to know what had happened to Peryl or Strigoi. Robin didn't doubt for a moment that Eris' fury would have been something to behold. He still couldn't get the image of those golden eyes out of his head.

If Peryl's failure followed the same pattern as Strife's, she would be back at the bottom of the pile by now, and her treacherous green-haired brother back in his rightful station, having schemed his way back into the Empress' good favour.

He wondered where she was. If Peryl was still abroad in the Netherworlde, or if she was in the pits of Dis, disgraced and imprisoned like tragic Mr Moros. He also wondered why he seemed to care so much.

It was announced, shortly after Hawthorn's departure, that as well as the new addition of Jackalope to the erstwhile rebels of Erlking, an extended offer of hospitality had been laid out to Mr Ffoulkes. On the strictest conditions by Irene that he behave, and that he make penance for his attempted theft by agreeing to help to lighten the load of teaching with Calypso. He was to assist in the tutoring of the Scion.

Ffoulkes, who by this point had regained all of his former pomp and new clothes brighter and more bedazzling than ever, accepted this offer with thanks, smoothing his perfectly waxed moustache and beard. Hestia had managed to find some wax for him, and he was almost like his old, rather irritating self again, save for the fact that he had elected not to procure a new wig. His bald head, he had told them all, despite absolutely no one asking, was a dashing sign of virility in itself.

The news of his appointment as tutor-in-residence was greeted by the nymph with a world-weary sigh, which she made no attempt whatsoever to conceal, her book drooping listlessly from her hands as she rolled her eyes into the back of her head.

Well, Robin thought. *This is going to be interesting.*

Karya recovered slowly but steadily. The other companions spent much time in her room keeping her company as the days passed. More snow began to fall outside, the last of the autumn leaves drifting down from the nearly-naked trees of Erlking. Hestia occasionally shoed them out, flapping her hands and insisting the girl needed peace and quiet, not to be constantly bothered and harassed by three loud boys and a faun. None of them mentioned her unnatural healing. None of them really knew how to bring it up in conversation.

It was late in the evening on a Sunday, when the subject, amongst others, was finally breached.

They'd had supper in the hall downstairs, Ffoulkes insisting afterwards on entertaining them all on the large harpsichord which stood in the corner of the room. He had actually been surprisingly good at it, though of course, he had been the first to exclaim and applaud his tremendous skills.

Afterwards, Irene had taken Robin briefly to one side and spoken with him in private, and now, while she, Mr Drover, Calypso and Ffoulkes retired to the drawing room for rather dull adult conversation, Robin and the other Erlkingers had come up to Karya's room.

It was dark outside, night closing in, and the girl sat propped up in her bed on roughly a million cushions, the twined flowers twisted through her headboard at her back. She was eating her dinner from a tray, 'like a bloody invalid' as she put it, confined most sternly to bed-rest until she was fully healed.

The room was cosy and comfortable. A fire crackled in the hearth, where Henry sat on the floor, determinedly trying to teach Jackalope how to play cards, the frowning Fae scowling down suspiciously at his carefully concealed cards, as though suspecting Henry of trying to cheat at every turn, which, of course, he was.

Their enmity, Robin noticed, had mellowed into extreme competitiveness. And besides, Henry was sulking tonight because Jack had received a much larger portion of pudding than he had. The miserable old housekeeper insisted that the Fae needed feeding up, although Henry cried favouritism and injustice at this.

Elsewhere in the room, Woad sat in a deep windowsill, curled up in a ball, Inky the kraken cradled peacefully in his arms. Both the blue boy and the small, tentacled thing were asleep, softly snoring after too much dinner. Woad sounded like a quiet but peaceful chainsaw. The kraken, Robin reasoned, could well have been purring.

He himself sat at the foot of Karya's bed. He was twirling Phorbas on its tip on the footboard, lost in thought. Karya was looking at him oddly.

"What?" he said, a little self-consciously, catching her staring.

She shook her head, "Nothing … just … I can't get used to your eyes. You look so … odd."

Robin's eyes had not changed back. Even now, days after their safe return. One was blue as the sky, the other as green as jade. He was still getting used to it himself.

"Wow, thanks," he said, half joking.

"Not *bad* odd," she said hurriedly. "Just … different. You're more … I don't know … Puck than you were."

Robin considered this a moment. He shrugged. "We've come to an arrangement, he and I," he joked. "Anyway, don't you think it makes me look a bit like David Bowie?"

"Who?" Karya asked blankly.

"Just the greatest human who ever lived," Robin grinned. "Well, according to my gran, that is."

Karya looked over to Henry, confused. "I thought you told me the greatest human who ever lived was Bobby Charlton?" she enquired.

"He is," Henry muttered immediately, not looking up from his cards.

"You're all so confusing," she said to Robin, eating a spoonful of jelly from the bowl resting on the tray before her. "As is this curious human dessert. I cannot bring myself to trust a foodstuff that shivers as you eat it. Are you certain it's not self-aware?"

Robin nodded, grinning. "No more than our friendly neighbourhood faun over there."

Karya chuckled, wincing a little. She was still not fully healed.

They sat in amiable, comfortable silence for a time while she ate, and Robin polished Phorbas. Listening to Woad snore and Henry and Jackalope quietly swearing at one another over the slapping of playing cards on the hearth rug. It was a comfortable evening.

"What did your aunt find out in London?" she asked him eventually, out of the blue. "About the book? I know she found out *something*. Henry said she dragged you off to one side for a chat after dinner."

Robin gave Henry a sly look.

"Yes, she did," he said. "She didn't find out much to be honest. The trail of the cubiculum is cold, whatever it is. We might have gained an

Earth Shard, but we're not much closer to knowing which book was so important to Oberon and Titania. Or why." He leaned in a little. "But… she said she did find out *something* that was interesting."

Karya's golden eyes narrowed with interest.

"Apparently, she's not the *only* person who's been enquiring after this lost volume," Robin told her. "There's another interested party. They've been all over London, contacting libraries everywhere. All very innocent and polite, very vague, but Irene thinks it's very odd. They kept popping up everywhere she was looking herself."

Karya frowned. "Who are they?"

Robin shook his head. "No idea, and neither does she. She only knows that they're a private firm in London. Old school establishment. They have interests in all sorts of things. Medical research, property, law firms. Private transport. You name it, they're into it. They own a series of those old gentlemen's clubs too, in the city. You know, all brandy and cigars, proper cabal. They're called Sire Holdings."

"Never heard of them," Karya admitted. "Sounds a bit pompous."

Robin agreed. "Aunt Irene tried to contact them, see if she could get an appointment to see their director, maybe find out what their interest is in all this. But she kept getting the brush off. She showed me one of the letters she got in reply while she was down there. It was all business-speak. Consultations by private appointment and invitation only, that sort of thing. Even the letterhead was pompous. Old school logo like a coat of arms. She's going to try and see what else she can find out about them. Dig up some dirt."

"We will need to step up our game you know, Scion," Karya warned. "We made a fool of Eris back at the Hive, even if we did only escape by the skin of our teeth. She won't like that. And the fact that Lady Irene came in person, an open display of conflict, destroying her forces like she did. It changes everything."

Robin looked at her, questioningly.

"We're not just a nuisance anymore," the girl explained. "Not just a quiet underground resistance faction, skulking around in our safe house. What we did, what Irene had to do. That was an open declaration of aggression. Erlking is at war now. Open war."

Robin knew this was true. He nodded. "Good," he said gravely. "Bring it on. I can't wait to see Strigoi again. He has to pay for what he did, to the Sidhe-Nobilitas." He sighed. "All we wanted was peace. But things are getting darker out there, aren't they?"

"*Si vis pacem, para bellum*," Karya said darkly.

Her gravitas and serious face were only slightly ruined by the spoonful of raspberry jelly quivering on her spoon held before her.

"Karya …" Robin said hesitantly. "I have to know … You should have died. You didn't."

"I know," she replied blankly.

"What …" he hesitated, peering at here carefully. "What *are* you?"

Henry and Jackalope had stopped playing cards. They were both looking up across the room silently, watching the girl as Robin studied her.

Karya met his eyes, slowly lowering her spoon.

"The truth?" she said, looking rather lost. "The truth is, Robin Fellows, Scion of the Arcania … I honestly don't know. I don't … remember."

She looked out of the window, at the dark, cool night. "But I think … it's important *to* know," she said, her voice both worried and thoughtful. She glanced back to Robin, her eyes meeting his.

"But in order to find out," she said slowly. "We're going to have to go home. To Eris. To where I came from. Robin … we have to go to Dis."

Robin looked back at her solemnly. She looked both frightened and determined. He reached out and took her hand, lacing her fingers with his and squeezing reassuringly.

He thought of all they had been through together, these people in this quiet room, since first they met. All they had survived.

"Well then," he said, smiling slightly as his eyes twinkled puckishly. "That sounds like quite an adventure, doesn't it? Eris had better watch out. We're coming for her."

And he meant every word.